ALL MY HOLY
MOUNTAIN

THE BINDING OF THE BLADE

BY L. B. GRAHAM

Beyond the Summerland
Bringer of Storms
Shadow in the Deep
Father of Dragons
All My Holy Mountain

BOOK 5

THE
Binding
of the
Blade

ALL MY HOLY
MOUNTAIN

L. B. GRAHAM

P U B L I S H I N G

P.O. BOX 817 • PHILLIPSBURG • NEW JERSEY 08865-0817

For my father, Thomas Edward Graham,
who has entered already into the joy of his reward
and tasted of the restoration for which we long.

Page design by Tobias Design
Map by Stephen Mitchell © 2008

Printed in the United States of America

Library of Congress Cataloging-in-Publication Data

Graham, L. B. (Lowell B.), 1971–
  All my holy mountain / L. B. Graham.
    p. cm. — (The binding of the blade ; bk. 5)
  Summary: Sulmandir and the dragons have returned and, despite the
power of their adversaries, hope for victory is growing but before the bind-
ing of the blade can be broken, Benjiah knows he will have to make a sac-
rifice.
ISBN 978-0-87552-724-6 (pbk.)
  [1. Fantasy.]   I. Title.
PZ7.G75267All 2008
[Fic]—dc22

                                                           2008007580

CONTENTS

Prologue: The Prophecy   9

BLADE

1. No More   27
2. Back from the Brink   44
3. The Hammer Falls   63
4. Dread Captain of the Nolthanim   85
5. The Devoured   104
6. Reunion   126
7. Night of the Wolf   145
8. Last Rites   162
9. Facing the Future and Unveiling the Past   181
10. A Time for Love   202
11. The Last Campaign   222

BROKEN

1. A Prophecy Fulfilled   243
2. The Once and Always King   263
3. Their Separate Ways   282
4. The Kumatin   302
5. Saegan   323
6. All Roads Lead to the Mountain   342
7. Under the Hammer   360
8. Strength That Stoops to Conquer   375
9. The Last Titan   398
10. The Crystal Fountain   413
11. The Unmaking   431

Epilogue: All Things New   459
Glossary   467

Agia Muldonai

Avalione

ZAROS MTS.

FOREST OF GYRIN

PROLOGUE:
THE PROPHECY

CORIAN WALKED TO THE EDGE of the great pavilion and looked out over the tents fluttering in the stiff winter breeze. Midwinter and the New Year had come and gone two days ago, and still the Assembly bickered and debated. Malek had shut himself inside the Mountain after the fall of Vulsutyr some seven years before, but without Allfather's permission to go up after him, there was nothing the Kirthanim could do but wait.

He turned from the tents and looked to the Mountain itself. It rose, tall and imposing in the twilight. Not since the end of the First Age had any man dared set foot upon it, that is, until Malek and his hosts fled into its labyrinth of tunnels and caverns. Now the long-deserted Mountain teemed with dark and vile life. Some were made by Malek. All were obedient to him, living in subterranean darkness.

Corian sighed. If Allfather would not grant their petition to go up the Mountain after Malek, then the future defense of Kirthanin must be looked to. First and foremost on the list of essential matters, Corian believed, was the still-gaping wound held open by the interrupted and unresolved Civil War. While Kel Imlaris had not been in the center of the conflict that tore Kirthanin apart (indeed, Kel Imlaris was never in the center of anything), the division touched even his beloved home city. Corian could sense the deeper divide among his brothers on the Assembly, and it grieved him.

Stepping from the pavilion, he moved out into the gathering night. He had walked this ground each year for seven years, just like the others, and still Allfather was silent. No prophet came bearing word of Allfather's direction. In fact, Erevir had not even been seen since Malek's retreat into the Mountain, and no one knew where the prophet had gone. What's more, the Assembly's attempts to solve their problems had failed over and over again.

He needed to propose his plan. He knew it would sound crazy to the others. They were men of action with little on their minds beyond building defenses or finding ways to hem Malek in if Allfather disallowed direct engagement. The subtlety and long-term value of his idea would be missed by many, but nevertheless, he needed to try. When he listened to the debates and heard the bitterness in both what was said and, more poignantly, in what was left unsaid, he understood that hope for a real and lasting peace lay not with them but with their children.

Corian stopped between two large tents bearing the red and grey of Tol Emuna, the colors mirroring the rough terrain of that formidable city. Beyond them his own tent, brilliantly decorated in the vibrant blue and yellow of Kel Imlaris, reflected the brighter world of his sunny home. He looked up at the stars beginning to shine. He'd never been much use in things military, and even in the discussions and negotiations of recent years, where he should have excelled, he had failed. He couldn't afford to fail this time. He could feel the frustration mounting on every side. No, none of them was foolish enough to resort to blows again, not after all it had cost them, but they might well accept, even embrace, the cold disharmony that had settled upon the land. The once-vicious foes, though no longer at war, each looked only to their own cities and houses. Kirthanin could not afford that state of affairs to persist, not if they hoped to stand strong and stand together against the looming threat of Malek in the Mountain.

He would try to mediate an agreement that all would honor, but to do that, he would have to get Dalamere of Shalin Bel and King Sandrel of Amaan Sul to agree first. They were influential and respected men, and if they could shake hands over the agreement, then Corian could present it to the Assembly with support. The fact that such bitter rivals could agree would force the others to take notice. Yes, it had to be done, and soon.

Every year since Malek's retreat, the Assembly gathered at the foot of the Mountain a week before the New Year. Every year, they stayed for ten days. Every year, on the evening of the third day of the New Year, someone suggested that the Assembly should be concluded, that they'd accomplished all they could, that no word from Allfather had come and did not appear likely to come. Every year, the fourth day dawned to find the great tents coming down and each delegation preparing to ride. Every year, the fourth day of the New Year ended with the pavilion and the broad clearing empty once more.

Tomorrow was the third day, and no word from Allfather had come. He could wait no longer.

The sun rose over Gyrin, its expanse stretching to the eastern horizon. Though the delegates were gathered right at Malek's doorstep with only a token force of men from each city, Corian knew they were as safe here with the might of the Gyrindraal protecting them as they would be in far off Kel Imlaris by the shining sea. The absence of dragons in the sky was indeed alarming, but the Great Bear remained a stalwart buffer against attack from the Mountain.

Corian called for a runner, and four young men came quickly to his tent. Two of them he sent away. The first he sent with a written request to King Sandrel, and the second he sent to Dalamere. The Assembly was not scheduled to meet until after the midday meal, and while the leaders might have meetings that morning, Corian doubted it. None of the delegations had arrived at the Mountain without a clear agenda, and most attempts to form alliances had transpired in the dusk and twilight of the first few days of meetings.

Corian knew that both men would likely see his request as a nuisance. He was not an important man, and he came from a politically unimportant city. However, he had passed his seventieth birthday two years before, and age still commanded some respect among the Novaana. They would grumble to their stewards and to their subordinates and perhaps even to the runners, but they would come.

King Sandrel arrived first. Tall and robust, his sandy locks curled upon his brow, he appeared every inch the warrior he was reputed to be. Though only in his late twenties during Malek's Invasion, he had led the forces of Enthanin as the crown prince of Amaan Sul, and when his father fell in battle, Sandrel refused to take the crown until the war was over. He was valiant in war and wise in most matters domestic, but as stubborn and hard-headed as any in relations with the Werthanim or western Suthanim. He had inherited bitterness and hatred from his father and his father's father as surely as he'd inherited the valor and nobility with which he ruled Enthanin. Alliances against Malek did nothing to quell the animosity. What's more, with each passing year the common hatred of Malek that had eclipsed all other hatreds faded, leaving more room for the old rivalries to grow to their former intensity.

"Corian," King Sandrel said as Corian went out to greet him. "What requires my attention at this early hour? I had hoped to spend a morning in quiet reflection, since all hope of peace and tranquility will pass with the approach of today's meeting."

"And is that not a matter of grave concern, Your Majesty?"

"A nuisance, yes, since I dislike the constant bickering as much as the next man, but a grave concern? No."

"With Malek hidden in the Mountain and Kirthanin still deeply divided over disputes that are older than I am, disputes that should have been long since forgotten, that is not a grave concern?"

King Sandrel looked at Corian with barely masked annoyance. "Enough of the lecture, Corian. It is easy enough for the men of Kel Imlaris to forgive wrongs that were not primarily directed against them."

Corian held out his hands and motioned with them to King Sandrel to relax. "I do not wish to lecture you, and I am aware of my city's lesser role in the divisions I spoke of. I am also aware that if Kirthanin falls to Malek in the future, my people will suffer as much as yours, and avoiding that common fate should be the common cause that trumps all other matters, for *all* of us."

"I agree, which is why I continue to come to these meetings year after year, though they have produced precious little of value."

"You are correct that little of value has come from most of these gatherings." Corian nodded. "Hoping to change that, I have summoned you, you and another."

"Who?" King Sandrel tensed.

Corian indicated the figure approaching through the nearby tents. King Sandrel's response was predictable. "Dalamere! You have wasted my time, Corian. I have had all I need of Dalamere and the Werthanim in the Assembly meetings. I will not suffer them when I do not have to."

"That's a pleasant greeting," Dalamere said. He stopped and stood with arms crossed, glaring at both King Sandrel and Corian. "Perhaps when you have finished your business with the *king*, Corian, you can come to my tent and tell me whatever it is that is so important."

"Our business is already concluded," King Sandrel replied, turning to go.

"Peace, both of you," Corian scolded. "Treat each other like children all you want in the Assembly. Yes, perpetuate there the foolishness of your fathers that almost ruined us all, but don't waste my time with it. I am as old as the two of you put together, and you will hear what I have to say."

Neither man replied, but neither moved away either. In fact, both followed Corian into his tent, carefully positioning themselves in places equidistant from Corian and each other, taking wooden chairs to sit in awkward silence. Corian took a deep breath. *Allfather, grant me success and grant us peace.*

"All right," Corian began. "Despite the way in which I just spoke to the two of you, you are here because I think you are wiser men than many of your peers. I have a proposal that I want you to consider. It is simple and will take only a moment of your time, but I believe it could have far-reaching benefits for Kirthanin. Perhaps it might even mend the divide that has separated us too long."

King Sandrel snorted, and Dalamere ignored him, looking blankly at Corian. He said at last, "You must be a very optimistic man."

"Hopeful," Corian answered. "I am hopeful that enough common sense remains in the Assembly to pursue the common good."

Neither responded, and Corian continued. "My proposal is simply this: The Assembly should establish a haven somewhere in Kirthanin. To my mind the distant southlands would be preferable, as far from the shadow of the Mountain and the divisions of the past as possible. I thought perhaps Sulare, now that it is no longer needed to keep watch on the waters of the Southern Ocean, but it isn't pressing that we resolve that issue now. I propose that every seven years, for half a year, the Assembly should send all Novaana between the ages of eighteen and twenty-five to that haven."

"What?" King Sandrel blurted. "What for? Who would run this 'haven'?"

"I envision men from Werthanin, Suthanin, and Enthanin working together to run it," Corian replied.

Dalamere laughed. "You really are an optimist."

"I am hopeful."

After a brief silence, King Sandrel said, "Corian, I'm not following you. Aside from the obvious impossibility that the Novaana of Enthanin would trust their sons and daughters to a place run even in part by Novaana of Werthanin, what would it accomplish if they did? How does this solve our problems?"

"The purpose of the sojourn would be to forge relationships with the Novaana who will lead the Assembly in years to come. They would be old enough to understand what is at stake and yet young enough, I hope, to lay aside regional rivalries and learn to see each other as friends."

King Sandrel frowned at Corian, and Dalamere sat silently, merely watching him. Corian took their silence as a chance to press his point. "Don't you see? By the time most of us start coming to the Assembly, and by the time we're old enough to have a voice anyone will listen to, we're so steeped in our region's squabbles we can't see past them. But what if each new generation could get to know one another as people, as men and women, outside of the realm of politics? What if they learn their shared humanity firsthand from one another and from wise and compassionate men of other realms? The men we send could teach them about the world before the Civil War, when Kirthanin was united and strong. They could train the young Novaana for a better tomorrow. Could we not unlearn the bitterness and contempt that the Civil War and Malek's lies have taught us? Could we not, through our children, undo the folly of our fathers?"

"I hear what you are saying," Dalamere said at last, leaning forward with a look that seemed to Corian to be almost mournful, "but it is impossible. There is too much distrust. My daughter is twelve, and I would be as reluctant to send her into the care of an Enthanim as King Sandrel would be to entrust Prince Arindel to the care of a Werthanim."

"On that," King Sandrel added vehemently, "Dalamere and I agree. What you suggest is not only impossible, it is unnecessary."

"Unnecessary?" Corian replied in disbelief. "Can you not see the danger we are in so long as our divisions remain unmended?"

"No, I cannot," King Sandrel replied. "Two men need not be friends to guard the gate to my city together. They need only do their job. The men of Enthanin will do their part in the east, and if the Werthanim will do their part in the west, we will protect Kirthanin from Malek. How we feel about one another has nothing to do with it."

"But Your Majesty . . . "

"No more talk, Corian," King Sandrel replied, standing and holding out his hands to prevent Corian from speaking further. "I have heard your proposal and have no interest in it. It is impractical foolishness, and I will not distract the Assembly from important matters of Kirthanin's defense with it. Arindel will be taught and trained by no one but me."

"Then he will learn your hatred, and another generation will be lost."

"He will learn what is necessary."

With that, King Sandrel stepped from the tent and started away. Corian looked to Dalamere, who also stood. "Don't waste your breath, Corian. I can see the sense in what you are proposing, but it can't be done. There are far too many who feel as King Sandrel does to ever approve it. Even seeing the sense of it, I don't know if I would approve it until I knew who would be running the place, and I can imagine that choosing those men could be as divisive as the idea itself. I just don't see how it could be implemented. Not in our lifetimes. Maybe the idea will be more palatable to our children's generation."

"Yes? And how will that be if they learn their view of the world from us?"

"I don't know."

Dalamere left the tent. Corian sighed and placed his head in his hands.

Corian looked at the stone memorial around which they were gathering. It had been established at the beginning of the Second Age, over a thousand years ago. It had been erected to remind future generations of the words Erevir had spoken to the Assembly in this place on that occasion:

So says Allfather:

There is blood on the Mountain.
It stains the City
And soaks the ground.

The Fountain is defiled.
It no longer flows
And cannot cleanse.

The deep waters will flow again.
And then the stains
Will be washed clean.

But until that day shall come,
The Holy Mountain is
Forbidden to us all.

The warning and the hope that message contained had once been sufficient to bind all Kirthanim together. No longer, it would seem.

The Assembly meetings that afternoon had been as useless as Corian expected. He supposed that he should take some consolation in the fact that King Sandrel and Dalamere were two of the least inflammatory voices in the disputes, but it was small consolation. Thinking back over their meeting that morning, though, had brought a little more comfort. He was still disappointed, but as the day passed and he gained some distance, his hope returned. The failure had not been total. He had expected the real antagonist in the conversation to be Dalamere, and to his surprise, Dalamere had almost been supportive. King Sandrel's bad mood and vehement rejection could be partially attributed, no doubt, to Dalamere's mock reverence of Sandrel's royalty. When and where ridicule of Enthanin's political structure had entered the more complex issues dividing east and west, Corian had no idea, but he did know that insults of the monarchy remained one of the biggest obstacles to productive dialogue. He was far too old to enjoy traveling very much, but he resolved to travel constantly between Amaan Sul and Shalin Bel to keep at each man separately. Perhaps the following year he would have more luck.

Now, though, he waited with the rest of the Assembly for the formal blessing upon Kirthanin. These men gathered around him would echo the words, wishing peace to men they had barely been civil to for the last ten days, and then they would return to their tents, eat supper, sleep, and go

home as convinced as ever that they were wise and benefi-
cent and their enemies malicious fools. He could barely
stand to be in their midst.

As the gathering fell quiet for the words of blessing, a rider
came out of the forest, thundering toward them along the
foot of the Mountain. As he grew closer, Corian thought that
the man was the most wild and striking figure that he had ever
seen. His flowing green robe flapped in the wind along the
side of the black horse. The man's white hair stood out in all
directions, a thick shock of unkempt tangles, and the man's
eyes, they were as blank as a page without words, as white as
his hair, devoid of color. Even so, despite the man's evident
blindness, the eyes were wide open and seemed to be gazing
at the Assembly. He drew his horse up not far beyond the elder about to begin the blessing.

"Who are you?" the startled elder cried.

"I am Valzaan, prophet of Allfather, and I come bringing
an answer to your petition, rebuke for your folly, direction for
your future, and hope for the dark days that must come."

Though his arrival had triggered murmurs, there was complete silence now. Corian, like the rest of them, stood transfixed by this wild stranger and his wilder words.

"Allfather has heard your request to be allowed onto the
Mountain in order to pursue Malek, but He forbids it. The
Mountain is closed. As He told your fathers through Erevir, so
He tells you. Until the Fountain flows again, washing Avalione
clean, you will not go up. Ask no more for this, for He will not
change His mind and you will receive no answer but this one.
So says Allfather."

The prophet on the horse paused to let his words resonate
among them, and then he continued. "What's more, Allfather
has held back this answer for seven years, giving you all a
chance to recognize your greatest need, to seek His forgiveness for the Civil War that ravaged this land and to repair the

breaches that caused it. You have not done so, so I bring this rebuke. For seven years Allfather will hold back the rain, and you will learn that none of you rises up in the morning or lies down at night except by Allfather's hand, which sustains you. You will learn that these men beside you whom you despise are your brothers. If you do not learn to stand together, you will perish together. So says Allfather.

"And yet," Valzaan continued in a gentler voice, though it still carried to the farthest edge of the Assembly. "Even in His judgment, there is mercy. Allfather will grant you a spring harvest like none you have ever seen. Your grain fields will produce beyond your imagining, and your fruit trees will sag under the weight of their yield. All this will come to pass to prepare you for the drought and famine that is coming, so long as you obey Allfather's command and enact the wise proposal of Corian of Kel Imlaris."

Corian was stunned to hear his name, and all nearby turned to look at him as the prophet continued. "You will not leave this place until you have agreed to the plan, settled on a place, and selected a date this spring for the training to begin. Corian will show you what you are to do, and those among you who already know the plan are charged to support it wholeheartedly. This will be done, or the harvest that I have spoken of will not come, and the seven-year drought will be disastrous beyond measure. So says Allfather."

At this point, a voice other than Valzaan's broke the silent reverie that had fallen upon them all. It was the bellowing voice of Trevarian, one of the most difficult and fractious Novaana in the Assembly. "This is absurd, brothers. Who is this man who comes before us without credentials to testify to the authority he claims, ordering us about as though we were children? Without such proof, why should we heed him?"

The man on the horse raised his hand, silencing any who would have replied. "The drought I have prophesied will ultimately confirm my authority, but that you all might know I am who I say I am, and that I speak for Allfather as I claim, I will give you more immediate proof. This man who calls you to question my authority, to doubt my claims, has long been in the service of Malek, and he remains among you like a serpent in the grass to poison those voices of wisdom and moderation who have tried to speak for peace these last seven years."

"That is a lie!" Trevarian cried.

"Silence!" Valzaan commanded, and Trevarian obeyed as Valzaan dropped from his horse and moved through the Assembly. All parted to let him pass until he stood a few spans from Trevarian, where a small clearing formed around the two men.

"Most of you already realize that what I have said is true. Now that I have said it, you can sense it, but that you may know it beyond doubt, I will give you proof." The prophet faced the man with his blank and fantastic stare, addressing him directly. "Even now, Trevarian, it is not too late for you. Acknowledge your wrong, beseech Allfather for His mercy, and you will be forgiven. Deny it, and you will perish."

Trevarian trembled, looking not at the prophet but at the men staring at the spectacle unfolding in their midst. He began to shake his head slowly. "No, it isn't true."

"So be it," Valzaan replied quietly. He turned and headed back through the crowd toward his horse. Without warning, a ball of fire fell from the clear sky, striking the place where Trevarian stood. It struck and disappeared, leaving nothing but scorched earth and ashes, blowing low along the ground in the cold evening breeze.

Corian gazed at the space, amazed. As soon as the prophet had spoken the accusation, Corian saw the logic of it. Wherever the deepest divisions lay, the most virulent dissension and most bitter arguments of the Assembly, Trevarian was never far away. Corian felt, if anything, embarrassed not to have considered that something more than folly motivated the man. Now Trevarian had been punished and the legitimacy of the prophet established in a single moment. In that same moment, Corian's great hope for Kirthanin's future had become not only likely, but almost certain.

"So far I have given you the answer, the rebuke, and the direction. Now it is time for the hope, for indeed, dark days lie ahead. I cannot say when, for Allfather has not revealed it to me, but though you may not go up after Malek, he will come down after you. Be sure of that. A third great war is coming, and it will be terrible. Even so, fear not, for Allfather has not abandoned you. Hear now the words he has spoken:

> ' *With a strength that stoops to conquer*
> *And a hope that dies to live,*
> *With a light that fades to be kindled*
> *And a love that yields to give,*
>
> '*Comes a child who was born to lead,*
> *A prophet who was born to see,*
> *A warrior who was born to surrender,*
> *And through his sacrifice set us free.* '

"So says Allfather." Valzaan added. His blank but staring eyes swept over them. "In the dark days that shall come, remember these words of hope and cling to them, even as you cling to the words of the mound rite that Allfather spoke from of old concerning the days of restoration: *'I shall cleanse Agia Muldonai. It shall be cleansed forevermore, as indeed all Kirthanin shall be cleansed. Never again will sword and spear be raised in war, for even they will be made anew, and all implements of war shall be made implements of peace, and no one will dare to harm or destroy on all My Holy Mountain.'*

"You have work to do."

With that, he wheeled his horse around and was off, galloping back the way he had come.

BLADE

1

NO MORE

WYLLA LOOKED UP through her tears at Benjiah, strung
between the two poles. Watching him rolled through the
crowd in his wooden cage had pained her, but when he'd
emerged looking defiant and unbroken, she thought that perhaps she could endure this after all.

He had looked so noble, noble and beautiful. She saw Joraiem in Benjiah's quiet strength. They pushed him toward
the scaffold, and he walked up the stairs without comment,
pride and strength in his calm demeanor. Surely he was on his
way to death, for short of Allfather reaching down from the
heavens and plucking him out of their midst, she could see no
way out for him now. And yet, though his death seemed inescapable, she hoped she would be able to watch with the
same unbroken pride and defiance.

She had hoped this until she saw him chained to the poles.
The way they jerked the chains tight, pulling his arms up so

hard into their unnatural position, smashed any defiant courage, any vision of standing before her people in this dark hour as the strong queen unmoved in the face of defeat. She was reduced to the role of tearful mother, weeping for her only son.

"Why do they need to be so tight?" she whispered through her tears to Yorek.

He placed his hand upon her shoulder. She felt his fingers squeeze her slightly as a sign of reassurance, and then he left them there to remind her that she did not stand alone.

Tashmiren, in his ornate coat of dark blue with a scrolling red pattern embroidered upon it, moved to the front of the scaffold. He turned his back to the crowd and whispered quietly to Benjiah. She couldn't hear what he was saying, but she'd seen the man around Malek's camp and knew him to be a smug, smirking fool. She could imagine the cruel taunts rolling from his lips, and for a moment, anger overcame her sorrow and she clenched her fists by her side.

Benjiah raised his head slightly, and Wylla could see from where she stood that he was saying something in reply. Whatever it was, it seemed to bring the short conversation to a close, for after just a moment, Tashmiren turned back to the crowd.

The next few moments were almost unbearable. Tashmiren walked slowly back and forth across the front of the scaffold, saying the most ridiculous things. He spoke of their rebellion against Malek and their surrender as though they had been naughty children who refused to come to supper when called. He mocked their celebration of the Mound rites and their worship of Allfather. He went so far as to suggest that Allfather was a fabrication, that Malek was their true god.

A cold shudder passed through Wylla. What if what Tashmiren was saying was true? It was a terrible thought, but even as Tashmiren rambled, Wylla couldn't quite dismiss it. After all, there was a certain logic to his argument: If Benjiah truly was Allfather's prophet, why was he chained to these poles, about to die? If Allfather could not save his prophet from this ignoble death, then perhaps Malek really was the one great power of Kirthanin. Not a god perhaps, but a malevolent demigod toying with lesser beings.

Wylla composed herself and pushed the thought away. There was evidence, counterevidence, that a power in this world was arrayed against Malek, at times an apparently stronger power. She couldn't think clearly at the moment about exactly what it was, but she knew it was there. Still, as Tashmiren turned to face her son once more, having enumerated the charges against him, she couldn't help but feel unsettled by this scene and Allfather's abandonment of her son. At times she had felt anger at Allfather for allowing her husband to die as he had, and now Benjiah's life neared its end. She couldn't help but wonder if she'd been naïve to believe all her life in a God who'd not seen fit to protect either her husband or her son, though apparently both had been His chosen instruments.

Benjiah's head jerked up from where it had been hanging as he stared at the platform. She was once more caught up in the scene.

"So," Tashmiren was saying, "having heard the charges that Malek brings before you, have you anything to say?"

Wylla looked past Tashmiren at her son, who met Tashmiren's gaze with little expression. *What could he possibly say?* She thought. *Don't bait him, Benjiah. He only wants an excuse to make your death more painful.*

Benjiah said nothing for a moment, and then his eyes moved past Tashmiren to the crowd. Wylla realized that he was looking at her. Involuntarily she lifted her hand and stretched it out toward him, as though by doing so she could touch his face and comfort him.

Benjiah looked into her eyes, and she treasured the love she saw there. She gazed back, trying to make an imprint of that moment upon her heart for however long she should have left to live. His eyes flickered back from her face to Tashmiren's, and she could see his lips move, though she heard no sound. She sighed. She wanted his death to be as painless as possible, but if Benjiah needed to speak, so be it. If by looking to her he had found the strength, even to lift his voice in a whisper, she was glad she could be here.

Wylla lost sight of Benjiah's face. Tashmiren had all but turned his back to the crowd and moved closer to Benjiah, and it seemed from where Wylla stood that a series of hostile whispers passed between the two men. Then Tashmiren stepped back, and she could see Benjiah's face once more.

She gasped at what she saw. Gone was the impassive face of calm defiance. It had been replaced now with a kind of ecstatic exuberance. He lifted his head as high as he could hold it. His blond hair fell away from his eyes, and she could see them clearly, no longer cold and resigned but bright and shining. At that very moment, he opened his mouth again, and this time his voice boomed, every bit as loud as Tashmiren's had been. His voice resounded above them, and to Wylla's surprise, she realized he was singing.

> *Peace, my son, and lay you down,*
> *The sun has gone away.*
> *Wake and find the dawn at hand,*
> *Tomorrow is today—*
> *Tomorrow is today.*

What song was that? What words were those? What did they mean? Wylla looked to Yorek as though to ask, but before she could, Benjiah started the song over again, this time even louder, more clearly.

Peace, my son, and lay you down,
The sun has gone away.
Wake and find the dawn at hand,
Tomorrow is today—
Tomorrow is today.

Tashmiren seemed incapacitated by the bizarre turn of events. He stared dumbfounded at Benjiah. Once more Wylla turned to Yorek as the song ended, but the sky seemed to crack and brilliant sunlight burst through the grey clouds. She looked up at the tiny crack, which quickly widened, magnifying the intensity of the light and blue sky many times over. She raised her hands instinctively, for her eyes weren't ready for the brilliance of a sun they had not seen in more than half a year. Her eyes flickered shut despite her desire to gaze at the blue.

The piercing bright light shone through her closed eyelids, making it only just bearable. Gasps and groans rose around her, and she felt jostled by the crowd as people shifted and squirmed, trying to shield themselves from the light. Both friend and foe alike, having lived and moved in semidarkness for so long, had been similarly stunned by the sudden burst of the full light of day.

Then, over the mumblings and murmurings she heard Benjiah call out, clear and strong. "Behold, he comes!"

The words rang out across the plain, and still Wylla could not open her eyes to look at her son or to try to see what he meant. Despite her inability to look for herself, Benjiah spoke again and her question was answered.

"The Father of Dragons! He comes!"

Benjiah stared at the golden forms approaching. An image of dozens of dragons winging their way through the air had flashed rapidly through his mind, their powerful wings beating as they flew eastward toward Tol Emuna. As the image passed and he looked west at their barely visible approach, he thought to himself that he'd never seen anything so beautiful.

The crowd started to move as though waking up from a daze. Benjiah looked down at men and women, Malekim and Great Bear, and even Vulsutyrim opening their eyes as they began to get used to the bright sunshine. The break in the clouds had continued to expand, and now as Benjiah looked heavenward, blue sky stretched across the horizon. It was almost as beautiful to Benjiah as the dragons.

Despite the confusion in the crowd, three facts became apparent to Benjiah. The first was that the Vulsutyrim had heard his cry and were moving to prepare. The towering forms of the giants were in motion, and all around the moving giants was a growing commotion of men, Malekim, and Great Bear scrambling to get out of their way. Some Vulsutyrim were gathering in the middle of the crowd, generally away from the scaffold and piles of weapons where they had been stationed, while others were moving away from the crowd, back in the direction of Malek's camp where Benjiah had started his day.

At first Benjiah wondered why, but then he thought of the great shields that he had seen the Vulsutyrim use in the skirmishes and battles against dragons along the Barunaan. Whenever dragons appeared, the Vulsutyrim came together under those shields, which did a remarkable job of protecting them from the dragon's fire. They had seemed from a distance to be wood with some kind of inflammable cured hide stretched over it. Surely the giants were headed to the camp to defend themselves.

The second fact that became clear to Benjiah was that the Great Bear were taking advantage of the Vulsutyrim's distraction to reclaim their weapons. A brief struggle took place around both mounds of weapons. The Nolthanim left behind by the giants were quickly overpowered by Great Bear, who armed themselves, established a perimeter around the weapons, and began distributing swords, bows, and axes as quickly as they were able. The sight of the furious Great Bear wielding their staffs excited Benjiah almost beyond reason. He strained against his chains, but they held him tight. He felt discouraged by his inability to break free, but he did not despair. The dragons were coming, the enemy was in disarray, and the Kirthanim were beginning to rearm. Hope rose in him, even though he was still held fast.

The third fact that came to him was that the crowd nearest the scaffold was in utter turmoil. He couldn't see exactly why. He imagined that there had been far less room for the crowd to maneuver as the Vulsutyrim started moving away. The waves of displaced bodies had nowhere to go as they came crashing up against the great structure. Also, the captains of the Kirthanim had been near the scaffold, off to Benjiah's right. Likely they had the same idea the Great Bear did—get to the weapons. That the general confusion was an opportunity for them to break free of their guards and rally to the weapon deposits, he didn't doubt.

Mother. He surveyed the crazed scene swiftly to try to see her. He scanned the place where she had been, but he saw few distinguishable faces in the seething mass.

A movement on the scaffold drew his attention to something happening even closer to home. Tashmiren had summoned the large Nolthanim soldier, the man Benjiah assumed was his executioner. They stood close by, not two spans away, heads bent together so they could hear each other above the gradually increasing din. Tashmiren was looking sideways at Benjiah and pointing to the man's sword.

The wave of bodies that had pushed Wylla sideways past the scaffold had been irresistible. Had she not gone with it, she would surely have been trampled. As it was, it was all she could do to keep her footing. Yorek had almost gone down as well, and both of them probably owed their lives to Rulalin, who first steadied Wylla and then grabbed Yorek, who had started to fall. When the sideward movement ceased, more or less, Wylla looked back up at the scaffold. She was too close to the side to see Benjiah, though the near pole rose high enough that she could still see the top of it.

Wylla turned from the scaffold to Rulalin. She knew what she must ask of him, and she knew that he'd have good reason to resist. She must persuade him, and quickly.

"Rulalin!" she called above the groans and chatter as she grabbed the man's arm.

He turned to look at her, then leaned in close to hear her.

"Benjiah," she said loudly into his ear as she pointed toward the scaffold.

Rulalin pulled back slightly and searched her eyes.

She reached up with both hands and took hold of his face, firmly but tenderly. "I need you. You were willing to help last night, and you are the only one who can help me now."

Rulalin looked up at the scaffold, then back at her. "I will do what I can."

Rulalin pushed through the crowd, his face still tingling from the touch of Wylla's hands. It was that touch, even more than the break in the clouds, that brought light to his darkness. The night before, he'd had some hope that he might be able to free Benjiah and get away from the camp. Maybe, he'd thought, they'd be able to evade capture for as much as a day, and for that day, he would be Wylla's hero and protector. Here, now, there was little hope of that. Whatever was going on, whether the dragons really were coming or not, he wasn't going anywhere with Benjiah even if he did manage to free Wylla's son. It was, quite literally, broad daylight, and that scaffold was surrounded by servants of Malek. Rulalin was under no illusions about getting Benjiah free and getting away.

Even so, when Wylla touched his face and looked into his eyes, he knew that he would do everything in his power to save the boy. Rulalin had lived much of his life in disgrace for what he had done in service to his obsession for her, and he was willing to die doing what he could in service to her, to Wylla herself. He owed her more than that, but he would give her what he could.

It was only a span or less to the stairs that led up to the platform, and yet getting there was like wading upriver through rapids. The tide of humanity pushing against him was almost impenetrable. Almost miraculously, he was able to find cracks here and there, tiny gaps between people, and the next thing he knew he had reached the bottom of the stair.

It was there that he met his first deliberate rather than incidental obstacle. A clear-headed Nolthanim soldier had escaped the drift of people a moment earlier by gaining the second or third step. He'd also managed to keep anyone else from using the stairs as a haven from the mad pushing and shoving. Rulalin had no doubt that he was looking out for more than his own welfare. He was there to make sure no one gained access to the prisoner.

The man had not yet noticed Rulalin's interest in his location, for there were many people before him, and Rulalin had approached from beyond the edges of the Nolthanim's peripheral vision. Even so, Rulalin had no illusions about being able to draw his sword. Even if the quarters hadn't been so close that it was all but impossible, that movement would betray his intent long before he could attack. He needed another way.

There was no time to waste, and Rulalin had but one idea. He let himself drift behind the stairs with the natural movement of the crowd until he stood a half step behind the stair where the soldier stood, then he raised his right hand slowly and cocked it. Striking quickly, he grabbed the man's knee and pushed it forward. As he'd hoped, the man's leg buckled and he teetered. Holding tight, Rulalin seized his opportunity and pulled.

It worked. The soldier pitched off the stairs into the crowd of people, and Rulalin immediately pulled himself up onto the stair. Another Nolthanim close by saw the first man's fall, which cleared a space for him, and he leapt onto the bottom stair to come after Rulalin.

Rulalin did draw his sword now, and only just in time. The Nolthanim drew his and Rulalin was able to deflect the first stroke, though the force of it pushed Rulalin down against the stairs. He was desperate, lying on his back and in a vulnerable position. With his left hand he grabbed the hair hanging loose on the Nolthanim's head. He pulled it sideways at an awkward angle and heard the man grunt with the sudden jerk of his head. With the man's neck exposed, Rulalin swung his head forward and hammered it with his forehead as hard as he could, twice. The first time he hit mostly chin, but he pulled the man's head back harder and the second time he struck the exposed, fleshy part of the neck.

The soldier sputtered and Rulalin jerked up violently as he continued to pull the man with his left hand, and he managed to roll the Nolthanim off the stairs. The soldier fell into the jostling crowd, and Rulalin wasted no time in turning and scrambling the rest of the way up.

The executioner drew his sword and handed it to Tashmiren. The long, shiny blade gleamed in the bright sunshine, and Benjiah strained again against his chains, pulling with all his might. Allfather had spoken to him and assured him that this day was not his last. Benjiah knew what he'd heard hadn't been a dream or an illusion. Even so, he could not break the chains, and Tashmiren was drawing nearer with the sword, an even crueler, more insolent grin on his face than before. Benjiah kept pulling.

Tashmiren walked slowly, savoring Benjiah's helplessness. Though not entirely rational, the thought occurred to Benjiah that if he was to be cut open while chained between these poles, he'd rather the executioner do it than Tashmiren. The executioner drifted closer to Benjiah as well, but he had stepped to the side in deference to Tashmiren, who had obviously pulled rank and laid claim to this kill. Benjiah felt his anger and frustration returning. He wouldn't die by this man's hand. He just wouldn't.

Tashmiren stopped and held the sword up to Benjiah's neck. He could feel the sharp point against his vulnerable flesh, where Tashmiren pressed none too gently, and he stopped pulling against the chains for fear his motion, though slight, would get his throat cut. Tashmiren laughed softly. "Boy, dragons or no dragons, nothing can save you now."

Benjiah didn't reply, but he met Tashmiren's gaze evenly. Despite what he thought Allfather had promised him, he found it difficult to be hopeful in his current situation. Even so, though he might die, he wasn't about to plead, beg, or grovel, or lose his composure in any way that might suggest Tashmiren had gotten to him.

Benjiah was vaguely aware of the sounds of a scuffle not far away. Tashmiren must have heard it too, because he turned his head for a second and then turned back. He must not have seen anything of note, because his face betrayed no concern. "For whatever reason, your death is important to my master. Had things gone as planned, though, I would have been only a spectator to it. Now, I get to do it myself, and when this little commotion is over, I'll stand before him and take the credit and glory for making sure his will was done despite what has transpired. All in all, this day is working out well for me."

"The storm is broken and the dragons are coming," Benjiah said quietly. "I would be cautious about dreaming of your reward too soon."

Tashmiren lowered the sword so he could move in even closer. He stepped up until his coarse hair brushed Benjiah's cheek. "Your dragon friends couldn't deliver your army before, and that was before we'd decimated your ranks of men and Great Bear. They certainly won't deliver you now."

Tashmiren motioned with his free hand to the crowd. "The Bringer of Storms is here, as are his brothers and the rest of Malek's host. The coming of the dragons is only a momentary delay at best. In fact, it is fortuitous. They're saving us the trouble of climbing the mountains to find their gyres and hunt them down. It would have been a time-consuming and tiresome process."

Again, Benjiah held his tongue. The man made him so angry, and he knew that was exactly the point. He wanted to see Benjiah's frustration and anger so he could laugh as he struck the killing blow. Benjiah clenched his teeth and said nothing.

Tashmiren stepped back and raised the sword to chest level this time. "All right, boy prophet of Allfather, no more talk. Now you die."

As the last phrase slipped from Tashmiren's mouth, Benjiah felt the pull of *torrim redara*, and suddenly Benjiah found himself in slow time. He was struck, as always, by the instant silence, and he closed his eyes for a moment and breathed a sigh of relief. He opened his eyes again and looked at the man holding the sword. This was but a temporary stay of execution. When he entered the normal stream of time, Tashmiren would move quickly and swiftly to kill him.

Benjiah. It was the voice he had heard clearly for the first time in the storm while sailing south from Col Marena and most recently just moments ago. It was the voice of Allfather; he was sure.

Benjiah.

"Yes, Allfather, I am listening."

Can you break the chains?

Benjiah strained against them again, but even in slow time, they held him fast. "No, I cannot."

Nevertheless, they will be broken. Can you deliver yourself from the man before you?

Benjiah looked at the raised sword. "No, I cannot."

Nevertheless, you will be delivered. You will be delivered, and when you are delivered, you will know that the fate of men is in my hand and no other. You will know that all I have promised, I will do. Look to your left.

Benjiah turned left as far as his chains would allow. At first, he saw only the executioner's big body, for he had taken up his position there and stood frozen, watching Tashmiren threaten Benjiah. Beside the executioner was the pole, and more than that, Benjiah couldn't see.

"I don't see anything."

Look more closely.

Benjiah refocused, noticing for the first time something that was mostly obscured from his vantage point. Between the pole and the executioner he saw a glimpse of what appeared to be a crouching man moving from the side of the scaffold where the stairs were toward the pole and the Nolthanim guard.

He craned his neck even farther back, despite the pain that shot through his arms as he stretched them awkwardly in an attempt to get a better glimpse, and he was stunned by what he saw.

I have raised up a deliverer, and he will save you from the hand of your enemy.

"But that's Rulalin Tarasir, my father's murderer."

It is. He murdered your father, but today he will deliver you.

"I don't understand."

You will. For now, just see and understand that my arm has not grown short so that it cannot save.

"I see and understand."

Good, now return to real time and see what I will do.

Benjiah felt the pull and knew by the noise and commotion emanating from the crowd that he had left *torrim redara*. He looked up at Tashmiren, whose mouth was just closing behind a final taunt. Benjiah looked at the man's mocking eyes and said, "You fool, you're already dead and you don't even know it."

Before Tashmiren could react, a cry of pain drew his attention to the side, and both he and Benjiah turned to see the body of the Nolthanim executioner sliding off Rulalin's blade onto the platform. Benjiah turned quickly toward Tashmiren to drink in the sudden appearance of surprise and fear on his face as realization of his predicament set in.

"What are you doing?" Tashmiren said, turning defensively toward Rulalin, Benjiah now forgotten amid the more pressing matter of self-preservation.

"What I've wanted to do for a very, very long time."

Tashmiren stepped back slowly. "You wouldn't dare."

"Oh I would," Rulalin answered, stepping forward.

"You swore your allegiance."

"I did."

"You're breaking your oath."

"I am."

"Malek will kill you."

"Not before I kill you."

Tashmiren, holding before him the sword he'd had to borrow, nervously glanced sideways at Benjiah. "If you want the boy, just take him."

"I will, after I kill you."

Tashmiren lunged and tried to land a desperate stroke, but Rulalin easily deflected it, and with Tashmiren off balance, he slashed the back of the man's leg. Tashmiren howled as he dropped to his knees, blood seeping through the back of his cloak.

Grimacing, the wounded man looked up and directed seething hatred at Rulalin. Through clenched teeth he said, "You fool, you treacherous fool."

"Yes." Rulalin nodded. "That is exactly what I have been, but I am a traitor no more. I serve Malek no more."

With that, Rulalin drove his sword through Tashmiren's gut, just below his rib cage, until the tip of the blade came out of the man's back. Benjiah watched him drive the killing blow home, swiftly, deftly, almost effortlessly. He held Tashmiren upright, and then, after a moment, when he was sure Tashmiren was dead, Rulalin withdrew his sword and let the body fall.

Rulalin looked down at the dead man and turned with a grin to Benjiah. "I've been waiting to do that a long time."

Benjiah looked at Rulalin, a mixture of wariness and gratitude within. Allfather might have raised up Rulalin to deliver him from Tashmiren, but the traitor was still his father's murderer. How exactly Benjiah was supposed to respond to this turn of events was something Allfather had neglected to mention.

Rulalin did not wait for Benjiah's response. Glancing quickly left and right at the stairs on either side of the scaffold, Rulalin stepped closer to Benjiah. "I don't know how much time we have up here before we get company, so I'd better see about getting you down."

As Rulalin moved aside to examine the chain that held Benjiah's right hand tight, Benjiah saw that at the front of the scaffold, directly behind the place where Rulalin had killed Tashmiren, a man had been lifted up onto the stage and was now crouching, moving stealthily forward. It was the man Benjiah had noticed moving through the crowd, fury in his face as Benjiah sang.

As soon as the man realized that he'd been seen, he leapt toward Rulalin. Sunlight glinted off the dagger he was holding in his hand. Benjiah called to Rulalin, "Look out!"

It was too late. Rulalin had just begun to turn when the man buried the dagger up to its hilt in the small of his back. Benjiah saw the look of pain and surprise on Rulalin's face as he heard the blade go in, be withdrawn, and then be thrust in again.

Rulalin's sword clattered to the platform floor, and Rulalin fell past Benjiah with a crash and lay still.

"You have served your purpose," the man murmured as Rulalin fell. "I have no more need of you."

The turn of events caught Benjiah completely by surprise. Allfather had said Rulalin would deliver him but nothing about any of this. Now Benjiah seemed to be right back where he had been. Where was his deliverance going to come from now? This man intended his death as surely as Tashmiren had.

He looked into the man's eyes. They were dark and cruel, and the hate that burned in them was far deeper than Tashmiren's. He bent over and grabbed Tashmiren's body, which was lying right in front of Benjiah, and roughly pulled and tossed it aside. The man seemed strong, but Benjiah noticed he limped a little. He faced Benjiah again, this time with nothing separating them.

"I have big plans, and you can't be allowed to ruin them, child of prophecy or no," he said, stepping forward with the dagger, ready to strike Benjiah's exposed chest.

As the blade rushed in, the light and warmth that Benjiah had felt beside the Kalamin flowed through his body. The dagger kept coming toward him, but it seemed to be moving slowly now. Benjiah felt a rush of strength as he pulled with his right hand, ripping the chain from the iron ring on the pole and slashing the chain across the face of his lunging attacker.

The blow was sudden, fierce, and startling. The man's head snapped back as the chain struck him, lacerated the side of his face, and drove his stab attempt wide of the mark. In fact, the dagger flew out of his hand and dropped over the edge of the scaffold. Benjiah pulled with his left hand and again ripped from the iron ring the chain that had only moments ago withstood all his struggles. He dealt the man a second blow, this one across his chest, sending him staggering back a few steps.

Benjiah felt the relief in his arms, free of their painful positions at last. Half a span of chain dangled from each wrist, but his arms were loose and he was free. The man who had stabbed Rulalin was dazed and off balance. Benjiah lowered his shoulder and struck the man hard enough to send him tumbling backward. He rolled over completely and fell off the front edge of the scaffold and into the crowd. Benjiah quickly looked around him for any other surprises, but he was alone on the scaffold.

He was alone on the scaffold, but he knew he had to get off it. An almost inexhaustible supply of men could be sent to kill him up here. He had to get away. The question was how.

He looked up at the horizon, which had been lost to him in the dramatic events of the last few moments. Swooping down out of the sky was the golden form of a dragon, dropping lower and lower and flying faster and faster. The dragon was flying right toward the scaffold, right toward him. As the dragon's intent dawned upon him, Benjiah braced himself. In a matter of seconds, he was firmly gripped in the talon of the dragon and soaring up above the scaffold, the crowd, and the battle beginning down below.

BACK FROM
THE BRINK

ALJERON AND KOSHTI RAN with Valzaan, Evrim, and Saegan in the war party of the Kalin Seir. The ground was soft, grassy, and essentially level, as they had left the foothills of the Zaros Mountains far behind some time ago. Naran was just ahead of them, as he had been all the way from their village in Nolthanin, even though his role as liaison had been rendered almost unnecessary. Keila ran nearby as well. She'd kept her distance from them, or more likely, from Aljeron, since coming down from the mountains, but today she had settled in a little behind Naran.

Aljeron watched her run. She was fluid and graceful, even at the great speed they all had maintained since the break in the cloud cover brought the sunshine flooding down, the sunshine that moment by moment was radiating outward in a growing circle, its center above the city of Tol Emuna and the great red rock, which was now visible in the distance. Aljeron watched and wondered if his feelings toward her would have been different had he not felt so deeply the joy of running toward Aelwyn.

Though her mask, like those worn by the rest of the Kalin Seir, obscured part of her face, enough showed that Aljeron knew she was beautiful. Even watching her run, he felt attraction toward her, an attraction that had grown, much to his dismay, over the days of their journey as they spent time in close proximity. Even so, there were reasons other than Aelwyn to suspect that they would not have made a good match. The first was that she was a Kalin Seir, and they were a proud and unusual people. There would no doubt be "complications" for such a union.

What's more, she was a great deal younger than he was. Aelwyn was too, but as she was twenty-five and a Novaana, the whisperings over the age difference would be minimal. Aljeron figured Keila to be still younger than Aelwyn, perhaps twenty—of marrying age, but much younger than he. He could imagine returning home at the end of this war, if he lived to see that end, riding into Shalin Bel with his wild young bride. There would be more than whispering then.

Aljeron stepped awkwardly upon the top of a rock buried in the ground and largely obscured by the grass. He stumbled slightly and then regained his footing, but the arch of his foot ached from the unexpected blow. He grumbled to himself about his ill fortune, then sought to pull his attention away from Keila. The only bride he'd be returning to Shalin Bel with, if Shalin Bel even still existed, was Aelwyn. Ahead lay the city of Tol Emuna, which when Valzaan had seen it last was surrounded by Cheimontyr and Malek's hosts. Blue sky or grey, they were running toward the Bringer of Storms and trouble.

Of all the things he should be thinking about, the suitability of a marriage to Keila was pretty low on the list.

All around him, the snow leopards running amid the Kalin Seir began to wheel to the right, toward the southwest. As they did, the Kalin Seir began to follow. Aljeron had not seen any signal among the people and their battle brothers, and yet they swung around in a great, fluid arc as one. As they did, he noticed Koshti's attention had also turned that direction. Though his connection to Aljeron kept him from racing alongside the snow leopards, Aljeron could tell his battle brother was feeling pulled in that direction. He slowed and scrutinized the southwestern horizon, trying to see what had attracted the animals' attention.

"Black Wolves." Valzaan supplied the answer to the riddle. "Several packs of them, approaching quickly."

"How many is several packs?"

"I would estimate a thousand."

"They are outnumbered then," Aljeron replied, now able to see the black forms moving swiftly toward them.

"Yes, but they will slow us down, and battle is brewing before the gates of Tol Emuna."

The line of snow leopards and Black Wolves crashed together, and the sound of fierce howling and snarling reached Aljeron. Kalin Seir archers and spearmen had moved forward, assisting their battle brothers. From what Aljeron could see, the wolves were not faring well.

Even so, not every Black Wolf was engaged immediately, and some were weaving their way through the Kalin Seir, deeper into the war party. Aljeron drew Daltaraan in order to be prepared. A great brute of a beast made a dash in their direction, but Koshti intervened, leaping on the creature's back. He used his powerful forelegs with his claws buried deep in the wolf's back to pull the beast down. With the creature below him, Koshti opened his great mouth wide and sunk his teeth into the wolf's neck. Aljeron could hear the neck bones snap as Koshti shook the head and neck while using his weight to keep the body still.

In the meantime, another wolf was coming toward Aljeron and Valzaan. Aljeron moved sideways to be in a better position to protect the prophet, but Valzaan raised his hand and stretched it out in the direction of the wolf. Immediately the wolf burst into flames. It ran a few more steps and swerved, yelping and howling as it burned. Its front legs buckled, and it fell down head first and rolled over on its back, where it lay smoldering in the grass.

Aljeron looked at Valzaan. "I guess I shouldn't have worried about protecting you."

"We are wasting time," Valzaan said, his face turned generally in the direction where the battle between the Kalin Seir and Black Wolves was now fully underway, and Aljeron heard a rare note of irritation in his voice.

Valzaan stepped forward and closed his empty eyes, raising both hands to the sky. His lips moved swiftly, but Aljeron heard no words. Then, all over the battlefield, Black Wolves starting bursting into flames. It was like watching a spill of lamp oil catch fire, for the flames seemed to zigzag and ripple across the battlefield in multiple directions at once, like waves of flame radiating outward from the prophet. All over, startled Kalin Seir and snow leopards disengaged and leapt back from the burning wolves that ran howling in circles or dropped to the ground to try to extinguish themselves.

After a short moment, the flames all but died away, leaving behind simmering piles of fur and bone smoking in the morning light. The Kalin Seir and their battle brothers drifted back to Valzaan. They gathered around him with amazement in their eyes.

"If any of our people doubted that you are Allfather's prophet, let them doubt no longer," one of the Kalin Seir elders said. "You have wielded great power."

"You are right to say I am Allfather's prophet," Valzaan replied, "for the power I wielded was not my own."

"No, but it was great power, and though this was a battle we would have won, you have spared us many casualties."

"The power was given that we might not be delayed. A much larger battle than this one is waiting." Valzaan motioned back toward the southeast and the red rock rising in the distance. "We must not lose time. We must run."

"Then we shall run," the Kalin Seir elder replied. "Duran, take twelve men and their battle brothers and remain behind with the wounded. If all can move, then come after us as swiftly as you may. If some cannot be moved, wait, and we will send help should the battle at the city go well for us."

The Kalin Seir Duran moved quickly, selecting his twelve helpers and moving out among the fallen wolves to the few injured men and leopards. With that, and with no further prompting, the war party turned southeast and began to run again. As they did, Saegan and Evrim appeared, one at each of Aljeron's shoulders.

"That was something," Saegan said in his understated way.

"It was something, all right." Evrim laughed, then added more soberly, "It would be a handy trick to pull out when we get to Tol Emuna."

"Indeed," Aljeron replied. "It would put an end to this war, with style no less, would it not?"

"Yes," Saegan said, "but somehow I doubt it will work that way. Valzaan doesn't seem able to do such things at will."

"No, not at will," Aljeron agreed.

"Still, I'd love to see Cheimontyr running around on fire, wouldn't you?" Evrim added, smiling.

"I would, but I'm not holding my breath," Aljeron replied. "Now, let's run."

Caan stepped cautiously over to Pedraan, both men watching three Nolthanim soldiers huddled together in the midst of the pandemonium. Pedraan tried to make sense of the events unfolding around him: the crowd had been silent and subdued, in total submission to their fate as a defeated people, and then Benjiah had started to sing.

The words of the song, strange though they were, had awakened something in each of them, just as it had appeared to do in Benjiah. Then the clouds had parted and the sun burst through, seemingly as a response. Whatever the truth of the matter was, as the people in the crowd opened their eyes to the bold light, the submissive hearts wearily accepting their fate disappeared. Pedraan knew this to be true, for no one had been more resigned to defeat than he, but no longer. For the first time since he'd watched Pedraal be struck down, he felt both the desire and the will to fight burning in him.

"Any time now, these soldiers are going to realize that the smartest thing for them to do is just kill us instead of trying to guard us," Caan whispered in his ear. "I suggest we kill them first."

Pedraan looked at Caan and saw that Corlas Valon, Talis Fein, Gilion, and several of the other officers had followed Caan to Pedraan and were watching him. He smiled in response. "What are we waiting for?"

"Let's go then," Caan said, turning from Pedraan toward the guards.

Had the three men been huddled together with their swords drawn, they might have had a chance, but they weren't and they didn't. Pedraan slipped around them to get the one farthest away, the one who would have had the best chance to draw his weapon. Pedraan seized him as the blade was perhaps a hand's length out of the sheath, and he took the man up in his arms and squeezed him. He didn't just choke or suffocate him, he crushed him. The man's ribs snapped, and he screamed as he met a quick and awful end. The scream was lost in the cries and sounds of struggle, and the three dead Nolthanim were quickly relieved of their swords. The officers looked in the direction of their own surrendered weapons.

Pedraan took the sword off the soldier he'd killed and handed it to Caan. "Here, you take it. I'm not good with this thing."

"I know," Caan said, smiling. "I gave you that war hammer and you never looked back."

"I didn't, and now I'm no good without it."

Caan looked at the broken body at Pedraan's feet. "I'd say that you're still holding your own."

The other two swords found their way into the hands of Gilion and Talis, and Gilion said to Caan, "Secure the weapons piles sir?"

"Yes."

With that they began to move through the chaos toward their objective. At first glance, despite the confusion, it appeared to Pedraan they'd never be able to get there. Although the Vulsutyrim between them and the piles had moved off when Benjiah announced the coming of the dragons, the officers still had to deal with Malekim and a small host of Nolthanim. A small band of men with three swords wouldn't ordinarily have had much hope for success. What saved their lives, all of their lives, was the arrival of the dragons. Their golden forms came rushing in and swooping down over the assembly, talons at the ready and eyes peeled, looking for opportunities to aid the Kirthanim and Great Bear now struggling to rally together. Pedraan saw dragons snatch up Malekim and Nolthanim, carry them off, and then dash them to the ground away from the crowd. There seemed to be too many people too close together for the great creatures to use their fire, at least at this point, but their intimidating presence kept the servants of Malek distracted, moving slowly and hesitantly, always with at least one eye on the heavens. It was this distraction that gave Pedraan and the others hope.

And yet, even with the aid of the dragons, the task before them wasn't easy. The dragons, though fierce and fast, couldn't be everywhere at once, and the crowd was rapidly expanding as waves of people moved outward. Lulls in the action overhead did come, and when they did, the Nolthanim and Malekim looked to the situation around them and their own hides.

One such lull came as the officers were trying to slip unnoticed past a large pocket of Nolthanim. Most of the Nolthanim had recently been forced to their knees by the low pass of a dragon, and they were only just straightening when they saw the officers only two spans away.

The result was predictable. The Nolthanim moved with swords drawn in their direction. Pedraan could see the confidence in their approach increase as they realized only a handful of the Kirthanim bore swords. Pedraan started to drift away from the other officers, hoping to draw one or two of the Nolthanim away from the rest to increase the chances for his armed friends.

His ruse worked, and a pair of Nolthanim detached from the others and came toward him, weapons in hand. Their first attack was hesitant and poorly coordinated, and Pedraan, having anticipated it, dodged without much difficulty. They spread out and continued their approach, this time taking advantage of their numerical superiority. Pedraan knew that evading their next attack would not be so easy.

Pedraan was starting to run out of time as he prepared for their next assault. While Pedraan tried to anticipate their move, a brown flash came from his right as a Great Bear on all fours came barreling into the scene, knocking the surprised Nolthanim completely off his feet. The other Nolthanim soldier looked up in surprise as his friend sailed past him in the air. He reacted quickly, redirecting his attention to the Great Bear, who had now risen to his full height. As he stepped toward the Great Bear, however, Pedraan tackled him, making a grab for the man's sword arm.

He missed. Though he succeeded in taking the man down to the ground, his sword arm remained free. Even so, Pedraan went down on top of the man, and his weight knocked the wind out of him completely. All the Nolthanim could manage to do was bring the hilt crashing down on Pedraan's head, which hurt tremendously but gave Pedraan the chance he needed to finish his enemy. He raised himself up off the man, and with surprising speed and agility drove his clenched fist into the man's exposed throat. Pedraan watched the man shudder and thought that perhaps he had killed him, but to make sure, he quickly took the man's head in his massive hands and snapped it sideways sharply enough to break it. He relieved the man of his sword and stood quickly.

The other Nolthanim was also dead, having been ripped open by the powerful claws of the Great Bear, who had moved on to help the other officers. They had also received the help of more Great Bear, and now all of them were continuing toward the nearest weapons pile. Pedraan jogged after them, his eyes roving in all directions, looking for any sign of attack.

The remaining distance to the weapons pile was surprisingly easy, a fact that Pedraan understood better when they found a circle of Great Bear with staffs encircling it. They passed through this perimeter and started extracting and disseminating weapons to every Kirthanim soldier who made his way to them.

Pedraan took up a place in the defense and helped push back the intermittent assaults that came from the Nolthanim, and on one occasion, Malekim. These attacks were repelled as the number of armed Kirthanim and Great Bear grew, but the attack that involved the Malekim was almost the end for Pedraan. As one of the Voiceless came toward him, Pedraan stepped forward without hesitation and aimed a vicious stroke at the creature with the sword he'd taken off the Nolthanim. The blade struck the Malekim's thick hide and bounced off, doing no damage and leaving Pedraan quite vulnerable. Only a stumble on the part of the creature, hit by another Malekim engaged with a Great Bear, saved him. Pedraan dodged the awkward sword stroke from the Silent One and retreated, allowing the Great Bear to take care of the Malekim.

He examined the sword in his hand and found the blade notched. He felt sheepish, recalling Caan's lessons on the density of the Malekim's hide. He had been used to the war hammer and his ability to defend himself against Malekim by sheer force, and he realized that unless he somehow came into the possession of a Firstblade, he'd better be more cautious when it came to engaging this particular foe.

"Pedraan!" a familiar voice called to him, and he turned in surprise to see Karalin, Mindarin, and Aelwyn coming toward him inside the perimeter of Great Bear. He ran to Karalin and caught her up in his arms, carefully, for he kept hold of the sword.

"I thought I'd lost you," she whispered into his ear.

"I thought I'd lost you," he replied.

He set her down and looked from her to the others. "As good as it is to see you, why did you come here?"

"We were looking for you," Mindarin said.

"Me? Why?"

"We're trying to organize the civilians to lead them back into the city," Mindarin replied, "but they're too afraid to go anywhere. They keep huddling together like sheep."

"We thought maybe you or one of the other officers could help."

Pedraan nodded. "I can. I'll grab a few men and come with you."

A few men turned out to be about thirty by the time Pedraan made his way toward the cowering mass of frightened people. Chaos was growing as the situation on the battlefield spun out of control. The dragons were now fully engaged, and from time to time great bursts of flame erupted from golden forms flying quite close by. Those bursts of light and heat, although not directed against them, could be quite alarming, and Pedraan found the people much more willing to be led away than the women had indicated.

There was initial resistance from the enemy, though not a great deal, not until a contingent of about fifty Nolthanim approached Pedraan and his thirty men to engage them. Before they could close in combat, though, a pair of dragons came from opposite sides and blew terrific bursts of flame at the Nolthanim. The blasts momentarily obscured them from view, and but for the brilliant flames and screams, Pedraan wouldn't have known they were still there. The initial bursts faded and what was left was terrible. The sight and smell of it was, even for Pedraan, sickening beyond words. Karalin tucked her face away from the scene and Pedraan held her tight. The few surviving Nolthanim moved out of their way.

Before long, the stream of mostly women with children and older men broke away from the growing battle, and they ran unimpeded across the open plain to Tol Emuna's gates. Pedraan stepped aside and watched the steady stream of people flee.

Looking back at the battle and lifting his gaze to the heavens, he marveled at the golden dragons flying against the backdrop of the blue sky.

"They're beautiful," Karalin said, taking his arm.

"They are."

"Beautiful and terrible."

"That too."

Pedraan then noticed a large contingency of Vulsutyrim returning from their camp, moving in close formation behind their great shields. As he watched, the formation broke up and the giants began to spread out as they worked their way into the battle. Pedraan felt his body tense. More than once he'd seen the Vulsutyrim neutralize the effect of the dragons. In those cases, the Nolthanim, Malekim, and Black Wolves used their superior numbers to drive the Kirthanim from the field.

To be sure, Pedraan had seen no engagement involving this many dragons, but that didn't mean that the Vulsutyrim wouldn't be able to effectively relieve the Malekim and Nolthanim. The battle, he realized, was far from over.

"I need to go back," Pedraan said, turning to Karalin.

She looked into his eyes, and reaching up, touched his face. Her hand was soft and trembling. "I know you do, just come back to me."

"I will."

"You'd better."

"I love you, Karalin."

"I love you too."

"Whatever happens, stay inside the city. The walls will afford you some protection if things go badly."

"I will, but come back to me."

"I'll try." Pedraan hugged her tightly and bent over to kiss her. He lingered for a moment at her lips, then let her go.

Rulalin was dreaming and knew it. He didn't know how he knew it, but he did. He was walking through the quiet streets of home, of Fel Edorath, and he knew somehow that he had not been there in a long, long time. The sky was blue and the sunshine was bright and warm. A light breeze played with his hair. He stopped and breathed deeply, the scent of spring heavy in the air.

Ahead of him was the western gate. The road that ran through it passed through some of the greenest plains and pasturelands of all Werthanin. He felt an urge to go down and look upon it again, so he walked down to the gate. When he got there, he saw a young blond-haired man standing in the grass, looking at him.

"Benjiah?" he said, recognition dawning on him.

"Yes," the boy replied.

An image of the boy chained between two poles flashed through his head. Rulalin remembered. "I didn't free you?"

"No, but you did save me. Tashmiren would have killed me."

"What happened?"

"Allfather granted me the power to break the chains, and a dragon took me from the scaffold."

"You are safe?"

"I am."

Rulalin nodded, thoughtfully. "I'm glad."

"Rulalin, I have offered twice before a chance for you to turn from your path. I ask you again what I asked you before, and for the last time. Will you renounce what you have done and who you have become? Will you not come out?"

Rulalin looked at Benjiah, then raised his eyes and surveyed the beautiful land. "I will," he said and stepped out of the city.

A fiery pain burned in Rulalin's back. He lifted his head up off of the rough wooden platform. Bright sunshine like that in his dream greeted his attempts to open his eyes. The beautiful grasslands and Benjiah were gone. He saw nothing clearly at first, but his vision gradually returned as he tried to focus on the tall dark object rising beside him.

It was one of the poles to which Benjiah had been chained. Tilting his head a little to the side, he looked as far up it as he could and saw that indeed, a chain dangled down beside it, ending in a broken link.

The pain in his back erupted again, and Rulalin groaned, his head falling back. The memory of turning to see Synoki drive the dagger home flooded back. Rulalin tried moving his arm a little to lift himself up onto his hands and knees, but his movement only brought more pain.

He heard feet and voices from the stairs as men came rapidly up. He lay still, in part because he found it hard to move, but also because he suspected the men meant trouble for him.

They stepped onto the scaffold, and Rulalin thought from the sounds they made that there were just two, though two were more than enough to finish him off. He was relieved when they bypassed him, moving first to the executioner, and then to Tashmiren. Over both men they said something that Rulalin could not quite catch, but he could tell from their grim, hushed tones that to them the scene was disconcerting.

He held his breath, waiting for them to come examine him. He could try to lie still and play dead, but the pain in his back was so severe, he knew he wouldn't be able to hide it if they handled him roughly. He waited, but they did not come. After a quiet moment of mental agony, unable to see what they were doing or what they were looking at, Rulalin heard them descend, talking earnestly to one another.

Rulalin exhaled and groaned, the pain in his back intensifying. It throbbed and radiated outward. He sensed how damp his cloak was, and he wondered how much was sweat and how much was blood. He wondered, but felt reasonably sure that he didn't really want to know.

He heard another pair of feet on the stairs, this time a softer pair, and without thinking he tried to lift and turn his head that way. The movement sent more pain shooting through his body, and darkness washed over him.

Benjiah had little time to process his dramatic and strange return to the gates of Fel Edorath and Rulalin. The vision that had suddenly taken him ended just as suddenly, and Benjiah's eyes popped open to find the great red rock of Tol Emuna just below. The dragon carrying him began to circle and descend. He remembered the first vision involving Rulalin, and discussing it with Valzaan, but what had just happened and what it signified was not clear to him. So much was happening all at once that he almost felt dizzy trying to keep track of it all.

As the dragon slowed above the smooth red rock, its talon opened and Benjiah dropped lightly onto its surface. The dragon alighted as well. Though large, strong, and fierce, he was every bit as graceful as the most delicate bird in flight. He faced Benjiah, peering down at him from his most impressive height.

Benjiah had dealt with Eliandir and Dravendir and a few other dragons before being captured by Malek, but this dragon appeared to be almost, if Benjiah could trust his eyes, a full span taller than they. Not only did he appear larger, but as Benjiah looked more closely, he realized that he could see no tinge of coloration in his scales, no red, no blue, no green. He looked down at the talon that had held him, the telling location of any dragon's color, and he saw nothing but gold.

"You're Sulmandir," Benjiah said, awestruck.

"I am."

Benjiah nodded slowly, recognition filtering through him that he'd just been rescued not by a dragon but by *the* dragon. "Thank you. I thought I was going to die down there."

"Not today, Benjiah," Sulmandir replied, his deep voice resonating as he lowered his head to look more closely at him.

"You know my name?"

"Yes."

"How?"

"Allfather spoke to me as I was approaching the city."

"What did He say?"

"He said, 'The boy chained to the poles, his name is Benjiah. He is my prophet. He has need of you. Before you join the battle, take him up and remove him a safe distance away.' So I did."

"Did He tell you anything else?" Benjiah inquired. "Like what I am supposed to do now that I'm here?"

"No," Sulmandir replied, his great golden eyes gazing intently at him.

Benjiah nodded again, looking for the first time at the great red rock from which the city was carved. The vista overlooked the tops of the tallest towers in the city, and he could see the open plain outside the city gates. There was chaos on the ground, and the sounds of battle rose, keeping pace with the brightly shining sun. The other dragons were swooping repeatedly, spouting fire, then rising rapidly back to the sky. Benjiah looked back to Sulmandir.

"The battle is intensifying, should I go back?"

"I can't answer that question for you," Sulmandir replied, "but I must go, that I know."

A great boom sounded across the plain, followed by half a dozen more just like it. Both Sulmandir and Benjiah turned to look. The first thing Benjiah noticed was the approach of a large detachment of Vulsutyrim. The next thing he noticed was Cheimontyr, emerging from their midst, his great hammer raised high above his head.

Though the sky above him was clear of clouds, his hammer still flashed with lightning, and bright surges of power erupted in every direction. They were flying up at the dragons and out toward the ground, and with each eruption another great boom rang out above the din of battle.

"The Bringer of Storms," Benjiah whispered under his breath.

"Cheimontyr," Sulmandir added, turning away from the view.

"You know him?"

"I do. He has sought and gained power from Malek since last I saw him, but I know him. We are enemies of old."

"Can you defeat him?"

"Before the sun goes down tonight," Sulmandir replied, "I will kill him as I killed his father before him."

With that, he leapt from the great rock and circled upward until he was high above Benjiah, then he flew out over the city in the direction of the battle. For a moment, Benjiah watched him go, then he turned his attention back to his own situation. He could stay here and wait, watching from a distance, or he could make his way down and head back out to help.

It occurred to him as he watched Sulmandir fly away that rejoining the battle could be difficult. Flying Benjiah to the highest point around for safety had probably been quite natural, especially for a dragon who felt at home in the heights, but Benjiah couldn't help wishing that Sulmandir had taken a little more into account Benjiah's own limitations.

Perhaps his location suggested that he should stay put, although Sulmandir hadn't said so. Benjiah needed to get moving, of that he was sure. Any way down would certainly take him into Tol Emuna, and once down and in the city, he could decide what to do about the battle.

It didn't take him long to find a great carved stair leading down from the top of the rock. It was long and the stairs narrow, but he didn't see any other way. He paused to look out over the city and plain once more. What a day it had been so far, and it wasn't even midday.

His mind went back to the scaffold. He saw Rulalin examining his chains, and then he saw the man who'd stabbed him, the limping man. The cold face and dispassionate scorn was very different from Tashmiren's gloating arrogance. Something about him had struck Benjiah as odd, although things happened so quickly he had no time to try to figure out what it was. It simply registered in his mind and was forgotten as Sulmandir swept him away. What had it been?

I have no more need of you. That was what the man had said to Rulalin when he struck him down. He hadn't said, "We have no more need," or, "Malek has no more need." He'd said, "I have no more need." And, when he faced Benjiah, he'd said, "I have big plans, and you can't be allowed to ruin them, child of prophecy or no."

Benjiah froze at the top of the long, narrow stair. Surely he was reading too much into a simple choice of words. Rulalin undoubtedly had many superiors, even as Malek must have many captains under him. It was silly to think that the limping man upon the scaffold was Malek himself. But what if he was? Benjiah followed that thought and recalled striking the man across the face with the chain and then across the chest before knocking him from the scaffold. Had he just fought Malek, striking three blows against the fallen Titan, the Master of the Forge and ancient nemesis of Kirthanin?

A chill ran through his body. Allfather had filled Benjiah with power right when the man turned toward him, and with Allfather's power Benjiah ripped out the chains that had held him fast all morning. With Allfather's power he had struck the man faster than he would have thought humanly possible, twice, and knocked him off the scaffold before he could recover from the blows. It was possible that Allfather had empowered him to do what otherwise he could not have done. That man *could* have been Malek.

He had thought earlier in the day, first when he announced Sulmandir's arrival and then later as he'd gazed out over the battle with the dragons circling above, that this day would mark the turning point in the war. The thought that he might have just escaped Malek himself only confirmed that suspicion. Today was the day. They had stood on the brink of defeat, and Allfather had reached out and seized them, preventing them from tumbling over the edge. Victory, which had seemed an impossible thought that morning, no longer seemed impossible.

3

THE HAMMER FALLS

WYLLA LOOKED UPON RULALIN lying face down, blood seeping through the back of his thin cloak. From the ground, she'd managed to see Rulalin's confrontation with both the executioner and Tashmiren. She watched him kill them and move to free her son, only to see Synoki take Rulalin from behind.

Rulalin had spoken to her of Synoki's allegiance to Malek before, during the long leagues from Amaan Sul to Tol Emuna. Wylla hadn't been sure what to make of the story. It wasn't that she doubted this particular tale so much as she simply perceived everything Rulalin told her with a fair bit of mistrust. Apparently Rulalin had been telling her the truth, because Synoki struck Rulalin down with a vengeance, and it appeared for a brief and terrible moment like he would strike Benjiah down as well.

What a wondrous sight had followed—Benjiah ripping the chains and using them as whips, then the dragon snatching him up into the blue sky. Her heart leapt for joy to see him taken away, hopefully far away, where he would be safe from the turmoil and chaos around her.

With Benjiah delivered, her thoughts had turned to Rulalin, and Wylla felt the hardness in her heart directed toward him these many years break. Compassion and pity poured out of her, and tears rose unbidden at the thought of what he'd sacrificed to try to save her son. She decided at that point that though Yorek pleaded for her to come away with him now that Benjiah was safe, she would not abandon Rulalin to his fate upon the scaffold. She would go up after him as he had gone up after Benjiah.

Her plan was compromised when two Nolthanim reached the stairs ahead of her and went up. She slipped back along the side of the scaffold with Yorek and waited, wondering what they were up there doing and if Rulalin was still alive. The soldiers did not stay long, and as soon as she was able, Wylla climbed the stairs as quickly and quietly as she could.

Rulalin lay beside the near pole, face down and as far as she could tell, dead. She stooped to feel his face and found it still warm, burning in fact. She watched him closely and kept her hand still upon him. He was breathing. It was faint and labored, to be sure, but he was breathing.

"He's alive, Yorek."

"What do you want to do?"

"I don't think we can safely move him," Wylla replied, looking back at the steep narrow steps.

"No, Your Majesty. He needs to stay here."

"Then so will I."

"Your Majesty, you can do nothing for him."

"That's not true, I can stay. I can stay and comfort him if he comes to."

"Is that worth your life?" Yorek asked, looking intently into her determined eyes.

"Yes, if that is what it costs," Wylla replied stubbornly. "Besides, you cannot guarantee me that we'd be any safer down there. For all we know, this might be the safest place for us to hide until the battle ends."

Yorek frowned. "Up here, you are visible for many spans in every direction. If any of our enemies are looking for you, they'll see you."

"Then we'd better sit down," Wylla replied, and following her own advice, she settled onto the warm wood next to Rulalin's head. Yorek got down too, lowering himself between the two great poles.

Wylla reached down and gingerly lifted Rulalin's head, taking his face in her hands, then slid over and lowered his head in her lap. Gently she stroked his matted black hair and pulled the few strands that had fallen across his face back.

Rulalin stirred, his eyelids flickering open. Wylla could see him struggling for comprehension, and she bent over him and whispered, "Shh, Rulalin, just lie still."

He seemed to relax, but his eyes remained open, now focused on her face. "I can't be dreaming," he said, struggling a little bit to be heard. "It hurts too much."

"You're not dreaming. We're on the scaffold. You were stabbed by Synoki."

Rulalin's head nodded ever so slightly. "My downfall again."

"Again?"

Rulalin looked away from her. Wylla could see the shame in his face, and she moved quickly to ease his mental anguish. "Rulalin, you saved Benjiah from Tashmiren. Thank you so much. You gave yourself for him."

Rulalin's eyes moved back to Wylla, intensity burning in them. "Don't thank me." He struggled with his words, but he seemed vehement and shook his head when she opened her mouth. "Forgive. That's what I . . . forgive me, Wylla. That's what I need. Don't thank, forgive."

His bloody hand clenched her cloak. She bent further and looked him in the eye. "I do forgive you Rulalin, for every-thing. Don't torture yourself about it anymore. Do you hear me? I forgive."

His hand relaxed and dropped back upon the wooden floor. The fire slipped from his eyes, and his gaze moved from Wylla's face to the bright blue sky. She thought that something nearly like peace appeared in his countenance.

"There was a soldier, Wylla, dying like me, from Fel Edo-rath. He followed me into Malek's service. He was lying on the battlefield, dying." Rulalin's voice was faint, and he struggled to roll even slightly onto his side so he could look up at Wylla's face with more ease. "He asked if I thought Allfather could forgive him. I didn't answer, didn't know what to say. I didn't think Allfather would forgive any of us. Can He, Wylla? Can He forgive me?"

Wylla's tears fell on Rulalin's face as she kissed his brow. When she raised her head from his face, she saw that he'd closed his eyes. She knew he wasn't asleep because his hand had once more taken hold of her cloak. She whispered, "He can, Rulalin. He can and he will, if you desire it."

Rulalin struggled to nod, but he didn't open his eyes. "Maybe that's what the vision meant."

"What vision?"

"The city, so quiet and beautiful, and the green fields. Ben-jiah said I had another chance."

"Benjiah?"

"Like before, at the gate. He told me I had one more chance."

Rulalin's voice was growing faint. His breathing was light and shallow, and his hand relaxed its grip on Wylla's cloak.

"Rulalin," Wylla whispered. "I don't understand what you're saying about Benjiah. What vision? What did you see?"

"Beautiful," he whispered. "Like you. No sound of battle there. I want to go back. Go back and rest."

The last phrase was so faint that Wylla wasn't even sure that she'd heard him correctly. Thin wisps of breath eased out of his mouth as he lay asleep in her lap. Wylla looked up from him and over at Yorek, who sat watching silently.

"Not long now," she said, though to whom she said it wasn't clear. She kept stroking his hair.

For the first time in a very long time, Pedraan found the midday sun beating down on him from almost directly overhead. For a Full Spring day, it was uncomfortably hot, and sweat was pouring down his face. The sword he carried was much lighter than his war hammer, but his unpracticed use of it made him work twice as hard to wield it effectively. He wanted to throw the thing away, and he would have, had he had anything close at hand blunt and large and heavy enough to pound and thump away with. He'd tried to take up the staff of a fallen Great Bear, but he'd been forced to admit that as big and strong as he was, it was more than he could handle.

The confusion that had covered the battlefield like a mist that morning had finally, for the most part, drifted away. In the wake of the coming of the dragons and the departure of the clouds that had hung like a permanent fixture in the sky since Autumn, the soldiers of Kirthanin and the Great Bear had been energized. They took back their weapons and drew together in violent resurgence. The Nolthanim and Malekim experienced just the opposite, as disorder and chaos settled over them like a pall. Now, though, both sides of the conflict were returning to a state of normalcy. The servants of Malek had regrouped and reorganized, and the Kirthanim's euphoria had slowly dissipated in the face of the hard work of battle.

The euphoria had dissipated, but the newly forged resolve inside them had not. The devastation Pedraan had felt after Pedraal's death a few days before had not returned. Instead, the coming of daylight and the sight of those golden forms overhead, fighting with them, had fueled his inner desire to win this battle and if possible, end this war.

Even so, despite the renewed strength and resolve that he saw in every Kirthanim face, the battle was beginning to slip away from them. The Vulsutyrim, the only ones among Malek's hosts who had responded to the events of the morning immediately and with calm and measured actions, returned to the battlefield with their great shields and began to take control. They spread themselves throughout the field, moving in pairs and groups of three, so that all had access to the cover and protection of their shields. When unopposed by a dragon, the giants were able to rally the Nolthanim and Malekim, organize and spur them on, not to mention wreak havoc with the Kirthanim and Great Bear, who were poorly equipped. When opposed by a dragon, these mobile Vulsutyrim units focused only on the dragon, avoiding the flames and talons and stepping out from behind the shields to strike with the great spears they had fetched for precisely this purpose.

These great spears were thicker than the staffs of the Great Bear and twice as long with long, wicked iron spear points bolted to the end. They were sharp enough to penetrate dragon scales, for perhaps as many as five dragons lay injured or dying around the battlefield from wounds inflicted by them. Pedraan had seen one of the fallen dragons pierced. He'd come roaring in, a long, slender dragon with green hues visible in the sunlight, winging low and fast above the battlefield toward one of the giants engaged in directing a large number of Malekim. The Vulsutyrim saw the green and raced for the protection of a giant shield, but the beast had caught him first and overwhelmed him with flame. And yet, as the dragon blew fire at the exposed Vulsutyrim, another stepped out from behind the shield and drove his great spear deep into the side of the dragon. The dragon dropped to the ground and writhed there, lashing out with talons and tail, but a handful of giants converged and finished him.

And so, increasingly, the thirty or so dragons that remained became occupied with engaging the Vulsutyrim, leaving the Great Bear and Kirthanim with ever decreasing aid against the superior numbers of Malekim and Nolthanim. This process was greatly accelerated by the emergence of Cheimontyr as the central, destructive force.

As Pedraan returned to the battlefield after escorting the civilians back to Tol Emuna earlier that morning, he saw Cheimontyr moving in the distance, great surges of power and sound erupting from his hammer in all directions. *Boom! Boom! Boom!* The deafening sound raced across the plain, bringing to mind his first glimpse of Cheimontyr outside Zul Arnoth, hurling lightning strikes laterally at the ancient walls and dashing them to pieces. It was even more bizarre now to see this Bringer of Storms wielding such power, because the sky was clear as could be. Whatever had happened to the actual storm that Cheimontyr had conjured and controlled for the last half year, the giant was creating a storm of a different kind on the battlefield.

Fortunately for Pedraan and the rest of the Kirthanim, the great golden dragon—which Pedraan figured must be Sulmandir, for he was bigger than any of the others and pure in color—had come flying into the fray and focused solely on Cheimontyr. He had made it his task to shadow Cheimontyr wherever he went and to keep him occupied. And so it was that the Bringer of Storms, who had brought down two or three dragons in the space of less than an hour after arriving on the battlefield, had been to some degree neutralized by

Sulmandir. The two moved back and forth in a dangerous dance of attack and retreat.

Now it was midday, and Pedraan found himself with Caan and Gilion, talking to Turgan, the leader of Elnindraal, who had assumed command of the remaining Great Bear and organized them into the front line of defense. The Kirthanim captains had done their best to form a manageable and effective fighting force, but they were outnumbered and knew it.

"They are intent on flanking us on our right, in the north," Gilion said, pointing in the direction that troubled him. "Every time we stretch our line thinner to avoid being flanked, the Vulsutyrim usher up a new unit of Nolthanim or Malekim."

"Fortunately," Turgan added, "there are a pair of dragons who have made it their mission, from what I can see, to frustrate their attempts to extend the line northward."

"Yes, but even so," Gilion said, "the enemy line is growing steadily, if slowly. We will soon be flanked."

"There's nothing we can do about that," Caan said, frustrated as he looked northward. "We're stretched impossibly thin as it is. Gilion, you'll just have to start bending the northern end of our line back, like a hook, to protect our exposed flank."

"Yes, Caan," Gilion said, evidently not pleased with that prospect, for he knew that such a maneuver without a natural barrier to anchor it or reinforcements was desperate and rarely effective.

"What worries me," Pedraan said, "is where the Black Wolves are. There were thousands and thousands of them in the battle a few days ago, but I haven't seen any of them today."

"Neither have I," Turgan said.

"Perhaps Malek didn't think he would need them here anymore," Caan said, "and maybe he sent them elsewhere."

"Perhaps," Pedraan said, "but if they return from a direction where we're exposed, they'll rip us to shreds from behind."

"There's nothing we can do about that either," Caan replied, sharply. "We may not even be able to field a force large enough to defeat the enemies we can see. We can't be worried about ones we can't."

"So what do we do?" Gilion asked.

"Hold the line," Caan replied. "Our only hope is for the dragons to break the Vulsutyrim. They're the backbone of the enemy. If we break them, we may win the day. We just can't break first."

As Caan was speaking, an eerie silence fell upon the field, and the three men and Great Bear looked up to see what had happened. Across the field, before the Nolthanim, a figure in bizarre black armor had emerged on horseback, trotting nonchalantly through their midst.

"The dread captain of the Nolthanim," Caan said as they all watched, transfixed by the mysterious man. In every engagement they'd fought in their flight up the Barunaan, he'd been a constant, immovable force in the center of the battle.

"I thought they recovered rather quickly from their disarray this morning," Gilion said. "I should have known he was why."

"He and the Bringer of Storms are the heart of this army," Pedraan said. "If we could kill them, we'd stand a chance."

"We tried for Cheimontyr once already." Turgan sighed.

"I know, and you almost did it," Pedraan replied. "I think we'll have to leave him to the dragons. This man, though, no matter how brave, is only a man."

"Pedraan, no foolish risks, not today," Caan said. "We just need to hold the line."

"I understand," Pedraan answered, but he kept his eyes on the captain. That man was the heart of the Nolthanim, he was sure, and even the Malekim seemed to go where he willed and to do as he wished. He and the Bringer of Storms were like twin pillars upon which the rest of them stood. Cut them down, and the Kirthanim would have a chance.

Benjiah appeared to be at an impasse. The long, narrow stair down from the top of the great red rock of Tol Emuna ended at a narrow ledge. The view from this ledge was spectacular. As he looked directly down at the roofs of most of the houses and buildings, he realized he was still perhaps ten spans above the streets, and they were the high streets that sloped downward into the rest of the city and out toward the great stone wall and gates. He could still see out over the wall from this ledge, though he wasn't so far above it that he had the panoramic view he'd enjoyed from up top. And yet he felt no closer to his goal, for there were no stairs leading down the outside of the rock from this ledge, and the only door he'd found, a great iron door, was locked from the inside.

As he examined the great rock he had descended, he quickly realized that many rooms must lie within, for windows and other ledges were scattered here and there, at least in the surface he could see from the ledge. He was reasonably confident that if he could get inside, he'd be able to find his way down. The door was heavy, however, thick and locked, and there were no windows within reach that he might try to force so he could get inside.

He had found one possibility after examining what lay below the ledge, but it was risky. Beyond one end of the ledge was a straight drop all the way down to the foot of the great rock, but at the other end, Benjiah saw another ledge half a span over and a span and a half down. A span and a half was a long distance to drop, but he thought he could make it. The problem was that there was but one door connected to this second ledge, which could as easily be locked as the one on his ledge, and there were no stairs leading back up to the top of the rock. In short, if he jumped and found the door locked, he'd really be stuck, because jumping down was feasible, but jumping back up was not.

He had almost conceded that the wisest move was to trudge back up that long, narrow stairway to the top of the great rock, when a rather bold and intriguing plan occurred to him. He moved back to the edge and looked down at the second ledge. He ran his fingers through his hair, wondering if he dared. In theory, it should work, but his theory was based on the incomplete knowledge he'd gained of *torrim redara* from Valzaan during his all too brief prophetic apprenticeship.

He decided he'd try it, and he found himself forcing the transition into slow time. He had certainly grown in his ability to control his entrance to and exit from *torrim redara*. Controlling his access, however, was not the same thing as controlling the whole process, and it wasn't in the timing of his exit that the trick would lie.

He squatted so as to minimize the distance he would fall, and without waiting jumped down and out so as to clear the distance. He landed roughly on the ledge, and his momentum carried him forward so that he sprawled out on the hard stone. He picked himself up, his hands scraped and body bruised, but otherwise he was unhurt. He walked over to the door and tried the handle. It swung open and outward. Looking inside, he saw a dark corridor with stairs at the end. That was all he needed to see. If he jumped down here in real time, the door would still be unlocked and the stairs would still be there, and then he could be about the business of finding his way down.

He pushed the door shut and looked back up at the ledge from which he'd leapt. Here was the part that concerned him. If his theory held true, the stream of real time would pull him from this lower ledge back up to the higher one, placing him back where he'd begun, so he could repeat the process of dropping down in real time with the certainty that an open door awaited. The problem was that Valzaan had been clear that it was best to return to the approximate place from which one entered slow time, so that the return didn't hurt too much. Benjiah didn't really want to be slammed into the underside of the thick stone ledge above if the pull toward the place from where he'd jumped was too direct.

He moved farther along the ledge he was now on, away from the upper ledge. The further out he went, he reasoned, the less likely that a direct line of pull would bring him crashing into the ledge. He moved as far as the lower ledge would allow him, then decided there was nothing for it but to see what happened. He willed the move back into real time and felt himself jerked off the lower ledge and flung up through the air. He was quite pleased and relieved to find himself in the end upon the higher ledge, facing out, with no bumps or bruises from the return trip. As soon as he regained his orientation in real time, he leapt down a second time onto the lower ledge.

This leap was no smoother or more graceful than the first, and once more he picked himself up from the hard stone, grunting with the aches and pains of his none too soft landing. He looked back up at the ledge he had started from and felt quite happy that there would be no need to do that again. Walking to the door, he opened it and passed inside in search of a way down into the city.

The corridors and stairs inside the great rock were narrow and dark, but he kept his head and negotiated them quickly and without incident. Soon he was out in the sunshine again, walking along the clean, hard streets.

He wasn't familiar with Tol Emuna, and without his vantage point from the top of the great red stone, he didn't really know which roads led where. At first, it was relatively easy to just keep moving downhill, using the towering rock as a point of reference behind him. As the streets leveled out, however, he found that the interlocking rows of houses and buildings would sometimes cut off the street he was on, leaving him with little alternative but to trace his way back and start hunting for a new route. Unlike the generally straight and predictable streets of the more spacious Amaan Sul, Benjiah found the winding streets of Tol Emuna frustrating.

When he turned onto a larger-than-usual street and found women and children streaming the opposite direction, he knew he must be on the right track. These must be refugees from the battle, flying back into the safe haven they'd been forced to vacate that morning. It stood to reason, then, that if he moved against the current, he would find the gates and his way out, for by now he was decided. He was going out to help if he could, in whatever way possible. He even harbored a vague notion that perhaps his earlier success against the limping man, whoever he really was, was a pledge of sorts, though of what exactly he didn't know. He trembled a bit to think of squaring off with the ancient enemy of Kirthanin, but this was why Valzaan had burst into the palace in Amaan Sul in the middle of the thunderstorm that Autumn night, was it not?

Benjiah began to make his way along the street, drifting to the side to escape the growing stream of people flowing in the other direction. Some looked at him curiously, making him wonder if they recognized him from the scaffold, but most of them seemed intent on reaching their own destination and paid him little heed. Before long, he was within sight of the great gates, which were open to receive the return of its people.

Getting out of the gate, he realized, was going to be a little more difficult than getting to it, because of the growing mass of people eager to get back in. Here, as in the street that had brought him here, his best chance appeared to be at the margins, though he'd have to cross the large crowd to get to the wall adjacent to the gate. He pushed off boldly and began wading through.

It wasn't easy, and he received some scathing looks from people who couldn't understand, he was sure, what fool would be going the wrong direction. Still, he persevered and gradually made it to the wall. He slid along the wall until he almost reached the gate. To his surprise, he heard a familiar voice calling his name from above. He looked up and saw Aelwyn's smiling face beaming down at him from a walkway a few spans off the ground.

"Come up," she called excitedly when she caught Benjiah's eye.

"How?" he called back.

She pointed back along the wall the way he'd come, and he noticed then a small stair that went up to the walkway. He looked back up and smiled. "Just a moment."

It didn't take him long to negotiate his way to the stair, for it wasn't a great deal farther than he'd already come. He ascended rapidly to be greeted not just by Aelwyn, but by Mindarin and Karalin too.

"So good to see you," Aelwyn was saying as she threw her arms around him. The hug was short-lived as he was passed off, first to Mindarin and then to Karalin.

When the enthusiastic greetings were complete, Mindarin asked what had happened. How had he gotten from the scaffold, where they'd last seen him, to Tol Emuna? He told his story in abbreviated fashion, and all three went back to the same detail.

"You say it was Rulalin who killed the two men on the scaffold?" Mindarin asked, a look of mixed sorrow and joy on her face.

"Yes."

"And the man who came up from the front of the scaffold stabbed him?"

"Yes."

"Do you think he was dead?"

"I don't know. Rulalin was stabbed twice before the man turned his attention to me."

Mindarin nodded and said no more as Aelwyn turned to the others. "What does it mean, I wonder, his helping Benjiah?"

"Who can say?" Karalin replied. "Maybe he thought better of his allegiance to Malek and wanted to help."

"Or maybe he was always an unwilling accomplice," Mindarin said, peering at Benjiah. "Do you know?"

"I think," Benjiah began, "that he has always been conflicted, but that he went to the Mountain and offered his service to Malek freely, even as he chose to help me of his own free will."

"Still, it is great to see you free of those awful chains and safely removed from the battle," Aelwyn said, obviously steering the conversation away from a protracted discussion of Rulalin and his motives. She turned back to Benjiah, putting her hand upon his shoulder. "As soon as the bulk of the crowd outside the gates is in, we are going to start reorganizing the volunteers to minister to the wounded, since it looks like the battle had been renewed. Do you want to help?"

"I can't," Benjiah replied, "I'm headed out to the battle myself."

"Don't be ridiculous," Mindarin said, frowning at Benjiah. "You're scraggly and unkempt, and even I can see you haven't been fed properly. You're in no shape to fight. You don't even have a sword or spear."

"I don't want a sword or spear," Benjiah answered. "They've never fit comfortably in my hand, and I'm not good with them.

Besides, it wasn't with a sword or spear that I held back the enemy at the Kalamin River."

"We heard about that," Aelwyn said, standing back and taking a fresh look at him, a look that told Benjiah he had succeeded in his purpose for making the statement, namely reminding these increasingly maternal women that he was a prophet of Allfather, even if not yet of age.

"Well, you know what you need to do," Aelwyn continued, "and I for one say that we should let you be on your way."

"Wait," Karalin said, reaching out for Benjiah's arm. "You can take Suruna with you!"

"Suruna?" Benjiah answered. "You have it?"

"Yes, or at least, I know where it is. Pedraan has it in his room. He said you entrusted it to him for safekeeping."

"I did."

"Do you want me to take you to it?"

Benjiah was torn. He wanted to be on his way as soon as possible. What's more, he knew he would be of limited aid as an archer, but as a prophet, he could wield much more power on behalf of the Kirthanim and Great Bear. At the same time, the power he could wield was not his own, nor was it at his beck and call. He had no guarantee that this morning's surge would be repeated to any degree. Having Suruna would at least mean that he could both defend himself and do damage to the enemy if he received no such gift of power from Allfather. Besides, with Valzaan's staff destroyed, he had found himself longing for the familiar curves of Suruna at times while lying in his wooden cage.

"Yes," Benjiah said, "Take me to it."

Benjiah stared down the shaft of his arrow, waiting. He held it firmly against Suruna, both because the shot wasn't clear, not yet, and because the arrow was cyranic and he couldn't afford to let it slip.

The close quarters of the fighting and the relative flatness of the plain had minimized his effectiveness since joining the Kirthanim forces. He'd moved north toward the flank, in part because that was where the Kirthanim seemed to need the most help, and in part because it was the point on the battlefield farthest from the scaffold. He felt a strong internal urge to stay far away from there.

Now he was watching a Great Bear hold a trio of Malekim at bay. The bear wielded his staff quickly but defensively, as he had little opportunity to put down one of the enemy with two others waiting for their moment to strike. Ordinarily, Benjiah would have had a shot already, but a second struggle between a small cluster of Kirthanim and Nolthanim was also going on in the space between the Great Bear and himself, and he didn't want to let the arrow go until he knew he had a clear shot.

A surge from the Kirthanim thrust the Nolthanim soldiers backward, and Benjiah released the arrow. It flew across the field and struck one of the Malekim squarely between the shoulders. The creature flailed, reaching backward to pull it out, but the poison had already begun its work. He staggered sideways and pitched over onto the ground.

Relieved of the burden of guarding against three Malekim, the Great Bear quickly finished the two who remained. Benjiah watched the Great Bear work, wondering at the strength, speed, and agility these otherwise gentle and patient creatures demonstrated when necessary. They were indeed remarkable, but he needed to be moving on.

Benjiah moved back from the front line and started making his way southward. Great golden forms flashed overhead as dragons flew across the sky, this way and that, constantly in motion, making the most of their ability to both protect and attack. The sun hung low in the western sky, and Benjiah wondered what would happen at sunset if the apparent standoff between the two armies was not resolved.

For his part, Benjiah resigned himself to the fact that he needed to go where he didn't want to go, to the scaffold. There were a couple reasons for his decision, one of which was the obvious: that from even that minimal elevation he might be more effective as an archer in this battle. The second, less obvious but more important reason was that he was looking for a vantage point from which to see Cheimontyr. Benjiah had begun to feel a strange inner conviction that if he indeed wanted to find the limping man, he would need to find Cheimontyr. That meant he would need to go south toward the center and left flank of the battle. For most of the afternoon, the *Boom! Boom! Boom!* and wild surges of light and power had emanated from that direction.

A great flash of light, almost perpendicular to his current position south of the line, shot straight into the sky. Benjiah knew it couldn't have come from more than twenty spans away, and turning in toward the battle, he quickly saw Cheimontyr towering over the battlefield. Benjiah had seen his face before, but he was struck again by the intensity of the rage. The giant held his hammer aloft, high above his head, and ripples of energy moved up and down the shaft between the great fist that held it and the hammerhead.

A second blast flew upward in a brilliant vertical slash, and this time Benjiah saw it strike its target. A smoking dragon fell to the ground, crashing loudly into the midst of the battle. Benjiah began to weave through the men and Great Bear until he reached the edge of his own line. A small clearing had formed around Cheimontyr, and now that the dragon had been brought down, the Bringer of Storms moved in and brought a furious blow of his hammer down upon the smoldering body. Benjiah peered anxiously at the dragon, thinking that perhaps he could see a tint of blue in the reflection of light on its scales.

Benjiah was searching the ranks behind Cheimontyr for a glimpse of the man from the scaffold when a piercing cry rang out from the raging form of the giant. Benjiah's focus was once more arrested by the towering form. Cheimontyr's eyes were on the heavens, and as Benjiah looked up, he saw Sulmandir swooping down.

A pair of Vulsutyrim, great shields in hand, moved to offer protection to their captain, and the great blast of fire that blasted out from Sulmandir's mouth was deflected. *Boom!* A surge of energy erupted from somewhere in the midst of the fire and smoke and shot up, just missing Sulmandir's outstretched wing as he reeled left and flew upward.

As the smoke from Sulmandir's attack cleared, a half dozen dragons came in low and fierce. The first two blew great blasts as Sulmandir had. As the Vulsutyrim crouched behind the shields, the rest flew into the fire, and Benjiah heard a great clatter as the dragons struck the shields themselves. As the fire and smoke dissipated, Benjiah could see that the two giants who had been shielding Cheimontyr had been knocked down by the blows.

Immediately Sulmandir returned, winging his way fast and straight for Cheimontyr. The Bringer of Storms dived headlong to the side to avoid the next blast of flame, and when he came up, he had in his free hand one of the shields that had been dropped by the dazed and wounded Vulsutyrim. Cheimontyr wielded it adeptly as a second wave of dragons followed Sulmandir again. This time, the last dragon did not rise fast enough to avoid Cheimontyr's hammer, which caught his tail, sent him spiraling sideways, and almost brought him down.

More Vulsutyrim came to aid Cheimontyr, but now a host of dragons appeared, working in concert to hold them back. The Vulsutyrim, for all their efforts, were effectively separated, and Cheimontyr was isolated in the clearing.

Sulmandir returned, this time blowing fire to force Cheimontyr to use the shield, and then driving talons into the shield. They struggled over the shield itself for a moment, and Benjiah saw Sulmandir's tail lash hard to the side and strike Cheimontyr's arm as he tried to wield his hammer. A moment later, Sulmandir had succeeded in ripping the shield from Cheimontyr's hand and was rising into the air.

Boom! A surge of energy flung from the hammer at the rising dragon struck and shattered the shield, and Benjiah watched as Sulmandir staggered in midair. The shield fell to the ground in shards. Sulmandir circled awkwardly over Cheimontyr and then dropped onto the ground. Cheimontyr flashed across the intervening space, and before Sulmandir could unleash another burst of flame, Cheimontyr had landed a blow with his hammer that knocked the dragon sideways.

Benjiah winced as he saw the hammer connect. It was a thunderous blow, and the sound of the metal striking Sulmandir's great golden scales drowned out all other sounds. Sulmandir rolled to the side. Benjiah almost couldn't watch as Cheimontyr raised the hammer to strike a second time, but he couldn't look away either. What he saw, though, was not what he expected.

Before Cheimontyr could land the blow, Sulmandir raised his head, and at the same time, his tail lashed out with amazing speed and curled around Cheimontyr's wrist, stopping his blow mid-strike. With a powerful motion, Sulmandir wrenched Cheimontyr's arm downward at an awkward angle, and the hammer was jarred free so that it fell to the ground. Wasting no time, Sulmandir raised himself up and with the talons of his near foreleg, slashed Cheimontyr across his exposed chest.

Cheimontyr stumbled backward, bleeding and empty-handed as Sulmandir released his wrist. Instinctively, the giant pressed his arms inward to protect the painful wound. Sulmandir righted himself immediately and faced the dazed giant. Then he pounced, leaping into the air with a single powerful thrust from his wings and gliding swiftly across the intervening distance. Cheimontyr started to raise his arms, but he was unable to defend himself at all.

Sulmandir sunk the talons of his rear legs deep into Cheimontyr's stomach and side, ripping through the giant's thick muscles. Likewise, the Golden Dragon drove the talons from his forelegs into either shoulder, pinioning the giant's arms to his sides. The whip-like golden tail flashed downward and wrapped itself several times around both of Cheimontyr's legs, holding them firmly together. For a brief moment Sulmandir just hung there, attached at each of those points with his back arched so that his great golden head hovered in front of Cheimontyr's exposed face.

The Bringer of Storm's rage only increased. It seemed to Benjiah that he was positively shaking with hate and anger as he defied his adversary. If there was fear or submission anywhere in him, it wasn't evident.

Sulmandir began to open his jaws, and Benjiah watched in wonder as his mouth kept expanding. He was sure that Sulmandir must have unhinged his lower jaw like an Eola snake that swallows its prey whole, for the dragon looked as if he could swallow Cheimontyr's entire head. In fact, he very nearly did just that. He slid his lower jaw under the giant's chin and sank his teeth into the soft, fleshy part of his upper neck. His upper jaw he brought down firmly on top of the giant's head.

Then Sulmandir summoned from deep within a tremendous blast of fire and heat that consumed everything above Cheimontyr's shoulders. Smoke billowed upward as the flame swirled out for spans in every direction. Gradually, the flame died down and the mass of smoke drifted up and off across the battlefield. Sulmandir pulled his head back, his jaws now closed.

Benjiah could see nothing where Cheimontyr's head had been. There was empty space above his shoulders and nothing more.

Sulmandir released the giant's body and dropped back to the ground on all four legs, his wings raised in a gesture of defiance to all of Malek's watching host. The headless body of Cheimontyr teetered upright for the briefest of moments, then fell straight backward and crashed into the ground with a thud.

4

DREAD CAPTAIN OF
THE NOLTHANIM

BENJIAH DIDN'T MOVE. He stared at the body of the fallen Vulsutyrim captain. Cheimontyr slain? Could it be? His mind flashed back to the giant's approach to Zul Arnoth, which he had watched with Valzaan and his uncles from inside the ruins. His eyes blazed, visible even in the distance, and as he'd raised his hammer to the sky to summon the lightning, Benjiah had thought nothing and no one would ever stand against him.

Of course, Benjiah himself had stood against Cheimontyr with aid from Allfather. Even so, Benjiah felt he had been granted power only to slow the Bringer of Storms. Consequently, he had wondered, as he passed day after dreary day in his wooden cage, what order of power would be required to slay Malek's most terrible captain. Now, as Cheimontyr lay headless and quite dead on the battlefield, Benjiah looked from him to the golden form of Sulmandir, his wings still outstretched and threatening.

Before the sun goes down tonight, I will kill him as I killed his father. That's what the Father of Dragons had said to him, and though Benjiah hadn't doubted his word exactly, he had been almost afraid to believe. Cheimontyr was dead, though, and Benjiah felt unbridled joy and elation. What could stop them now? Surely the day would be theirs, and if the war didn't end here, it would end soon hereafter.

At that moment, the world around him, which had seemed for a brief time to be frozen and silent like some scene from *torrim redara,* burst again into motion and sound. Benjiah saw a wave of Vulsutyrim, apparently not overwhelmed and dismayed as he might have hoped after their captain's fall, begin to move out with their great shields raised in a row of protection. Sulmandir hopped backward, and Benjiah realized for the first time that the blow he'd been dealt by Cheimontyr had wounded him.

A half dozen dragons descended from the sky, swooping in to protect their great father. The Vulsutyrim advanced, enduring the intense bursts of flame as Sulmandir slowly withdrew from the field. After several moments like this, several more dragons appeared, large red dragons Benjiah thought. Surrounding Sulmandir, they took him in their talons and with a great, concerted effort, lifted him from the ground. For all their majesty and grace, the removal looked awkward. Benjiah wondered how far they could really fly with their great father in their talons like this, but his question was soon answered. When they had raised him several spans above the ground, the red dragons released Sulmandir, and he began to fly haltingly toward the city. They made steady progress toward Tol Emuna, where Benjiah imagined they were headed for the high ground.

The battle between the Vulsutyrim and the dragons intensified. More giants arrived, but the dragons, emboldened by their father's victory over Cheimontyr, held their ground. Benjiah took an arrow from his quiver and nocked it on Suruna, ready to deal a blow wherever he could be of service.

His mind returned to the limping man. Now that Cheimontyr had fallen, Benjiah wasn't sure where to look for him. He scanned both sides of the engagement between the giants and dragons. Men moved around behind the giants, some on horseback, some not. His eyes were drawn to a dark-cloaked man standing beside one of the Vulsutyrim, one not engaged in the fighting. Benjiah felt suddenly cold and knew that this was the man he was seeking. Whether the man was truly Malek, he couldn't say.

He moved around to the side, jogging slowly along behind the Kirthanim, who mostly watched the engagement of dragons and giants. Most of the Nolthanim and Malekim had likewise fallen back and become mostly spectators in the contest. In fact, to Benjiah the enemy lines seemed in disarray. No doubt the fall of Cheimontyr had been more disconcerting to the ordinary rank and file of Malek's host than to the Vulsutyrim, whose determination and resilience continued to impress.

He kept his eyes upon the man in the dark cloak while seeking the place from which to take his shot. The man had moved so that he now stood some distance behind the melee of giants and dragons in the middle of the field, but also some distance in front of the main enemy line of men and Malekim. His attention seemed fixed on the encounter, and Benjiah felt little rivulets of sweat run down his forehead as he tried not to think about what a successful shot could mean if the man really was Malek. He tried not to think about it, but it was no use. The stakes were high. He needed to get into position and shoot before he lost the opportunity.

Benjiah finally reached an advantageous spot. About thirty spans away was the wooden scaffold, but he couldn't bring himself to look at it, only in part because his attention was elsewhere at the moment. While the scaffold might afford a nice elevated view, it would make his shot unnecessarily long. From where he was, he had a clear view of the limping man, and barring wind or other interference, Benjiah could take him down.

He knelt. Looking down the shaft of the arrow, he took aim at the man's chest. He would have liked to put the arrow through the neck or in the head, a more certain kill, but he wanted to be sure of a hit with his first shot, just in case he didn't get a second. He had nocked a cyranic arrow. Was Malek vulnerable to cyranic poison like an ordinary man? Benjiah could only hope so, if this was him.

He was about to release the arrow when a giant stepped closer and obscured his view. Benjiah relaxed his hold upon the bowstring and looked up and over the field. He could see a part of the man, now turned to speak to the giant, but he knew it would be wiser to wait until his shot was truly clear again.

The giant moved away and the man was once more in plain sight. Benjiah took aim and, fearing the opportunity might once more slip away, let the arrow fly.

The arrow sped across the bloody field, accurate, a good shot. It arced up just a bit and then started down, accelerating. Benjiah felt his stomach tighten with expectation as he waited for it to strike its target.

Inexplicably, the man turned and looked right in Benjiah's direction. Seeing the arrow, the man raised his hand almost nonchalantly and plucked it out of midair. Benjiah had never seen anything like it. The man's hand simply reached up and closed around the arrow's shaft as though it had been hanging there, suspended motionless. Benjiah watched as the man tossed the arrow to the ground. Not knowing what to do next, Benjiah reached back for his quiver to draw another one. The man was still looking in his direction. Not waiting for Benjiah to ready another arrow, he lifted his hand with his fingers spread wide and his palm opened toward Benjiah.

An invisible wave crashed into Benjiah with terrific force. He was physically lifted from the ground and hurled backward through the air a great distance. He sensed himself passing over a small crowd of men who were as taken aback by his sudden trajectory as he was. He tumbled through the air, and then after a brief but dramatic flight, landed roughly on a small pile of bodies. He felt sharp pain as every bit of his body ached and his head swam. He thought he should try to get up, but his thoughts were jumbled and confused. Darkness washed over him.

Pedraan grabbed the wounded Nolthanim soldier who had started to stumble away after losing his sword. Pedraan's hand clamped down on the man's shoulder and finished him quickly, mercifully. The man dropped to the ground and Pedraan turned away. He'd taken up this sword because it had been necessary, but the part of him that had reacted to the bloody art of war so strongly and with such disgust after Pedraal's death stirred uneasily within.

"The enemy is falling back," Carrafin said as Pedraan approached.

Pedraan let his sword arm drop and bent over at the waist, drinking in great draughts of air. He looked up at the captain of Tol Emuna, who looked as weary as Pedraan felt. From the moment Cheimontyr fell, everything seemed to stop except the fierce skirmish between the dragons and giants. But with Sulmandir gone and many of the dragons engaged elsewhere, that conflict had effectively been a stalemate, and both sides apparently realized this. The dragons did not pursue as the giants withdrew together.

Pedraan and the others had barely taken a breath to consider what they should do next when a massive wave of Malekim and some Nolthanim came charging across the field. The attack was as sudden and unexpected as it was disorderly and poorly executed. That was fortunate for the Kirthanim, lulled into a false sense of security by the giants' falling back. The charge was repulsed far too easily, Pedraan thought, not that he was complaining. All he could conclude was that whatever had driven them forward was not strong enough to sustain them when their charge met with stiff resistance. It was stiff, for the Kirthanim fought with renewed vigor, encouraged by Cheimontyr's fall. Caan had instructed them from the beginning in Sulare that morale was the military intangible for which no simple assessment of numbers or strategic planning could fully account. A demoralized foe with superior strength could be routed when a heartened core of defenders stood their ground. This Pedraan had just witnessed—a lecture of the past come to life in the present.

"By the Mountain, that was too close," Pedraan replied, lifting his head to look at Carrafin, who nodded. "If they'd persisted at all they would have broken through, and then where would we have been? Even with Sulmandir's victory, we would have been in a bad way."

"Indeed," Carrafin said. "Had the enemy any captain who could rally them and hold the line, we might yet lose the day."

Pedraan thought of the Nolthanim in the bizarre armor, the 'dread captain' as he had become known. He mumbled, mostly to himself, "They do have one."

"Yes they do," Carrafin answered, and Pedraan looked at him, surprised that the other man had heard and comprehended his remark. "Let us hope he is currently organizing a retreat."

"Let us hope," Pedraan said. A voice called out to them from farther up the line, and both men turned.

"Carrafin! Pedraan! You're both all right."

"We're all right, Caan," Pedraan answered for both of them. "Though we easily might not have been."

"I know it," Caan answered soberly, then he smiled. "But you know, it is about time we had some good fortune. After all, Sulmandir's slaying of Cheimontyr really was spectacular. It had to be worth a little demoralization of the enemy. Don't you think?"

"Absolutely," Carrafin agreed.

Pedraan nodded, recalling the image of the great dragon latching onto the Bringer of Storms and finishing him in such a terrible and yet magnificent way. It had been a majestic display, if majesty could be displayed in such a way.

"So what now?" Carrafin asked Caan, and Pedraan's attention was back on the issue at hand.

"Yes, what now?" Caan answered, looking up into the evening sky.

"The days are grown long," Carrafin said, as though anticipating the question in Caan's mind. "There might be as much as two hours left before it is too dark to fight."

Pedraan looked up as Caan had done. The sun, hanging in plain view, remained at the end of the day as jarring a sight as it had been in the beginning. It was almost as hard to believe the sun was free from its cloudy captivity as it was to believe that the one who had kept it hidden was dead.

"Even if we could organize pursuit, that's not much time," Caan mused.

Their discussion was interrupted by a rider coming hard from the north. The rider had seen the small huddle of men and was making straight for them. Caan turned and stepped toward the rider, who slowed to halt.

"Master Caan?"

"Yes?"

"I've been sent from the northern flank. We're under heavy attack and are giving ground. Gilion says to come quickly and bring as much help as you can afford to bring."

"They're pressing where we're weakest," Pedraan muttered.

"Yes," the messenger replied, "and with a vengeance. We're in danger of being overrun."

"Why were they not demoralized there by Cheimontyr's fall as the enemy was here?" Pedraan wondered out loud.

"It seemed at first as though they were," the messenger replied, "but then the captain of the Nolthanim in the black armor pulled them together. He led the attack, and now the situation is dire."

Pedraan inhaled deeply. He could envision the dread captain of the Nolthanim on his horse, sitting tall as he directed the attack, holding the enemy forces together with the strength of his iron will.

"That settles the debate," Caan said, turning back to the others. "I'll go now. You two organize as many of the men here as you can afford to bring, but leave a defensive detachment behind in case the enemy regroups. It looks like the day isn't over for us yet."

"I'll come with you," Pedraan said. "Carrafin can organize the men here without my help."

Caan looked from Pedraan to Carrafin. "All right with you?"

"I'll be fine. Go."

"All right," Caan said, motioning to Pedraan. "Come on."

The din of battle had faded. Though the enemy charge came quickly after Cheimontyr's fall, the latest scuffle now seemed to be over, and from her seat on the wooden scaffold, Wylla could see the enemy forces withdrawing. She hoped that this meant the battle was over, at least for the day.

The encounter between the dragon and the giant was visually arresting, even from a distance, and she'd been unable to look away. Benjiah had spoken of the Father of Dragons just as the sun burst through the clouds, and Wylla couldn't help but think it had been him, Sulmandir, who'd faced and killed Cheimontyr. Who else could have withstood that mighty blow with the hammer and still prevailed? She hoped that he was all right.

She looked down at Rulalin's lifeless face and stroked his hair. Her tears, only recently dried, began to flow down her cheeks again. She turned to Yorek. "You must think me mad, to weep for him like this."

"No, Your Majesty, I don't."

"He killed my husband."

"He did."

"He betrayed Kirthanin by helping Malek."

"He did that too."

"And you don't think I'm mad to weep?"

Yorek returned Wylla's gaze. "It is a sign of Your Majesty's character that you weep for your enemy."

"He repented and asked my forgiveness, Yorek. He's not my enemy anymore, no matter what he did."

"I suppose he's not anyone's enemy anymore," Yorek replied.

"No," Wylla said, wiping the tears from her face. "I suppose not."

Wylla lifted Rulalin's head and slipped out from under it. Her legs ached and tingled a little as she uncrossed them. She'd been sitting in the same position so long, it felt good to stretch them out. "I suppose, in a way, he could have remained my enemy, even in the grave. I've known others haunted by their bitterness toward the dead, and I could have been one of them. I was fortunate to be here, Yorek, to see what I have seen today and to have heard what I have heard. I just wish I could have done something for him."

"You did enough. You gave him what he needed most—your forgiveness."

"I did, and I think it helped ease his spirit, if not his pain."

"It did. I could see it."

Wylla, her legs no longer tingling, struggled to her feet and stretched. Several bodies lay motionless around the scaffold, but there appeared to be no living soul nearby. Not far from where she had been sitting with Yorek, trying to ease Rulalin's passing, lay Tashmiren and the other Nolthanim that Rulalin had killed.

"I don't want to leave him here with them," Wylla said to Yorek, motioning to the others.

"What do you want to do?"

"I don't know, but I don't want to leave him here."

"Tol Emuna is too far for us to carry him."

"I know, but maybe we could take him part of the way," Wylla answered.

"We could, but there are so many fallen, it might be hard to locate him again."

"True," Wylla said, gazing down at Rulalin and then back out over the land stretching north and east toward the city.

"We could leave him at the bottom of the stairs and then come back later with men who could carry him wherever you wish," Yorek suggested.

"We could." Wylla sighed. "But we might as well leave him where he is if the plan is to come back for him later. I just don't want to leave him here long."

"I will organize his retrieval as soon as it seems feasible."

"Thank you, Yorek. I appreciate your help, very much."

"Your Majesty knows it is my heart's desire to be of service."

"I do." Wylla smiled at Yorek. "And now, I think it is time to go look for Benjiah. I don't know where exactly the dragon took him, but they headed toward Tol Emuna."

"Then let's head back to the city."

"It will be good to see him Yorek, alive and free."

"It will."

They started for the stairs, but Wylla hesitated at the top, turned and walked back to Rulalin. She knelt beside him and laid her hand tenderly on his chest, above the bloodstains on his cloak. "You took Joraiem from me, but you gave Benjiah back. You gave yourself for my son. Rest in peace, Rulalin. We are enemies no longer."

She rose and returned to the stairs, where Yorek waited for her. "Ready?" he asked, offering her his hand.

"Yes," she said, taking Yorek's hand and beginning her descent. "Let's go. I want to see my son."

The scene on the northern flank was dismaying. The pressure from the renewed enemy assault had bent the north-south line until it was slanted almost as much east to west. Gilion was doing what he could to hold back the enemy, but it was obvious to Pedraan that the current state of affairs was untenable.

Turgan, his massive wooden staff clutched tightly, was engaged in the center of the line with a few other Great Bear fending off a cluster of Malekim. They were driving forward like a wedge in advance of the main body of the enemy. Nolthanim and Malekim were engaged elsewhere all along the line, and to the credit of the Kirthanim under Gilion, they were holding their formation as best as they were able. The scene was dire, but it was not yet chaotic.

Riding on horseback not far from the front line, Pedraan could see the dread captain of the Nolthanim. Even the sight of him in that nightmarish phantasm of black armor made Pedraan shudder: head and body, arms and legs, hand and foot covered, riding with his great dark sword lifted high so that he could direct his minions with but a wave and point. A chill ran through his weary body. This man, if man he could possibly be seemed to have taken no notice of Cheimontyr's fall. Pedraan's own musings on the importance of the Nolthanim captain came back to him: *He and the Bringer of Storms were like the pillars upon which the rest of them stood. Cut them down, and the Kirthanim would have a chance.* He had known it to be true when he first conceived it, but it had been proven true beyond any doubt. With one of the pillars destroyed, the enemy tottered, but it had not fallen. The other pillar remained. *If Cheimontyr can be killed, then surely this dread captain can be killed as well.*

Pedraan's attention was pulled back to the skirmish between Turgan's Great Bear and the Malekim. He'd missed the intervening action, but he could see Turgan's staff had been dislodged from his hand. Turgan seemed to be, at least for moment, all right. With one mighty paw he grabbed the sword arm of the Malekim and held back the blow the creature had been hoping to deliver. With his other mighty paw, he placed a firm grip on the Silent One's neck. A moment later he let go, and the Malekim fell in a heap upon the ground. Pedraan couldn't imagine the strength required to crush a Malekim's throat with all of its thick, dense hide protecting it. Turgan retrieved his staff and rejoined the larger defense against the resurgent enemy.

Pedraan could see the line slipping. Even in the short time since he'd arrived with Caan, the end of the line had been further bent by the assault. They were losing ground, and Pedraan knew that they might not be able to hold back this tide much longer. He looked back down the line along which he had ridden, but he couldn't see any glimpse of reinforcements making their way north, nor could he reasonably expect that Carrafin had had enough time to organize any yet. Redeploying soldiers took time, especially on a day like today when so much of the battle had simply happened without clear direction or advance planning.

Pedraan joined Gilion and Caan, talking intensely in close quarters. He didn't know what they were debating, but there wasn't time to wait any longer. He headed in their direction.

"We need to do something, now!" he said as they looked up at him. "These men and this line are about to break."

"We know," Caan said, his frustration evident as he turned to the younger man. "We're planning our withdrawal."

"Withdrawal? We're conceding the field?"

"We'll try to hold the line as we back toward the city. With good fortune, as we draw nearer to the walls and as the line grows more compact, the enemy will realize that success against the exposed flank is not the same thing as success against us. Maybe he'll pull back as well."

"And then what? We'll head back into Tol Emuna and be right back where we were this morning?"

"No, we won't be right back where we started," Caan answered sharply. "We came out from behind the walls, if you'll remember, at least in part because we believed the Bringer of Storms could knock them down. He won't be knocking anything down today, or ever again for that matter, so there is some reason to hope the walls may afford us both time and protection to figure out what we do next."

At that moment a shadow, as if cast by a fast moving, low flying cloud, swept over the land. All three men looked up. It was no cloud, but a handful of dragons flying high above. They began to circle. Pedraan counted five, although at the height and speed they flew, it took him a moment to be sure of his count.

"By the Mountain, they're a welcome sight," Gilion said, putting the relief they all felt into words.

The dragons had not attacked anyone or anything yet, but their presence had an immediate effect on the enemy offensive. Their line seemed to be detaching. Concerned about what was above them, they withdrew out of reach of both staff and sword. To Pedraan's surprise, the Malekim seemed more affected by disorder and fear than the Nolthanim, though with the Nolthanim's captain on horseback right there, Pedraan understood their incentive to hold themselves together.

The dragons dropped out of the heights and swept low across the field. The enemy line began to scatter, creating some separation between themselves and the Kirthanim and Great Bear. Pedraan knew from having watched the dragons all day that this strategic division was necessary to make their flame attacks both possible and effective.

And yet, when the dragons circled back around, they did not come from multiple angles onto the field, throwing flame in all directions as Pedraan had expected. They focused on the center and, Pedraan soon realized, the dread captain. They came in low, together, flying quickly toward him. Pedraan felt his excitement rising; the dragons had also realized that killing this one man would do more for their ultimate cause then killing a thousand men and Malekim.

For his part, the dread captain of the Nolthanim sat upright on his horse, exposed before his attackers. Most of those under his charge had fallen back behind him, so that he sat for the most part alone at the front of the enemy's disintegrating line.

As the dragons flew in low and together, he held his ground. Hot, vivid bursts of flame erupted from the dragons' mouths, and the captain with remarkable control of his horse dodged, evading one after the other. Pedraan couldn't believe his eyes, but when the dragons had passed on and were swooping up and around to come back, the captain remained in his seat, sitting tall.

The next time the dragons came staggered, from different directions. They resembled to Pedraan's eyes a closing net as they surrounded the man. Again, with remarkable control of his steed, the captain managed to evade the initial attacks, but he found himself running out of room to maneuver. At that moment, the last of the five to approach swooped down upon him from the side. The captain, seeing his doom, ducked his face away from the blast as the dragon sent forth an explosion of light and heat that swallowed up both man and horse in an instant.

The dragons, already headed in the direction of the Kirthanim line, flew back overhead. Pedraan felt elation every bit as strongly as he'd felt it when Cheimontyr had been killed. He turned to Caan and grabbed his arm in his ecstatic, strong grip. "He's down!"

Caan turned, a great smile beaming on his face. "He's really down."

"You remember what I said this morning? Kill him and kill Cheimontyr, and we can win both this battle and this war."

"Can win?" Caan said, his smile breaking into laughter. "We've just won! They won't recover from this loss."

"Look!" Gilion called out to them, moving forward and pointing in the direction of their fallen enemy.

Pedraan looked up and across the field at the place where the flame and smoke from the dragons' strike was just beginning to rise and drift away. On the ground there, he could see a black heap, the bodies indistinguishable and smoldering, with smoke trailing up from the scorched remains. Then Pedraan understood why Gilion had called out. Incredibly, unbelievably, something was moving. Pedraan's heart and mind told him it was impossible, but his eyes told him it was happening anyway.

The dread captain of the Nolthanim, smoke rising in thin wisps from his arms, head, body and legs, rose to his feet beside the motionless remains of his incinerated horse. He stood and gazed across the battlefield at the line of the Kirthanim. Quiet fell on the entire field, in both camps, as all eyes were riveted on the surreal figure.

"Is he a man?" Pedraan said half to Caan, half to himself.

"Who knows what he is!" Caan replied.

"Perhaps he is a ghost or spirit of some kind," Gilion said.

Though the suggestion would have normally prompted laughter and even ridicule from the two hardened soldiers, neither laughed now, though Caan replied, "I'd be open to just about anything that might make sense of this, but surely a spirit wouldn't still be smoking from the dragon's blast."

"Maybe it's neither a man nor a spirit," Pedraan said.

Caan looked at him, "Malek, you mean?"

"Couldn't it be?"

"I guess," Caan answered, "though I always envisioned Malek pulling the strings from some invisible height. I don't remember any stories of him actually leading troops after his fall."

The dread captain turned to face his own line, and raising his sword high above his head, gave a loud cry and motioned to them to come on. A great shout erupted from the Nolthanim. They had watched their captain swallowed up in fire only to emerge from his own ashes. Their confidence restored and their purpose renewed, they came like a wave across the field.

"Here they come again," Caan said, waving the Kirthanim and Great Bear forward to meet the enemy.

Pedraan reached out and grabbed him, holding him back. "Hold on, Caan."

"What?"

"I don't think it's Malek. I think it is just a man, but a man with armor that's made from something pretty incredible."

"What makes you think that all of a sudden?" Caan asked.

"Did you see what he did just before the flame hit?"

Caan furrowed his brow, then realization crossed his face. "He turned away."

"That's right. He turned and raised his arm to protect his eyes from the blast. He was counting on his armor absorbing the blow."

"I think you're right."

"He's a man," Pedraan said. "He's a man and he can be killed. We know his weakness now—the opening in his helmet. I'm going after him."

"Don't be foolish. Wait for the dragons to come back."

"Why? They may be back at the city by now. They must think he's dead."

"They'll hear the battle start up again."

"Even if they do, he'll be hard to isolate from the rest of the battle now. And besides, if they break through before help comes, it may be too late. They'll sweep down our exposed side and wreak all kinds of havoc. They have all the momentum now. He's got to be stopped."

Caan looked at Pedraan. "You're right, but you're not going."

"Why not?"

"Pedraan, be realistic. You're no swordsman. You are strong and brave, but you can't win this battle. I'll go."

"Caan," Pedraan started, looking from the battle beyond them as it swelled in intensity back to his old teacher. "You are a great warrior, but your time has passed."

"Maybe," Caan conceded, "but I'm still a better swordsman than you. I will find him."

"I'll come with you."

"You'll keep your distance. Without Aljeron, this army will need you to lead it if I fall. I'm not being noble, Pedraan. This is serious. Gilion is a great second in command, but he's no leader. You are."

"I'm still coming."

"I'll argue the point no further. You're still under my command, and I expect you'll honor my intentions."

The two men moved through the battle as it raged on. They met with occasional opposition, but they were able to pick their way through the chaos. The dread captain wasn't hard to find, for he was fighting in the thick of the front line, wielding fear as much as he wielded his sword, being equally destructive with both.

As they drew nearer, Caan reached back and planted his hand momentarily on Pedraan's chest. Against his own will, Pedraan stopped as Caan moved toward the man in his hideous black armor. From this closer vantage, the figure of the man struck even more fear into Pedraan's heart. Tiny curls of smoke still rose from him, and the two eyes that peered out from the recesses of the helmet were cold and intense. Pedraan watched Caan move toward him and felt that there could be no hope of victory in this encounter.

Caan was, however, more successful than Pedraan had thought possible. He engaged the dread captain and for a few moments, matched him stroke for stroke. Caan wielded Kurveen masterfully, blocking the swift and fierce attacks of his enemy, and even from time to time pressing the Nolthanim captain back with counterattacks of his own. It became obvious to Pedraan, though, that these counterattacks were growing more and more infrequent. Before long, it was all Caan could manage to defend against the captain's advances.

Then a vicious cut from the Nolthanim's sword opened up a wound on Caan's upper left arm that bled fast and freely, soaking his sleeve. Pedraan hesitated for an instant, held for the moment by Caan's command, but then decided some orders needed to be ignored. Before he could rush in to Caan's aid, however, Caan burst out in an unexpected and furious rush of counterstrokes, driving the Nolthanim captain backward across the field. At the culmination of his counterattack, Caan knocked the dread captain off balance, and he thrust Kurveen forward for the kill.

The Nolthanim captain turned his head, and the tip of Kurveen, Firstblade though it was, glanced off the side of the man's helmet. Caan, who had put everything he had into the strike, was winded and off balance after his miss. The captain recovered quickly, then stepped up and drove his sword through Caan's exposed chest.

Caan's eyes rolled back in his head and as his body fell lifeless to the ground. Pedraan, horrified, was on the verge of rushing forward when the howling of hundreds of wolves broke out across the battlefield. He stopped, looking past the dread captain and saw the ominous black forms sweeping in like floodwaters bursting through a levee, rushing here and there and everywhere among the engaged combatants. Caan had fallen. Black Wolves had come. The dread captain lived.

Their doom was upon them.

5

THE DEVOURED

FOR A MOMENT PEDRAAN could only watch the rallying enemy, who just moments ago had been in disarray. The end of this day, this battle and even this war had seemed within their grasp. And yet even as they had reached out to grab it, it had eluded them. Their enemy was not only still alive, he was leading his resurgent forces, sweeping over the battlefield toward the exhausted men and Great Bear who were trying to hold the Kirthanim line together.

What's more, Caan was dead. Pedraan had watched him fall. As he watched the enemy surge and swell like waves in a mighty ocean, he struggled to wrap his mind around the thought of Caan dead. Images of the younger Caan in Sulare, training them in the art of war, mingled with images of the older Caan leading them through the interminable rain and holding them together as they retreated the length and breadth of Kirthanin. Pedraan suddenly felt weary like he'd never felt before. He was immediately and completely aware of every ache and pain in his body, every scratch, cut, and bead of sweat upon his skin, every muscle twitch, and every rock underfoot. He wanted to sit down. He wanted to run back to the city. He wanted to head home to Amaan Sul. He wanted to do anything but attempt to rally the Kirthanim and Great Bear, though that was exactly what he needed to do. Caan had ordered him to stay away from his fight with the dread captain for this very reason. Pedraan needed to pull things together, or they would be swept away before the growing tide of the enemy.

Without conscious awareness, Pedraan found himself in motion. He was directing Gilion and calling out orders as he ran along the line. He organized the Great Bear and Kirthanim into the simplest, tightest formation he could manage, and he started leading them backward, slowing the overall pace of their disorganized retreat with a steadier and more orderly one. With weapons drawn they fell back, fending off the leaping attacks of the snarling wolves.

Gilion ran up to Pedraan in the midst of their retreat. "We're going to be cut off from the line farther south if we keep falling back like this, and both they and we will be exposed if we do. We need to pivot, swinging the northern section of the line southward like a gate upon a hinge."

"Can you direct the maneuver?"

"I can."

"Then do it."

Gilion raced off southward, and a moment later he was back, barking out orders to the retreating men. It took a moment for the line to figure out what they were being told to do, but eventually they did it. The desperate attempt to keep the line from being flanked exposed the Kirthanim for a time. Especially at the point in the line that had become the hinge, they were vulnerable to attack from multiple directions. Without reinforcement, they would buckle eventually.

Pedraan ordered an end to the movement. They needed to hold their ground now. He stepped forward from the line with his sword raised, meaning to give encouragement to the weary warriors. To his surprise, many of the black wolves pulled up and turned from their pursuit, peeling around to head back in a northwesterly direction. In fact, the Nolthanim also ceased their advance and turned away like the wolves.

Pedraan looked around to see what had happened. Surely his stepping forward hadn't frightened them off, but he could see nothing that would have caused the retreat either. Was the enemy trying to go around the end of their line, to flank them even after the Kirthanim's maneuver? Were they being called to regroup before striking again en masse? He couldn't understand it. The enemy had been on the verge of victory. What had happened?

And then he saw it. Flooding into the great tide of black bodies were hundreds and hundreds of large, fierce cats. They were smaller than the wolves, but long and sleek, spotted like leopards but white, and they were moving among the Black Wolves, attacking them. Roars and howls mingled in the spring evening, and Pedraan turned to look for Gilion.

The older man was not far behind him, having come to see what was going on as well. Pedraan had to shout to be heard above the din.

"What are these creatures?"

"Snow leopards," Gilion replied.

"Snow leopards?" Pedraan answered. "Where have they come from?"

"They live in the northlands, I think," Gilion replied. "I've heard tell of them in the Zaros Mountains, but I've never seen any before, and certainly not a pack of them, or whatever this is."

"Snow leopards," Pedraan repeated, glancing back.

"Yes, Snow leopards. What I don't know, though," Gilion continued, pointing past the sea of animals, "Is who are they?"

Pedraan followed Gilion's hand and saw a large company of wild men and women—at least it appeared to Pedraan that some might be women—were approaching the engagement between the wolves and leopards with long spears in hand. They wore silver masks, giving them an eerie look in the approaching twilight.

"By the Mountain," Pedraan said, "this is most strange. First a pack of wild cats, and now a pack of wild people."

"If they're here to kill the wolves and they break the Nolthanim charge in doing so, I don't care who they are," Gilion said.

"Well, whoever they are, we should probably take advantage of their diversion," Pedraan said, looking around at the men and Great Bear drawn in by the curious scene.

"Should I signal for the attack?" Gilion asked.

"Yes," Pedraan replied. "Send everyone."

Not long after, Pedraan found himself at the front of a charge into the confused enemy, faced suddenly with a battle on two fronts. If Pedraan had been concerned about how the snow leopards and wild men and women would treat their entrance into the battle, he wasn't worried anymore. Neither man nor beast among these strange new arrivals showed any interest in the Kirthanim or Great Bear. They were intent upon the enemy, and they were having much success.

As Pedraan hacked his way through the seething sea of Black Wolves, he saw a flash of orange out of the corner of his eye, and he turned to see what third creature had joined the wolves and leopards. It was a tiger, his brilliant orange fur a striking contrast against the backdrop of black and white. In fact, unless Pedraan was hallucinating after so long and so hard a day, it wasn't just any tiger, it was Koshti.

Hardly had the realization of all that this might mean struck him when he saw Aljeron. He was standing not far away from Koshti, Daltaraan flashing, soaked already with the blood of his enemies.

"Aljeron!" he shouted.

He received no visible response, so he shouted again, even louder. "Aljeron!!"

This time Aljeron looked up, and Pedraan saw a grin break across his friend's scarred face. On a day of such intense emotional swings, this was the pinnacle of it all. Seeing Aljeron meant more to Pedraan than the coming of the dragons and the fall of Cheimontyr. His friend had returned. After all this time, Aljeron was back, and Pedraan could not help but wonder at this strange but timely help he appeared to have brought with him.

Without fanfare, a host of dragons roared by overhead, and what fight was left in the enemy disappeared. Rapidly and chaotically, men, Malekim and wolves all began to fall back. Where the Nolthanim captain was in all that mess, Pedraan didn't know, and at this moment, he didn't care. The war might not be over, but they would survive to fight another day.

Something else became apparent to Pedraan as the battlefield began to clear. Some of the Black Wolves still engaged in the fight with the snow leopards began, without evident cause, bursting into flame. He looked up to see if there was a dragon casting small, targeted bursts of fire at the ground, but he saw none. Searching the battlefield, he saw a sight even more startling than Koshti with Aljeron.

Valzaan.

Valzaan was walking through the middle of the battlefield with no weapon, pointing with his hands at Black Wolves. Each targeted wolf burst into flames instantaneously. Pedraan gaped.

"It can't be," Pedraan murmured to himself. It had occurred to him that morning, with the arrival of Sulmandir, that Aljeron might still be alive and on his way, though he never imagined that he would see his friend that very same day. But Valzaan was a different matter entirely. The prophet had been blown into the sea by the Bringer of Storms. He'd passed his staff along to Benjiah because he knew he was going to be destroyed. At least, that was what they'd all assumed for the last half a year. How Valzaan had come to be here, and in the company of Aljeron and Koshti and their wild and mysterious friends, Pedraan could not begin to guess.

He turned his back to the retreating enemy, and he allowed himself to release the sword that he had grasped tightly in his hand all day. It fell to the ground. He'd taken it up when the dragons first came, and he had wielded it as best as he was able as long as he needed to. It had been necessary, and the blade served him well. It had been necessary, but he was glad to be rid of it, at least for a little while.

Aljeron drew Daaltaran. For some time now, they had been running toward Tol Emuna, which was clearly visible in the background. The foreground was a confused scene, as indeed most battles are when viewed from a distance. The ability to see, really see, what is happening in battle is a rare gift. Fortunately for Aljeron, it was a gift that he possessed and had cultivated. What he saw as they drew nearer was that the retreating Kirthanim were in danger of either having their line broken or being flanked. The situation was serious, even dire.

The snow leopards of the Kalin Seir, with Koshti running in their midst, were the first to engage the enemy. Like a cascade of snow and ice falling from a mountain peak, the leopards fell upon the enemy in an unfaltering wave of white. Both men and Black Wolves went down under the force of their attack, and gradually, the great hosts of Black Wolves detected the scent of the new enemy and began to wheel away from the retreating Kirthanim lines to defend themselves. *Good*, Aljeron thought, *our presence already begins to turn the tide of this battle.*

The Kalin Seir were not far behind their battle brothers. A thick cloud of Kalin Seir arrows flew over the snarling animals, striking their marks in men, Malekim, and Black Wolves in reserve. Kalin Seir spearman moved forward into the surging fray to aid their battle brothers, taking advantage of the reach of their spears to strike down Nolthanim before ever coming within reach of their swords. They were, however, at a disadvantage closer in, as the swords were more maneuverable in close quarters and the metal blades stronger than the wooden spears.

Aljeron, with Saegan and Evrim both following nearby, were cast upon the enemy as well, and the luxury of broader observation was lost as Aljeron found himself for the first time in a great while back in the chaotic fury of a pitched battle. This sudden return to the madness of battle was exhilarating, and adrenaline pulsed through his body as he felt again the thrill wash over him. Daaltaran whistled through the air, here blocking a stroke from an enemy soldier, there cutting open another so that his foe fell, lifeless and staring, to the ground. He advanced until he was fairly embedded in the heart of the fight, and movement in any direction put him face-to-face with the enemy—man, wolf, or Malekim. He greeted them each alike, bringing to bear months of pent-up rage and frustration as he dealt death right and left without mercy.

The battle fever was full upon him now. Aljeron had only felt it like this a few times before. The feeling was not unlike euphoria, as he gloried in the defeat of each and every enemy he faced. He delighted in knowing he was helping to deliver his friends, delighted in knowing he was helping to advance the cause of Allfather. Honesty, though, required that he admit there was more involved, even than this. He delighted in besting his enemies, in soaking his sword with their blood and avenging at least a few of his friends and countrymen who had fallen.

The thick of battle began to wane and thin. Plenty of Malek's servants fought madly for their lives, so Aljeron remained focused both on their immolation and his own survival. He heard though, in the midst of his killing reverie, a voice crying out his name. He looked up, spotted one of the Someris twins across the battlefield, and grinned as he went on with his work.

Not long after that, dragons came roaring across the sky, their great golden bodies passing gloriously above. Aljeron paused and stared, awed by their grandeur and moved to think that by reaching Harak Andunin and summoning Sulmandir, in a way, they had done this. They had brought the Kalin Seir and sent the dragons. Allfather had rewarded him and all the Kirthanim for the long journey through the barren and inhospitable Nolthanin wilderness.

The battle was over. The enemy pulled back, disengaging completely. The isolated enemies left behind were quickly dispatched, and the eerie calm that comes immediately after the cessation of hostilities fell all around him. He heard little more than the moaning of the wounded here and there around the field. The battle fever had passed, and the elation and euphoria were replaced by weariness. They had run for leagues before joining the battle. His legs ached as much or more than his arms, and his mind, freshly relieved of the responsibility to be hyperalert, felt the fatigue of the day.

Aljeron saw Valzaan moving across the field, stopping wherever a wounded Kalin Seir was to be found. He couldn't tell what the old prophet was doing for them, but it was apparent even from a distance that his presence comforted the injured. Aljeron looked for Saegan and Evrim, and seeing only Evrim, moved toward him.

"Are you all right?" Aljeron asked, looking at a darkening red patch on Evrim's side.

"I think it looks worse than it is," Evrim replied, looking down at his wound. "I sidestepped the sword thrust of a Nolthanim soldier, but I wasn't quite fast enough to avoid the blow entirely."

"We should get you to the city as soon as possible to have that wound attended to."

Evrim nodded, then pointed Aljeron back in the direction he had come from. Aljeron turned to see Gilion coming. With him was the twin, though Aljeron still couldn't tell which one. This man had been holding a sword, a weapon neither brother ever used, and now he appeared to be carrying no weapon at all.

"Aljeron!" Gilion called out, starting to jog.

Aljeron had never seen Gilion like this, running with tears on his face. He was always formal and fastidious, dealing with everything in a subdued manner in its own proper time and place, but not now. He threw his arms around Aljeron and embraced him tightly.

Gilion stepped back after a moment and looked up into Aljeron's face, but he kept his hold on Aljeron at the shoulders. "You have returned at a most opportune moment. We were running out of options."

"I could see that."

"Who are these you've brought with you?" Pedraan asked, for now that both men were close, Aljeron could see it was the younger twin.

"That," Aljeron said, "will take some explaining, but suffice it to say for now that they call themselves the Kalin Seir. They have dwelt in hiding in Nolthanin since the First Age and consider themselves the true heirs of the Nolthanim of old."

Pedraan and Gilion both stared at Aljeron and then past him at the Kalin Seir, their masked faces gleaming faintly in the twilight. Eventually Pedraan murmured, "Strange help, but welcome."

Valzaan joined them, greeting both Gilion and Pedraan warmly. Pedraan spoke for both of them when he asked, "What happened, Valzaan? We thought you were dead."

"I will tell you my story soon enough, but for the moment, more pressing matters need our attention, like whether to pursue the enemy."

"That's right," Aljeron said. "Our light is fading, so we need to assess the situation and decide quickly. Where's Caan? Was he not directing the battle today?"

"He was," Pedraan answered.

"Well, then where is he?"

"He's fallen," Pedraan said. "Up until a short while ago, he performed both wisely and well the role you entrusted to him. If he were here now, though, I'm sure he would readily return to you the authority you entrusted to him."

"Caan is dead?" Aljeron said, his face clouded by a frown.

"Yes."

"How did it happen?"

"He was slain by the dread captain of the Nolthanim, the mysterious rider in the black armor. He thought to forestall the enemy's advance by killing their leader, but he lost."

"And you say it happened just a short while ago?"

"Yes, not long ago."

"By the Mountain," Aljeron exclaimed, "had we been but a little faster, he might have lived, then."

"You cannot change what has already transpired," Valzaan interjected. "Many have died, and none of them can be brought back by pondering what might have been. What remains is to decide what to do."

Aljeron did not acknowledge Valzaan's words directly, but he returned his attention to the situation at hand. "Who assumed command after Caan's fall? You, Gilion? Or you, Pedraan, or would it have been Pedraal?"

"Pedraal fell a few days ago," Pedraan answered.

Aljeron looked for the first time carefully into Pedraan's eyes. He could see now another reason why Pedraan had seemed to him different than he remembered. The laughter that had always been in his eyes was gone. "Pedraan, I'm sorry."

"He died defending the city. He gave himself to save me."

"I'm sure you would have done the same," Aljeron replied.

Pedraan did not answer, turning rather to the issue of command. "Caan asked me to lead if he should fall. Between Gilion and me, we can probably tell you whatever you need to know."

"All right," Aljeron said, looking steadily from one to the other. "What's your read of the situation? Should we go after the enemy or fall back?"

Pedraan looked to Gilion, but the older man made a deferential gesture and Aljeron looked to Pedraan. "Well, if it were up to me, I'd fall back. We started this day in defeat and surrender, marching out from the city to lay down our weapons, but after the dragons came and freed Benjiah—"

"Freed Benjiah?"

"Yes," Pedraan said, "he was captured by the enemy just south of the Kalamin during our retreat. He was supposed to be executed, but Sulmandir rescued him. After this the battle began anew, and we thought we had won when Sulmandir killed the Bringer of Storms—"

"He's dead?" Evrim said, his eyes widening.

"Thanks be to Allfather," Aljeron added.

"I knew Cheimontyr's power had been broken," Valzaan said. "I could feel it. Sulmandir killed him as he killed his father on the slopes of Agia Muldonai."

"Yes, he fell earlier, and we thought that would end the battle and possibly the war, but the dread captain of the Nolthanim rallied and counterattacked. Even a direct hit from the fire of a dragon couldn't stop him, and we were in real danger of being overrun when you came. I think that in light of the long day, the many fallen, and the general emotional and physical fatigue, we should fall back and regroup."

"It sounds, though, like the enemy is in disarray," Aljeron replied. "This may be a rare opportunity for us to seize."

"It is possible," Pedraan said, "but if I might add two observations?"

"Go on."

"The first is obvious: The day has been won at high cost. Our forces, especially the Great Bear, suffered heavy losses prior to our surrender this morning. Now, even with the reinforcements you have brought, I'm not sure if we have a numerical advantage."

"All right, and what is the other observation?"

"Well," Pedraan said, motioning to the great stone walls. "We surrendered because we believed that the Bringer of Storms could knock down those walls. With his death, though, there may be hope that the defenses of Tol Emuna will prove safer than we first thought. What I'm saying is that if the enemy has more to throw at us than we know, I'd rather wait and see what it is from the other side of those walls. That's wiser, I think, than finding out tonight in the dark."

"Gilion?" Aljeron asked. "Do you agree?"

"I agree," Gilion replied. "The men are spent. Take them into the city. Let the morning bring what it may."

Aljeron nodded. "All right, then. Let's not waste any time. Organize the retreat."

"Yes, Captain," Gilion said, smiling. "It's good to have you back."

Aljeron acknowledged the compliment with a nod, and Gilion turned to begin organizing their withdrawal. Aljeron stepped over to Pedraan. "Do you think you could find the place where Caan fell?"

"I think so."

"Would you take me there?"

"I will."

Aljeron turned to Evrim. "Help organize the retreat as you can. I'll be back as soon as possible. And find Saegan, will you? I haven't seen him since we were separated in the battle."

"I will," Evrim replied.

"Good," Aljeron answered, then his eyes fell on Evrim's wounded side. "No, Evrim, go to the city. I'm sorry. I forgot about your wound."

"I'll be all right."

"Evrim, just go to the city. We can manage things without you."

"I will go, don't worry," Evrim said. "I just want to find Saegan first."

"All right," Aljeron nodded, knowing that Evrim was determined and that there was little use in fighting over the matter.

Pedraan guided Aljeron through the battlefield, and Valzaan followed quietly. Aljeron wasn't sure why the prophet chose to come, but he neither asked nor objected.

After some time spent searching the battlefield strewn with the bodies of the dead, Pedraan found Caan's body, lying stiff and bloody in the grass. Pedraan squatted beside him, as did Aljeron.

Aljeron spoke after a moment. "He was a great teacher."

"Yes, he was."

"All I know about the art of war, I learned from him."

Pedraan did not add anything, and the two of them looked at the lifeless body a while longer. Eventually, Aljeron reached down and picked up the sword that lay beside Caan in the grass.

"Caan's Firstblade, Kurveen," Aljeron said. "It was his most prized possession."

"No one should have a weapon for a most prized possession," Pedraan answered, rising and stepping away. "Even an Azmavarim."

Aljeron looked up over his shoulder at Valzaan, who stood like a silent sentry, neither speaking nor moving. Beside him stood Pedraan, with his back to Caan and Aljeron, looking back across the battlefield at the troops preparing for withdrawal. Aljeron turned back to Caan. "We'll bury you properly when we get the chance. For now, though, I'll take care of this."

Aljeron took up the sword, rose and headed back with the others.

"You need to leave him."

Yorek's words penetrated the thick fog that shrouded Wylla's mind. She looked down at the face of the young Kirthanim soldier. He wasn't much older than Benjiah, which is why she'd stopped to help when she heard his moans. She stopped to help, but as with so many other dying men on that battlefield, the only comfort she could offer was to hold his hand as he died.

"So much death," Wylla said, looking up at Yorek. "Werthanin, Suthanin, and Enthanin, they're all soaked with blood."

"War is an impartial and indifferent taskmaster," Yorek replied. "Regardless of why a man fights, war takes whom it will."

"When will it end?"

"This war or all wars?"

"Both."

"Hopefully soon," Yorek said, placing his hand on Wylla's shoulder. "Perhaps this battle is the prelude to the end. The dragons came and the Bringer of Storms has fallen. It may be that the tide has finally turned."

"Let us hope so."

"I do, but in the meantime, I think we should be on our way back to the city. The hour grows late."

Wylla did not protest but rose and followed Yorek. She trained her eyes ahead so that the bloody field would not be so disturbing. She wanted, no, she needed to find Benjiah. She needed to take him in her arms again and remind him of how much he was loved.

As they approached Tol Emuna, Wylla was struck by how many soldiers were winding their way back through the gates. She looked northward and neither saw nor heard evidence of ongoing battle.

"Do you think it's over?" she asked Yorek.

"It seems to be," he replied. "For today at least."

They continued toward the column of men. Wylla observed them as they passed, noting that beyond the weariness, something else was present in their faces, something that hadn't been present that morning—hope. There was hope in their eyes, hope and pride, and their faces were uplifted, not downcast as they had been when they'd shuffled out to surrender their weapons earlier that day.

"Wylla?"

She turned to see her brother approaching from farther back in the column. She smiled and opened her arms to receive him. "Pedraan, so glad to see you well."

Pedraan took her in his arms and held her tightly. He offered no light words or jokes, none of the levity that had always come so easily to both of her brothers, no matter how serious the situation. Reluctantly it seemed, Pedraan let go, and Wylla took Pedraan's face in her hands. "I am sure that you have served bravely and well today, my brother, and I am sure that Pedraal would have been proud of you."

"I just feel like something's been taken out of me, taken from here," Pedraan said, thumping his chest lightly. "I don't feel whole."

"Pedraal was my brother too," Wylla said softly, "but he was your twin. We both miss him, but you've never known life without him. You two have always been together. From the time you both crawled into the hearth in the main hall and covered each other in ashes when you were barely a year old, you have been inseparable. It's going to take time."

Pedraan said no more, and Wylla lowered her hands. "Pedraan, you should know that Rulalin Tarasir is dead."

Pedraan looked at her as though something was coming back to him. "I remember now. I thought I saw him on the scaffold not long before the dragon came, but in the jostling and madness, I didn't see what happened exactly."

"He saved Benjiah's life."

"How?"

"They were going to kill him, that awful man Tashmiren and the guard on the scaffold, but Rulalin stopped them. He killed them both, but then Synoki killed Rulalin."

"Synoki," Pedraan said, disgust evident in his voice. "If anyone deserves to meet a bad end, it's him."

"Well, I don't think it killed him, but Benjiah somehow broke his chains and struck Synoki with them, more than once."

"Broke the chains?"

"Yes, then the dragon came and took him away."

"That I saw. I'm glad he's all right, at least."

"Yes," Wylla agreed, "that's why we're headed to the city, to find him. I just wanted you to know how Rulalin died. He asked my forgiveness as he was dying, and I gave it. I hope we can all forgive him for what he did."

"It was obvious to me when I was with him yesterday that he had grown through his sufferings. I think he was a tortured man."

"I think you're right."

"He reaped what he sowed, but I guess we all do in a way."

"That we do," Wylla agreed. "I hope Rulalin finds the forgiveness he desired, not only from me and the rest of those he betrayed, but from Allfather."

"So do I."

"Well," Wylla continued, "I want to get back to the city. Are you coming now?"

"Yes, soon, but Aljeron wants me to stay here a little while to keep the men moving."

"Aljeron?"

Pedraan turned red. "Yes, I'm sorry. In the midst of it all I forgot to tell you, Aljeron has returned along with most of the others. Saegan was slashed by a Black Wolf but is all right, and Evrim was cut in the side. Even Valzaan is back."

"Valzaan! How can that be?"

"I don't know, but he's back."

"Where are they? I must see them."

"They're north, bringing up the rear."

"Good, we'll be back," Wylla said as she and Yorek started moving out alongside the column.

"Wylla?"

"Yes?"

"Evrim lost an arm somewhere along the way. I didn't get the story, so I don't know how yet."

Wylla thought of Kyril waiting somewhere in Tol Emuna, and tears came to her eyes again, but she choked them back. "Thanks for warning me," she said, and quickly she was on her way.

Finding Aljeron and the others stirred up so many emotions and memories in Wylla that she wasn't sure whether to laugh or cry. After the initial exchange of greetings and news, she stepped back and said, "Look at us. After all these years and all these leagues of struggle and hardship, we can still rejoice in one another. Whatever else went wrong, the Summerland certainly succeeded in binding us together, didn't it?"

"That it did," Aljeron said, smiling at Wylla. "It is good to see you again."

"And you. You've come a long and difficult way to be here."

"Yes, and with Evrim and Saegan both wounded, we need to get to the city so they can be looked after."

"Saegan wounded," Wylla said, looking at Saegan, who was sheepishly holding his arm, which a wolf had clawed. "I never thought I'd see the day when you were injured. I thought you were invincible and untouchable, Saegan."

"Quite the contrary, Your Majesty," Saegan replied. "I appear to be just as susceptible to injury and harm as the next soldier."

"I'm sure that's not the case," Wylla said, glad Saegan's good humor was still intact. "You are a remarkable soldier, and we all know it."

Turning to Evrim, she stepped up to him and smiled. "Kyril will be so happy to see you."

Evrim lowered his head, his lone arm hanging awkwardly at his side. "She's here then? And all right?"

"Yes, along with the girls and her father."

"Monias?"

"Yes."

Evrim nodded but didn't say anything else, and Wylla continued. "Evrim, I'm sorry about your arm, and I know Kyril will join all of us in weeping with you over it, but really, she'll be so happy to see you. You should just go to her."

"Indeed you should go," Aljeron echoed. "We all should. Darkness is falling and we need to get everyone inside the city and shut the gates, just in case."

"There is one other thing," Wylla said as they prepared to move out.

"What?"

"Rulalin is dead."

The men looked at her silently. She told them quickly what had happened, and when she finished, Aljeron said, "Take me to him."

"Now?" Wylla asked.

"Yes, if you don't mind," Aljeron said, as though just realizing he was addressing a queen and not one of his officers.

"All right, but we'll need to go quickly."

"That's fine."

"Let's all go," Evrim said.

"No," Aljeron said, shaking his head vigorously. "You and Saegan are going back to the city, now. As for Valzaan, he can choose for himself whether to come with us or to go to the city."

"I will come with you," Valzaan replied.

"All right then," Aljeron said, looking back to Wylla. "Lead on."

Aljeron stood on the scaffold, looking down through the near darkness at Rulalin's dead body. He swallowed and tried to gather himself. How much of his life had he dedicated to finding Rulalin again? Though he'd caught glimpses of Rulalin during the war against Fel Edorath, Aljeron hadn't actually been this close to him since the morning Rulalin killed Joraiem in Sulare. That was a long time ago, and the majority of that long time had been dedicated to bringing justice to Rulalin. Now justice had overtaken Rulalin at last, but Aljeron wasn't sure how he felt, let alone how he should feel.

"I thought I'd feel hatred," he began, "but I don't. Not really."

"I'm glad," Wylla said while Valzaan looked on and Yorek stood near the top of the stairs they had ascended.

"To be completely honest, I don't really know what I feel."

"I know. It's confusing. He took my husband from me and betrayed us all, but he saved Benjiah's life. What makes it even more confusing is that I think he did all those things for me. He took away Joraiem, and he gave me back Benjiah, all out of some strange sense of devotion."

"In a way, perhaps, but it was not exactly the same kind of devotion," Valzaan said. "It was a selfish obsession with you that led to Joraiem's death, but it was sacrificial love for you that led him to lay down his life for Benjiah. Rulalin changed."

"I'm glad to hear you say that," Wylla said. "It makes me think there might be hope. When he was dying, he asked me for forgiveness. I forgave him, but do you think Allfather will forgive? Can He, after all Rulalin did?"

"Can He? Of course He can. All fall short of Allfather's laws and requirements. We all bear the mark of Andunin's first betrayal. And yet Allfather has made it clear that all may be clean. Did Allfather forgive Rulalin? Well, that's between Rulalin and Allfather, for Allfather alone knew Rulalin's heart."

Aljeron knelt to examine Rulalin more closely. The blood from the stab wounds had soaked his cloak and stained the scaffold. "You say Synoki stabbed him with a dagger?"

"Yes."

"Forgiven or not, it would seem that Rulalin died in the manner that he killed, stabbed by a trusted friend. He devoured with his blade and was devoured by it."

"That he did, and that he was," Valzaan agreed. "Of course, as we look around us at this battlefield strewn with corpses, we see many others who were devoured by the blade as well. I suppose we could say that even Caan, in his own way, lived by and for the blade, and in the end, it devoured him."

Anger flared in Aljeron. "You're comparing Caan to Rulalin? You're comparing a hero who fought to protect Kirthanin to a traitor who sold us all out to save himself? You're saying there's no difference between these men?"

"Don't be foolish," Valzaan said. "There are many differences between them. Caan and Rulalin had different motives for going to war. One was dedicated to using his blade for good, the other used his for evil. And yet, the outcome this day for each was the same. Was it not?"

Aljeron did not reply.

"The blade is unforgiving, Aljeron," Valzaan continued more gently. "This you must know and understand by now. It devours the strong and the weak alike, the good and the bad, the noble and ignoble. All who live by and for it will be blessed when Malek is finally defeated and the binding of the blade is broken. The blade, all blades, perhaps more than anything else, display proof that this world is broken and has gone wrong. We can never lose sight of that, least of all when we hold those very blades in our hands.

"Remember the words of the prophecy:

'On that day, the fountain will flow again.
The Mountain will be cleansed
And all will be made new.
All instruments of war will be destroyed.
They will be unmade;
They will be reforged.
Recast as implements of peace, as plows
These blades will work and till
The ground forevermore.
No one will ever harm or kill again,
And Peace will be restored
On All My Holy Mountain.'"

Aljeron looked at Valzaan when the prophet finished. "Say what you like, but Caan died today standing against our enemy. It dishonors him to compare him to Rulalin."

"I meant no dishonor to Caan, nor do I believe I have brought any upon him. I think that if Caan, of all people, were here right now, he would understand what I am saying. You need only to look around from this platform and open your eyes, really open them, and you would see what I mean. The blade devours, and until they are all broken to pieces, melted down and remade, we will have no peace."

REUNION

ALL THINGS CONSIDERED, the city wasn't nearly as chaotic as Wylla expected to find it. To be sure, they encountered a mass of people immediately upon entry, for the well were trying to help the wounded to any of a number of locations where they could be tended. The process of sorting the healthy from the hurt and the severely wounded from the less so slowed progress sufficiently enough that for a while, Wylla and Yorek could hardly move. Even so, as they gained their bearings and gradually made their way forward, Wylla thought it could have been worse.

Wylla had not been to Tol Emuna in some time, and the last time she was there, of course, there was no siege or war on, so the streets were clean and all but deserted. Now, though, the city, exceeding capacity, struggled to cope with its burden. And yet, she was proud of the Enthanim, proud of their resilience in the face of difficulty. Though they faced confusion and hardship, she could see the calm persistence of the citizens of Tol Emuna as they bustled to and fro, doing what needed to be done despite their exhaustion. They were in many ways removed from the rest of Enthanin, but they were still her people.

"Benjiah may be difficult to find," Yorek said to her.

"He may well be," she answered. "We best start looking."

Their search proved slow and trying. There were so many people, and more than that, they were constantly moving. Everywhere they went and everywhere they looked, the people were in constant motion. Wylla realized quickly that she could never really rule out a street or building they'd managed to examine, for people constantly poured into and out of places where they'd just been. She stopped where she was in the middle of a street and threw her hands up in frustration.

"There must be a better way. We'll never find him like this."

"We need help, Your Majesty."

"We don't have help."

"Then perhaps we should split up. We could cover more ground."

"We could, but what would we do if we found him? How would we ever find each other again?"

"We could agree to a meeting place and time."

Wylla considered Yorek's suggestion. It certainly made sense to divide and conquer, though she wasn't optimistic that the two of them would be able to cover that much more ground apart then together. More than that, she felt so drained, the thought of wandering the city alone through the dark watches of the night was almost more than she could bear.

Before she could respond to his suggestion, though, a voice called out to them from down the street. Wylla peered through the crowd and saw Pedraan and Karalin coming toward them.

"Good, Pedraan," Wylla said as she hugged her brother. "I knew you were going to look for Karalin." Wylla hugged her friend also, whispering, "Good to see you again, Karalin."

"And you, Your Majesty."

"How'd you find her so quickly?"

"That was easy." Pedraan smiled. "She's predictable really. Just look for the place with the greatest need, in this case the large hall where the most severely wounded soldiers are being tended, and there Karalin will be."

"And you've whisked her away from all those men in need?" Wylla asked, smiling at them both.

"That I have, Sister, for she's been on her feet helping them since the battle began and the wounded began filtering back earlier today. She needs rest, and I was about to walk her home."

"Rest sounds good," Wylla said wearily.

"Why don't you come?" Karalin said gently. "There's more than enough room where I've been staying. After all you've been through, surely you could use a good night's sleep in a real bed."

"That sounds wonderful, Karalin," Wylla answered, "but I can't. I'm looking for Benjiah, and I won't be able to really rest until I've seen him. I know the dragon brought him into the city, but I can't find him."

Karalin grew pale, and Wylla could see the change in her, even in the half-light of the shadowy street. "What is it, Karalin?"

"I saw Benjiah earlier today."

"Was he all right?"

"Yes, he was."

"Where was he?"

"Here in the city, down by the walls."

"That's great," Wylla answered. "It confirms what we already know, that he's safe and in the city, right?"

Karalin hesitated, "Not necessarily. When I saw him, he was headed out to the battlefield again."

Wylla looked closely at her, trying hard to hold back the fearful images that crowded the edges of her imagination. "When was this?"

"Perhaps midday."

"And did you see him go out of the city?"

"I did, because I fetched Suruna from Pedraan's room for him. I thought he might need it."

A cold knot tightened in her stomach. "So we don't really know if he's all right, or even if he's in the city at all."

"Sister," Pedraan said, "let's not jump to any conclusions. Last any of us knew, Benjiah was fine, and we should assume he's fine until we know otherwise."

"I can't do this," Wylla said woodenly, a glazed look coming over her eyes. "I don't even know where to begin looking. There's so much city and so many people, and he's just one person. I can't do it."

Tears interrupted her, and she put her face in her hands. Pedraan stepped forward and took her in his arms. "We'll help you."

"But you need sleep, both of you," Wylla said.

"Never mind that now," Pedraan continued. "We can help. We'll keep going as long as we need to."

Wylla looked from her hands and Karalin nodded, "Of course we'll help, Wylla. Gladly."

"Should we each go alone or look in pairs?" Yorek asked.

"Let's go in pairs," Wylla said, looking to her advisor. "I really can't bear the thought of being alone right now."

"Yes," Pedraan said, "I think that's for the best."

"All right," Yorek said. "Then let's agree on a time and place. It's almost the end of First Watch now. I suggest we meet at the main gates by the end of Second Watch, all right?"

"Sounds good," Pedraan answered, nodding. "We'll head up toward the interior of the city. Why don't you two go back down toward the gates? If Benjiah was hurt at all in the fighting, he should be down there."

Wylla nodded, the thought of Benjiah lying hurt and in pain flashing through her mind. The thought sent a chill through her. If he was hurt, she just hoped he'd managed to make his way back into the city. The thought of him not being here, safe inside the walls, was something she just couldn't let herself think about.

Pedraan and Karalin moved deeper into Tol Emuna, farther and farther from the crowd near the gates, and Pedraan felt the tension in the silence between them. They had been talking easily before running into Wylla and Yorek, but now, although Karalin kept pace with him despite his long strides and her bad foot, she had all but stopped speaking.

"We'll find him, Karalin," Pedraan said, trying to sound reassuring.

Karalin walked on as though she hadn't heard him. Pedraan looked at her, persisting doggedly, eyes fixed ahead.

"I gave him Suruna," she said without turning. "I should have joined the others in trying to dissuade him. Maybe if we'd all persisted, he wouldn't have gone out."

"Don't count on it," Pedraan replied. "I know him well. He's not the boy who left Amaan Sul in Autumn. He's grown beyond that. If his mind was made up, you couldn't have dissuaded him from going. Better that he had Suruna to defend himself if need be. It was well done, giving him back the bow. Don't you dare blame yourself, no matter what's happened since you saw him last."

Karalin did not object, and Pedraan slipped his arm around her as they walked. He examined the people moving in either direction on the narrow street. For a while, their conversation was put on hold as they came to a large building with doors and windows open. They realized quickly that many soldiers, most with minor wounds, had been moved here to make room closer to the gates for the more pressing cases coming in.

As they moved through the room, looking for Benjiah among the men who sat or slept, Karalin caught her breath when they saw a young man stretched out along an interior wall. Pedraan moved forward and peered down, only to turn back to Karalin and shake his head. They made their way back onto the street once more. For a moment they stood and looked at one another before silently making their way up the street.

"So many wounded men," Karalin said softly as they walked. "It must have been awful again today."

"It was," Pedraan answered. "Not as bad as two days ago, maybe, but it was bad. I've had my fill of war these last few days."

"I'm sure you have."

"So many have fallen. Even from the small group of us who were together in Sulare. Pedraal, of course, and Sarneth, but Caan too earlier today." Pedraan turned and looked at Karalin, "Even the loss of Rulalin is strangely sad to me."

"Strange, as in unexpected?"

"Yes, unexpectedly sad. He betrayed us, but he was one of us, there in Sulare, and now he's dead. That's four in just the last few days."

"It is very sad."

"It is, and I'm sick of it. This battle, this war, the whole thing. I'm sick of it all. I want it over."

"Maybe it nearly is," Karalin said, seeming to grow excited at the thought of it. She took Pedraan's hand in her own. "Too long the fear of Malek and the need to wage war against him has dominated the hopes and dreams of Kirthanin."

"Yes, and too long the cares of this war have come between us."

Karalin squeezed Pedraan's hand. "You are caught in something bigger than the two of us. It isn't your fault."

"Yes," Pedraan said, looking over at Karalin, "even so, it has been too long."

Pedraan stopped and stood in the street, still holding Karalin's hand. She looked curiously up at him. "What?"

"I'm just thinking about that day in Sulare when my sister married Joraiem."

Karalin smiled and blushed. "I remember that day."

"I know you do," Pedraan answered, stepping closer. "We were all standing there in the beautiful gardens of the Summerland, listening to Master Berin and Valzaan and watching the ceremony. I was standing by Pedraal, trying to behave, when, out of nowhere, I just noticed you."

"I noticed you noticing me," Karalin laughed.

"I knew you did, but I couldn't help it. There was something about that setting or that event or that day. I don't know what it was, but it was like seeing you for the first time. I know I must have stared or gawked—"

"Not too badly."

"—but I couldn't help myself. All I could think about was how beautiful you were."

"Why thank you," Karalin said. "Of course, you were just a young thing, so I wouldn't have said so at the time, but I thought you were rather handsome too."

"Tell me the truth," Pedraan said, his mischievous smile somewhat at odds with his serious tone. "Did you know which of us I was? I mean, could you even tell Pedraal and me apart at that point?"

"Yes," Karalin answered definitely, but as she looked into Pedraan's eyes, she added, "I think."

Pedraan shook his head and feigned hurt while Karalin laughed. "Well, you can't be too hard on me. It isn't like either of you ever paid me any attention. Even after the wedding, it took you almost five years to get up the courage to speak to me."

"I know," Pedraan sighed. "What can I say? I'm a coward."

"That you are not," Karalin answered. "You're one of the bravest men I've ever known, without exception."

"In battle, maybe, but not in life," Pedraan replied. "Anyway, I'm sorry I've moved so slowly."

"We don't need to go over that again," Karalin said, raising her hand to stroke Pedraan's face. "It just gave me a chance to practice patience."

"You were already patient." Pedraan took Karalin's hand from his face and gripped it earnestly. "You've been waiting for years, too many years. You shouldn't have to wait any longer."

Karalin trembled and looked closely into his eyes. "Are you saying . . . ?"

"Yes, I am. That's exactly what I'm saying." He pulled Karalin in and held her tight. "It could have been me, Karalin, not Pedraal. On that field, cut down by the enemy. It could have been me. And then what? You'd have become a virtual widow, but without ever having been a bride."

Pedraan stepped away from her, both her hands now firmly in his own. "It's time. Whatever tomorrow brings to our walls and gates. Whatever our next move is, or theirs, it's time. That is, if you'll have me."

"Of course I will," Karalin said as she leaned her head against his chest and closed her eyes. "Of course I will."

For a long moment, Evrim stood before the door of the house he'd been shown. He shifted uneasily from one foot to the other, his fingers fiddling with a button on his cloak. It had been so long, and so much had happened in the interim.

He took a deep breath, raised his hand, and knocked. After a long moment, he heard a hand on the latch and the door swung open to reveal Monias, the candlelight from the room behind him casting shadows out the door. His eyes shone with tears as recognition came over him, and he took Evrim in his outstretched arms. "My boy," he said, "welcome home, for you are home you know. You are home."

He stepped back and smiled as he looked into Evrim's face. "Come in, come in. Let's get you inside. Come, sit."

Monias closed the door, and he soon found himself sitting at the table in the outer room while Monias poured him water and brought it to him. "Rest, my boy, and set your burdens and cares down for a while. You've come a long way, but you're here now."

Evrim looked at the short stumpy knob that protruded from under his cloak, and Monias followed his eyes. Evrim gazed down at the floor, embarrassed.

"Don't you worry about that now, my boy," Monias said firmly, although Evrim could hear the emotion in his voice. He looked up, and tears were rolling down Monias's face. "I've had a son brought back to me, body rotting and draped over a horse, and now I've had one come home alive but wounded, and I can tell you, there's nothing but joy in it. We'll weep with you tomorrow and for years to come over the price you've paid to do what you had to do, but make no mistake about it, there's nothing but joy for those in this house tonight. You're home safe."

Evrim was about to reply when he noticed movement at the doorway on his right. He turned and looked, and there was Kyril with Roslin and Halina. Evrim rose silently to face them.

"I was just putting the girls to bed," Kyril said as she gazed at Evrim.

"Hello, girls," Evrim said, looking from Kyril to them.

With that, Roslin rushed across the room and threw her arms around him, crying, "Father," and Halina did likewise. Before long, they were standing all four of them together in close embrace as Roslin babbled excitedly through a brief history of raids, rain, retreats and war, with something tossed in about juggling that Evrim couldn't quite square with the rest of it. After this had gone on for a few moments, Kyril gently hushed the excited girl, and Evrim walked both of his girls back to their beds.

For a long time Evrim sat and listened to them as they lay in their beds, spilling out their hearts to him. He heard their hopes and fears from the past year in what they said and didn't say, and he marveled at how much they'd grown. With his hand he caressed their long soft hair, and each of them, in the midst of their storytelling, broke down into tears. He didn't try to stop them, but held them close and cried with them. Much had been lost, more than just his arm, in the years that had slipped away from them while he fought first against Rulalin and Fel Edorath and more recently against Malek.

Eventually, he whispered good night to them both, kissing them as he blew out the candle and left the room. In the outer room of the small house, at the table, Monias sat close beside Kyril as she leaned against his shoulder. Though both were tearful, Evrim could see in Kyril the love and devotion he'd longed to see. Despite the many leagues and the deformity, her love had not faded. From their youth she had been constant and faithful, and he was ashamed that he had ever doubted her.

She rose and walked to him. "Do you want to go sit outside? The clouds are gone, and I haven't seen the moon or stars in ages."

"I'd like that," Evrim said, and both bid good night to Monias as they slipped outside.

They stood for a while in the open street, gazing into the nighttime sky, but soon they settled in on a small wooden bench against the front of the house. Though people were still moving along the street, no one paid them any attention. Evrim waited for Kyril to sit, then sat down on her right side so he could put his arm around her, and so his missing arm wouldn't be so obvious.

Kyril leaned her head against him and put her hand on his chest. Slowly, she ran it back and forth, caressing him. "Allfather brought you back to me. I thought I'd never see you again, but here you are."

"Here I am."

Kyril worked her hand back and forth across Evrim's chest, gingerly, carefully, lovingly. Evrim relaxed under the soothing touch of her fingers. How many nights had he dreamed of her touch? And yet when her hand strayed closer to his lost arm, he flinched.

"Did I hurt you?" Kyril pulled her hand back, looking a little startled.

"No, you didn't," Evrim answered sheepishly. "I'm sorry, I'm just feeling, well, I'm not really sure how I feel."

"Don't apologize, Evrim. It's all right. We've got time to figure it out. I'm sorry about what's happened, and at some point, maybe you can tell me about it and about your journey, but I don't want you to worry about that tonight. I just want to hold on to you. It's been so long."

"It has been," Evrim said, squeezing Kyril tightly and closing his eyes as he rested his head against the house. "As you said, Allfather brought me back. He's brought us both a long way, hasn't He?"

"He has," Kyril answered. "I thought today was the end. I thought we were done for. When I woke up, I expected to be Malek's slave by nightfall, but the dragons came, and now you've come. I thought I was going to lose everything today, but instead, I got you back."

"I'm back."

Kyril looked up at him, excitement shining in her eyes. "Perhaps it's almost over. Do you think it might be?"

"The war you mean?"

"Yes, with the dragons here and the Bringer of Storms dead? Do you think it might be over?"

"I don't know, Kyril. Despite their losses, I don't think the enemy will give up. They have lost some of their strength, maybe even much of it, but I suspect they're not finished yet."

Kyril leaned back into him. "Well, never mind. We can worry about that tomorrow. Tonight you're here, and we're safe. That's all that matters."

Aljeron walked quickly along the street. After stowing Kurveen in the room he would share with Gilion, he had thought to go quickly in search of Aelwyn, but he was out of sorts and hadn't wanted to be reunited with her while in this mood. He stayed with Koshti for a little while before eventually leaving his battle brother behind, curled up on the floor of their room.

It was now fairly late, because he had been delayed even before going to the room. He'd been delayed because the first order of business for him after entering the city had been solving the predicament of the Kalin Seir. Their wild appearance and masks aside, they had been given a warm reception by the normally wary and by now quite weary inhabitants of Tol Emuna. However, as Aljeron and the other captains had soon discovered, the Kalin Seir seemed ill at ease with their celebrity and were reluctant to intermingle. Aljeron thought that perhaps this was due to concern that the host of snow leopards brought potential for trouble, but having talked with the Kalin Seir elders more, he was now convinced it had something to do with their long years of isolation and sense of corporate shame. Despite their name, they were but Nolthanim to the rest of Kirthanin.

Aljeron could empathize with them, though he knew his situation was very different, having felt shame in his dealings with others on account of his marred face on more than one occasion. So, he'd negotiated a solution with Carrafin, the officer who seemed to be directly in charge of Tol Emuna. Carrafin found a less crowded corner of the city where the Kalin Seir could stay together with their battle brothers. The Kalin Seir elders seemed pleased with this plan, and the people parted in the streets as best as they were able to let the Kalin Seir pass, watching with gratitude as the men, women, and snow leopards moved silently through their midst. Aljeron had seen the occasional Kalin Seir still moving among the rest of the crowd in the city since then, but by and large they seemed to have settled into their own self-imposed isolation.

At last Aljeron arrived at the building he had been looking for. It was lit brightly, far more so than any of the others around it, and he paused at one of the open windows to look inside. Here many of the more seriously wounded soldiers were receiving aid, and though he didn't see Aelwyn, he recognized several Werthanim women of the auxiliary Aelwyn and Mindarin had formed. He searched the room and was about to move on, convinced that Aelwyn wasn't there, when he saw her enter through a door on the far side.

He had tried, all the leagues of his long journey, to keep her image alive in his mind, but seeing her again in person was jarring. She was beautiful, every bit as beautiful as he remembered, but he felt a strong and almost overpowering fear that he'd distorted or possibly even invented the words and feelings that passed between them upon his departure. Yes, he'd known her since she was a little girl, but except for those brief encounters in Shalin Bel and their retreat together to Col Marena, they had never hinted, let alone talked, of love. Maybe the swirl of emotions surrounding those events had deceived them both. Maybe when they were face-to-face again, he would be as strange to her as she now seemed to him.

She was moving along the row of wounded soldiers, giving them water, when she turned in the direction of the window where he was standing. Instantly he withdrew until he was hidden in the shadows. He stood there, against the outer wall, holding his breath. After a long moment he stepped away from the window so as to be less easily seen by anyone inside, and looked for her again. She was still there, working, and as far as he could tell, she had not noticed anything. He sighed and backed away.

As he stood there, torn between going in and facing the truth, whatever it was, or walking away, a voice called to him. "Aljeron Balinor."

He turned to see the lean form of a Kalin Seir woman not far away, likewise using the shadows to avoid notice. "Keila? What are you doing out here on your own?"

"I went for a walk."

"You should go back," Aljeron said, though he lacked a convincing reason.

"I can take care of myself."

"That I know," Aljeron answered, stepping closer to her. "You fought well today."

"As did you," Keila answered. "You are a great warrior, even if you are a Blade-Bearer. It still seems strange to me, but no one who saw you today could accuse you of serving the Forge-Foe."

"I hope not," Aljeron answered, thinking of Valzaan's words on the scaffold. "I have opposed him with all of my strength, all of my life."

There was silence between them for a moment, then Keila continued. "What do you look for in the window? Is she here?"

"She is," Aljeron answered.

"Is that her?"

Aljeron turned to see Aelwyn standing in the doorway. He looked at her, framed in the room's light, and he felt everything else around him fall away. Suddenly there was only Aelwyn, and she was stepping out of the doorway into the street in his direction.

"Aelwyn," he said, stepping toward her, feeling suddenly nervous.

"I had hoped you would find me," Aelwyn said, and Aljeron thought he could detect nervousness in her as well. "I saw Gilion earlier. He told me you were in the city."

"Yes, I had to help Carrafin figure out what to do with the Kalin Seir. If you haven't heard, they're the people from the north who accompanied us from Nolthanin."

"I've heard," Aelwyn answered. "Was that one of them?"

"Yes," Aljeron said, noticing as he looked back toward the shadows that Keila was gone. "We were briefly prisoners of the Kalin Seir until we could convince them we weren't servants of Malek. She was one of our guards."

"A guard?" Aelwyn asked.

"Yes, both the men and women are armed and fight among the Kalin Seir."

"A woman after your own heart," Aelwyn said, but Aljeron couldn't tell if she meant it as a joke or not.

"No, Aelwyn," he said after a pause, "I could only say that about you."

Aelwyn needed no further invitation. She came the rest of the way to Aljeron and slipped her arms around him. "I've missed you so much."

"And I you."

"I was afraid for you. Afraid of never seeing you again."

"But I'm here, and so are you."

"Yes," she answered, holding him tightly. "I'm here."

After a moment Aelwyn relaxed her grip on him and stepped back, looking up into his face. There was silence, and Aljeron felt the uneasiness return.

"Do you need to go back in?" he asked.

"No," Aelwyn answered. "Mindarin has forbidden my return."

"Forbidden?"

"Yes," Aelwyn answered, smiling. "She saw you through the window and sent me out, telling me that I wasn't to come back."

"Well, I'm sure you're weary, as I am," Aljeron began, "but if you're up for it, let's walk together a while."

"That would be lovely," Aelwyn replied, and they turned away from the brightly lit building and started down the street.

Walking, arm in arm, Aljeron began to feel more confident that he had not in fact imagined their closeness during the extremity of his journey through the miserable, snowy wasteland of Nolthanin. Their conversation flowed with increasing ease, focused mainly on the events of that very day. After Aelwyn summarized her own account of things, she listened as Aljeron talked about their long run and timely arrival. What surprised her, and even Aljeron a little bit, was how visibly disturbed he grew, not when describing the battle, but when describing the aftermath and the visit to see Rulalin's body on the scaffold.

"So at first," she said, "you thought Valzaan was somehow questioning or impugning Caan's honor?"

"Yes, I did, and despite what he said after, I still feel like he did. There's no comparison between them."

"But Valzaan explained that he hadn't meant to say they were the same."

"Yes, but he still compared them, Aelwyn." Aljeron looked at her, feeling the same swirl of emotion he experienced on the scaffold rising in him now. "I mean, by his logic, almost any soldier in this army could have been compared to Rulalin, and certainly any captain. Gilion, Pedraan, even me, and that's not right. I've spent the last seven years of my life in direct opposition to Rulalin, trying to bring justice to him. Yes, we were both fighting and we've both used the sword to kill, but we were not the same, not at all. All who wield the sword are not the same."

"No," Aelwyn answered after a moment, "but that doesn't seem to have been Valzaan's point. Maybe his point is that the people who wield the sword aren't the same, but the sword is the same no matter who wields it."

They had reached an intersection where the smaller street they were walking along met a larger road. A few people were moving along this larger, more brightly lit way, and Aljeron stopped to look at her. He could see that she was waiting for him to respond, but he didn't know what to say. He smiled and hugged her close.

"You do hope for a day when this war is over, when the sword can be put down, don't you?" she asked.

"Of course," Aljeron answered. "Yes, I would like that very much. I'm as weary of all this as anyone."

Aelwyn nodded, leaning against his chest. "Then let's not worry about such things tonight."

"I agree," Aljeron replied, trying to smile warmly and restore the ease that had been between them. "Allfather has brought us back together after two long and treacherous roads. Tonight we will be happy, and we will not worry ourselves about it."

Wylla reached the stairs at the base of the wall and began to ascend, her feet moving rapidly. She could feel the same sense of urgency pulsing through her that she had felt all night.

Even though she hadn't expected that the four of them would be able to find Benjiah in the city on their own, she was still distraught to find that her assumption was correct. She and Yorek met up with Pedraan and Karalin not long ago, and they confirmed her suspicion. He might be in the city, but if so, they didn't know where. Pedraan offered to keep looking, but Wylla rejected the offer and told them both to get sleep. Her insistence was motivated partially by genuine concern for her brother and for Karalin, and in part by the realization that when tomorrow came, she might well need many well-rested people to help her cast the net wider.

"Your Majesty?" Yorek called from below.

She kept going until she was on the walk that led along the top of the wall. Then she paused and looked down. "Yes?"

Yorek was climbing, though not at her pace, and he didn't answer immediately. "Nothing," he said when he reached the top, breathing heavily. "I just wanted you to slow down. I was worried you'd fall in your haste."

Wylla didn't answer but walked a few paces. She passed one of the many sentries posted on the wall to keep watch for any threatening nighttime movement of the enemy. She moved several spans beyond him and turned to the parapet. Leaning against it, she looked out over the broad plains.

"Why are we here?" Yorek asked.

"He's not in the city."

"We don't know that."

"No, maybe we don't, but I can feel it. He's out there, Yorek. He's out there and he may be hurt. He could be bleeding to death, right now. He could be dead already."

"You're right, Your Majesty. Either of those things could be true, but we have no evidence that they are. The city is jammed with people, and just because we didn't see him, that doesn't mean he isn't curled up safe and warm in some bed somewhere. There are thousands of buildings here, and we didn't exactly conduct a room-to-room search."

"I know," Wylla answered, "but I still think he's out there."

Wylla looked up at the full moon. It was big, bright and luminescent, and like everyone else, she hadn't seen it in ages. In almost any other situation, she would have greeted the sight with joy and delight. It would have been comforting to gaze at the moon and stars and contemplate the dissipation of the unnatural clouds, but not tonight. For all its brightness, the moon did not provide adequate illumination of the vast plain. There was only just enough light to tease her with impressions of the fallen, dark and shadowy shapes upon the ground. Yorek was right, of course. Other than the confirmation that Benjiah had left the city earlier in the day to fight, there was no specific evidence suggesting he was still out there. None. Why then did she feel it with such certainty? She lifted her eyes from the battlefield to the bright moon and faintly twinkling stars.

"Oh, Allfather," she whispered. "Watch over him and keep him safe."

7

NIGHT OF THE WOLF

DARKNESS SURROUNDED HIM. He felt like he was floating. Then, suddenly, there was light. He looked around.

There, across the open plain, was the enemy army. The limping man stood, looking on the fallen form of Cheimontyr. Benjiah noticed that the body of the Bringer of Storms was already decaying. It seemed odd to him, since Sulmandir had only just killed him, or had it been longer? Benjiah was struck by the strange thought that ages had passed since Cheimontyr fell, but if so, why were they all still gathered as though it had just happened? However long it had been, the flesh on the giant was grey and in places caved in as though the body it once covered was hollow. As Benjiah watched, the Vulsutyrim's bare, outstretched arm collapsed into dust.

Benjiah pulled his eyes from the rapidly deteriorating body and looked back to the limping man. He nocked an arrow to Suruna and took aim. Vaguely, he was aware of having tried something like this before, and there was a distant tremor somewhere in his body like a warning as he let go of the string. Even so, he watched the arrow fly true, heading straight for the limping man.

And then, as the arrow was about to strike its target, the limping man disappeared, as did the giant's body and the whole battlefield. For the briefest of moments he was alone on a vast plain, but that too disappeared. He felt a puff of wind that tousled his hair, and then all was darkness as once more he found himself floating.

Gradually he became aware that he was no longer floating. Under his body was solid ground, stone in fact. It was cold and smooth and brought goosebumps to the back of his neck. He also became aware that the darkness was not entirely dark. Some distance away there flickered light as though from a fire.

Slowly, for now he felt that his body ached, he rose to his feet. His legs were stiff and his knees creaked as he straightened out. It was as though he had been lying in an awkward position for hours, though he was sure he'd only just arrived in this place, wherever it was.

His eyes adjusted to the dark, and looking around he saw that he was in a hallway. Ahead, the hallway opened into a much larger room, and the flickering must have been coming from a fire outside his line of vision. He wasn't sure where he was, though the hall had a familiar feel. He took a careful step, attempting not to make too much noise. Until he saw what lay ahead, it seemed prudent to be cautious.

Stealthily, he slipped up to the entryway. The room beyond was indeed large. It was a great hall, largely empty except for a single, scarlet-upholstered, high-backed chair that sat before a large stone fireplace. At the same moment, Benjiah recognized both the chair and the great hall as belonging to the royal palace of Amaan Sul, and immediately he felt relief wash over him. He had been away for so long and traveled so far, and when he'd finally returned to Amaan Sul, he'd been wheeled through it in a cage. Now he was home, really home.

And yet, despite the relief, he didn't feel quite at ease. A creak came from the chair as its occupant shifted positions. He almost said, "Who's there?" but he thought better of it and continued quietly, angling in such a way as to get a glimpse of the person sitting there.

Mother, he thought as he drew nearer, for indeed, now he could see that the person in the chair was his mother, the queen of Enthanin. She was wearing one of her formal dresses, a long blue gown with a high collar and embroidered sleeves. He'd seen her wear it on special holidays and festive occasions a handful of times in his early youth. Why she wore it now in this dark, drafty, and essentially empty room, he couldn't imagine.

"Mother?"

"He's gone," she said in reply, though she did not turn to look at him but continued gazing into the fire. As Benjiah grew closer, he could see that she appeared sad, indeed forlorn. Tears were running down her face.

"Who's gone, Mother?"

"My son. He left this morning."

"But, I'm here—" Benjiah began, wondering why his mother would not look at him.

He stopped speaking, though, for the body of his mother seemed suddenly to dissolve and disappear, and the blue dress deflated and fell in a crumpled heap on the chair cushion. The fire still crackled, burning bright and hot in the fireplace, but the chair was uninhabited, as the blue dress lumped on the scarlet upholstery gave the room a small splash of color in the darkness.

"Mother?" Benjiah called out, fear and worry washing over him as he recovered from the momentary daze. "Where are you? Are you all right?"

He felt a draft of cool air sweep through the room, and the chair and the fireplace appeared to grow smaller and recede. The last glimmer of the fire disappeared from view, and he was once more in darkness, floating.

Again he found himself upon stone, but standing this time. Before him was a low wall, beyond which lay a great open plain. He was standing atop the great outer wall of Amaan Sul, gazing across the plains to the north and west between the city and the distant forest of Gyrin.

The night was cool and quiet, but the moon hung low on the horizon. It was full and bright, casting down its silvery beams, illuminating the twin peaks of the distant Agia Muldonai. Benjiah's eyes were drawn to the Mountain. For a long moment, it seemed peaceful, shimmering slightly at this distance in the moonlight, but then something changed. Darkness began to spread out from the Mountain, but it wasn't a cloud, not exactly. It was more like an inky blotch growing in all directions at once, until after a moment Agia Muldonai was obscured from view. Still the blotch grew until it eclipsed much of the horizon.

Then the darkness began moving across the moon, and before long, the moonlight also disappeared. One by one and cluster by cluster, the bright and twinkling stars winked out of the nighttime sky. The darkness grew blacker, so black Benjiah couldn't make out anything around him. He could not distinguish his own hand from the wall beneath it. A chill ran down his back, and he shivered as a gust of cool wind tickled his face.

And then, all at once, a myriad of yellow gleaming eyes appeared across the great plain. As far as he could see, the eyes stared up at the wall where he stood. They were not motionless, hanging suspended before him in the dark, but rather they bounced lightly up and down as the feet beneath them glided noiselessly through the soft grass.

They are beyond numbering, Benjiah thought, but as he reached for Suruna and his quiver, he found that he was carrying neither. He wore his clothes and a light cloak and nothing more. He shivered again, and then the scene faded away. Once more, he floated across the darkness.

Benjiah's awareness gained a new level of clarity. He recognized it was odd to know he was dreaming while still dreaming. What's more, he was aware of the sequence of images from the battlefield to the great hall to the city wall. The images themselves made no more sense to him now than they had when he first saw them, but just the distance he felt from them even now, still inside his dream, was a comfort.

A new scene appeared. This time there was no growing awareness of a change in surrounding; he was fully and completely aware all at once. He stood upon a plain, but in the distance he could hear the sound of waves crashing upon the shore. He could even see the white-tipped tops of waves rolling in. A strong wind was blowing from off the sea, bringing the unmistakable scent of saltwater to his nose. He breathed deeply, taking the smell in as he saw a flash of lightning streak horizontally through the dark clouds. The flash lit up the clouds, and a moment after the flash disappeared, a great roar and rumble of thunder rent the air. He felt himself trembling at the mighty sound.

Silence returned, and he stood still, not sure what to do. He felt, somehow, less constrained than before, like he was less of a spectator and more of an actor in the scene. This shift, this change, was not comforting.

Another great flash of lightning ripped open the sky, but this time it fell vertically toward the earth. At first Benjiah leapt back as though to avoid the strike, but he saw it hit the water a hundred spans away and felt foolish. As the last glimmer of light from the strike faded, though, he saw to one side a small mound raised up from the ground with something like a cave mouth appearing in it. Without hesitation, he started walking toward it.

Stepping into the mouth of the cave was a strange experience. Benjiah stepped out of the cold wind coming off of the sea and into a warm wind coming out of the cave. It was as though the mouth of the cave were the mouth of a great, earthen beast, and it was breathing its warm, moist breath in Benjiah's face. He hesitated at the opening, but just for a moment, before making his way into the cave.

His way was not entirely dark, for blue luminescent stones embedded near the base of the walls at even intervals provided faint light for his journey. Had he not felt compelled to keep going, to keep penetrating the narrow tunnel, he might have stopped to examine the stones and the light they created.

He was drawn, though, and he could feel it like a magnetism tugging at him insistently, pulling him with irresistible will into the hot breath of the mysterious cave. His feet moved mechanically, one after the other, even as the downward slope steepened, so that he had to lean back to counteract his tendency to stumble forward. He could envision himself pitching over and sliding down this long, dark tunnel, tumbling over and over into the very center of the earth. *Toward what nether region am I heading, and what will I find when I get there?*

At last, Benjiah found the slope so steep that he sat down and allowed himself to slide with his feet out, bracing for whatever shock might await him. He did not slide far, and the end of his slide was less painful than he had feared. He fell off a slight drop and landed on a smooth, level stone floor.

A few moments of investigation revealed he was in a round room, not overly large, with an opening that led to another, larger room. What took even less than a few moments' investigation to discover was that he had found the source of the hot breath blowing up the tunnel and out the mouth of the cave. No sooner had he dropped onto this stone floor than he felt a marked increase in temperature, blowing in from the larger room.

A loud, insistent clang rang out through the stifling air, and Benjiah moved into the entryway to this second, larger chamber. Several things greeted his senses all at once. He heard even more clearly now the echoes of what sounded like metal on metal. The sound rang out, and from the nature of the echoes it created, he judged the room to be cavernous. He was also greeted by a bright glow of eerie reddish light. Silhouetted by the reddish light was the frame of a powerful man leaning over the source of the light and wielding a hammer adeptly.

Benjiah hesitated to enter the room. He still wasn't exactly sure where he was, but he felt no doubt about whom he was seeing. The man at the forge, for that was surely what was giving off the reddish glow, could be no one else but Malek. *He will look up. He will see me, and then I will die.*

But the man at the forge did not look up. He continued working intently, and after a moment, Benjiah overcame his fear and moved through the dark room. The large and powerful frame of the man impressed him, as his sweating muscles heaved and flexed while he moved the hammer up and down in a rhythmic fashion. The man's shoulder-length dark hair moved up and down as he worked, the glowing hot metal taking shape on the forge. Benjiah peered at it and saw a long, slender blade with a cruel, razor-sharp point extending to some length. The man, still apparently unaware of the observer who had come so close and watched him work, set down his hammer to admire the blade. With a pair of tongs he picked it up and turned it over and over, examining it closely. He set it back down and took a few more strokes, these more precise but no less forceful than those that had come before, and once more he examined it.

At last, seeming satisfied, he plunged it into a vat of water beside him, and steam rose hissing.

Beyond the mist-enshrouded figure, Benjiah heard a sound unlike any he'd heard in his dream to that point, a sound that pierced the darkness. It was, unless he was mistaken, the bleating of a sheep.

Awake, called a voice, and his surroundings disappeared. Benjiah was no longer floating in darkness.

Benjiah opened his eyes. He was instantly aware that he was no longer dreaming. He moved and felt the painful ache—not the echo of bodily ache as he had felt it in his dream, but the fullness of it: The ache from being struck by a wave of energy or power hurled at him by the strange, limping man. The ache from being cast many spans through the air before landing roughly on the hard ground. The ache that came from lying unconscious in an awkward position for many hours.

The limping man. The man in the last of his dreams, if it had been Malek, looked different from the limping man—bigger, stronger, more of a commanding physical presence. Benjiah knew that this might not mean anything; after all, Valzaan said that Malek had the power to change his physical appearance. Even so, Benjiah couldn't help but wonder if his earlier suspicions had been misdirected. Perhaps the limping man, like Cheimontyr, only wielded power entrusted to him by his master. Perhaps Malek remained unidentified and at large.

Benjiah started to sit up, and he was suddenly aware of something else entirely, something outside of himself. Danger. There was danger. He felt it in his skin, his blood, his bones. A dark blur flashed toward him through his peripheral vision. Instinctively he reached out for something to defend himself with, and he rolled as fast as he could, going up and over the corpse of a dead soldier. As he dodged, he was vaguely aware of the warm breath of the Black Wolf that just missed him, sinking its sharp teeth into the dead body instead of his own soft flesh.

Benjiah continued to scramble away, knowing his reprieve was momentary. In fact, the wolf had already raised its bloody jaws, now clearly discernible in the bright moonlight. Benjiah's eyes had adjusted fully to the waking world, but he could see no simple way out of this predicament. With no other recourse, Benjiah slipped quickly into *torrim redara*.

The wolf, a great brute, paused crouched and ready to spring with eyes narrowed upon Benjiah's exposed neck and face. The crimson bloodstains on the matted fur around the wolf's mouth were eerie in the moonlight, and Benjiah looked around him for some kind of help. The first thing he saw was not the cast-off sword of some Kirthanim soldier, but his own quiver, full of arrows. It must have sailed across the battlefield with him and fallen a span or so away when he'd landed. It wasn't his weapon of choice for facing a Black Wolf in the darkness, but it was available. He stared at it as though to commit to memory its exact location, and when at last he felt he was ready, he stepped out of slow time.

He felt the rush of time as he emerged from *torrim redara*, and already he was diving toward the quiver as the wolf leapt through the air. Again the beast just barely missed, and Benjiah felt the leather quiver in his hand. He rolled over and back up onto his feet in a stooped position. Unable to clasp a single arrow quickly, he withdrew several. The wolf was already upon him, and he raised the arrows and jammed them up into the animal's underbelly as it landed on top of him, knocking him onto the ground.

With his left hand he pushed the arrows home, driving them deeper and deeper into the wolf while he raised his right hand to try to hold off the snapping and snarling jaws just a hand's length above his face. He got hold of the wolf's lower jaw and held on, pushing the arrows harder. His right arm trembled to hold back the angry beast's head, but then, in a moment, the creature grew limp and collapsed heavily upon him.

By the time Benjiah managed to push the wolf off and extricate himself from underneath it, his shirt and cloak were soaked with the creature's blood. Fortunately, the Full Spring night was fairly warm, and the wet clothing didn't feel too uncomfortable, despite the stickiness. He fanned it to keep it from drying onto his skin. He rose, shaking from the experience, feeling the nerves that adrenaline had energized during the brief encounter. The dreams had been unpleasant, but waking up was worse.

For the first time, he looked up and surveyed the battlefield. His heart sank. Moving stealthily around him were scores and scores of Black Wolves, their dark coats so shadowy that even in the moonlight, their movements were all but hidden from his eyes. Benjiah felt desperation well up inside, and he looked around more extensively, hoping to find Suruna nearby. It might not do him a great deal of good against so many, but he was better with bow and arrow than with a sword. It was a faint chance, but possibly his only chance.

None of the other wolves were especially close or seemed particularly interested in him, but he knew this would soon change. Their eyes, capable of surveying their surroundings in darkness, would soon see him, and their noses, capable of tracking even faint scents, would soon smell him. He dropped to his hands and knees and worked through the grass, looking for his bow. Then he saw it, the smooth curved wood of Suruna.

He scrambled over to it with elation but then gasped with dismay. The bow was broken. A crack ran lengthwise from the handle, so that the upper half of the bow hung by long slender threads of wood. Involuntarily, tears welled up in him. It wasn't just that his hope for defense was gone, though that was certainly part of it. At that moment, he felt suddenly and completely cut off from his past. This bow had been his father's, and he'd never felt closer to the father he never met than when he drew its string. Now that link was shattered, and with it any prospect for defending himself.

Do not fear.

Why not? I'm surrounded.

Yes, but I am with you.

Suruna is broken.

I know. You will not need it again. The battles you have left to fight will not require it. Only one remains where physical weaponry would do you any good, and in that battle you must refuse it.

I don't understand.

You will. For now, it is enough that you know.

Benjiah looked around. Though he knew the conversation was inaudible to the wolves, he could tell that a couple of them had taken notice of him at last. He could see by their silhouettes that they had stopped moving and pricked their ears in his direction. His time was running out.

What should I do?

Run.

Run?

Yes. I will empower you to outrun your foes, but they will pursue you. They will all pursue you. You will lead them away from this place, and when you have, then I will show you what has been to prepare you for what must be. Of what is to come we have already spoken.

Two of the wolves bounded across the field, and Benjiah did not wait. Dropping the useless quiver of arrows, he ran south.

The wolves ran after him. He turned toward the city as the small pack behind him kept growing. Again he was turned out of his course by the sudden appearance of a small cluster of wolves. He turned again, this time northward, and he ran with the lights of the distant city walls on his right, like a beacon from a friendly harbor that was out of reach and steadily being left behind.

He came upon more wolves, but never so many at once that he had to completely change course again. Even so, he had to be nimble and his way was never straight, for he was constantly dodging and zigzagging. And yet he could feel the sustaining power of Allfather, and he ran with a fleetness and strength not his own. As the darkling plain stretched out before him, he felt something almost like joy as he ran through the moonlight, a great host of wolves gathering behind him.

Despite the fact Benjiah had been running for hours, he felt no fatigue. Even the aches and pains he'd felt when he awakened from his strange dreams seemed to have gone. The bright moon shone on the plain, which now sloping steadily upward. He kept going, almost directly due north, his outward focus on each step. Inwardly, the words of Allfather were running through his head. *I will show you what has been to prepare you for what must be.*

What could that mean? Benjiah had no idea. All he knew was that the promise of speed and strength had been true. None of the vast host of Black Wolves behind him had even come near. He had outstripped them all.

He looked over his shoulder, realizing he hadn't done so for a while. What he saw amazed him. There had been many hundreds of wolves trailing him, but now there were thousands. There they all were, their sleek bodies a great black sea, bobbing up and down in the moonlight. Like an ominous and inescapable tide, this sea swept over the plain.

Why are they all chasing me? He assumed they were following him because Allfather had drawn them to him. His words certainly implied something along those lines. *But how do I know they weren't already looking for me? Maybe the limping man knew I'd been hurt but not killed, and maybe they were sent to finish me. Why else would every last one be running behind me now?*

He turned back forward and came to a sudden halt. There before him, lining the crest of the long hill he'd been ascending, was another great sea of Black Wolves.

Benjiah felt the supernatural strength and speed leave him, and the aching in his muscles returned. He stood in the tall green grass, turning around and around, looking at the thousands and thousands of wolves that encircled him for as far as he could see.

The tug into *torrim redara* came without warning, for Benjiah had not yet summoned it. Something or someone else pulled him there.

You have done well.

I am surrounded.

Yes, but that is what I desired.

Why?

You will see, but first, it is time you knew the fullness of what you have already done, the fullness of what I have done through you, that you may see what it is that you are about to do.

The dark hillside covered with wolves disappeared. Benjiah was hurtling through the darkness, but he felt almost no motion at all. And then he was standing still again, this time in a darker place.

Under his feet was a stone floor, smooth and hard. He could not see anything around him, but above him, some light fell in through what appeared to be a rectangular hole in a solid roof. He took the sight in, and then he knew where he was.

I am in the dragon tower again.

Yes.

Benjiah would have asked more, but a burning and brilliant flash erupted from nearby, and Benjiah turned to watch. The light was so bright he should not have been able to look, but he did not even blink as he gazed at what was taking place. He saw himself, holding Valzaan's staff, and his uncles dropping to the stone. Above, the wooden doors burst into flame and disappeared in black smoke billowing out into the night. Beyond where he was standing, he saw the dark and terrible figure of the Grendolai being burnt into the stone wall behind its mock dais and makeshift throne.

The searing white light glowed as the silhouette of the Grendolai was etched into the dark stone. Then the light disappeared. Still, he was able to see his uncles slowly rise from the ground. They looked with wonder at him, standing still, holding Valzaan's staff firmly in his hands.

The scene slipped away, and he was once again racing through the darkness. This time, he was vaguely aware of landscapes zipping by below him at speeds beyond his imagining. Soon he saw rising up in the darkness another dragon tower. As they approached the tall, dark structure, he could see dazzling light shining up through the center of the tower, shining out beyond the shelter, so that thin rays of light shot up into the night sky like starlight being retracted into the heavens.

The tower slipped behind them as they continued moving, and before he knew it, they were approaching another dragon tower. Like the preceding one, a strong and dazzling light was exploding out of the storage area at the top into the nighttime sky. They passed it and soon approached another and another. Benjiah started to keep count and continued until at last they left the last one behind. Then he came to a stop, back on the hillside where the great sea of wolves waited patiently, a small circle of bare grass kept open for him.

All of them?

Yes.

Every Grendolai?

Every one.

The enormity of what Allfather was showing Benjiah overwhelmed him. The thought that he had been used by Allfather to kill a Grendolai was astonishing enough, but all of them? That was too much.

I don't understand.

Why not?

How could it be?

Why should it not be? It is as easy for me to kill all as to kill one. The judgment you pronounced upon the usurper you faced was spoken into the darkness of all the towers. All the Grendolai heard your voice and My words and knew their time had come. At the very moment I destroyed the one, I destroyed them all. Every last dragon tower in Kirthanin has been cleansed.

Benjiah felt a tingling in his body as he recalled that moment, the flood of light and heat that had filled him. In some strange and mysterious way, some part of him had known that something larger than the destruction of a single Grendolai had happened. Now he understood what had been happening through him.

Malek's creations are a blight upon my world, and through you I have begun the process of cleansing it. The cleansing began there, that night, but it is not finished, and it will not be until the Fountain flows again and the stones of Avalione are washed clean. The time for that is not yet, though it will be soon. Tonight, however, the cleansing continues.

Benjiah looked around himself at the great dark sea, still frozen in its sweep up the hillside.

You understand?

I do.

As the words went forth from his mind, he felt himself slipping out of slow time. The slight evening breeze resumed, blowing upon his cheeks and lifting his wet and matted blond locks from his neck. The wolves also resumed their course, approaching from all sides at once.

Benjiah lifted both arms into the air, his hands clenched tightly. He felt the light and heat, like the source and sweetness of life itself, coursing through his veins.

"Children of Rucaran the Great. Servants of the Master of the Forge. Too long have you run by night and terrorized Allfather's world. Too long have your bodies, bearing inside them the seeds of their own destruction, run free across our fields, a mockery of Allfather's good creation. No longer. Not one moment longer. Here and now, I call down Allfather's fire upon you. You are finished. Your time is ended."

Zigzagging through the darkness, lines of fire crisscrossed above them all, a vast and intricate web of flames racing back and forth. The wolves stopped moving and gazed up at the curious and fearful phenomena. With every moment more and more of the sky lit with fire, and the flames glowed brighter and hotter.

Benjiah looked from the sky to the wolves and saw that many were cowering, crouching and lowering their bodies down to the ground as though to put as much distance as possible between themselves and the terrible sky.

Bursts of flame began to shoot down all around him. Benjiah watched as streaks of flame fell, hundreds and hundreds at a time. Shrieks and howls rent the night air as the wolves not yet on fire began jostling against their neighbors, both the living and dead, both the burning and the not burning. There was nowhere for them to go. They had gathered themselves compactly into this one, single location, like sheep herding themselves into a pen. In no time the howling began to die away, for the fire was consuming and their deaths immediate.

Soon, the fire stopped falling, and the delicate streaks began to retrace their initial courses until, at last, the final few threads disappeared back into whatever wondrous place they had come from. Benjiah stood upon the hill, now gazing into the face of the bright moon, which smiled gently upon him as though nothing at all unusual had come between them.

Benjiah surveyed the hillside in every direction. There were no wolves or wolf corpses. Their dissolution had been absolute. Thin wisps of smoke rose from each small pile of ash, the last remains of each of Rucaran's children. Benjiah squatted near the pile closest to him and peered carefully at it. The ash was no more substantial than if a sheet of parchment had been burned. There was no sign of hair or bone, and no wriggling of the vile worms that characteristically emerged from their dormant hiding places in the wake of a Black Wolf's death. They, along with their hosts, had been burnt from the face of the earth.

They're all gone?

All of them.

Now what?

The night is far spent and the dawn is at hand. Return to the city. I will give you strength, for you have run far.

There was more that Benjiah wanted to ask, but he was learning to recognize when all had been said. He turned his back to the crest of the hill he had never reached, and being careful not to step in any of the myriad piles of ash, began to jog back down.

8

LAST RITES

FOR WYLLA, THE LONG NIGHT had seemed endless. Yorek had encouraged and implored her to lie down, even if she thought she couldn't sleep, but lying down had only made the waiting worse. Sitting outside in the fresh spring air beneath the shiny moon was at least somewhat soothing, though the watches of the night moved agonizingly slowly. Yorek, faithful as he was and unwilling to leave her alone, had come outside to wait alongside her, but fell asleep and now lay dozing with his back against the wall of the house, snoring quietly.

At long last, the moment Wylla had been waiting for arrived. The first faint sliver of dawn showed itself in the east, above the towering red rock. *Now they will open the gate of the city for me, and I will be able to go out and look for my son.*

She rose from the bench, and Yorek, not the heaviest of sleepers, opened his eyes. "Your Majesty?" he asked with a sleepy voice.

"The dawn is coming," Wylla replied. "I will go down to the gate and have them open it."

"Go down to the gate and have them open it?" a third voice echoed, and Wylla turned to see Aljeron appear from around the corner of the nearby street. Trailing behind him were Koshti and her father-in-law, Monias.

"Yes," Wylla said, feeling slightly irritated at the tone in Aljeron's voice. "That is what I said."

"Why?"

"Because I can't find Benjiah in the city, and I'm convinced he is outside the gate. After Sulmandir rescued him yesterday, he brought him here, but Benjiah took up Suruna and went back out to help. He was seen leaving, but no one has seen him since."

Aljeron nodded thoughtfully as he considered her words. He looked at Yorek, who rose to stand beside his sovereign, and from him to Monias, who was also weighing Wylla's news. "I am sorry that Benjiah is missing," he said, "and I'm sure you passed an uneasy night, worrying about him. But I don't think you're going to be able to go outside just yet."

"And why not?" Wylla asked.

"For a couple of reasons, Wylla," Aljeron replied, trying to sound calm in the face of her mounting opposition. "The first of which is that Valzaan has sent me to inform you that the rites of Midspring will be celebrated formally this morning, as soon as word can be spread throughout the city."

"Midspring?" Wylla said, testy. "That was yesterday."

"I know, but Valzaan seems to think it appropriate that we fulfill the rite today."

Wylla couldn't really argue with this; indeed, it seemed on the surface to be a good idea, given what everyone had been through the previous day. In fact, had it not been raised as an obstacle to what she wanted, she would have welcomed it.

"That sounds fine, I suppose," she said in a tone that made it clear it was anything but fine, "but why should that prevent me from going outside now that the dawn has come? Surely Valzaan can proceed without me."

"I'm sure he can," Aljeron answered, "but he's requested that you join him beside the Mound. As the queen of Enthanin, the celebration of the rites in Tol Emuna is officially under your governance. What's more, given your recent captivity, it would be heartening to the survivors of the recent battles to see what civic and military leadership of Kirthanin remains, though much of it has been lost."

The logic was clear and the point sensible, so Wylla sidestepped it entirely. "Look, Aljeron, my son has been in the hand of Malek for weeks and weeks. Yesterday, he was on the verge of being executed right in front of my eyes, when suddenly a dragon appeared out of the sky and rescued him. For a few brief hours I thought he was safe, until I discovered last night that he wasn't."

"Your Majesty," Yorek spoke up timidly, "we don't know for sure—"

"*I* know." Wylla started walking down the street in the direction of the gates. "I tell you, I know he isn't inside the city. He's out there, somewhere. He's out there, and he isn't dead. Don't ask me how I know, I just do. He could be hurt, though, and I'm not going to go play at being queen to give Kirthanin a morale boost when I could be looking for my son. You can let Valzaan know that I'll be there if I can, but right now my duty lies with my son."

"Your duty?" Aljeron said, anger rising in his voice as he started after her. Koshti, Yorek and Monias came behind them. "Does your duty include having the gates of this city opened in the half-light of morning when we have no idea where our enemy is? Does your duty include possibly giving them an opportunity to assault this city?"

Wylla kept walking, her flowing dark hair flickering in the morning breeze. "They only need open the gate long enough for me to slip out. I seriously doubt an army will slip past me as I go."

"Oh, and if the enemy is lying in wait somewhere near at hand? What then?" Aljeron asked. "You'll fend them off with your blind fury, will you? You'd allow yourself to fall back into the hands of our enemy? You'd lay down your own life when you don't have to, demoralize your people for no good reason?"

"No good reason?" Wylla stopped on the street and turned to Aljeron, raising her hand and poking him in the chest as hard as she could. "No good reason? He's my son, Aljeron. You don't know what that means, I know, but if you had a child of your own, you would. He's out there, and I'm going."

She started to turn away, and Aljeron caught her by her arm. "Let go of me."

"Wylla—"

"Let go of me."

"All that can be done to find Benjiah will be done, I promise," Aljeron said, all hint of aggravation or confrontation gone from him. Instead, Wylla could hear compassion and sorrow in every word. The sudden shift in him disarmed her, and she stopped resisting and looked at him, listening.

"You must trust me," he continued. "I will see to all of it. Even so, it will not be for you or for me to do. The Enthanim need to see you at the Mound, even as the Werthanim need to see me. We were both lost to them, but now we are found. Don't you see? We must stand side by side to show them that Allfather protected and delivered us both—out of the hand of the enemy, out of the Nolthanin wild—even as He protected and delivered us all yesterday, and even as He can protect and deliver Benjiah, with or without your involvement. Come with me to Valzaan, Wylla. Let others go out and look for Benjiah when it is time."

"What others," Wylla asked quietly, "and when will it be time?"

"I have already arranged for a sortie of soldiers to be sent from the city when it's light enough to make sure that no enemies are hidden anywhere among the dead or beyond what we could make out by moonlight. Their instructions are to seek any wounded who survived the night. These soldiers can be instructed to look for Benjiah in particular."

"But if he's unconscious, they might pass him by. They don't know him."

"I will find Enthanim soldiers from Amaan Sul to go out. They would know Benjiah," Aljeron answered.

"And I will go with them," Monias added.

They both turned to Monias. Wylla looked into her father-in-law's face and saw the gentle compassion and sadness that she had seen when first they met. She did not speak but stepped to him and took him in her arms. He hugged her tight. "He is my flesh and blood too, Daughter. I will search every span of that battlefield before I return without him."

"Thank you, Monias."

"Then you will come with me, back to Valzaan?" Aljeron asked as Wylla let go.

"I will."

"I'm sorry, Wylla," Aljeron said, looking intently at her. "I didn't handle that well. I didn't mean to anger you."

Wylla stepped up to him and hugged him also. She had not seen him for so many years, and she was grieved that they had exchanged such angry words. "No, Aljeron. You were only doing your duty. I'm sorry." She stepped back from him. "You're right about needing to attend the rites. We were lost, but now we're found. Everyone should see that. Everyone should look on us and take heart."

"They will, Your Majesty," Yorek agreed. "Your people will look upon you and rejoice. For them, and for us all, this is a great day."

Wylla nodded, then she turned with the others to make their way back up the street. As they walked, though, she turned and looked back over her shoulder at the tall city gates, a few blocks down behind them. She would do her duty, but it was hard. He was out there, and she knew it.

The Mound was not far from the wall of great red stone into which the city was built. There, the streets of the city reached their highest point. Turning back to face the city sprawling west and downhill provided Aljeron with quite a view of the buildings, the great walls, and the plain.

The Mound in Tol Emuna was not smaller than anywhere else, but next to the towering stone, it appeared little larger than a dirt hump. As Tol Emuna, circumscribed by stone, had little room to grow, the open area surrounding the mound had gradually been encroached upon by buildings of various shapes and sizes. Mound rites here, even under normal circumstances, meant many people had to stand in the streets out of sight, and today, with so many soldiers and refugees, the crowd overflowed down each and every street, lane, and alley. Even so, except for those on duty on the wall and those in the sortie he'd directed to search the battlefield, everyone able to walk had gathered here. After the city had awakened the previous day to surrender, they came home to victory—or at least something that felt very much like victory to people who had expected to end the day in slavery. What's more, the legendary prophet Valzaan had appeared out of the Nolthanin wilderness and was said to be leading the Mound rite. Even had their cause for celebration been less than it was, his presence alone would have drawn them together. The mysterious Kalin Seir, also drawn to the Mound rites, appeared occasionally in the margins of the crowd, though Aljeron had no idea if there was anything in their own tradition similar to what was about to take place.

Wylla, who had borrowed a clean dress from one of the prominent ladies of Tol Emuna, stood in front of Aljeron. They had reason to celebrate Allfather's goodness, for though their paths had taken them through very different trials, they both emerged tried and tested. Whatever weaknesses and failings were theirs, they had not been abandoned. Now they stood here together, shoulder to shoulder in the lovely spring morning, a testament to hope.

It was a testament that the people needed, for whatever measure of victory had been won the previous day, Aljeron was not so naïve as to think the war with Malek was over. When the rite was past and while the people celebrated, those Kirthanim captains who remained would need to gather and decide on their next move.

Valzaan, dressed in a flowing white robe and carrying an ornate golden bowl, made his way through the small cluster of city elders. As he approached the foot of the Mound, the silence in the assembly, if possible, grew deeper. Aljeron pushed all distractions and martial thoughts away. It was time to focus. It was time to worship.

Valzaan stopped at the foot of the Mound, set the golden bowl on the ground beside him, and turned to face the crowd. "The Mound rite has been the central fixture of our corporate worship since the beginning of the Second Age. Generations have gathered here and at mounds like this all across Kirthanin, to acknowledge not only our collective guilt over Andunin's betrayal, but also our collective hope. We are united in hope. Hope that Malek will be destroyed. Hope that the Fountain will flow again. Hope that the Holy Mountain will be cleansed. Hope that peace and restoration will be known throughout the land. Today, that hope is near. It is not here yet, and though many have given their lives in its pursuit, more will be required. Even so, it is near. Today, people of Kirthanin, today we gather once more in hope. Today, we observe the Mound rite for the last time."

With that, Valzaan raised his countenance to the beautiful blue sky, and the light of the morning sun fell upon him. He raised his arms, and Aljeron closed his eyes as the prophet began the traditional lament.

"Far away, Allfather, far away. We are cut off from the Holy Mountain and the healing waters of the Crystal Fountain. We are wanderers in the world, estranged from home and living in shadow. Avalione lies empty, stained with blood and closed to all living creatures. Agia Muldonai has spewed the evil that infested it out into the world, and yet it is not at rest. The memory and taint of Malek's spawn and Malek's presence still linger there.

"Where is peace, Allfather, where is peace? For you made the world in peace and established harmony between the earth and the sky, between the forest and the field, between the mountains and the plain, between the sea and the shore. Once, all living things knew and understood their place in the fabric of life, before it was rent from top to bottom. In tatters it is and has been. How long it shall be, only You can say.

"What shall we do, Allfather, what shall we do? The sin of Andunin stains us all, for we are the children of a bent and twisted race. Though we curse his treachery, we are but flesh and bones and are not without blemish. Though we denounce Andunin's choice, we know it might have been ours, his shame and punishment with it. We know that we have sinned in other ways and share responsibility for the land's need of atonement.

"This is our lament. This is our grief. This is our shame, our sorrow, and our sin. We cry out to you, Allfather, and ask that you forgive. Hear us we pray."

"Hear us!" the men cried together.

"We also pray, Allfather, that you would restore peace. We ask that you would bring about the restoration that you have promised. We long for it, eagerly desiring the day when it will be, when all things will be made new. We long for the day when Malek will be no more, thrown down for a second and final time. We long for the end of evil and the death of death. We long for the day when the waters of the fountain will flow again, cleansing the streets of the city and tumbling down the Holy Mountain. We long for the restoration of life and the peace of Allfather and ask that you will hear our prayer."

"Hear us!"

Valzaan lowered his hands and appeared to gaze out over the crowd. "You have heard the lament?"

"We have heard."

"You have heard the prayer?"

"We have heard."

"You have agreed in your hearts?"

"We have agreed."

"You have come in humility?"

"So we have come."

"You have come in repentance?"

"So we have come."

"You have come in hope of forgiveness?"

"So we have come."

"You have come *with hope for restoration?*"

"So we have come."

"So have you come, and may Allfather hear your prayers and bless the work of your hands. So be it."

"So may it be."

Picking up the golden bowl, Valzaan made his way to the top of the Mound. Turning in the direction of the Mountain, Valzaan knelt with his face to the west. Likewise, the whole assembly fell to their knees. Aljeron dropped to his, and leaning forward, felt the warm stone of the street with his hands. He thought of all those days and nights in the snow of Nolthanin's winter, and his mind was transported to the great Water Stone they'd found on Andunin's Plateau, the collective guilt from Andunin's betrayal. Already, as the Nolthanim prepared to march to war, they had felt it. It wasn't just Andunin's guilt. It was their guilt. *It isn't just their guilt,* Aljeron thought, *it is my guilt.* He thought of the words of the rite and of his own failings. For a long time he meditated on who he was and the gap between that reality and who he wanted to be. But as the time of meditation passed, he found himself envisioning the picture of restoration Valzaan had painted. He tried to picture Avalione, the blessed city, its streets running with water from the Crystal Fountain. What would it be like? What would restoration look like? Feel like? What would it mean for him to be made new? He didn't know, but he knew that he wanted it. And then, as though only moments had passed, he heard Valzaan begin again.

"The promises of Allfather are sure. What He has spoken, He will do. This is so and always has been so. Allfather has spoken of the future of this world. His words are truth and His purposes are certain. Is this not so?"

"It is so."

"Evil shall be destroyed. So be it?

"So may it be."

"Malek shall be cast down and punished. So be it?"

"So may it be."

"Peace and life shall be restored. So be it?"

"So may it be."

"Allfather shall make all things new. So be it?"

"So may it be."

"Allfather shall cleanse the Crystal Fountain. So be it?"

"So may it be."

Valzaan tipped the golden bowl, and a trickle of water fell upon the Mound. It splashed into the red-brown dirt and slid down its side.

"Allfather shall cleanse Avalione. So be it?"

"So may it be."

A second time Valzaan tipped the bowl, this time further, and more water streamed down the Mound.

"Allfather shall cleanse Agia Muldonai. It shall be cleansed forevermore, as indeed all Kirthanin shall be cleansed. Never again will sword and spear be raised in war, for even they will be made new, and all implements of war shall be made implements of peace, and no one will dare to harm or destroy on all His Holy Mountain. So be it?"

"So may it be."

Valzaan tipped the remaining water out of the bowl, and it poured down upon the Mound. Aljeron watched as the dark streaks moved down, forked, and divided into smaller ones until they reached the foot of the Mound.

Valzaan, raising his hands once more, said, "Rejoice, Kirthanim! Rejoice in the promise of a new dawn. Rejoice, for even as the sun has returned, bringing light and warmth back to the earth, so the age of peace will return, and once more the land will know harmony without discord and life without war. Rejoice, for before Midsummer morn, Kirthanin will be free. So says Allfather."

Reflexively, Monias reached up to wipe sweat from his brow, and it was only after he wiped his hand on his pants that he stopped to think about it. He looked up, squinting, into a blue sky almost entirely devoid of clouds. The morning sun was rising higher, and the pleasant spring warmth was bordering on being hot.

How impossible had it seemed only weeks, if not days ago, that the world would be bright and hot again? Monias had always been in love with autumn, the colors and crisp mornings before winter wrapped the world in its cold grip. And yet this burning sun, and even the sweat running down the side of his face, was most welcome. *At least for a little while,* Monias thought, smiling to himself. He was old enough to know how fickle men could be about such things. He didn't doubt that if the sun kept blazing, day after day, there would be a morning or afternoon not too far away when he'd find himself wishing it were cooler. Such was the nature of man's continual discontent.

He directed his focus back to the work at hand, moving across the immense battlefield with the other soldiers from Amaan Sul, looking for survivors. The soldiers had all volunteered, and more would have come had Aljeron and Pedraan not set a limit. So moved was the army by their queen's return and by the events of the previous day, every Enthanim among them wanted to find Benjiah and bring the young prince to Wylla.

Monias thought back over the years. The distance between Dal Harat and Amaan Sul had prevented frequent visits, but still, he had many cherished memories of his grandson. Benjiah looked so much like his father, right from the beginning, that the child had always triggered Monias's memories of Joraiem as a boy. And yet Benjiah was his own person. He looked like Joraiem, sometimes acted like him, but he wasn't Joraiem. As Benjiah grew, Monias came to appreciate, love, and care deeply for his grandson, not simply as a surrogate for his own lost firstborn, but as his firstborn grandchild, and to date, his only grandson.

He moved on from a small pile of bodies. Not only was none of these men alive, he doubted if any of them had survived to see the setting of the sun. Their wounds were horrific. In fact, the sortie had found few survivors so far. It was disheartening to see so many Kirthanim dead, but Monias took some comfort in the knowledge that the vast majority of survivors had been taken into the city the previous night. Those who had survived the long night out on the battlefield bore a distant and shattered look in their eyes that made Monias want to turn away. He wanted to find Benjiah, but he didn't want to see that look in his grandson's eyes.

Monias was working at the far right of the sortie as they moved outward from the city gates. To his left were a handful of soldiers whom, he suspected, had been given clear directions to stay near him. They did their best to look nonchalant about it, but no matter how far to the right or how far forward Monias drifted, they always ended up drifting the same direction. Someone evidently thought he needed looking after. The young always felt the old needed looking after. Maybe they were right, but it was an irritating presumption all the same.

"Monias?" a voice called from behind him.

He turned and shielded his eyes from the bright sun with his hands. It was Yorek, the advisor that Wylla had picked up somewhere along the way. Though Monias wasn't clear how he fit into the picture, it was evident that his daughter-in-law held this man in high esteem, and that he had been an invaluable support. For that reason alone, even if there were others, Monias thought he could give the man the benefit of the doubt.

"Yes, Yorek, here," Monias answered, lifting one hand in a half-wave.

Yorek came to him, and the nearby soldiers worked hard at paying no attention.

"You've come alone?" Monias said, surprised. He had expected to see Yorek trailing his monarch, and she was nowhere to be seen.

"Yes, I'm alone," Yorek answered, stopping before Monias. "Like you, I was surprised by Her Majesty's decision not to come."

Monias smiled at the man's directness. He guessed Yorek to be close to his own age. As the affairs of this war and world were being largely conducted by his children's generation, it was nice to share a peaceful moment with another man of so many years. "What happened?"

"Well, it was strange. As we were heading to the Mound for the rites, Her Majesty kept going over and over her exit strategy for getting away quickly when it was over." He chuckled. "It was like being briefed on a battle plan by a general who wants every officer to know his role by heart. She kept wanting to confirm with me the plan to disentangle ourselves from all possible obstacles. I felt that she was nearly frantic to get to the rite and get it over with. She was walking faster than these old bones have gone in many a year."

"I can just see it," Monias laughed.

"And I can still feel it." Yorek winced, stretched, then wiped sweat from his brow and peered for a moment up into the bright sky. "Well, when the Mound rite was over, I prepared for our immediate departure, but when I turned to the Queen, she put her hand up and motioned for me to wait. She was standing by Aljeron Balinor, and neither moved as Valzaan descended from the Mound. Then she gazed out over the crowd with a settled peace in her face that I haven't seen in a very, very long time. She was completely calm.

"After a few moments, she turned to look at me at last. She said, 'Yorek, go, find Monias and help him however you can.'

"I said, 'What about you, Your Majesty? Aren't you coming?' And she answered, 'No. Benjiah is needed for what is to come. He's all right, or at least he will be. Today, my people need to see their queen celebrate their hope with them. Come find me when you have word of him.'

"So I made my way out, and now here I am."

Monias nodded. "It sounds as though the rites really moved her."

"I think so."

"Good, I'm glad. She has found what she needed most today. Besides, there isn't much here that she could add to what is already being done, despite her being a queen. She will do more good in the city."

"She will do much good," Yorek agreed. "I am sure of it. It even did me good to see her like that."

"And we will do what she has asked," Monias answered, turning to another pile of bodies. Yorek came after, and together they kept working across the field.

They looked through the scattered dead until the sun rose to its full height and the sweat freely flowed down them both. In the growing heat, the stench of the dead bodies thickened. Monias knew the smell of death, but so many rotting bodies in the warm spring sun created an uncommonly potent odor.

They had just given up on the pile they were looking through when Yorek tugged on Monias's arm. He looked up to see what had caught Yorek's attention. A solitary figure was working his way south across the bright field. It was hard to make him out clearly, but Monias was certain the man was alone. If he was hostile, the soldiers a short distance away would no doubt have little trouble with him.

As the figure drew nearer, Monias felt his heart race. The man was of slender build and had blond hair—that much was clear. Monias watched him come, and he could tell from the halting gait that whoever it was was bone tired. Each step was heavy and labored. The figure looked up and saw them, hesitating, and while at first the features of his face were in shadow, Monias soon made out the face clearly. He felt trembling waves up and down his body, but without hesitation, he started to run as rapidly as the rough terrain and his aging body would allow, across the field in Benjiah's direction, his arms open to welcome him.

Recognition dawned in Benjiah's tired face, and he started toward his grandfather. They met in an embrace that lasted several moments, and by the time they let go of one another, Yorek and the soldiers had gathered at a respectful distance.

"My boy," Monias said, "you are safe."

"Grandfather," Benjiah said, tears beginning to slip down his face.

"Yes, Benjiah, I am here."

"It is so good to see you."

"Likewise."

"It's been a long night."

"I want to hear all about it, but come with me, and we'll go find your mother. She's been anxious about you, and I'm sure she'd love to hear your story too."

Benjiah nodded. "Yes, there is much to say."

"I'm sure there is," Monias agreed, stepping forward and taking Benjiah by his shoulders. He regarded Benjiah with a close and admiring eye. "So much like your father, and yet so much your own man." Monias smiled, clapping Benjiah good-naturedly. "Come, the sooner we take care of what is needful, the sooner you can rest."

Monias put his arm around Benjiah's shoulders, and they turned and walked back toward the city.

Aljeron shut the door behind him as he and Aelwyn entered the small private parlor outside his room. "I'm sorry it took me so long."

"Don't apologize," Aelwyn said, smiling at him. "The Werthanim needed to see you and greet you. You've been gone a long time, and now you've returned to them, like a miracle."

She sat down at the table, and he served her a glass of water. She drank eagerly as Aljeron served himself one. He had been holding out for this, for the day was growing warm and he was thirsty. "Seeing you again, after all you've been through, it's a lot like a miracle," she repeated.

"Likewise." He smiled as he took his own seat and drank deeply again. "What did you think of the rites?"

"They were amazing. Valzaan was amazing."

"Yes, indeed," Aljeron nodded. "I guess the question I meant to ask you was what did you think of *during* the rites?"

"A lot of things," Aelwyn said, smiling at him. "All of them images and dreams and ideas born out of hope."

"That's the word, isn't it?" Aljeron said. "I don't know how to put it, but the hope was almost palpable. The air smelled of it, the images in my mind shone with it. I'm usually more reflective in a self-critical way, and I started out that way this morning, but the sense of hope, it lifted me up out of myself. I don't know. It's hard to explain."

"It's a little jarring, feeling so much hope ripple through you so soon after so much despair."

"Yes, but jarring in a healing way, if there is such a thing."

"It's hard," she started, but then she looked down, faltering.

"What's hard?"

"Thinking that the war isn't actually over yet, that more needs to be done. That more lives must be lost."

"Yes," Aljeron said, reaching across the table and putting his hand on hers. "It is hard."

"When do you have to go to the council?"

"Soon," Aljeron answered. "I think a messenger will come for me, but if no one comes, I'll need to go by Eighth Hour at the latest."

"And what do you think will be decided?"

"I don't know. I've been gone for so long, Aelwyn. I'll try to listen mostly, just to get a better feel for what has been going on here. Until I have more information, I don't really know what needs to be done."

"You don't know exactly, but you know there will be more fighting, and you know you'll need to be a part of it."

"Yes," Aljeron said. "I think we can safely say we know that."

"I'm not asking you not to fight," Aelwyn said softly. "I'm just wanting to tell you that I wish you didn't have to."

"I know."

"There's talk that maybe the Kirthanim women of the medical auxiliary won't be able to come with you if you take the battle somewhere else."

"I know. There are many wounded here, and they need your care. Not to mention, life behind Tol Emuna's walls will be safer than life on the road with us."

"Safer, but lonelier."

"Some may be allowed to come with us."

Aelwyn looked at him. "Would you want me to come?"

"Yes," he said, "and no. I'd love to have you along, you know that, but I'd rather march to war knowing you're safe here in the city. I think, though, that this is one of those questions we can't really contemplate until we have more information. I'd like to know more about what we're marching out to do before I speak definitively about whether I want you to come."

"That's fair," Aelwyn said.

They sat for a long moment, silently, just looking at one another. Aljeron breathed deeply, thinking about what he wanted to say but feeling unsure how to say it.

"Have you heard about Pedraan and Karalin?"

"Have I heard? Of course I've heard. How long do you think it took the news of their engagement to travel among the women this morning?"

"What do you think?"

"It's about time."

Aljeron laughed. "Yes, well, we all think that. What I meant was, what do you think about the fact they're getting married tonight?"

"Well, given that Pedraan might be marching out to war again any day, I think it's a great idea."

Aljeron took a firmer grip on Aelwyn's hand and gazed at her. She looked back, and he thought he saw a flicker of realization.

"You're asking me?"

"I'm asking."

She smiled broadly, and tears started rolling down her face. "Well then, Aljeron Balinor, ask properly."

"Aelwyn Elathien, would you marry me?"

"Yes."

"Tonight?"

"Yes," Aelwyn replied, but she hesitated before going on. "I'd love to marry you tonight, Aljeron, but maybe we should ask Pedraan and Karalin first, you know, just to make sure it's all right with them."

"I've already spoken to them both."

"You haven't!"

"I have."

"When?"

"This morning, when they told me the good news."

A mixture of astonishment and delight crossed her face. "And they said it would be all right?"

"Yes. In fact, they said the more, the merrier."

"Well then, I suppose there's only one thing left to do."

"What's that?"

"Come kiss me."

"Fair enough," Aljeron pushed back his chair. He rose and went to her. A moment later, he had pulled her to him tightly and was kissing her just the way he'd dreamed.

9

FACING THE FUTURE
AND UNVEILING
THE PAST

BENJIAH FOLLOWED MONIAS through the quiet
house. Outside, the sun was bright and hot like a summer day.
Benjiah felt its strength in the heated red stone walls of Tol
Emuna and in the warmth radiating off the streets beneath his
feet. Here, though, inside this home built right into the great
rock, the air was cool and refreshing.

In the full light of morning, as he had walked back from
the distant hill on which he faced the wolves, the dark dreams
and adventures of the previous night seemed surreal. Even so,
as fantastic as his encounter with the wolves had been, he
knew it to be reality. They had pursued him through the long
night, running under the bright moonlight, until at last he'd

been surrounded. They must have felt his defeat to be as imminent as any defeat could be. They must have salivated at the thought of ripping him to pieces and stripping the flesh from his bones. But whatever thoughts passed through their dark and twisted minds were fleeting, for Allfather sent the fire and consumed them, one and all.

Now Monias was taking him to see his mother. Other than their brief meeting under Rulalin Tarasir's supervision while he was a prisoner in Malek's camp, he hadn't spoken to her since he departed Amaan Sul in the Autumn. Memories of their uneasy parting had accompanied him across every league, and he had lots of time to grow apprehensive about their reunion. While he had no doubt that the finer details of their squabbles would be overlooked, he knew the specter of it would remain. His mother never forgot things like that, and in all fairness, neither did he.

Monias stopped in front of a wooden door that appeared at first glance to be simple enough, but as Benjiah moved closer, he could see it was delicately and beautifully carved. Monias stepped aside, and Benjiah paused in front of the door, tracing the beautiful patterns beneath his fingertips. The wood was smooth, like Suruna had been, and he felt the urge to tell Monias what had happened.

"Grandfather," he said, stepping away from the door and whispering softly.

"Yes?"

"I forgot to tell you about Suruna," he said hesitantly, searching Monias' face for his reaction to that name, but if the mention of Suruna affected Monias, he did not show it.

"Yesterday, in the battle," Benjiah continued, "I was flung backward by . . . well, by something." The image of the limping man catching his arrow and thrusting an invisible force across the intervening distance flashed through his mind, but he didn't know how to begin to explain that whole situation. "It's hard to explain. Anyway, Suruna was broken. I, I'm sorry about that. I know it was your bow, and Father's, and I have tried to take care of it—"

Monias put his hand on Benjiah's shoulder and smiled. "Never mind that now, Benjiah. In the end, it was only a piece of wood. Suruna served our family well, and if it is broken, it is broken. You are far more important. Better to have Suruna broken and you returned safe and sound than the other way round. Now, if that is all you were worried about, go, see your mother."

Benjiah nodded and turned back to the door. He spoke without looking back. "We didn't part well, Mother and I, when I left."

"It'll be all right, my boy, just go ahead."

Benjiah wiped the sweat from his palms onto his ragged pants. He'd not yet had time to get new clothes, and he felt self-conscious about how he looked. His mother had never liked him to look disheveled.

He raised his hand at last, and rapped lightly on the door. He held his breath, but no answer came from within. He looked back to his grandfather, but Monias simply nodded toward the door as though to encourage him to knock again. He did, but still there was no answer.

"Try the latch," Monias whispered.

Benjiah reached down and tried the latch. The door quietly swung inward, and Benjiah caught it, stopping it from opening any farther. "I'm not sure I should just go in."

"Sure you can. She was up all night and is probably just sleeping."

"She doesn't like to be surprised in her sleep."

"I'm quite sure this will prove an exception to that rule."

"But—"

"But nothing. No more excuses, Benjiah, go!" Monias said, and placing his hand on Benjiah's shoulder, he all but pushed the boy through the door into the dim room.

Benjiah stepped inside. A span or more from the door was a bed, where his mother was indeed lying asleep. On the far side was a lamp, still burning. He closed the door and walked across the floor to the bed. For a moment he stood beside it, then he sat down beside his mother.

She was fully clothed, and Benjiah didn't doubt that she had lain down with no intention of sleeping. Even she, though, couldn't fend off sleep forever, and if she hadn't slept last night, she had been a very long time without it, because she hadn't slept well the night before he was to be executed. He knew it because he'd seen sleeplessness in her face when he'd been chained to the wooden poles. He'd seen the weariness in her eyes. He'd seen the signs of a restless night.

Looking at her now, he could still see lines of worry etched upon her. Seeing this, he was encouraged that waking her might alleviate her concern. He knew that whatever hurt still lay between them, seeing him again, alive, would be a balm to her heart and refreshment to her soul.

He placed his hand upon her and said, "Mother," nudging her ever so softly.

She stirred and opened her eyes, which took a brief moment to adjust to the lamplight, but they soon fixed upon his face. She sat up and took him in her arms.

"Even in my dream, I knew it was you. I knew your voice, calling to me," she said, crying as she held him close.

He let her hold him. He let her hold him like he was a little boy again, and after his long night and the long days and nights in the cage, her embrace soothed him in a way words cannot describe.

After a long moment, she loosened her grip and sat back to get a look at him. Before she could speak, though, he said, "Mother, I know it's been a long time, and I know we've both been through a lot. In fact, for a while there, I didn't think I'd get the chance to do this, I've been meaning since

I left to apologize for the way I treated you and the way I spoke to you when—"

"Oh, Benjiah," Wylla said, silencing him with her fingers on his lips. "I'm the one who's sorry. I should have told you what I knew about your father and what I suspected about you. You were just a boy, and I shouldn't have left you to wonder about it all on your own. Anyway, what happened then is no longer important. I hope that after all we've both been through, we can forgive each other and start anew, now that Allfather's brought you back to me. Can we do that?"

"Of course, Mother." Benjiah said.

"Good," she answered, the tears falling steadily. "I'm so glad. It's so good to see you again, not in that cage and not chained to those poles."

"Yes."

"I was so afraid for you. I thought I was going to lose you, like I lost your father."

"I thought you were going to lose me too. I thought I was going to lose myself."

"But Allfather sent the dragon, Sulmandir himself, I hear. He sent help when you were beyond all help but His, and He rescued you."

"He did, and here I am."

"Here you are." She smiled as she looked at him. Moving both hands to his face, she felt his skin with her fingers, like she was checking to see that he was really there and not an apparition or mirage.

Benjiah reached down and pulled up from under his tunic the golden cord that Wylla had tied around his neck before he left Amaan Sul. "I'm still wearing it, Mother. Across all the leagues and through all the adventures, I still have it."

Wylla lowered her fingers to the cord. It was worn and grimy, having been tied to Benjiah's neck all this time. She could still see it, new and clean and whole, wrapped around her wrist and Joraiem's, joining them ceremonially as one. "I'm glad to see it's safe."

"Do you want it back?"

"No, dear," Wylla answered. "It was a gift to remind you of him. Keep it, and think about how proud he'd be of you."

"Would he be proud?"

"Oh, Benjiah, I know he would."

Benjiah sat in the comfortable high-backed chair in the snug little parlor, eating voraciously. Allfather must have granted him some sort of supernatural sustenance, for he hadn't eaten since the day before he was chained to the poles, and yet throughout the long night running from the wolves and the long morning walking back, he'd hardly thought about his stomach. Now that he was back, he was hardly able to think of anything else. So now he sat, not far from his mother, who watched him with a bemused look as he devoured his third plate of cold meat with bread and butter. When he'd cleaned every scrap and crumb off the plate, he sat back, feeling full and contented at last.

"Shall I send for more?" Wylla asked, sounding serious despite the twinkle in her eyes.

"No thank you," Benjiah replied. "I think that will hold me for a while."

"I should hope so," she answered.

Benjiah looked at the large stone fireplace across the room, standing empty. "All those long days and nights in the wet and the cold, and I would have given anything to be in a cozy parlor before a roaring fire. Now I'm here, and it's too hot to burn a thing."

"Yes," his mother agreed, "but I'm glad that the weather has turned warm. It smells of spring, and spring smells of hope."

"It does indeed," a third voice joined theirs from the door.

Benjiah stood to his feet in astonishment, his plate falling with a clatter. "Valzaan! It can't be. You . . . you were cast into the sea."

"I was cast into the sea, but I am back."

Benjiah looked from the face of the prophet to his mother, who had also risen to her feet. "I don't understand."

"I'm sorry, Benjiah," his mother said, looking embarrassed. "So much has happened. I didn't realize you were still unaware of Valzaan's return."

"That's all right," Benjiah said, aware that her apology for this particular oversight was rooted in past failures to disclose. "I'm sure I've missed plenty. It's just that I was so sure you were lost to us, Valzaan, and I'm so glad to see you are not."

"I am also glad to see you well, given what you have lately endured." Valzaan crossed the room and directed his attention to Wylla. "I'm sorry to have to ask this of you again, Your Majesty, for I know your reunion has been all too brief, but I need to borrow your son again."

"You're not asking to take him through Gyrin into a civil war or anything like that, are you?" Wylla asked, and it sounded to Benjiah like she was only half joking.

"No, I am not. I will need to make an appearance with him at the council, and then he will accompany me on another errand, but I assure you, we will not set foot outside this city. What's more, I promise to have him back tonight in time for the weddings."

"Weddings?" Benjiah and Wylla both said simultaneously.

"You mean wedding, right?" Wylla added. "Pedraan and Karalin?"

"Uncle Pedraan?" Benjiah said, looking from the prophet to his mother.

"Weddings," Valzaan answered, "for I have just learned that Aljeron Balinor and Aelwyn Elathien will be joining them."

"Aljeron!" Wylla said.

It was his mother's turn to be shocked, but Benjiah just smiled and added, "I'm glad for them both."

"What a day," Wylla said at last, looking amazed at them both.

"So I may borrow Benjiah?"

"You may borrow him, Valzaan."

Benjiah turned to his mother and gave her a hug. "I'll see you at the weddings, I guess."

Wylla hugged him and then let go. "Yes, I'll see you tonight."

As they reached the door, she called out after them. "Benjiah?"

"Yes?"

"When I said earlier that your father would be proud of you, well, you know that I'm proud of you too, don't you?"

"Yes," Benjiah said, "I do now."

Benjiah walked along beside Valzaan, still amazed by the prophet's reappearance, a return as though from the dead. As they walked, Valzaan told him his story, and when at last Valzaan finished, Benjiah found his mind reeling no less than before.

"It is remarkable," he said at last.

"No more remarkable than your own journey, I understand," Valzaan replied. "Much of your story is known to me, but I am only vaguely aware of the events of last night. Would you share them with me?"

Benjiah thought for a moment, then began with his waking on the field and sensing the wolf nearby. From there he told Valzaan everything about how he killed that first wolf and about Allfather's words to him, about the long chase and the final confrontation.

"So now you know," the prophet said.

"Know what?" Benjiah asked.

"About the Grendolai."

"Yes," Benjiah answered. "Did you know already?"

"Yes," Valzaan answered. "When you entered the dragon tower with your uncles, Allfather granted me a vision of the three of you ascending the long spiral stair in the dark. I saw what happened there."

"You saw it?"

"I did, or much of it, anyway."

"And you knew about the other Grendolai?"

"I did."

"Allfather showed you the light coming out of the dragon towers, like He showed me?"

"Yes, but even before He did, I knew. I felt, even from afar, the power that destroyed them, and I sensed their destruction. It was like a fresh wind blowing across the land, for Malek's darkest and most frightful creation was swept away in that moment."

"So you knew about last night too?"

"Not in detail, but I also felt the wolves being destroyed, if that's what you mean."

"It is."

"Allfather has used you to begin the work of cleansing this land from the vile presence of Malek and his creations. Their time is running short, for He will no longer be mocked by their warped devotion to their twisted creator."

Benjiah stopped in the street. "Valzaan?"

"Yes?"

"Before I woke to find the wolf near me last night, I had dark dreams."

"Tell me."

He did, in as much detail as he could remember, from beginning to end. When he was finished, he waited for Valzaan to comment. When the prophet remained quiet, he asked, "What do they mean, Valzaan?"

"I cannot say for sure, for Allfather has not revealed their meanings to me, but I suspect that they signal what I already know."

"Which is?"

Valzaan lifted his face to Benjiah, and tears were running slowly from those empty, white eyes, down across the ridges of the prophet's wrinkled cheeks. "Valzaan, what is it?"

Valzaan reached out and put his hand on Benjiah's shoulder. "You have come so far, through so much, but your journey isn't over yet."

Benjiah wanted to speak, but feeling the hand upon his shoulder and seeing the look on Valzaan's face, he found that he had no voice. "Benjiah, there is one more dark and heavy burden for you to bear, and it will be harder than all the rest. It will be harder, because you will know that victory lies at hand, but you will not be able to take it up. You will have to lay aside what another could not, what even then might save you, and in doing so, you will break the binding and set Kirthanin free."

"But it will cost me?"

"It will cost you."

"What will it cost me?"

"Not more than you can pay," Valzaan answered, "but all that you have."

Benjiah swallowed. "Will I be alone?"

"You will be alone, but not completely. My feet will accompany yours as far as they can go.

"So, you'll be with me?"

"I will, Benjiah. I will not leave you again, but the final steps, those you will take on your own."

The gathering in the Tol Emuna council chambers was marked by a strange mixture of tears and high spirits. Aljeron felt the tension inside himself. There was elation following their unexpected survival and the stirring spectacle of Valzaan proclaiming the coming age of peace. There was camaraderie in reunions too long delayed, for though Aljeron and those with him had returned, so much attention had been paid to organizing the withdrawal, the care of the wounded, and the celebration of the Mound rite, that all greetings had been cursory.

And yet, mixed with both the elation and the camaraderie was a sort of melancholy that curbed his own enthusiasm and restrained the celebration. The war with Malek wasn't over, whatever respite they'd been temporarily granted and whatever promise Valzaan had made about eventual triumph. Aljeron felt the absence of too many familiar faces, men who had helped to hold this army together, men who had given their lives in pursuit of what had seemed an impossible task—survival in the face of overwhelming opposition. With so many lost, he wondered what hope there was that they'd ever gather and not feel incomplete.

Aljeron looked around the table at the many gathered there, which now included Valzaan and Benjiah. He had only briefly been able to talk to the boy, but Aljeron hoped to have more time to spend with him soon. From the bits and pieces he had picked up already, Benjiah had been used by Allfather in remarkable ways while Aljeron was in the Nolthanin waste. In fact, it sounded like Benjiah had, to some extent, been the hand of deliverance Allfather had provided for Kirthanin. He thought he could see in the boy's demeanor a marked change from the lad he'd met at Zul Arnoth just half a year ago. Gone was the uncertainty and the youthful eagerness to be known and approved, replaced by a settled maturity and understanding of who he was and the place he rightly occupied in this council. Joraiem's boy, it seemed to Aljeron, was now a man.

"I suppose," Aljeron began, "That I ought to call this assembly to order. I for one, have plans later."

The assembled men and women, for Bryar and Mindarin were also there, laughed at his joke. It was as much for his sake as for theirs, for Aljeron had determined to hold Aelwyn in his mind as much as he could as they proceeded. He could not forsake his duty to Kirthanin out of his love for her, but it was possible he might undertake what he need not, and thereby forsake her out of a misguided sense of duty. That possibility, he was determined not to allow.

"The business of this meeting is important, and many of you may feel it a mistake to delay it even a moment longer, but I would ask that we take a moment first to honor those no longer among us."

Aljeron looked around the room. He saw no reluctance there, no impatience, and for that he was glad. He would have proceeded anyway, but he felt now in a new way how much he disdained fighting useless battles among those who should be friends, while larger and more important battles with true enemies remained unfought.

"First of all, I want to pay tribute to Caan. He was my instructor at Sulare, even as he was for many of you. He was a friend as well as a teacher, and he was an excellent soldier. When I realized I must go north to Harak Andunin, the decision to go was made easier knowing that Caan would lead the army.

"Sarneth likewise will be missed. He brought help to stand beside us, and of course, the help was timely and essential in every possible way. Where would we be today had not the Great Bear come? It is a question painful even to ponder. However, the Great Bear did come. They came, and we remain alive and free. No man or Great Bear in all Kirthanin did more to advance our reunion than Sarneth, and his contribution to our survival cannot be exaggerated.

"I want us also to remember Pedraal. Pedraan's marriage is a thing for celebration, but Pedraal's absence will hang heavy with him." Aljeron focused his eyes directly on Pedraan. "Old friend, we fought together on the Forbidden Isle and many times since. I cannot take the place of your brother, but I want you to know that to me, you are like a brother. I'm sure many here feel that way. We have come through many trials and forged a bond of brotherhood and sisterhood that is like family in every way. We will rejoice with you tonight, but we weep with you now. We loved Pedraal. He was a mighty man. He was a good man. He will be missed."

Pedraan and many others nodded in acknowledgement of Aljeron's words, some with tears in their eyes. Aljeron fought off the temptation to lose himself in memories of Caan and Sarneth and Pedraal, and he pressed forward.

"I am afraid that I must also be the bearer of more bad news. Not long ago, Corlas Valon of Fel Edorath succumbed to injuries sustained yesterday. I was informed on the way here that he is dead."

Aljeron had expected murmurs to go around the room, but they did not. Though he could tell by their looks that many of those gathered were surprised, and all were saddened by the news, no one spoke. There was something hallowed in the silence, a marking of Valon's passing, perhaps.

"I did not know Corlas very well, but I know this: When it counted, he stood up for what really mattered and gathered his men and marched out of his city to stand shoulder to shoulder with us. He did not let the war between Shalin Bel and Fel Edorath color his judgment. That took strength and courage and conviction. Like the others, he should be honored in our memory."

Nods of agreement were scattered around the room, and Aljeron gathered himself for one final tribute. He had wrestled with whether to say anything, but now that it was time, he felt compelled. It was, perhaps, a personal need more than a collective one, but he was going to say it.

"Some might think my next remarks inappropriate, but I feel they are necessary. No one wanted justice brought to Rulalin Tarasir more than I did, save perhaps Brenim or Evrim, but it should be said that in the end, Rulalin helped save Benjiah. Rulalin killed those who would have killed Benjiah, which kept him alive until Sulmandir could rescue him. In doing this, Rulalin laid down his own life. This does not erase his past misdeeds, but it shows, I think, that even in Rulalin, something of his old allegiance to Kirthanin against Malek remained alive, despite his betrayal.

"Whether we each choose to honor him in our hearts or not, these others represent all three regions of Kirthanin, people who worked together to stem Malek's evil tide. I thank them, and I also thank each of you. Divided, we would have perished, but united, we survived."

After a moment, Aljeron sat down. When he had gathered himself, he motioned to Valzaan. "Do you still want to begin?"

"I do," Valzaan replied.

Aljeron bowed his head deferentially. "Then the floor is yours."

"Thank you," Valzaan said, though he did not stand. "As we look to the fight that is coming, even as we have remembered those who have fallen, it is good for us to remember that the blade, which has destroyed so many, will be broken. Indeed, the work of Malek is already being unraveled, for the Grendolai and Black Wolves are no more."

Now gasps and murmurs did erupt around the room. Aljeron joined in, as astounded as the rest. "What do you mean?"

"To answer that," Valzaan said, "I will yield the floor to Benjiah."

Benjiah looked up into the afternoon sun. He was glad to be back outside.

"You did well, Benjiah," Valzaan said as they walked through the city.

"Thanks," Benjiah answered.

"They were a bit surprised by our news, weren't they?" Valzaan said, mirth clear in his voice.

Benjiah looked at him, grinning at the ancient prophet's childlike delight. "Yes, they were."

"That's the kind of message I like to deliver," Valzaan added.

"What do you think they'll decide?"

"I have no idea," Valzaan replied.

"Why'd we leave the meeting early?"

"The hard road we've all been walking has taught those men and women wisdom, and I'm confident they will be fine without my guidance. Besides, we have something else to do."

Benjiah looked up at the prophet again. Valzaan had hinted as much earlier, and Benjiah hoped for more specifics. "We do?"

"Yes, we do."

They continued, and just when Benjiah had decided Valzaan just wasn't going to tell him, the prophet said, "Have you heard anything yet about the Kalin Seir?"

"The people from Nolthanin?"

"Yes," Valzaan replied. "So you have heard."

"Not much, really, just something in the streets on the way through the city on my way to see my mother. The soldiers were talking, but what I heard, I didn't understand."

"Which was?"

"Something about a pale northern people and masks, I think. Is that true? Do they wear masks?"

"Yes, they do."

"Why?"

"I'll tell you if you'd like."

"I would," Benjiah answered. "Are we going to see one of them?"

"We are," Valzaan replied. "In fact, we're going to see all of them."

"All of them?"

"Yes, but that also is part of the story."

"The Kalin Seir are Nolthanim, though they dislike the term, associating it with those who betrayed Kirthanin. Their ancestors would not follow Andunin, because following him meant following Malek, and so they hid in a remote wood while the rest went with Andunin and Malek south across Kirthanin. There they built a life while the rest of Nolthanin became desolate."

"What are the masks for?"

"They wear them symbolically to cover their shame."

"What shame?"

"The shame of being Nolthanim."

"But you said they refused to follow Andunin and Malek."

"They did, but they felt guilt by association. Their brothers, cousins, and friends marched south and threw Kirthanin into disarray."

"And they've been there all this time?"

"Yes, waiting for the day when they would have a chance to make amends."

"Coming south with you and Aljeron, you mean. Helping to fight Malek even as the other Nolthanim have helped him."

"Yes, that's right."

Benjiah nodded. "How did you find them?"

"We didn't," Valzaan answered, "they found us. We were on our way south from Harak Andunin, and a large party surrounded us. They made us prisoners."

"Prisoners?"

"Yes."

"Why? You're both on the same side."

"The Kalin Seir have foresworn metallic weapons as an invention of the enemy. We had them, and they couldn't accept at first that men who carried swords could be opposed to Malek's ways."

"That's strange," Benjiah said.

"In a way," Valzaan answered, "but not so strange in another."

"What do you mean?"

"Have you never wondered about your own aversion to swords?"

"Aversion? I wouldn't have said I had an aversion. I just never really took to them."

"Does that not strike you as strange? You're a prince of Enthanin. In fact, you're *the* prince of Enthanin. Wearing a sword should be as natural as breathing for you. You had the finest teachers in the land, I'm sure."

Benjiah couldn't argue there. He had been instructed by the best. Even so, he'd always thought of it as just one of those things. He was much better with a bow, excellent in fact.

"Your father didn't take to the sword either."

"He didn't? I mean, I know he preferred Suruna, but, that's not the same thing as an aversion either."

"Like you, he was an excellent archer. With the smooth wood of Suruna in his hands, he was lethal. You were both trained in the sword, but you both turned away from it. Do you see?"

"You are saying that as prophets of Allfather, something inside us rejected the sword?"

"Perhaps something in you, or perhaps Allfather led your steps away from the sword. For whatever reason, you've turned away from it subconsciously, but the Kalin Seir have turned away deliberately."

"But they do carry weapons, right? They fought yesterday in the battle?"

"Yes, and though their weapons are wooden, they are very good with them. They haven't entirely grasped the idea that beyond the act of forging metal into blades, it was the use of those things to kill that bound Kirthanin to the blade. Regardless, they have done what they believed right."

Benjiah tried to imagine a great assembly of people with wooden weapons and masks. This would be interesting. "Anything else I should know about these mysterious people?"

"They've retained from the First Age, virtually as an entire people, the link between battle brothers that Aljeron and Koshti have."

"That's why the stories about white leopards?"

"Yes, they are called snow leopards."

"This really will be interesting," Benjiah replied as they turned into a part of the city far from the main gates. The streets seemed nearly deserted. A handful of Kalin Seir and their battle brothers appeared ahead, far down the street.

When they reached the small group of Kalin Seir, Valzaan took one of them aside. As they talked, Benjiah stood awkwardly not far from the others. Now that he was closer, he saw that their skin was indeed pale, their hair a deep and most curious shade of red, and the masks plain and nondescript. The snow leopards were not so big as Koshti, but they were big enough, long and lean and aware of Benjiah's presence, or at least they appeared to be.

After a moment, Valzaan returned to Benjiah as the Kalin Seir he'd been speaking with conferred with the others. They dispersed, except for the one with whom Valzaan had been speaking, who led them through the streets to a large warehouse. Benjiah deduced that this part of Tol Emuna was used mainly for commerce and storage, and that it had been turned into housing for the Kalin Seir. Why exactly they'd been kept apart from the rest of the Kirthanim, Benjiah couldn't guess.

The Kalin Seir who led them was tall and strong, not bulky like Benjiah's uncle, but sinewy and tough. His movements were stealthy, and Benjiah thought that the trait was likely just his nature, not the result of effort. Inside the warehouse, they found a large number of Kalin Seir already gathered.

Some of the older people, whom Benjiah took to be elders, approached them. Valzaan introduced Benjiah as a prophet of Allfather, like himself, and for the first time since they'd arrived, Benjiah felt like the Kalin Seir really looked at him. It was strange, those intense eyes peering from behind their masks at him, but he stood tall and strong and quiet. After a few moments, the elders moved away, and Valzaan and Benjiah stood more or less alone.

The warehouse filled up quickly with men, women and snow leopards, and Benjiah marveled at all the great cats. He wished he could have seen them on the battlefield, but he knew that opportunity might yet be granted him. As he scanned the crowd, he noticed in the midst of the Kalin Seir, though seeming to stand on her own, a slender woman holding a spear. Most of the Kalin Seir were armed, so the spear did not surprise him. He could see pride in her regal stance, her long red hair falling down her back. Her arms, like those of the man who had led them here, were muscular but not bulky, and even with the mask, Benjiah thought that she was beautiful. He was taking the sight of her in when she saw him looking. He turned away, embarrassed.

A moment later, one of the elders came to stand beside Valzaan. He motioned for quiet. He did not, however, speak. Instead he stepped back as Valzaan stepped forward.

"Fellow servants of the Master-Maker, I come to you now with a message from Him whom you serve."

Murmurs rippled throughout the crowd, and Benjiah watched the people watch Valzaan. *Master-Maker* must have meant *Allfather* to the Kalin Seir, for he'd never heard Valzaan use that term before.

"You have aided the Master-Maker's prophet, followed the Sun-Soarer, and fought against the Forge-Foe. You have marched south, leaving behind your homes in the north like your ancestors of old, but you have done so to avenge their shame, to serve rather than to rebel.

"Today the rest of the Kirthanim, your brothers of old, have celebrated the Mound rites for the last time. Some of you were there and beheld it, a ritual that anticipates the final cleansing of Kirthanin from the Forge-Foe's mark and stain. The Mound rite looks back to the shame of the past, but it also looks forward to the promise of renewal and restoration in the future.

"Kalin Seir, today I say to you, the shame you feel for Andunin's betrayal is a shame we all feel. It is not yours alone. It stains us all. Today I say to you, you have kept your ancient vow. It is time to remove your masks."

There was silence in the assembly, and at first no one moved. Valzaan waited, his head erect and unmoving. Benjiah scanned the crowd, wondering if the people were going to refuse. But then, near the front, one of the elders turned around to face the crowd and slipped his mask off. Benjiah could not see his face from where they were standing, but he saw the mask fall to the ground. Soon, others among the elders were doing the same, and masks began to fall all around the warehouse.

Benjiah watched the unveiling of the Kalin Seir and felt strangely moved. He didn't know these people personally at all, but he felt as if he was being allowed to watch a private reunion or blissful homecoming too long delayed, some great and momentous yet private occasion. Soon the quiet in the room was gone, and the Kalin Seir were chattering warmly and hugging each other, their martial appearance replaced at

least for the moment by something more open and more cel-
ebratory. He turned to Valzaan.

"It's beautiful to see. Thanks for bringing me."

"It's a harbinger of things to come," Valzaan replied. "Allfather is already at work."

"Already at work?" Benjiah said, not quite following him.

"Making all things new."

Benjiah understood and nodded, turning back to the assembly of Kalin Seir. He thought of the beautiful woman he'd
seen and felt a strong desire to see her face. He scanned the
crowd where he'd seen her for the first time. She wasn't hard
to find. She was caught up like the rest in the rejoicing, but
her back was to him now. He watched her, willing her to turn
around.

She did, and Benjiah was taken aback. It wasn't her beauty
that stunned him, for he had somehow known, even with the
mask on, that the face beneath it would be beautiful. He was
stunned because she didn't look to be much older than he
was. He watched her talking to the Kalin Seir, exchanging
words and embraces. He was transfixed and couldn't look
away.

Then she did it again. She caught him staring. This time
he felt himself blush, but he didn't look away. He tried to
smile, but he felt so embarrassed, he didn't know if he succeeded. She hesitated with her eyes upon him for a moment,
intense and unreadable, then looked away.

A TIME FOR LOVE

Aᴇʟᴡʏɴ ꜱᴀᴛ ᴠᴇʀʏ ꜱᴛɪʟʟ. Mindarin had been working on her hair for a long time it seemed, pinning large curls tightly to her head and allowing some loose tendrils to dangle here and there. This last curl had been the object of much frustration for Mindarin, as she wanted to get it just right. Voicing her irritations had never been difficult for Mindarin, but she had grown strangely quiet. Another tug and Aelwyn thought her sister might pull the hair right out of her head, but just as she groaned under the strain, she felt the last pin slide in.

"Aha!" Mindarin exclaimed as she stepped back to admire her handiwork.

"Did it come out all right?" Aelwyn asked.

"See for yourself."

Aelwyn rose and stepped to the mirror. She almost gasped at what she saw. Her sister, who prided herself in giving all due attention to the finer details of feminine upkeep, had done a beautiful job. Aelwyn couldn't remember the last time she'd felt so beautiful. In fact, after being on the road, dirty and bedraggled, league after league, she hadn't thought she'd ever feel beautiful again. She couldn't wait to see Aljeron's face when he saw her tonight.

"It's beautiful, Mindarin," she said, turning to and hugging her sister.

"You're beautiful, you mean," Mindarin replied. "And that dress is spectacular."

"That was a lucky find, wasn't it?" Aelwyn agreed, looking down at the flowing white silk. It fell around her feet in a small pool, and the bright green silk sash tied around her waist cascaded down her side.

"It wasn't luck, my dear." Mindarin laughed. "It's one of the benefits of marrying in Enthanin and having the queen as a personal friend."

"Yes, I suppose so." Aelwyn laughed with her sister. "Come to think of it, she didn't really elaborate much more on the dress than to say she found it. I hope some poor debutante out there isn't shedding tears over her favorite dress."

"Darling, whoever owned this dress isn't poor, and if Wylla acquired it from someone who cared, I'm sure she was well compensated for parting with it. Don't you worry about that tonight."

"I won't," Aelwyn answered, smoothing out the folds and feeling the lovely soft silk with her fingers.

"Are you nervous?" Mindarin said.

"A little bit."

"Don't be," Mindarin answered. "Aljeron is a good man. I'm sure the two of you will be very happy."

Aelwyn looked at her sister and saw warmth tinged with sadness in her eyes. When Mindarin had married Ralon, Aelwyn was only a girl, but even then she realized the marriage was based on less than love. Despite her tendency to have a joke or two at Ralon's expense, though, Mindarin was surprisingly tight-lipped about their life together, even after he died. Even so, Aelwyn knew that the marriage had been a disappointment for her sister, even if it hadn't been quite disastrous.

"Mindarin, you don't talk about it much, but I know you never found life as Mrs. Orlene to be quite what you'd hoped. I'm sorry about that."

"My marriage was a mess of my own making," Mindarin answered, crossing her arms. "And as for it not being what I'd hoped, it was more or less what I expected. Either way, let's not discuss it tonight. Down the road, when you've had some time to digest married life a little bit for yourself, perhaps we'll speak of it again."

A light rap came at the door, and Mindarin walked over. "Who is it?"

"Karalin," came the soft voice.

Mindarin opened the door. Karalin was also dressed in a beautiful white silk dress that Wylla had produced that afternoon. Her dress did not have a sash like Aelwyn's, but a thin sapphire-blue cord snugly encircled her waist, tied in an intricate knot.

"I thought you might be Aljeron, come to sneak a peek," Mindarin said as Karalin stepped into the room. "I was prepared to abuse him soundly and send him away."

"I'm sure Aljeron will behave himself," Karalin answered. "Pedraan, on the other hand, well, I'm not as confident that he's to be trusted."

The thought of her husband-to-be mischievously sneaking around where he didn't belong was apparently not too upsetting, for Karalin could barely contain her laughter.

"Oh Karalin," Aelwyn said, walking over to her. "You're positively radiant. I'm so happy for you."

"Thank you, Aelwyn," Karalin said, embracing her, "but if you think I look radiant, you need to have a look at yourself. You look absolutely beautiful. Aljeron will be speechless when he sees you."

"Thank you." Aelwyn blushed. "So will Pedraan. You look wonderful."

"Karalin," Aelwyn said after a moment, "Thank you for being willing to share tonight with us. It is very generous of you."

"Nonsense," Karalin replied. "We had no exclusive claim on tonight. Besides, the more joy we can bring to this city and our friends, the better. I am positively delighted that you and Aljeron will be joining us."

"All the same, I'm very grateful."

"Well, I'm grateful too. To me it is an honor. This is a moment we'll always share. Fifty years from now, we'll look back at this night and remember how we looked and how Aljeron and Pedraan looked, and we'll be delighted together."

"I certainly hope so," Aelwyn said, trying not to let anxiety enter her mind. Karalin spoke so easily of the future, but it was less than certain that they'd have fifty years with their husbands, and Aelwyn found it harder to wholeheartedly embrace Karalin's vision.

Karalin seemed to understand, and rather than saying anything else, she embraced Aelwyn again, this time holding her tighter, as though to reassure her.

"Enough of that, you two," Mindarin said, making as though to separate them. "It took me long enough to get Aelwyn ready the first time, I don't want to have to put either of you back together again. There's just not time for it."

Aljeron fidgeted with the golden cord that Valzaan would soon be using to tie his arm and life to Aelwyn's. Not that long ago, he'd thought he would never marry anyone. Then, when he least suspected it, Aelwyn changed all that, but he'd had to go north. He'd thought then that he might not marry because he might never see her again, but here he was.

"Why don't you put that down," Evrim said, pouring Aljeron another cider from the pitcher on the table. He was grinning. He'd been grinning all evening as he and Saegan sat having a drink. Ostensibly, they'd come to help Aljeron get ready, but by *help* they really meant they'd sit, stroke Koshti's fur, make jokes mostly at Aljeron's expense, and drink cider while he dressed and moved nervously around the room. Evrim was especially delighted to drop knowing remarks about marriage in general and about Aljeron's future married life. He seemed to be quite enjoying the role of the wise, experienced married man.

Aljeron tossed the cord on the table and took a drink. When he'd finished the cup, he put it down, rose, and paced some more.

"Relax, Aljeron," Saegan said, looking up from where he sat sideways on his chair, leaning back against the wall.

Aljeron was about to snap at Saegan when he saw the smirks on both of his friends' faces, and he restrained himself. They were just enjoying themselves, and he knew they didn't mean him any harm. They probably thought that by joking around with him they were helping to keep him from getting too nervous. He took a deep breath and sat back down. "He should have been here already."

"Well," Evrim said, filling their cups again, "I for one am glad he isn't, because it's time to be serious."

Aljeron looked closely at his friend to see if this was some new jest, but as far as he could tell, Evrim was indeed serious. Saegan also looked soberly at Evrim, to see what he would say next, so if Aljeron was being duped, he wasn't alone.

Evrim raised his cup. "We've come along way together, haven't we?"

"We have," they said.

"But the next step, Aljeron," Evrim said, looking fondly at his friend, "the next step you have to take alone."

"Hear! Hear!" Saegan chimed in. "We've been with you through thick and thin, old friend, against wild beasts and snow storms and all manner of troubles, but when it comes to your wife, you'll be on your own."

With that his friends took a drink and smiled at each other and at him, as he drank too. Though he knew Saegan was just teasing, there was some truth buried in the jest. He'd faced Malekim and Black Wolves, a Vulsutyrim, and even the great gaping jaws of the Snow Serpent. All these he'd faced, sword in hand, ready to do what was necessary. And yet there was something new, wholly unknown and a little bit overwhelming about the thought of being a husband. He knew how to fight a battle, but he didn't know how to build a marriage. He was going to have to learn.

"It'll be your turn next," he said at last, looking at Saegan.

"That's right." Evrim took Aljeron's bait, and for a few moments at least, the conversation moved away from him.

It didn't stay away long, though, for a moment later, Saegan leaned in toward Evrim and said conspiratorially, "Remember how innocent Aljeron tried to look when we mentioned Aelwyn in Nolthanin? 'Girl? What girl? I don't know what you mean. There's nothing going on!'"

Evrim laughed at Saegan's imitation of Aljeron playing innocent, and even Aljeron had to chuckle. He'd tried to play it cool with his friends and completely failed. "I wasn't trying to keep it a secret."

"No?" Evrim said, "then what were you doing?"

"Protecting myself," Aljeron answered.

"Protecting yourself?"

"Yes, from hope. I didn't know if I'd ever see her again, and not talking about her was how I dealt with that."

Evrim and Saegan nodded. Aljeron knew Evrim understood what he was saying. During the years of the war with Fel Edorath, talk about Kyril and the girls was a subject Aljeron had learned, for the most part, to let Evrim bring up. Discussions about them were not always welcome. Increasingly, Aljeron realized that fighting a war was something a man could do, and do well, only if he shut down some other areas of his life. It was one of the hidden costs of war, the things that got pushed away, or discarded and left behind, to make the warrior.

"Those days traveling from Avram Gol to the Andunin Plateau and beyond," Saegan said, "they seem so long ago now."

"They do," Aljeron agreed. "And the war with Fel Edorath that claimed so many years and so many men? It feels like a lifetime has passed since then."

"What is keeping Pedraan?" Aljeron added after a moment.

"Oh," Evrim said, "you know Pedraan."

"Yes." Saegan laughed. "He's probably taking a nap."

"Or maybe," Evrim said, getting in on the fun, "he might be out somewhere, smashing rocks with his war hammer."

"Speaking of which," Saegan said, "did you notice that he wasn't carrying it yesterday?"

"I did," Evrim replied. "I wonder why?"

A strong knock came on the door. Aljeron opened it to reveal Pedraan, standing tall and dressed immaculately. His thin coat was dark blue and hung to his knees. Gold thread had been used in the delicate needlework that adorned the sleeves in a subtle but elegant way. His shirt was white and his pants a light brown, tucked into his high boots.

"Well, well," Pedraan said as he entered and surveyed the room. "Things are a little subdued in here."

"We're just relaxing," Saegan answered.

"Well, cheer up now," Pedraan said, slapping Aljeron on the back. "We're getting married."

"Yes you are," Evrim said, rising, "so I'll be on my way to meet Kyril. It's just about time."

"Yes," Saegan added, for he had risen quickly after Evrim. "I'll come with you, Evrim, and get out of the way of these two. We'll see you fellows later."

When they had slipped from the room, Pedraan turned to Aljeron. "What's going on with them?"

"Oh, nothing. They were just here to keep me company until you came. A drink?"

"Sure." He took the cup Aljeron handed him. "I've been thinking a lot today about my sister's wedding in Sulare. That was a beautiful day, wasn't it?"

"It was," Aljeron agreed. "She and Joriaem made a wonderful pair. I wish he could be here tonight."

"So do I."

"And Pedraal too," Aljeron said. "I'm sorry he won't be able to see this."

"Thanks," Pedraan said, and then added after a pause. "Are you nervous?"

"A little."

"For me, it's mostly about the fear that I'll let her down, you know what I mean?"

"I think so."

"She's so steady and reliable," Pedraan continued. "I just don't want to disappoint her."

"I'm sure you won't."

"I'm sure I will," Pedraan said. "I just hope it won't be too often. What about you? Do you worry about that?"

"Yes, but mostly I worry about being too old to learn how to share a life. My father always said that was the challenge of marriage, learning how to think first about *us* instead of just *me*. I've been a *me* and not an *us* for so long now, I wonder if I'll adapt."

"You'll adapt."

"What makes you so confident?"

Pedraan smiled. "You'll have to."

Aljeron laughed. "There's one other thing, and it's a little more immediate."

"What's that?"

"Well," Aljeron said, "this euphoria—it can't last."

"You're worried about saying good-bye again?"

"Yes, aren't you?"

Pedraan nodded. "But they understand. They know we have to."

"Oh, I know they understand, but it isn't just them I'm concerned about. I'm afraid for us, for me. I'm worried I'll march away and not come back."

Pedraan traced the wood grains of the table with his finger. After a moment, he looked up. "Ever since Pedraal fell, I've thought for sure my time was coming. He died saving me, you know. Truthfully, that's one reason why I asked Karalin to marry me tonight. I'm afraid that if we don't, I'd die out there somewhere and she'll have a lifetime to regret that we never got married."

"We may come out of this all right," Aljeron said.

"We may," Pedraan replied, "or we may not. There's not a whole lot we can do about it, except do what we have to."

"That's right," Aljeron agreed. "We'll do whatever Allfather gives us to do and hope that when it's done, we'll be able to come home."

Pedraan poured himself another drink and filled Aljeron's cup too. "Today you said I was like a brother to you. Let's make a vow, then, right now, like brothers. If one of us falls and the other doesn't, let's promise each other that the one who makes it home alive will look after the widow of the one who doesn't. Agreed?"

"Agreed," Aljeron said. "If you should fall, Aelwyn and I will make sure Karalin has all she needs."

"And if you should fall, we'll do the same for Aelwyn."

They drank to it, stood, and clasped hands. After a moment, Pedraan released his grip. "Well, I think it is about time."

"It's past time," Aljeron said. "Let's go get married."

Benjiah stood with his uncle Brenim and grandfather on the side of the great stone hall. He had no idea where he was in Tol Emuna exactly or what this room was normally used for. He had simply followed the others to the wedding, stood where they stood, and watched.

He had seen his share of weddings as the prince of Enthanin. His mother was frequently in attendance at the weddings of prominent Amaan Sul citizens and their children. Those occasions were usually gaudy, artificial, and boring, at least in his opinion. His best experience with weddings involved stewards from the palace. Not only were these people he knew well, whom he cared about and who cared about him, but they always seemed to enjoy themselves a whole lot more than the wealthy. They seemed to appreciate the real joy and value of the occasion rather than focusing on things of little or no worth.

This wedding, though, had been like neither type of wedding he'd ever attended. It had neither the extreme self-awareness of a formal society occasion nor the wild and raucous abandon of a steward's celebration. It was, though, a shining moment of beauty and joy, a moment of levity and mirth after a season of darkness.

Aljeron and Pedraan, two of the men Benjiah admired most in the world, looked dignified in their fine and fancy clothes. They were big men, and even stripped of their weaponry and removed from the battlefield, they were imposing. Beside them,

Karalin and Aelwyn both seemed small and fragile, though Benjiah knew they were tougher than they appeared.

Seeing the women join Aljeron and his uncle before Valzaan had moved Benjiah. He'd known Karalin his whole life, and he could see the happiness in her face. As for Aelwyn, he was struck by how different she looked this night. He knew her only in the context of their flight from Shalin Bel, and this beautiful, even regal woman who stood beside Aljeron seemed like someone else entirely. Looking at Aelwyn, he found himself wondering what the Kalin Seir girl he'd seen that afternoon would look like in a fine silk dress instead of her plain and durable travel wear, but the thought embarrassed him and he tried to dismiss it from his mind, not altogether successfully.

The service passed quickly, and soon the room was transformed into a celebration to rival any he'd ever seen. Men and women, both young and old, from all over Kirthanin, danced and ate and milled about, enjoying the occasion wholeheartedly. They had stood on the brink of defeat and slavery, but now they were not only free and undefeated, they had something bigger than mere survival to rejoice in. Even Benjiah, who had felt sober since his exchange with Valzaan that afternoon, couldn't help but be invigorated by the life pulsing through his veins. Now, as the dancers whirled around the room to the music of pipers and drummer, Benjiah found his attention drawn to the conversation between his uncle and grandfather.

"So, what do you think that actually means?" his grandfather was asking.

"Well," Brenim said, "I'm not sure. It all depends on what the scouts find, doesn't it?"

"They leave at first light?"

"They do," Brenim confirmed. He nodded to Benjiah. "Despite the good news that the Black Wolves no longer run, we thought it would be best to dispatch the scouts tomorrow morning. We expect the dragons will help with the longer-range scouting, though no one is ready to presume they will without speaking to them first. At any rate, it is possible that Bryar and Saegan, who has resumed his post with the scouts now that he's back, will find only that the enemy is gone. Locating their exact position and number will more likely fall to Sulmandir and his sons."

"Which means we really don't know, do we?"

"No, we don't."

"What don't we know?" Benjiah asked, finally jumping into the exchange.

"We don't know when we'll be marching out from Tol Emuna," Brenim explained.

"But we know it won't be tomorrow, right?" Benjiah asked.

"Yes, I think we know that. If the enemy is still close at hand, depending on his strength, we might not march out at all. If he is farther away, we will need information before we plan our move, and time to reorganize as needed. I think it will be at least the day after tomorrow before we move, maybe later."

"Is there any concern that the enemy could put too much distance between themselves and our forces, should we delay too long?" Monias asked.

"Yes, but everyone agrees there isn't much we can do about that. Even with the aid of the dragons and the surprising appearance of the Kalin Seir, we only barely held the field yesterday. And no one wants to march out blindly, with no clear idea of where we're headed and what exactly we're up against."

Monias nodded. "I think that's wise. It is ultimately in Allfather we must trust, and not in our own strength. We must trust that even as He delivered us yesterday by means we could not foresee, He will continue to guide our hands."

"This is true," Brenim agreed. "I must say, despite the uncertainty of our immediate plans, there was more confidence at our council among the Kirthanim captains than I've seen in a long time."

"Success on the battlefield, even if only partial, goes a long way toward renewing morale," Monias commented.

"Yes, but I wasn't thinking primarily about that." Brenim looked from his father to Benjiah, again regarding him closely. "The return of Valzaan and Benjiah has done as much for morale as anything else. News of the demise of the Grendolai and Black Wolves has heartened everyone. Some have even begun to speculate that perhaps no more fighting will be necessary, that maybe Allfather will destroy what remains of our enemy by the hands of His prophets."

Benjiah looked at his uncle's expression and realized Brenim was asking a question as much as he was making a statement. "I don't mean to discourage you, Uncle Brenim, but I have no idea what Allfather intends to do. He gave me power to hold back the enemy at the banks of the Kalamin, but He allowed me to be taken captive. He gave me strength to break my chains yesterday, but not to break the wooden slats of my cage the weeks before that. His Divine endowments of power and strength come on His terms, not mine."

Brenim nodded. "I understand, Benjiah. No one expects you to do what you cannot, but there is hope that through you or through Valzaan, this war will end sooner rather than later."

"I'm sure we all desire that, however it might come," Monias said.

"I'm sure we do," Brenim agreed. After a moment he added, "Well, I've had enough talk for tonight of what's to come. I think I'll find a dance partner and forget the war for a moment."

"Sounds like a good idea," Monias said, embracing his son. "Enjoy."

Benjiah watched his uncle move through the crowd. Of all his relatives, he'd always felt the most emotional distance from

Brenim. While geography was undoubtedly a factor, he'd also come to see that his uncle, beneath the quiet exterior, was angry, or bitter, or something. At least, that's how Benjiah had always experienced him, until today. There was something calmer about him today, softer. Benjiah didn't know what it was, but he liked the change.

Benjiah watched the dancers as the celebration continued. Aljeron and Aelwyn, Pedraan and Karalin were in the center of it all, any initial nervousness about the ceremony now gone. They each seemed light and carefree. Not far from them, he saw his mother. She too was dancing, though not quite as vigorously, for her partner was Yorek. Benjiah was glad to see her looking happy and participating, but he felt sadness wash over him. *Father should be here. They should be dancing together.*

He looked from his mother back to the newly married couples. His mind returned to the war. Whatever Brenim and others like him might be hoping for, he had no reason to think that after all this time, Allfather would just grant him or Valzaan the power to obliterate the enemy. In fact, Valzaan had been quite clear that there would be more hardship to come, for him personally, but also for the Kirthanim as a whole. When the army moved out, Aljeron and Pedraan would move out with them. They might not come back to Karalin and Aelwyn. They might be widowed after less time together than his father and mother had enjoyed.

He looked back to his mother. She and Yorek had paused and moved aside, clapping and laughing. So many years she'd been alone. It wasn't right.

"Grandfather?"

"Yes?"

"Do you miss my father?"

Monias looked at Benjiah thoughtfully. "Every day."

"It's strange, I guess, for me to say I miss him, since I never met him. But there are times, like tonight, when that's how it feels."

"It isn't strange, Benjiah. It is perfectly natural. It is how you were designed."

"Even so, it still seems strange that I would feel his absence so much tonight. Yesterday morning, as I stood chained on the scaffold facing death, a lot of things went through my head, including thoughts of my father, but it wasn't like this. And now, after surviving that and coming to this time of celebration, I feel this deep and painful absence. Why should that be? This is a happy night, right?"

Monias had been nodding while Benjiah spoke, and even after he finished, his grandfather continued agreeing with him. "I don't know what to tell you about that, Benjiah. What you say is certainly true. All I can think is this, that perhaps joy and sorrow come from such a deep place within us, that whenever we experience one of them it sometimes opens the door to the other as well. I have often found strange hints of sadness in the best and most beautiful moments in my life, and also strange hints of joy and beauty, even in my darkest hours. That phenomena, I cannot explain."

"I suspect it was not always this way," said Valzaan from beside them, and both Monias and Benjiah turned in surprise, for he had come up to them undetected. "In the First Age, before Andunin followed Malek and they betrayed Allfather, I believe joy was not laced with sorrow. I also believe that there will be such a world again, when Allfather makes all things new. For now, though, joy and sorrow do seem inextricably interwoven.

"But," Valzaan continued, putting his hand on Benjiah's shoulder, "let us talk no more about melancholy things. There is a time for everything, and tonight is a time for love, and love is a time for celebration, a time for joy."

"You're right, Valzaan," Benjiah said. "I will throw myself into celebrating, and I think I will start with some more food."

Valzaan laughed. "By all means, do."

The night wore on and the celebration continued, unabated. Benjiah began to feel weary. He knew Allfather had sustained him through the long night. He had not felt all day like someone who'd gone without sleep, but he was tired now. A little while ago, Aljeron and Aelwyn, along with Pedraan and Karalin, said farewell to those assembled and made their way from the hall. And yet their departure did not curb the enthusiasm of those left behind. The music, food, and dancing continued as exuberantly as before. Benjiah had no doubt it would continue far into the night.

He decided to leave. He wasn't sure of the way to his room, but he knew the general direction and had little doubt he'd find it eventually. He wasn't in a hurry, really, and it was more important to him to slip out quietly than to have an escort take him directly there. If his mother knew he was leaving, she'd come too, but he wanted to go alone. He wanted to go alone because he wanted to be alone, and because he wanted her to continue to enjoy the evening.

He found the night air cool and refreshing. He hadn't realized how warm it was inside until he wiped the sweat from his brow. He looked up at the stars and felt strangely relieved and peaceful. From the events of last night to his talk with Valzaan to the whirling emotions of the weddings, he was glad to be walking the quiet streets of Tol Emuna alone.

For a time, he wandered somewhat aimlessly, his mind going over the many events of the past two days. Even so, he felt a sort of critical distance from those things, so that thinking about them didn't distress or disturb him. This too, he thought, must be a gift from Allfather.

After a little while, he stopped and realized that he had been so absorbed in his thoughts that he had lost all track of where he was. He felt like one waking from a dream, and as he looked around, he slowly recognized where he was. He was standing at the top of the long, winding road that led to the area where the Kalin Seir were staying.

He remained still in the barely lit street. She was almost certainly down there. The idea was at the same time a powerful draw and a powerful repellent. He wanted to see her again, and the thought almost started his feet moving. At the same time, he had no idea how to find her in the midst of all the Kalin Seir and absolutely no idea what he'd say to her if he did see her again, and that thought kept him firmly rooted.

After a moment, he moved off the street to a long wooden bench in the shadow of a large building. He sat down, instantly feeling relief in his tired legs. What was he doing here? He was exhausted and should be in bed. *Just a moment's rest here, and then I'll head back.*

He leaned back against the wall of the building and looked up again at the stars. The moon was high overhead, and Benjiah gazed at it, happy. He had no real time last night to admire it, but now there were no wolves around to distract him. He stared for a long time. Even when he closed his eyes, the silvery moonlight seemed to remain, hanging there in the darkness.

His eyes flickered open, and though it was still dark, Benjiah could tell he had been asleep for some time. The moon was no longer visible, having moved across the sky out of his line of vision. He rubbed his eyes and shrugged. His head had slumped to the side awkwardly as he slept, and now his neck was sore.

"I knew the city was short on accommodations," a voice said from nearby, "but surely those in charge could have done better for you than this bench, especially for someone with such good connections."

Benjiah's eyes adjusted to the faint light at street level and found the figure behind the voice not that far away, facing him. He blinked in disbelief. It was the same girl from earlier in the day, standing a little up the hill. Benjiah looked at her for a moment, then suddenly remembered she had spoken to him and replied. "Connections?"

"Yes," the girl replied. "You are the boy who was here with Valzaan today, are you not?"

"Yes, I was. I mean, I am." Benjiah paused and started over. "I was here with Valzaan this afternoon."

"That would make you connected, right?"

"Yes, I suppose I am connected," Benjiah answered. She could not, of course, know that his mother was queen over this entire land, including Tol Emuna, and he thought it might embarrass her and certainly him to mention it, so he didn't. "I have a place to stay. I just went for a walk, took a seat, and fell asleep here."

"You must have been tired."

"I had a long night last night."

The girl nodded, then moved a little closer. "You are not a Blade-Bearer."

"A what?" Benjiah said at first, then remembered what Valzaan had said about the Kalin Seir and swords. "Oh yes, no, I'm not."

"Most of your men are."

"Not normally, but during a war like this, yes, I guess most of them are."

"Do you not wear a blade because you are still just a boy?"

Benjiah was glad he was sitting in the shadows, because he was sure he was as red as the stone of Tol Emuna. "No. I have been trained with the sword, but I choose not to wear it."

"Why not?"

"Mainly because I prefer the bow, like my father, but also because I am a prophet of Allfather, like Valzaan, and I choose not to." Benjiah stood up as he said this, hoping it would help his case that he was not simply a boy.

He could not read the expression on the Kalin Seir's face. She said at last, "You are a prophet?"

"I am," Benjiah replied.

"The elders said there was another prophet here, not Valzaan, who destroyed the Black Wolves. That was you?"

"It was Allfather, really, but yes, I was the instrument he used."

She stepped closer, still peering at him. "You do not look like a warrior."

There was no malice or mockery in her voice, no attempt to belittle or shame, just simple observation. "I'm not," he replied, "though I'm pretty good with a bow and arrow."

At that the girl smiled, and she appeared to Benjiah even more beautiful. "Maybe one day, we will shoot together, young prophet, and then we will see how good you are with a bow. What is your name?"

"Benjiah."

"Benjiah," she echoed.

"What's yours?"

"Keila," she said, starting away down the winding road, a smile still on her face. "We will shoot together, and I will see what boys of this land mean when they say they are good with a bow."

"All right," Benjiah said, and for a moment he just watched her walk away. Then, almost without thinking, he called after her, "I'm sure you are good with a bow, Keila, but I'll wager you whatever you like when we shoot that I'm better."

Keila stopped abruptly and turned, and she appeared for the first time in their conversation to be a little surprised. He smiled, waved good-bye, and started up the hill.

Amontyr squatted a short distance away from the circle of Vulsutyrim as they gathered in the darkness. Pale moonlight shone down from above for the first time since Cheimontyr exited the Mountain. For his part, Amontyr welcomed the change in the night sky. He had missed the sight of the moon and stars. Now they were back, and while their light could not relieve their current predicament, he found some comfort in their presence.

Nirotyr approached, moving slowly from the circle. He squatted beside Amontyr. "The vote is unanimous. The choice has been made. What will you do?"

"What I must," Amontyr replied. He rose and followed Nirotyr back to the circle. His brothers kept still, watching as he rejoined them. Amontyr looked at them. He saw in many of their faces what he felt in his own heart.

"My brothers," he began. "Cheimontyr has fallen. We must present Malek and Farimaal with a new captain. You have chosen me, and while the burden of this task is heavy in these troubled times, I will not refuse.

"We were not made by Malek, and we are not men. We are the mighty sons of Vulsutyr. We are great. We are mighty. We will do what must be done."

THE LAST CAMPAIGN

THE AFTERNOON FOLLOWING the two weddings, which was the seventeenth day of Full Spring, Benjiah was relaxing with Valzaan outside in the sun. Both Valzaan and Benjiah's mother were staying in the same large house—at least he assumed it had been someone's house, though it might have been a small inn, for it had enough rooms. His was on the second floor, and one of the doors off of his hallway led outside to a small, open rooftop with some chairs. Here, he'd found Valzaan after lunch, soaking in the warm afternoon sun, and joined him. It was a stark place, the simple wooden chairs on the bare, reddish roof, but together they sat in pleasant silence for over an hour. While the afternoon was quite hot for this time of year, Benjiah found the inert, sun-drenched time to be quite restorative after the dramatic events of the past few days.

The sound of footsteps moving quickly on the street below interrupted his semidoze, and he opened his eyes to look down but saw nothing. He was about to sit back and close his eyes again when Valzaan spoke. "I think that messenger is coming for us."

"For us?" Benjiah answered, hearing the sound of footsteps first on the stairs and then in the hall.

"Yes," Valzaan replied, and the door that led back inside swung open. Benjiah turned to see one of the other Kirthanim who was also staying in the house point out onto the rooftop. The sweating messenger emerged from the shadows into the bright sunlight.

"Master Valzaan, and young Master Benjiah," the man said, appearing to Benjiah a little hesitant about how to address him. "You are needed at the gate."

"Who needs us?" Valzaan asked without moving in his seat or turning his face from where it was uplifted to the sun.

"Sulmandir, Master Valzaan," the messenger continued, and at that, Valzaan stirred, turning toward the man. "He arrived a few minutes ago and was met by the gate captain. The captains were immediately sent for, but he has asked specifically for you. Both. I mean, he sort of asked for both of you. He asked for the prophets of Allfather to be sent for."

Valzaan rose. "Thank you for the message. Please send word ahead of us that we are on our way." The messenger nodded, turned, and left. "Come," Valzaan said, rising, "let us go hear what news Sulmandir brings."

That was the last word that passed between them all the way through the house, through the streets of Tol Emuna, and to the gates of the city. Benjiah saw Sulmandir's majestic form not far off, with a small crowd of soldiers and Kirthanim officers gathered nearby.

One of those was Carrafin, Captain of the Rock and senior officer of Tol Emuna. Benjiah had only just met him briefly in the council the day before, though as Enthanin's prince, he had been aware of his name and position. Carrafin left the huddle of soldiers and met Valzaan and Benjiah as they approached.

"Thanks for coming so quickly," Carrafin began. "We think Sulmandir has word of Malek's host, but when we asked about it he said he would wait for the two of you. It would appear that in the chain of command around here, none of us ranks high enough to warrant an answer."

Carrafin did not sound upset; in fact, Benjiah detected the slightest hint of playful sarcasm in his tone and the barest of smirks at the corner of his mouth. Valzaan ignored these small signs of jest and replied, "He cares little for the hierarchies of men. He acknowledges the authority of the One we represent, otherwise, he would be as likely to tell the guard at the gate as he would the captain in the citadel."

"Yes," Carrafin replied dryly, "I gathered as much. Personally, I'm happy to leave the job of consulting with dragons to someone else. They're not the friendliest lot."

Carrafin led them toward Sulmandir, who had already fixed his piercing gaze on them as they drew near. Benjiah looked up at the great golden form of the Father of Dragons. He was almost certainly the most terrifying and the most beautiful creature he'd ever seen. It was an odd combination. Despite having been rescued by Sulmandir himself the other day, had he not been walking with Valzaan, he would have been afraid to approach so boldly.

"Greetings, Sulmandir," Valzaan called as they approached. "What news do you bring?"

"The hosts of Malek are moving along the road from Tol Emuna to Amaan Sul, apparently in full retreat."

Benjiah felt elation at the news. The siege on Tol Emuna had been repelled.

"Their numbers?" Valzaan continued.

"Less than one hundred Vulsutyrim lead the way, but behind follows men and Malekim, still a great host. We saw no Black Wolves with or among them."

"As I told you that you would not," Valzaan replied.

"You did say so, and now I have confirmed it." Sulmandir's gaze shifted from Valzaan to Benjiah. "One of my sons flew north, in the direction you indicated, and he found the place that you described. The ground was burned and charred in patches for leagues, but nothing of the wolves remain."

"They are completely destroyed, as are the Grendolai," Valzaan answered. "Your towers have been reclaimed."

"For that, we thank you," Sulmandir answered, and Benjiah realized the Father of Dragons was speaking to him.

"You are welcome," Benjiah replied self-consciously, but sounding to himself surprisingly even, as though he spoke with Sulmandir all the time.

"Will you and your children continue to keep watch on Malek's hosts?"

"We will. And we will bring you word of his movements as it seems necessary."

"Thank you, Sulmandir," Valzaan said. Moments later, the great golden dragon was rising in ever-widening spirals into the sky. By that point, both Carrafin and Gilion, who had joined the cluster of officers waiting for news, approached Valzaan and were filled in on the report.

"It might be a trap," Carrafin said. "They could be trying to draw us out of Tol Emuna, knowing that we would lose the positional advantage we now enjoy."

"They might be," Gilion agreed, "but what choice do we have? We may be able to avoid defeat behind the walls of Tol Emuna, but we cannot achieve victory there."

"No," Valzaan agreed. "Indeed, we cannot."

The sound of horses' hooves thundered across the plain toward them. The men looked northwest, and Gilion spoke for them all. "Our scouts return."

"The captains must be summoned," Valzaan said, turning back to the city.

"Aljeron and Pedraan as well?" Gilion asked.

"Yes," Valzaan said. "It is time we gathered what strength among us remains and end this war, once and for all."

Aljeron looked down at where he lay Daaltaran on the bed just moments ago. He picked it up in its scabbard and held it. Clasping the handle, he drew the long, sharp blade and grasped it firmly before him. It had been surprisingly difficult to leave the blade behind yesterday when he was dressing for the wedding, even though he knew full well that he wouldn't be leaving it for long. Still, Daaltaran had been with him for so long, it was as close to a companion as an inanimate object could get.

He looked down at Koshti curled up on the floor. The tiger looked sleepy and content. Aljeron stooped and ran his hand through the short fur on his stomach, and Koshti closed his eyes. He whispered to the tiger as he rubbed his belly, "Even so, I missed you the most, old friend."

He had wondered how Koshti would handle the wedding and separation, even if only for a few days, but the tiger seemed to understand completely what was going on. If anything, Koshti seemed more at rest yesterday as Aljeron prepared to go than he normally did. He wondered if Koshti's natural protectiveness over Aljeron would grow to include Aelwyn as well, now that they were married. He hoped so.

His battle brother had welcomed him back eagerly today after the brief meeting of captains from which he had just returned. Aljeron had likewise embraced Koshti playfully before getting about the business that brought him here, gathering his things for the morning departure. The plans were made, and the sooner he took care of the necessary preparations, the sooner he could return to Aelwyn and spend his last evening in Tol Emuna with her.

He sheathed Daaltaran and was just belting it on when a knock came at the door. "Come in," he called.

Gilion entered. "I think we've worked it out."

"Go ahead," Aljeron replied, continuing to gather his things as Gilion spoke.

"Talis Fein will take the Suthanim and the men from Fel Edorath."

"Good, that seems wise. There are likely to be fewer problems with them taking orders from Fein and his officers from Cimaris Rul than if they were under me or any other man from Shalin Bel."

"Though I still say there wouldn't have been any problems if they'd been placed under your command. I think everyone still alive knows who the real enemy is."

"I don't disagree, but it seems prudent that we not unnecessarily antagonize anyone, especially with Corlas Valon fallen."

"Agreed," Gilion said. "Pedraan has reorganized the Enthanim into three companies, each with a captain reporting directly to him."

"Good, with fewer divisions, they'll be able to respond more quickly to my orders."

"That was the thought."

"And the Great Bear?"

"Coming, and Turgan will act as their liaison with you, as we thought."

"The Kalin Seir?"

"Still no word."

Aljeron looked up at Gilion and shook his head. "I wish Valzaan could have been persuaded to be more forceful with them."

"As do I," Gilion replied. "But he was insistent. They were to be told in no uncertain terms that they had fulfilled their pledge and were free to go home if they chose. Coming with us was completely optional."

"But if we fail, then surely they will fall under Malek's thumb as well. The stakes of this fight are as high for them as for us."

"And we must hope that they will see it that way too."

"I suppose." Aljeron stepped over to Gilion. "Look, Gilion, I've probably not been as clear as I should have been on this, but you are indispensable to this army. I don't know that I could manage it all without you."

"You'd manage just fine," Gilion said calmly, but Aljeron could tell that he was pleased.

Another knock came on the door, but this time Aljeron was surprised. He'd not been expecting anyone but Gilion. He called out, "Who is it?"

"It's just me," Aelwyn said, stepping into the room.

"Hey," Aljeron said, smiling. "What are you doing here?"

"Just came to help you along," she answered, returning the smile.

"Well, I should probably be going," Gilion said. "I still need to organize the assembly of supplies and provisions and make sure the logistics of transport are taken care of."

"All right, Gilion," Aljeron said as the older man moved to the door, nodding to Aelwyn on his way past. "Let me know if you need me for anything."

"I will," Gilion said, disappearing. Aljeron knew he wouldn't, even had Aljeron not been newly married, but it was right to remind Gilion that he was available if needed.

He hugged Aelwyn, and she held him tightly. They stood there for a long time. At last she stood back from him. "Seeing you with your sword on again makes it all feel more real."

"Yes," Aljeron answered. "It is real. I'm sorry."

"Don't be sorry, it isn't your fault."

"I know it isn't my fault, but I'm still sorry. I would like nothing more than to linger here with you for a while, even forever. I am sorry that I can't."

"Well, you can't linger here, but I can come with you."

Aljeron lifted his hand and swept the hair that had fallen in front of Aelwyn's face to the side. "I suppose we can't avoid this decision any longer."

"No, we can't," Aelwyn agreed. "Both the captains and the officials here in the city agree that a small auxiliary corps can be spared from among those who have been taking care of the wounded. Mindarin has already accepted the charge of heading up that corps, and it would be perfectly natural for me to come along as well. After all, I was the cofounder of that auxiliary, and I did come all the way here from Shalin Bel."

"Yes, I know," Aljeron said, "and believe me, there is a part of me that wants nothing more than to have you along. I do. But there is another part of me that wants nothing more than to know you are here, safe behind these walls until I send for you when it is all over."

"But if something happens to you along the way?" Aelwyn asked, tears forming in her eyes. "I won't be with you."

"Being with me won't mean that you can keep me safe."

"I know, but we may only have a short time. We should spend it together. You can't stay, but I can go. I can and I should."

Aljeron looked at her looking at him, and suddenly he realized that he didn't have the strength to undertake another long march away from her. He couldn't do that again, whatever might happen.

"All right," he conceded. "Go tell Mindarin that you'll be coming and gather your things."

Aelwyn's face broke into an enormous smile, and she threw her arms around him. "I'm so glad."

"I'm glad too."

"Whatever the future holds, we'll face it together."

Benjiah sat at the table in his mother's parlor, eating the sumptuous dinner that she'd had prepared for them. The food was delicious, and after so long in that cage, being fed the scraps of tough, cold meat and stale bread in a less than regular fashion, this meal was an overwhelming sensory experience. Roasted meat, vegetables, fruit, cheese, bread and butter, and all of it fresh and delicious. He was being spoiled. He would soon be on the road again, and even if he was free and not in a cage, he knew better than to expect any meals like this one.

He looked at his mother. She was also eating heartily. She saw him look at her and smiled warmly. She seemed, strangely, to be in a good mood. He hadn't necessarily expected this parting to be as sad or difficult as the last one, but he thought it would be hard nonetheless.

"You keep looking over at me like you're confused," she said at last. "What is it?"

"It's nothing," Benjiah said, redirecting his attention to the meal.

"Nothing?"

"Nothing," he said after he had a chance to swallow. "Nothing important, anyway."

"If it is on your mind, then it is important."

"It's just that I expected this to go a little differently."

His mother nodded knowingly. "You thought I'd be sadder to see you going."

"Sadder, or something," Benjiah said, looking for the right words. "I thought it would be harder anyway."

"Well," Wylla said, looking thoughtfully at him. "It is hard, and it is sad. Don't for a moment think it isn't hard for me to see you go, or that you're not still the most important thing in this world to me. Every step that takes you away from me takes my heart with you. I'm not visibly upset this time, because I am at peace about what has to happen. You have to go. You are needed with the army. Your duty to Allfather and Kirthanin lies out there. Mine lies here, with my people. You must do what you must, even as I must. Besides, I trusted you into Allfather's hands before—unwillingly perhaps, but I did in the end—and He brought you back to me. I know He can do it again. Besides, I know I made your parting more difficult last time. I don't want to do that to you again."

"Thank you, Mother," Benjiah said, trying to smile.

She smiled back, then the smile faded somewhat. "What is it? There's something else."

Benjiah swallowed, not because he was eating, but because he had not intended to speak of this with his mother. Still, he thought she should know, and he didn't want to leave without saying it. "It's something that Valzaan said."

"Yes?"

"Well, he wasn't specific, so I don't know how exactly to put it."

"Put it however you like."

Benjiah looked at her as she waited patiently, expectantly. "Valzaan has said something hard is waiting for me, really hard." His mother tried to conceal the effect of those words on her, and had he not known her so well, she might have been successful. "I don't know what it will be, exactly, but I am afraid. I think that maybe I won't be coming back."

Tears rose unbidden to his eyes and began to flow down his face. He could feel his body trembling. "I don't want to die, Mother."

"Oh, Benjiah," she said, rising and coming quickly around the table. She knelt beside him and took him in her arms. She held him tightly, and it was comforting to be held so close. She whispered, "It's all right, Benjiah, it's all right."

When the tears stopped, and when he was no longer shaking, she relaxed her hold and leaned back so he could see her face, now wet from her own tears. "Benjiah, I don't know what hard thing lies ahead for you, but I know that whatever it is, you're ready for it. I know you are. You're not my little boy anymore, Benjiah, you're a man. A man that I'm proud of. A man that your father would be proud of, were he here to see you and tell you himself. I was afraid to let you go when you left last time, because I thought you might need me, but now I know that you're able to take care of yourself. I know that Kirthanin needs you more than you need me. Just go with Valzaan and do your best at whatever task Allfather sets before you. I know that whatever may happen, I'll be proud of you."

Benjiah nodded. "I will, Mother."

She stood up. "I think that we should try to get some sleep. You need to be ready early."

"All right." He rose, hugged her, then added, "Good night."

"Good night," she said, "I love you."

"I love you too." He turned from her and walked down the hallway to his room.

Benjiah sat on horseback beside Valzaan, and together they watched the army of Kirthanim march forth from Tol Emuna. The companies of men, bearing the colors of the cities they came from, marched out proudly. Aljeron and the Werthanim under his command came first, then Pedraan and the Enthanim, and after them the Great Bear. After the Great Bear came the Suthanim under Talis Fein and the men of Fel Edorath who'd been placed under his command.

As the men moved past, Benjiah thought back over the morning. His parting with his mother had been simple and yet hard. They did not speak of what passed between them the night before; there was no need for words. It was there, hanging over them, a great invisible cloud. His mother tried to recapture the lighter, assured attitude she'd brought to the supper table, but she could not. Benjiah could see she'd been crying and had probably passed a sleepless night. Whatever she might say to him, his news had shaken her. He was sorry for that, but on the whole, he was glad he had told her. The weight of that burden was no longer his to carry alone.

The rear of the Suthanim company was passing, and after them came the supply wagons. Benjiah could see the Kalin Seir coming behind those. No longer distinguished by their masks, they stood out now with their pale skin, reddish hair, and the sleek white leopards moving among them.

Benjiah watched them and noticed a man break off from the rest and come jogging over to where Valzaan and Benjiah were mounted.

"Greetings, prophets of Allfather," he said, looking from Benjiah to Valzaan.

"Greetings, Naran," Valzaan replied. "We are grateful to the Kalin Seir that they have decided to join us."

"We are one people," Naran said, proudly. "We all serve the Master-Maker, and we will throw down the Forge-Foe together. Maybe then, when the enemy is fallen, the Master-Maker will remove the curse from Nolthanin. Maybe we will be able to recross the mountains and settle in our ancient home."

"He will make all things new, Naran," Valzaan said. "I believe this includes all of Nolthanin."

"I hope so," Naran answered. "Perhaps we will see each other from time to time along the road."

"I will visit frequently among the Kalin Seir," Valzaan said, smiling. "You won't be able to get rid of me."

"You will be welcome," Naran answered. "Both of you."

With that he turned and jogged back to the ranks of the Kalin Seir. Benjiah had been listening to Naran, but his eyes were searching the Kalin Seir. There were many women among the men, so any doubt he had that Keila would march out with them if they decided to come had been removed. He couldn't say that he knew her well, but he couldn't imagine she would allow herself to be left behind.

"It is the last great campaign of the Kirthanim," Valzaan said. "Men from Nolthanin, Werthanin, Enthanin, and Suthanin march together once more, and for the last time."

"Four great peoples," Benjiah said, thinking of the prophecy he received during their flight from Col Marena. "And yet, not the four great peoples of the prophecy."

"No, I think not," Valzaan agreed. They had discussed this since Valzaan's return, and he agreed with Benjiah's speculation that men, Great Bear, and dragons were likely the first three. That the Kalin Seir might be the fourth had seemed possible, but to both of them, unlikely. Despite the unusual circumstances surrounding their alliance, they were Kirthanim, just like the men from Fel Edorath and Shalin Bel, Cimaris Rul and Amaan Sul. They had been long estranged, true, but they were Kirthanim.

Benjiah did not long ponder the mystery, for he saw Keila approaching the place in the road just opposite him. She was looking at him, and she smiled when he noticed her. He dismounted nimbly and walked toward the Kalin Seir. She stepped out of the column to speak to him.

"It appears we will have to wait for that shooting contest," she said, suppressing the smile and replacing it with a less expressive look.

"We will."

"But I will not forget your challenge," Keila retorted. "You have said I could wager anything, and I will hold you to it."

Benjiah grinned. "Please do. Maybe, if the march is long, we will be able to do it along the way."

"You are coming then?" Keila replied, and Benjiah understood. This had been her way of finding out if he was coming without asking directly.

"Yes, Valzaan and I will travel with the army. We may be needed."

"Not one but two prophets?"

"Not one but two."

Keila laughed. "I wouldn't have thought you were of age, and old enough to march out to war, but perhaps in these strange lands, where the blade is embraced by your men, other strange customs are also common."

Benjiah blushed at the statement. As with her comments the other night, the insult seemed unintentional, but the bluntness of the statement and the meaning stung.

"I am not only a prophet of Allfather," he said, "but I am the son of the queen of Enthanin. I ride with this army because it is both my duty and my right."

If his statement impressed her, it didn't show. She regarded him carefully, then said, "See, I could tell you had connections."

Benjiah was trying to think of what to say to this when Keila continued. "Let's not dance this dance any longer, boy prophet. How old are you?"

"I will be seventeen on the first day of Summer Rise."

At this, quite unexpectedly, Keila threw back her head and laughed. Benjiah felt flustered and angry, but he bit his tongue.

"Will be seventeen?" Keila said, then laughed again. "So the answer to my question is sixteen. You are sixteen, boy prophet. There are no *will be*'s, especially on the eve of war. No one knows how old any of us will be. We are what we are."

"All right then," Benjiah said, trying not to sound irritated. "And you, Keila? Old and wise as you are, how old are you?"

Keila checked her laughter, then drawing herself up to her full height, which was almost as tall as Benjiah, said simply, "Nineteen."

"Nineteen," Benjiah repeated. "And you believe that being two or even three years older than me gives you the right to speak to me as if I were a child?"

Keila stopped smiling. Again, she regarded him closely. "Before I was of age, those older than me spoke to me as though I were a child. I hated it. I am sorry if I have offended you."

Benjiah was unprepared for the ease of her about-face. "It's all right," he said. "I've just come so far, through so much. I don't feel like a boy anymore. My own uncles and other adults I've long known no longer treat me as one either. It's just a little unexpected and jarring."

Keila nodded. "I will not treat you like one anymore."

"I would appreciate that," Benjiah said, then blurted without thinking, "You know, my mother was two years older than my father, and it didn't bother her at all."

He realized too late what he was saying and how it would be taken and felt mortified. Keila stood there, saying nothing, and Benjiah wanted nothing more than for the ground to open up and swallow him whole. At last, after what seemed a long and painful silence, she spoke. "I wish you well on the road, Benjiah."

"Thanks," he said, quietly. "And I wish you well also."

She nodded in acknowledgement, then turned and walked away from him, rejoining the column of Kalin Seir. He watched her go as the first company of Enthanim under his uncle Pedraan approached and thought that he couldn't possibly have handled the exchange any worse, even if he had tried.

Nineteen days after leaving Tol Emuna, the army of Kirthanim was camped along the road, enjoying the dry, warm evening.

It was the seventh day of Spring Wane, and the weather since their departure from Tol Emuna had been perfect—warm and dry by day, and cool but not cold overnight. All those who had marched day after day in the endless rain of Cheimontyr's storm could well believe the difference being warm and dry made to their spirits. They were marching to war again, but in the evenings, their camps were filled with stories, laughter, and even music.

Not only was their morale higher when they camped, but it showed during the day as well, for they made far better time than on their trek north. To a certain extent, this of course made sense, given that they had marched through mud and mire the last time they moved along this road. In fact, the once-smooth road from Amaan Sul to Tol Emuna had been chewed up by feet, hooves and wagon wheels, so that even now, they could still see the effects of their last passage. Despite the adverse weather at the time, though, they had been fleeing before Malek. Now they were the pursuer and not the pursued.

For Benjiah, though, the surge in morale had a more limited effect. The last time he'd been on this road, he'd been rolling along in a cage, but proud defiance had kept him from despair. Now that he was riding with Valzaan and the army of Kirthanin, he should have been far happier, even ecstatic at the reversal of fortunes, but Valzaan's warning of difficulty to come hung over him like another endless storm. Even now, as he sat around the fire with the sun hanging low over his home of Amaan Sul, not too many days further on, he felt the sudden chill of fear. At the end of this road, whatever waited for the others, something dreadful waited for him.

He was sitting with Valzaan, and Aljeron was sitting with Gilion and Pedraan on the other side of the fire. They were talking, as they always did, about the two- or three-day gap between the armies. Though Kirthanin's army was moving as quickly as they could reasonably expect, the distance between Malek's hosts and them had not been shortened. They had entertained the idea of forcing the battle on ground of their own choosing, but this seemed increasingly unlikely. Instead, they would have to wait until Malek's army stopped.

As they spoke, three dragons flew low overhead, their majestic forms silhouetted in the reddish light of the setting sun. They began to circle and descend, and without waiting for the others, Benjiah was on his feet, following Valzaan off the road.

The dragons were down and waiting when they arrived, and Benjiah recognized all of them. Sulmandir had come this time with Dravendir and Eliandir, and although Aljeron and the others hastened to catch up, neither the dragons nor Valzaan waited for them to arrive.

"There has been a change in the movement of the enemy," Sulmandir said, no longer bothering with the formality of waiting to be asked for news.

"What change?" Valzaan asked.

"The men and Malekim have moved north, as though they do not intend to go through Amaan Sul but above it."

"Above it? Are they still heading more or less west?"

"Yes."

"Then perhaps they're heading for Gyrin."

"It appears so," Sulmandir replied.

"They may well be running for the Mountain."

"We cannot say."

Valzaan nodded, appearing deep in thought, then looked up toward Sulmandir again. "What of the Vulsutyrim?"

"That's the strange part," Sulmandir said. "They have not left the road with the rest. They are camped on the road itself, just two days or so due west of here."

By now, Aljeron, Pedraan and Gilion were present, listening, and Benjiah heard whispers pass among them at this news.

"What's stranger," Sulmandir said, "is that the Vulsutyrim stopped moving just after noon today. They stopped moving when the others left the road, set up camp, and have done nothing else all afternoon and evening."

"They haven't moved closer to Amaan Sul since midday?" Aljeron asked.

"They haven't moved at all."

"Not at all?"

"No, they spent all day sitting on the road, facing east."

"Facing us," Gilion murmured.

"There are about sixty of them."

"Sixty Vulsutyrim, a few days down the road," Aljeron said, and all heads turned west and gazed down the road stretching ahead of them, empty for as far as they could see. "Just sitting, all day. I wonder what it could mean?"

"It means our brief reprieve is almost over," Valzaan said. "The final act of this great drama is ready to begin."

BROKEN

A PROPHECY
FULFILLED

BENJIAH LAY STILL, staring up at the stars. Despite the excitement of the evening, with Sulmandir's appearance, news, and the subsequent discussions on what to do next, his inability to sleep came from a different source. He didn't seem to be able to push the image of Keila from his mind.

He had only seen her twice since the day they departed Tol Emuna. The first time had been from a distance, and as far as he knew, she had not seen him. The second time, just four days ago, they had spoken. Keila tried to joke good-naturedly with Benjiah that he had been avoiding her—apparently afraid of the archery contest. For his part, Benjiah felt so awkward at seeing her that he managed only a pathetic grin, little better than a grimace, at her jest, which effectively squelched any further lighthearted conversation. A moment later, with an even more pathetic attempt at an excuse, Benjiah took his leave of her.

It was the pained, quizzical look on Keila's face as he had turned away that haunted him now. What was behind that look? Annoyance? Anger? Relief? Disgust? He was reasonably confident that he'd ruined his chances with her, and his only comfort was that he probably hadn't had much of a chance to begin with, and that wasn't too terribly comforting.

Without warning, Valzaan's unmistakable silhouette appeared above him. He sat up and was about to say something when Valzaan sat down beside him.

"What is it?" Benjiah asked, turning to the prophet.

"I am uneasy," Valzaan said. A chill rippled up and down Benjiah's spine. It wasn't the kind of thing he was used to the old prophet saying.

"Why?"

"Something important is going to happen here, and soon, but I can't see what it is." He sounded frustrated.

"Is it good or bad?"

"I don't know."

"Well, it can't be too terribly long before morning," Benjiah said. "It must be Third Watch already. Your sense probably has something to do with the Vulsutyrim."

"Very likely," Valzaan said. "That's why I want your help."

"My help?"

"Yes." Valzaan answered. "I want to locate both the Vulsutyrim camp and the men and Malekim who are supposed to be moving around Amaan Sul, and I want you to help me."

"Supposed to be moving around the city?"

"Things are not always what they seem."

"You're worried about attack?" Benjiah asked.

"Just being cautious."

"But Aljeron already deployed an advance company along the road and sent scouts both north and south to provide us with warning of attack."

"So he did," Valzaan replied, "and very likely that will prove sufficient. Even so, please indulge me. The sooner the better."

Benjiah nodded. "Which would you like me to search for?"

"The Vulsutyrim," Valzaan added. "I will search for the men and Malekim. Tell me if you are successful."

Benjiah reached out, looking for a windhover, and before long he found one not too far away. The falcon was soon gliding over the southeastern portion of the city.

The moon was not quite full, but it was still bright. Benjiah was taken aback by the destruction he saw in Amaan Sul. The fires left burning by Malek's hosts had indeed wreaked havoc. Many buildings were roofless, just singed and charred walls clustered together around sooty remains. Debris littered the streets and alleyways, and what looked like wild dogs, or more likely, dogs that had been driven wild, nosed through the ruins. His heart sank as the windhover glided over more and more of it. He directed the bird to fly straight east until it found the city wall. When it did, it turned north, looking for the great eastern gate. Benjiah didn't want to see anymore of what was inside the city.

After a short while, the bird approached the gate, where a large fire burned. Stretched out all over the ground, the great sleeping bodies of several Vulsutyrim reclined both on the road and beside it. Several others sat by the fire, while several more stood in a row just beyond the makeshift camp, staring west. It struck Benjiah that the Vulsutyrim's position was just as defensive as their own. They certainly didn't appear to be up to anything aggressive, at least not at the moment, and if the dragon's count was accurate, nearly all sixty could be accounted for here. He had the windhover circle twice and, when he was certain that he had seen all that there was to see, released the bird.

"I have seen them," he said to Valzaan.

"And?"

"They appear to be right where Sulmandir said they were."

"Camped by the gate?"

"Yes, awaiting the dawn, like us."

"I see," Valzaan answered.

"And you?" Benjiah asked, curious. "Did you find the others?"

"Yes," Valzaan answered. "They are also where Sulmandir said we'd find them, camped along the outer wall a fair distance north of the road. If they only left the road this morning, they have made good time."

Benjiah sat, waiting for further comment or direction. None came, at least not right away. The sleepiness that had eluded him seemed to be coming on at last, and he yawned.

"I should let you get a few hours sleep," Valzaan said, turning back toward Benjiah. "I am sorry to have disturbed you for nothing."

"There's no need to apologize," Benjiah said. "Have you no other idea what it is you are sensing?"

"None," Valzaan said. "I feel as though something momentous is drawing nearer, and yet everything we see confirms what the dragons have already told us, that battle with the Malekim and Nolthanim is at least a few days away, probably more, and that the giants are more than a day's march down that road."

"If they send the dragons tomorrow to engage the giants, the outcome could be pretty significant," Benjiah offered, hesitantly. He was sure Valzaan knew this, but it was all he could think of.

"I agree. A clear victory for either side in that engagement would be most significant," Valzaan said, then he sighed and shrugged before standing back up. "Perhaps that is all it is, but I was so sure there was something else, something more, something . . . *unexpected*."

He tilted his head down so that Benjiah could not see his face clearly in the darkness. "Sleep now, Benjiah. Whatever it is will wait until its time is come, as all such moments must."

With that, the prophet moved off into the night, and Benjiah lay back down. He looked back up at the stars, his eyes heavier now. They flickered once or twice, then fell shut.

The large fire of the Vulsutyrim seemed even bigger now. What's more, the number of giants around it had also grown. There were scores and scores of them, all standing there, rank after rank, warming themselves in its glow. The firelight threw alternating shadows and illumination upon their intense and serious faces, and Benjiah felt once more the chill run up and down his body.

The scene seemed to shift, somehow, and Benjiah was aware that the fire had not so much grown as spread—the city was on fire again. He gasped. Fires crackled up and down the streets, and Vulsutyrim moved slowly between the rows of burning buildings. Here and there they would pause beside tottering walls and use the tips of their great swords to topple them. Nearby, a whole row of buildings collapsed in a burning heap, sending a myriad of sparks and embers whirling into the warm spring night. A tall and somber giant stood and watched it collapse, then slowly, he turned and walked away.

Benjiah saw a line of giants standing inside the outer wall, which was tall and strong and stone, and so not on fire. They had set their swords down and were leaning in together. The top of the wall, which had a few stones missing, it appeared, was a little lower than their shoulders. They pushed together and strained, but the wall did not give. They relaxed for a few moments, and Benjiah watched, holding his breath.

The Vulsutyrim threw themselves into their work again, and this time Benjiah heard a great crack as mortar dust burst from the wall and two great blocks of stone slid out and over the top. The Vulsutyrim set in upon the wall like locusts on full heads of grain, pushing stone after stone and block after block until the wall was fully breached for several spans in both directions.

Benjiah wanted to cry out, but he feared discovery. He didn't understand this wanton destruction. The city was empty. It had already been burned once. Why do this? Why burn it again? Why pull down the walls? Why reduce it to rubble and ash? What did Malek want to rule, exactly? A broken-down ruin of a world?

A light broke on the horizon, like dawn and yet not like dawn, and Benjiah looked up to see the sun already surprisingly high in the morning sky. Its rays brought warmth and comfort, and Benjiah felt his pain somewhat assuaged. He looked back to the wall, and what he saw puzzled him greatly.

The Vulsutyrim were lifting the stones they had knocked down and carrying them into the city. He watched a pair of Vulsutyrim take one of the stones and set it on a newly laid foundation for a large building not far from the wall.

This strange behavior was going on everywhere. Collapsed buildings were being restored, and leaning walls in structures still standing were being shored up. The Vulsutyrim were working like master masons, raising Amaan Sul from its ruined estate.

The sun rose higher, and now the walls and buildings of Amaan Sul glistened in the bright noonday light. Benjiah could see no trace of burning or brokenness. The city was completely restored. He looked around, realizing that the Vulsutyrim were gone. The streets were empty.

He found his feet heading toward the palace, and he navigated the city that had been his home since birth with wonder and delight. Not so much as a scorch mark from its prior burning was evident. *Perhaps this is how Amaan Sul will one day be*, Benjiah thought as he walked. *Made new, as all things will be.*

The thought passed as he found himself standing at the gate to the palace grounds. The great fountain was flowing in the courtyard and the palace rose tall and proud into the sky. Benjiah smiled. *Home at last.*

Aljeron and Gilion stood side by side on the road, peering at the western horizon. The grey morning light was growing stronger, and a warm breeze was blowing up from the south.

"We have to send them. There's no other way."

Aljeron turned his head slightly toward his companion but didn't take his eyes off of the horizon. "There's always another way."

"All right, there's no other way that makes any sense."

"Of course there is."

"What?"

"We don't send them, that's what."

"We don't send them." The sarcasm in Gilion's voice was unusual. Even when they disagreed, he was always respectful. "Aljeron, it is madness even to think about it. What would you have us do? Just march down the road right into them?"

"Why not?"

"Why not? Perhaps you've been away too long, but sixty Vulsutyrim could do a lot of damage to us before we stopped them, even with the dragons' help."

"That's precisely my thinking," Aljeron replied.

Gilion stared at him as if Aljeron were a lunatic. His eyes blinked a couple of times, as though he was trying to register something but couldn't. Aljeron continued.

"Listen, we're afraid of what they can do to us if we meet them head-on with our whole army *and* the dragons. Doesn't it make sense then to be a little worried about what they could do to the dragons if we send them on their own?"

"Sulmandir seems to think the dragons will be all right."

"Sulmandir doesn't speak all that he thinks. Maybe he knows that they are our best hope to win this battle, so he is willing to go. Maybe he and his children have a personal score to settle with the Vulsutyrim. Whatever it may be, we shouldn't underestimate what those giants can do. What's more, the giants must be expecting attack. What if they've prepared some sort of trap?"

"What kind of trap?"

"I don't know, I'm not a giant," Aljeron said, raising his voice, then controlling it again as he continued. "That's one reason why I'm hesitating. They've separated from the main force of Malek's host for a reason. They're not dumb brutes like the Malekim, who simply do what they're told. They don't seem like they'd just sacrifice themselves for no good reason, and if they're as mismatched against the dragons as we seem to think they are, then that is what they are doing."

"How do we know what has passed between Malek and them, or why they are doing what they're doing? Intelligent beings or not, I'm sure they are expected to follow orders. To assume anything else is just pointless speculation."

"Yes, it is speculation, but all speculation is not the same. You know as well as I do that it is not always enough to know *what* your enemy is doing. Knowing *why* your enemy is doing it is always an advantage."

"One rarely granted, unless your opponent is a simpleton."

"Agreed. Hence my reservations in favor of caution."

"Look, Aljeron, I understand about caution. You and I have often differed where I was the voice of caution. I hear what you're saying. Of course, our whole host added to the dragon's attack would increase our strength, but that's not the point. The point is that the best weapon against the Vulsutyrim is and has been, the dragons. I've seen it."

"Yes, and you've seen Vulsutyrim take down dragons. That's my fear, that this is some ruse on Malek's part to lure them away from us. Without them we're blind. Maybe this is part of a larger plan to decimate the dragons, to turn the tide of war back in his favor. I just can't seem to figure it out."

Gilion reached up and stroked his beard. "Not to quibble with your assessment, Aljeron, but we're not exactly blind without the dragons. We still have our scouts. There have been no reports of anything going on around us at all. I don't see how luring the dragons away for a few hours would do anything."

"All right, maybe we aren't completely blind without them, but our sight is severely reduced."

"I'm sure Sulmandir will be willing to send a few of the dragons to scout out the area before they go, just to make sure nothing is brewing."

"It should go without saying."

"It should also go without saying, Aljeron, that this isn't ultimately going to be your decision to make. Sulmandir isn't under your command, and though Valzaan might be willing to state your opinion to the dragons, he isn't under your command either."

"I realize all that," Aljeron said. "I just wanted to be clear in my own mind of what I thought was best before we met with Valzaan and Sulmandir."

"And are you clear now, sir?"

"I am clear. This is a war, and if Valzaan is to be believed, the last war ever to be fought. Much must be risked in war. Though I am uneasy about what these Vulsutyrim intend, sending the dragons seems to be our most advantageous course of action."

"Very good, sir," Gilion said, turning his back on the western horizon at last and looking back toward the camp. If he possessed self-satisfaction over Aljeron's decision, it didn't show. "Should I send for Valzaan?"

"Yes, I think it is time."

Benjiah stood on the side of the road, watching as the last of the dragons disappeared from sight. They were rising into the clear blue sky as they headed west toward Amaan Sul. They would soar high above what man and beast could see, then swoop down on the Vulsutyrim with all their might and fury.

That thought made Benjiah curiously uneasy. He had every reason to despise the giants, for he had seen the destruction they were capable of on more than one occasion. Consequently, in the battle before Tol Emuna's gates, he welcomed Cheimontyr's death. And yet, the strange image of Vulsutyrim rebuilding Amaan Sul remained vivid in his mind, even now that he was awake.

He knew his reaction wasn't really rational. After all, not only was the image of giants rebuilding Amaan Sul a part of a dream, it was only a part. Earlier in that same dream giants knocked down the walls and buildings, not to mention that the Vulsutyrim had undoubtedly played a role in the actual burning of Amaan Sul that had already taken place.

Benjiah thought back over the dream. The buildings they had burned and leveled were buildings already more or less ruined. The wall they had knocked over had been put to use in rebuilding parts of the city. Perhaps the dream couldn't be divided between two distinct phases: the Vulsutyrim as destroyers and the Vulsutyrim as rebuilders. Perhaps the whole displayed the giants at work cleaning out the old and rebuilding, just in different ways.

Benjiah had dismissed the dream upon waking as a strange but comprehensible creation of his weary mind. He greatly desired to see Amaan Sul rebuilt and restored. Further, he had gone to sleep knowing the Vulsutyrim were camped by the gates, so dreaming of the giants in the city, either destroying or rebuilding, wasn't hard to explain. Still, now that the dream seemed to make more sense as a unified notion of the giants at work on the city's behalf, he wondered if he shouldn't tell Valzaan about it.

He looked over at the small cluster of Kirthanim captains, for Valzaan was standing with them. They had been talking together since the dragons departed. Benjiah sighed. The dragons were already gone, far beyond recall, on their way to engage and destroy the Vulsutyrim. The notion that the ancient enemy of the dragons might help rebuild his destroyed home was a classic example of wishful thinking. His dream was but a dream.

Standing with the Kirthanim captains was the Great Bear Turgan. He stood at his full height, holding his great wooden staff. Benjiah admired his noble carriage, even if looking at him made him feel sad.

The news that Sarneth had fallen in battle when the Great Bear tried to kill Cheimontyr hit Benjiah hard. His adventures during this last year had been many and various, but the memory of entering Taralindraal with Sarneth was as treasured as any of the others. He knew that men among the Kirthanim looked at him and whispered. They whispered about the destruction of the Grendolai and the Black Wolves. Those who had been with the army since Cimaris Rul even whispered about the summoning of the dragons and the day he held back Cheimontyr and the rest of Malek's hosts at the Kalamin. He understood why they would—those things were remarkable manifestations of Allfather's power. For Benjiah, however, being the first man to enter one of the draals in a thousand years was perhaps his most cherished moment in the whole remarkable journey. The beauty and grandeur of Taralin Forest and the draal were enough to fill Benjiah with wonder.

Since discovering that Sarneth was dead, he had found himself often going back in his mind to their journey through Taralin. Following Sarneth on horseback as the Great Bear ran through the secret ways was tense and difficult but also exhilarating. Turning left and right time and again, and finding that the forest opened up before them where no way had been visible, at least not to Benjiah's eyes, was wondrous. What's more, sitting by the fire and listening to Sarneth comforted Benjiah in the wake of Valzaan's apparent demise. Sarneth was the closest Benjiah had come to having another mentor who possessed the wisdom of many ages.

Now Sarneth was dead, devoured like so many others by the blade. His uncle Pedraal had fallen, as had the others Aljeron paid tribute to in Tol Emuna, not to mention the legions of soldiers whose bodies lay strewn across the length and breadth of Kirthanin. So many dead, and the war not yet over.

Benjiah turned south and gazed out across the open grassland. In a sense, one could see Rulalin's treacherous killing of Benjiah's own father as the moment that had set in motion all the rest of this killing. That dagger, even if only a little blade, claimed the first victim in a great chain of killing that continued until this very day. Rulalin's murder created the tension between Shalin Bel and Fel Edorath that eventually swelled into a civil war. The civil war was obviously just the kind of opportunity Malek desired to exploit, because he chose to emerge only after the war had drained seven long years of men, supplies, and fight out of Werthanin. And here they were, still preparing to fight and to kill, that Kirthanin might be free of the very blades they wielded.

Benjiah turned from the grassland and looked back at the main body of Kirthanim. Starting all this was too great a claim to make for Rulalin's treacherous act. The murder was important, no doubt, but it had not been the beginning. If any mortal man could make that claim, it was Andunin. Rulalin was but one of many men who had since taken up the blade to advance his own purpose at the cost of another's life blood.

"Benjiah?"

He turned to see Aljeron approaching with Koshti beside him. "Yes, Aljeron?"

"Walk with me?"

"Sure."

Aljeron had often invited Benjiah to join him like this since setting out from Tol Emuna, and Benjiah enjoyed getting to know the man who had undertaken so zealously justice on his father's behalf. He fell in alongside Aljeron, with Koshti between them, and they walked west along the road. "Are we going to wait here for the dragons' return, or march on?"

"We will march," Aljeron said. "The captains are preparing the army as we speak. Whatever happens between the dragons and Vulsutyrim this morning, we can't let the Nolthanim and Malekim get any farther away. So we march."

"I see."

"Is it strange, to think of Amaan Sul empty and in partial ruin?" Aljeron asked, keeping his eyes ahead and his pace steady.

"Yes, it is strange."

"I have thought often of Shalin Bel since leaving her," Aljeron said, and Benjiah heard grief in his voice. "I wonder what Malek and his army did when they passed through. I wonder if I will ever see her again, and if I do, what I will find."

Benjiah felt an urge to say something vaguely reassuring, like, "I'm sure you'll see Shalin Bel again," or something similarly vacuous, but he kept his mouth closed. He had no idea if Aljeron would ever see Shalin Bel again, and he would not offer false comfort because he was uncomfortable with reality.

What he did say was, "I don't know if home will ever be quite the same for any of us after all this."

Aljeron looked at Benjiah, then smiled. "You are so much like your father. I could imagine him saying that if he were here."

"You still miss him?" Benjiah asked.

"Yes, very much," Aljeron replied. "I only knew him a short time, but we went through a lot together. In many ways, he was the best friend I ever had."

"Well, then I'm glad I remind you of him, even if I am just a boy." He had seen Keila's face in his mind's eye, and he looked down as he walked.

"Just a boy?" Aljeron asked. "Where in the world did that come from? You're no more a boy than I am."

Benjiah was surprised at Aljeron's vehemence and embarrassed to have voiced his thought out loud. Seeking to justify himself, he added, "I'm not of age. I'm not even seventeen yet."

"By the Mountain," Aljeron said emphatically. "There is no magical line that you cross to become a man, as though one day you're a boy and then the next you aren't. Being of age is a useful concept for the functioning of society, but everybody knows many boys and girls grow up long before they're of age, even as there are plenty of men and women who never really grow up at all."

Aljeron stopped and stared over Koshti at Benjiah. "Whether you feel like a boy or a man is in a sense, irrelevant. However you classify yourself, all of us here know that you are incredibly important to what is going on, even as you were incredibly important to the events that have kept us all alive. There's not a man, or Great Bear, or dragon for that matter, who is traveling with this army who would think of you as a boy."

Maybe no man, Great Bear, or dragon, Benjiah thought, *but there's certainly a girl who does.*

"Hadn't we ought to get back and mount up if we're heading out soon?" Benjiah asked, eager to change the subject.

"Yes, I suppose we should," Aljeron answered, and soon the three of them were on their way back.

The day was warm, and Benjiah's lack of sleep was catching up to him. The army's pace was slower with the scouts moving before them in anticipation of the battle going on somewhere up ahead. Benjiah, riding his sure-footed horse, began to drift off. His head nodded and bobbed a bit, occasionally snapping back up when moments of wakefulness startled him out of his dazed semislumber. His eyelids were heavy, and their tendency to close unbidden was only aided by the brightness of the sun, which seemed to encourage the squinting that led inevitably to sleepiness.

His head was sinking down on his chest once more when he heard what sounded vaguely like chatter and commotion. The rhythmic sound of horses clip-clopping along the road was broken up by the accelerated hoofbeats of more than a few riders. Voices called out, louder this time, and his head jerked up and his eyes opened.

It took a moment for him to catch the thread of the events, but he soon realized that Sulmandir had returned with only a few other dragons and was alighting some distance ahead. Valzaan and several others were already well on their way to meet him, and Benjiah spurred his horse on as he rubbed the sleep out of his weary eyes.

As he came up to the small gathering of men around the great dragon, he dropped from his horse and took his usual place beside Valzaan, who was already standing directly before the Father of Dragons. No one had said anything, not that Benjiah could tell, and he waited anxiously with the rest.

"Sulmandir," Valzaan said at last, when still the dragon had not yet spoken. "Tell us of your children and the Vulsutyrim. What news?"

"The eyes of the children of Vulsutyr are keen, so we approached from a great height, flying in wide circles. For their part, they were in no military formation that I have ever seen. They were, all but one of them, sitting in a tight cluster on the road, their shields in hand."

The Kirthanim captains exchanged puzzled looks with one another. All had expected stiff and clever resistance from the giants, and to think of the whole lot of them sitting together, where they could easily be assaulted by the flame of but a few dragons, just didn't make sense.

"The one who was not sitting was standing with his legs spread wide, facing east along the road, some distance off from the others. His arms were folded across his chest, waiting. As it turns out, he was waiting for us.

"After circling for a while, I eventually broke out of the great circle I was keeping and came low and fast toward the waiting giant, expecting with every beat of my wings that the rest of the giants would leap up with some hidden surprise. None of them moved, except the Vulsutyrim standing apart. He uncrossed his arms and held them up and to the side, so that they were a little bit higher than his head. He stood that way, gazing at me without blinking as I flew in faster and lower. I could have destroyed him, and I could see in his eyes that he knew his death might well be upon him. And yet, he did not move. He stood still as stone, apparently willing to be burned.

"I tell you now, the enmity between his father and me and between his brothers and my sons is deep. It was hard not to reduce the count of his kind by one, right then and there, but I understood that he was trying to signal a truce. I restrained myself, barely, and after soaring above him, pulled up and circled back around.

"After he again stood his ground on my second approach, I knew that I had read his intentions aright. I set down on the road, some distance east of him. Behind me, my sons alighted, and we waited for him, for he was already approaching us, alone and unarmed."

"The giant just stood there while you passed over him twice?" Benjiah asked, excitement mixing with his curiosity so that he inserted himself unbidden into the conversation.

"He did, prophet of Allfather, he did," Sulmandir replied.

The captains of the Kirthanim remained speechless. That they were flabbergasted by the whole story was apparent in their expressions. Valzaan, though, had turned to Benjiah, his blank white eyes for a moment fixed upon him. The older prophet turned back to Sulmandir, though, as the dragon continued.

"I greeted him none to gently, demanding that he stop when I thought he had come near enough and state his business. He identified himself as Amontyr, appointed leader of the Vulsutyrim now that Cheimontyr is fallen. His business, he said, would need to be conducted directly with the prophets of Allfather accompanying the Kirthanim army."

"Us?" Benjiah gasped, looking amazed at Valzaan.

"So we have returned to take the two of you to meet with him, if you are willing."

"This is unbelievable," Aljeron said, the first of the stunned captains to find his voice. "Valzaan, what do you think?"

"I think we must go," Valzaan replied. "Though I find the request as remarkable as you, I cannot see why we should not."

"You don't think this is a trap?" Aljeron asked, looking up at Sulmandir. "A way to get Valzaan and Benjiah away from the rest of the army?"

"It must be considered a possibility," Sulmandir replied. "I will take them to where my sons await us, and we will only let Amontyr approach. He will be unarmed, and even then we will watch him. If he attempts to harm either of them, he will die a speedy death."

"Come," Valzaan said to Sulmandir, as he turned his face once more to Benjiah. "Take us to him."

If traveling through Taralin behind Sarneth had been tense and exhilarating, it was not nearly as tense and exhilarating as being carried in the talon of Sulmandir. The dragon's grip was firm to the point of being a little painful, but Benjiah did not complain, for the security of the grip was reassuring from the height at which Sulmandir flew. The wind rushing past his face was incredible, and the land passing rapidly below them was equally so. The sights and sounds of the flight were a blur, though Benjiah could remember afterward wishing that Sulmandir had been in possession of a garrion.

The flight ended none too soon, and it took Benjiah a moment to gather himself once safely on the ground. When he had, he saw Valzaan smiling nearby. "Nothing in the world like being carried by a dragon."

"No, I don't think there is."

"The giant is nearby," Sulmandir said. "Should we bring him to you?"

"Yes," Valzaan said. "Tell him we will receive him."

A moment later, a few of the dragons surrounding them parted, and a Vulsutyrim came walking through their midst. *He does not walk like a defeated enemy*, Benjiah thought, and as he had done ever since Sulmandir brought word of this strange request, he wondered what in all the world this creature could want with him and Valzaan.

"Here are the prophets of Allfather, Amontyr," Sulmandir said as he held out his talon to let the giant know he had come close enough.

The giant peered down at Valzaan and Benjiah, then nodded to the dragon. "I recognize them both. Thank you for bringing them to speak with me." He turned from Sulmandir back to them. "I am Amontyr, as Sulmandir says, and I have been appointed by my brothers to lead the Vulsutyrim. This meeting was at my suggestion, but all of my brothers agreed to the decision. You should know that."

"What is this meeting about?" Valzaan asked. "And why have you camped here at the eastern gate of Amaan Sul?"

"We were bidden by Farimaal, captain of Malek's hosts, to turn aside here and do what we could to delay the pursuit of his army by your own. However, what we do now, we do of our own accord, without his knowledge or approval."

"And what is that?"

"We would like to express to you, prophets of Allfather, our desire to renounce our long service to Malek and swear allegiance to Allfather."

Benjiah felt his legs almost buckle, and he fought for control of his body so that he would not betray his wonder at the giant's remarkable statement. He succeeded, barely, while Valzaan answered Amontyr.

"Why should Allfather receive your service? For you and your brethren are His enemies of old."

"Our father, Vulsutyr, gave refuge to Malek in Nal Gildoroth against his better judgment, and he learned over time the folly of that decision, but not before he was far past too late to change it, or so he believed. Our brother Cheimontyr followed Malek more zealously and wholeheartedly than Vulsutyr ever did, and we followed him more out of fear and despair than the love with which we followed our father. His death has given us a new sense of freedom to choose for ourselves our own destiny, and we desire to help restore what we have helped to destroy."

Valzaan nodded slightly at Amontyr's words. "It is a fair answer, and we will consider your request."

Valzaan put his hand on Benjiah's shoulders as they turned and began walking away from Amontyr. "Tell me Benjiah, what do you think of this Amontyr and of his request?"

Benjiah stared into Valzaan's empty eyes. "I'll tell you what I think, Valzaan. I think the Vulsutyrim are the fulfillment of the prophecy. They're the fourth great people, and their decision to join with us signals that Malek's time has come."

2

THE ONCE AND
ALWAYS KING

"So says Allfather.

"The sin of Corindel was very great. His refusal to heed the warning of Valzaan, my prophet, was not least among his offenses. Take heed, lest Corindel's failure become your own.

"The clan of Taralin has been faithful and true. You have protected your families and this forest with great care. You have kept the draal safe. You have discharged your duty with loyalty, and in this you have done well.

"You can hide in your draals no longer, however. It is time to come forth, to rejoin the world that was and is and will be again.

"Hear me. A dark storm lies over the land, and even now the true extent of the darkness is hidden from your eyes. The days ahead will be darker still, but you must not fear. My hand is not grown short, nor have I lost the power to save. Remember this, when all hope seems lost.

Despair is a weapon of our enemy, and he will assault you with it in places where all other weapons cannot reach you.

"Malek's ultimate defeat will require the union of four great peoples. Then and only then will the last of his servants be defeated and the grip of his hand on Kirthanin be broken. The union of the Great Bear and men is the first step in that greater unity, and it must begin now.

"Even so, though man cannot stand alone and will not, it will be a man and his sacrifice that signals the end of Malek's oppression of my creation. As one man took up the blade, so another will lay it down, and the blade will pass from his hands and perish forever from the earth.

"This is what is and what will be. Know it as certainly as you know what has been. You are summoned now to come forth. The race of men does not call you. Sarneth does not call you. Your Maker calls you, the One who rules over the mountains and the forest, the land and the sea. It is He who calls you. It is time.

"So says Allfather."

The words of the prophecy that had been given to him at the meeting of the elders of Taralindraal came back to Benjiah in a flash. They passed through his mind in an instant, though every word was understandable and clear. The men and the Great Bear had been the first two great peoples, the dragons the third, and now the repentance of Vulsutyrim made way for the fourth. The prophecy was fulfilled. It must be.

And yet, despite the excitement at realizing the fulfillment was at hand, a different portion of those words ran a second time through his mind. *As one man took up the blade, so another will lay it down, and the blade will pass from his hands and perish forever from the earth.*

"Your words confirm my own suspicions," Valzaan said, his blank white eyes fixed upon Benjiah. "How sure of this do you feel?"

"Very sure," Benjiah answered, the words of the prophecy receding and the images from the previous night reappearing. "It fits with my dream."

"What dream?"

"Last night I dreamed of Vulsutyrim in Amaan Sul. At first, I thought they were burning it and tearing it down, but as the dream went on, I realized they were restoring the walls of broken-down buildings and rebuilding houses. When I woke I dismissed it as a fancy of my imagination, but with all that has happened today, I think it was preparation of sorts for this meeting."

"Perhaps so," Valzaan said. "Perhaps it was more than that."

"What do you mean?"

"Perhaps you have seen what will be later, in the restoration of all things. Maybe the Vulsutyrim will help rebuild Amaan Sul."

Benjiah looked up and peered into the distance, beyond the dragons and giants to the great walls of Amaan Sul. Beyond those walls the city lay largely in ruins, and the thought of giants helping to restore it filled Benjiah with a delight that was hard to express. "It seems too good to be true."

"All the more reason to think it may be Allfather's plan. He delights to give us better than we deserve, and His mercy toward us has always been great." Valzaan continued as Benjiah turned back. "But what may be when the Third Age is complete, we cannot say for sure. It is probably best to keep this vision between us until such time as you may have further confirmation."

"I will," Benjiah said, then added, "I'm sorry I didn't tell you earlier today. I thought about it, but after the dragons were sent to the giants, I thought it was moot."

"There is no need to apologize, Benjiah," Valzaan replied. "You are no longer my student. You are a great prophet in your own right. In the absence of specific direction to reveal your vision to me, you were free to keep your own counsel."

"Even so," Benjiah replied, "I feel as though I should have told you sooner."

"You are welcome to consult me whenever you wish, but as I said, there is no obligation."

"That will take some getting used to," Benjiah answered.

Valzaan smiled. "Given what you have gotten used to this last year, I am confident that you will."

It was Benjiah's turn to smile. "Perhaps you are right."

Benjiah turned and looked back at Amontyr standing between the two dragons that flanked him. Even beside the great golden forms of the dragons, Amontyr appeared indomitable. Benjiah was used to seeing men and Great Bear dwarfed by the creatures, but the fact that Amontyr stood almost as tall as the dragons made him impressive, even if he was submissive.

Beyond looking large and fearsome, Amontyr seemed, as far as Benjiah could tell, calm and undisturbed by his vulnerable position. His dark hair fell almost to his shoulders, and arms as thick as tree trunks lay crossed upon his chest. His muscled legs were planted solidly. Benjiah would have been trembling like a little boy had he been under such intimidating guard, but Amontyr showed no anxiety. Benjiah might have gone so far as to say the giant looked noble, waiting patiently for their reply to his remarkable request.

"Shall we return with our answer?" Valzaan asked.

"What exactly is our answer?"

"That we will take Amontyr's request to the Kirthanim captains and see what they want to do."

"And what do you think that will be?" Benjiah asked.

"Well, they may be reluctant to accept the offer, but we will just have to convince them to do so."

"All right, let's go speak to Amontyr."

Valzaan and Benjiah returned, and Amontyr watched them steadily as they approached. "Have you an answer for me to take to my brothers, prophets of Allfather?"

"We have," Valzaan replied.

"And?"

Valzaan nodded to Benjiah, and Benjiah understood that Valzaan intended him to address the matter. He took a breath to steady himself. "We believe your request is sincere. We will take the matter to the captains of the Kirthanim."

"When we've conferred with them," Valzaan added, "we will send word of their decision back to you."

"That is all we can ask of you," Amontyr replied, and Benjiah thought that perhaps the slightest look of relief appeared on the Vulsutyrim's face. It disappeared as quickly as it had come.

Valzaan and Benjiah were about to leave when Amontyr dropped onto one knee. He leaned forward with both arms on that knee and bowed his head. Benjiah stared at the humble form of the giant, realizing that the proud and mighty creature was giving homage not only to Valzaan but to him. He swallowed, looking at the still form, and felt a chill ripple up and down his spine.

The flight back was decidedly uncomfortable. Whatever excitement had mitigated the discomfort of the journey toward Amaan Sul, it was clearly insufficient for the trip back. When Benjiah closed his eyes to try to shut out some of the discomfort, he found the motion of the flight even more disruptive, so he fixed his eyes on the golden scales of the dragon above him and tried not to think about the ground below.

The dragon's elliptical descent was almost worse, and Benjiah found himself nauseated as the circles grew tighter and tighter and the dragon descended lower and lower. Only the prospect of reaching the ground kept Benjiah from giving up his battle against sickness, and he managed to hold on until the dragon set him down lightly. He stood too fast and doubled over, gingerly holding his stomach for a few moments. Then he took a deep breath, straightened, and walked to where Valzaan waited patiently for him.

"It's much easier in a garrion," the old prophet said.

"It would have to be," Benjiah answered. "You'd think that having felt the flying sensation many times while looking through the eyes of a windhover, I'd not be so susceptible to feeling sick while being held by a dragon."

"Flying in the talons of a dragon is a lot different. You never know whom it'll affect. Aljeron could barely keep his feet after Sulmandir flew him down from his gyre in Harak Andunin."

"Really?" Benjiah asked, the image of Aljeron weak at the knees flashing before him.

"Really," Valzaan answered. "Now, let's go see the Kirthanim captains. They're no doubt anxious for our report."

"No doubt."

The column of Kirthanim was marching westward toward Amaan Sul, just north of where the dragons had set Valzaan and Benjiah down. No fewer than five dragons had returned with the two prophets, and Benjiah felt very small in the company of such large and magnificent creatures—all the more so as he reflected on the image of Amontyr standing between his dragon guards.

As they began to move, he saw the captains and the Great Bear Turgan coming to meet them. Even having been prepared to some degree by his dream for Amontyr's incredible words, he was stunned by them. He wondered how these men, road-weary and battle-hardened, might hear the astounding proposition.

Aljeron led the group, walking rather than riding. He frequently walked rather than rode, Benjiah noticed as he watched him come, Koshti gliding along beside him. How often had he watched those two walking side by side on the wet and rainy march from Zul Arnoth to Shalin Bel? Benjiah didn't think that Aljeron was averse to horses, and he certainly handled one adequately, if not elegantly. Benjiah wondered if Aljeron's fundamentally restless nature wouldn't allow him to keep the saddle for too long at any one time. Riding required energy, to be sure, but it felt more passive than walking. Benjiah suspected that this feeling of inactivity tormented Aljeron, and that walking or jogging helped him feel more engaged in useful work.

"Well?" Aljeron said. "What happened?"

"We met the Vulsutyrim who has assumed leadership in the wake of Cheimontyr's death," Valzaan said. "His name is Amontyr."

"Yes?" Aljeron answered, and the eyes of all locked on the prophets. "What did this Amontyr want with the two of you?"

Valzaan did not answer this time, and Benjiah, who understood clearly enough that Valzaan expected this report and the larger task of gaining the captains support to be a shared responsibility, took the liberty of answering. "Amontyr summoned us to present a proposition from the Vulsutyrim."

"A proposition?" several of the captains blurted together.

"What possible proposition could the Vulsutyrim have for us?" Aljeron added when the initial murmur faded. "Did they offer terms of surrender? Are they that confident of victory?"

"Far from it," Benjiah continued. He allowed his gaze to sweep across the assembled group. "He came, at great risk to his own life, as you will recall from Sulmandir's account, to offer the allegiance of the remaining Vulsutyrim to Allfather."

"What?" Benjiah heard Aljeron say before his response was drowned out by exclamations. Not all voiced replies of incredulity, for he heard more than a few echo the mocking disdain of his uncle Brenim, who said, "This is preposterous."

"It is not preposterous," Valzaan said after Brenim's answer barely faded from his lips. Brenim's comment had been offered, Benjiah thought, as a summative judgment after most of the others gave their initial reaction. Valzaan took it to represent the doubts all of them must have been feeling to one extent or another. "The offer is timely, as I trust you are all quite capable of figuring out for yourselves, and we believe it is also sincere."

"You believe?" Aljeron asked. "What makes you believe it?"

"Aside from the behavior of Amontyr," Benjiah replied, "who stood in the road as Sulmandir passed over him, risking death in order to gain a hearing with us, I also suggest the following two reasons: First, last night I had a strange but vivid dream of giants helping to rebuild Amaan Sul. It seemed apropos of nothing at first, but in the context of what has just happened, I think it was given to me in preparation for this offer."

"And the other reason?"

"The prophecy which Allfather gave me to announce in Taralindraal suggested that Malek would not be defeated until four great peoples of Kirthanin unified. What's more, the prophecy suggested that men and Great Bear were the first two. Shortly after that, Allfather directed me to the dragon tower beside the Barunaan, where the Grendolai were destroyed and the dragons were summoned. The dragons seemed to me to be the third great people, and the coming of Sulmandir and even more of his sons only confirmed this in my mind. What had stumped me and all those who knew the prophecy before today was the identity of the fourth great people. Some suggested that perhaps this might be the Kalin Seir, but that suggestion seemed inconsistent with the fact they, too, are men, and that the first three peoples are distinguished by more than geographical division. I suggest to you that the Vulsutyrim are in fact the fourth great people, and that their offer of allegiance represents the fulfillment of the prophecy, foreshadowing Malek's ultimate fall."

"And you seriously think that the Vulsutyrim," Gilion said, "who gave refuge to Malek at the end of the First Age, who invaded Kirthanin with Malek at the end of the Second, and who have helped Malek to invade once more at the end of the Third, might be the fulfillment of the prophecy?"

"Yes, I believe so," Benjiah said, calm and confident.

"And you, Valzaan?" Aljeron asked, looking to the aged prophet. "Do you also believe the giants are the fulfillment of the prophecy?"

"Indeed I do," Valzaan said. "When Amontyr made his offer, it was the first thing that went through my mind, and when I consulted with Benjiah, I found that we both interpreted his intent in the same way. I am convinced."

"But neither of you have had any definite revelation," another voice asked, and Benjiah had to search for the speaker. It was Saegan, standing near the back, and his voice carried neither doubt nor belief, only curiosity. "No explicit word from Allfather has been given to suggest we should make this alliance?"

"No," Benjiah said, and he wondered if his face betrayed any embarrassment. He'd made the pronouncement so surely, and he was convinced this was the prophecy's fulfillment. Now, to admit that he had no definitive confirmation from Allfather felt like a setback.

"Nor do I, for that matter," Valzaan added, "but long years in the service of Allfather have shown me that direct words of confirmation are rarer than you might think, even for a prophet, especially when the matter is as clear as this one is."

"Clear?" Brenim asked. "What makes it clear? It seems anything but clear. Not only have the Vulsutyrim long been friends to Malek, they have long been the enemy of the dragons. Now we are to believe they have set all this history aside? For what reason?"

Benjiah said, "They desire to help right the wrongs that their brother and father—"

"Just so that we all consider what is at stake," Brenim said.

A flash of anger shot through Benjiah. Brenim would not have interrupted Valzaan this way.

"There is no margin for error here," Brenim continued. "If we are wrong about their intentions and we make peace with them, then who knows what damage they might do to us when we least expect it? To lower our defenses and accept a host of Vulsutyrim into our midst could be catastrophic. What if they turned against us during battle?"

"I am well aware of that," Valzaan said sharply. "Have you also considered the consequences of rejecting their offer if it is, as we have assured you, the fulfillment of the prophecy? Would you reject the aid we have been told we need to bring this war to successful conclusion?"

"No," Brenim answered, less boldly.

"Can we not all agree that much could be gained or lost in this decision?" Pedraan said in the silence that followed. Benjiah observed several reflective nods. He felt grateful for his other uncle's calming influence.

"Sulmandir is here with us. I would be curious what he thinks," Aljeron added. "His history with the Vulsutyrim is far more extensive than ours."

All eyes turned to the dragons behind Benjiah and Valzaan, including Benjiah's. He leaned back so he could see Sulmandir's head far above him. The great dragon considered the question for several moments, but eventually, he leaned down so that his head was only a span or so above them. "My own history with Vulsutyr and his sons notwithstanding, I would be hesitant to disregard the joint admonition of two of Allfather's prophets. Though they are my ancient enemy, I am not so full of hate for them that I cannot see the advantage their aid would bring."

Benjiah exhaled slowly and felt his body relax. Surely the matter was decided now. It would be a bold captain to object obstinately in the face of two prophets and the Father of Dragons.

For a moment, no one spoke. Benjiah examined the faces of the captains. The looks of astonishment and disbelief were mostly gone, replaced by sober reflection. He couldn't blame them for the difficulty of accepting this turn of events. He would have felt the same, if not for the dream and the connection between Amontyr's offer and the prophecy.

Valzaan broke the silence. "There is something else which I would offer as a final reason to accept the Vulsutyrim's proposal at face value. It concerns another prophecy, given long ago and long forgotten by even the most devout of Allfather's servants.

"Erevir, Allfather's faithful prophet throughout the Second Age, passed on the words of this ancient prophecy. It harkens back to the aftermath of Malek's departure for the Forbidden Isle. The prophecy is long and speaks of many things dealing with the restoration of Kirthanin. The part that is relevant to this current situation goes as follows:

> *"Every voice and every tongue,*
> *Every creature old and young,*
> *Will new songs raise*
> *Will offer praise*
> *Will join the chorus once more begun.*
>
> *"No voice will refuse to sing,*
> *Every plain and mountain ring,*
> *His wondrous fame,*
> *His glorious name,*
> *Allfather, the once and always King.'*

"It was long ago understood," Valzaan said as the words from the ancient prophecy lingered, "that Malek's failure to give the Malekim a voice was connected to this prophecy. They are voiceless because they cannot and will not praise Allfather, the true Lord and King of Kirthanin. The Vulsutyrim have voices because they are not Malek's creation. They are Allfather's creation, and I suggest to you that this reversal today is not only fulfillment of the prophecy of the four great peoples, but also of this other more ancient prophecy. With the Grendolai destroyed, only the Vulsutyrim of all the creatures of Kirthanin with a voice remained entirely aligned with Malek. And now they have betrayed him and returned to their Creator."

"Those words, or at least the effect of them, are not entirely forgotten," Turgan said. "The Great Bear have long remembered the reason for the Silent Ones' silence."

"Is there anything that you, as the representative of the Great Bear, might add to the discussion to help make our decision clearer?" Aljeron asked.

"I can add nothing to what has already been said. Like Sulmandir, I would be hesitant to disregard the conviction of two of Allfather's prophets. Add to that the words of the prophecies and the willingness of Sulmandir to accept the Vulsutyrim's offer as real, I have no more to say."

"Does anyone have anything further to add?" Aljeron said, and when no one spoke, he continued. "Can we then say it is unanimous, that we will accept the offer of the Vulsutyrim?"

"Could we accept their offer and still treat them with caution?" Gilion asked. "Perhaps the dragons could keep watch upon them, or something?"

"We will watch them, I assure you," Sulmandir said.

"Then it is agreed," Valzaan said. "Sulmandir, will you take word to your brothers and to Amontyr that we have decided to receive their help with gratitude?"

"I will."

"Please let them know also that our army should reach them tomorrow sometime," Aljeron added, "and when we do, the Kirthanim captains will confer with them."

Sulmandir leapt from the ground and spiraled up into the sky. Benjiah watched, grateful he wasn't along for the ride and excited about the unexpected turn of events.

Benjiah passed a restless night. Excitement like a child might feel on the eve of his birthday possessed him. He tossed and turned, but he could not sleep. In the end, he rose, stretched his legs and walked in the light of the almost-full moon.

They were camped only a few hours from the eastern gate of Amaan Sul, and Benjiah walked past the sentries, sitting at their fire, a little ways down the road in the direction of the city. The warm spring air had cooled noticeably, and he pulled his cloak around himself. He'd never had much insulation, and all those weeks in the wooden cage eating what scraps were brought him hadn't helped. He wasn't exactly skin and bones, but the cool night breeze seemed to penetrate his skin with ridiculous ease.

He thought of the Vulsutyrim waiting but a little farther down the road. They were evidence of the strange and mysterious hand of Allfather, which moved in ways no man could predict. Who would have guessed that the defection of the Vulsutyrim would be the final puzzle piece for not one but two prophecies of Allfather? They were the hammer and the sword needed to bring an end to this last great war. They were the tongue and voice needed to round out the choir of praise that would forever sing Allfather's name.

Perhaps because he had grown up the son of a murdered father, Benjiah rarely found himself surprised by evil. People sometimes treated one another badly, even horribly. Even in the palace of Amaan Sul, he had seen that. Of course, since riding from Amaan Sul the previous Autumn, he had seen up close the evil that Malek brought, and though it was at times overwhelming, it was not, in any deeper sense, surprising. The lust for power and gain or whatever else a man might desire, and disregard for whoever might stand in his way, was all part of the story. Rulalin's action had taught Benjiah that lesson before he was born. Evil was utterly predictable.

What had happened these last few days and weeks, now that was something else indeed. Rulalin rejecting Malek and laying down his life to save Benjiah—that was surprising. The Vulsutyrim repenting of their allegiance to Malek and offering their aid—that was surprising. Even gazing beneath the mask of a wild and warlike people and finding the face of beauty staring back—that too was surprising.

Goodness and beauty were hallmarks of Allfather, and perhaps His people bore inherently the creativity of their originator. Evil certainly bore the monotonous predictability of its originator.

Benjiah, feeling weariness in his legs, sat down on the road to meditate further upon the matter. Eventually, his meditations on the creative wonder of Allfather's goodness and beauty gave way to quiet meditation on the beauty of Keila's face. He lay back and gazed at the moon and stars, waiting for the dawn. There, lying in the middle of the road to Amaan Sul, he fell asleep at last.

Benjiah stood at the head of the column the next morning, the thirteenth day of Spring Wane, holding the reins to his horse. He'd ridden on the way in, of course, but as they drew nearer, the front of the column slowed down at Aljeron's command. Benjiah, restless to join the captains when they met with Amontyr, dropped from his horse and continued on foot.

The other captains were not as eager as he, it turned out, for it took longer than Benjiah expected for them to assemble. At last, the other captains gathered, and following Valzaan and Benjiah, they rode on horseback out to meet Amontyr, still under the close supervision of a handful of dragons, including Sulmandir. Benjiah could feel the hesitation of both horses and men as they approached the lone but towering figure of the Vulsutyrim. There was no arrogance or hardness in Amontyr's face, but even so, his strength bespoke a certain confidence that even his supplication could not nullify. As they drew to within ten spans of the mighty giant, he slowly dropped again onto one knee, as he had the previous day, and before any of the captains could speak, Amontyr addressed them.

"Prophets of Allfather and captains of the Kirthanim, I am Amontyr, captain of the Vulsutyrim, authorized to deal with you on their behalf in whatever manner is required. I offer you both our sincere apology and regret for the part we have played in Malek's schemes against you, and our utmost aid now in foiling those schemes. We seek nothing except Allfather's pardon and forgiveness and a chance to help make right what long ago went wrong with our world."

Without hesitation, Aljeron slipped from his horse and advanced alone, or mostly alone, for Koshti followed at his side to stand with his battle brother before the kneeling giant. "Amontyr," he said, his voice steady and clear. "I am Aljeron, captain of Shalin Bel and captain of the Kirthanim, and on behalf of all the Kirthanim gathered here, on behalf of the Great Bear and dragons, I accept both your apology and your aid. Your past offenses are between you, your brothers, and Allfather, but for our part, we willingly forgive and eagerly desire your assistance in bringing this war to final conclusion."

"Yes, Amontyr," Valzaan added, for he had joined Aljeron. "Arise, let the past lie with the past. We have need of your aid and counsel."

Amontyr stood back up again, and Benjiah and the rest of the captains moved up to join them.

"What counsel do you seek?" Amontyr asked.

"Any you might provide about our enemy's plans and intentions," Valzaan replied.

"And any guidance you might have about how we may best defeat him," Aljeron added.

Amontyr seemed to reflect upon the request before answering. "It would seem to me that we have two main problems. The first is that Farimaal is even now leading what remains of the Malekim and Nolthanim to the Mountain. He thinks that I and my brothers have remained behind to slow you down, to gain time for the remainder of Malek's army to seek shelter in the tunnels and caverns under Agia Muldonai. If they are successful in passing through Gyrin to the Mountain, they will be much harder to root out and defeat. They must be caught and defeated before they reach the Mountain if we are to be spared a long and bloody siege."

"They think you've stayed behind to slow us?" Aljeron asked.

"Yes."

"How long before they realize the truth, or can you say?"

"I cannot, not for sure, but he will expect some of our number to have returned within a few days. When none do, he will certainly wonder what happened. Whether he will suspect what has really happened, who can say?"

"The other problem?" Aljeron asked.

"The Kumatin," Amontyr said, and the name hung in the air like a foul odor. Benjiah had all but forgotten him, but now terrible memories came rushing back. "There has been no rain for weeks. The floodwaters of the great rivers and even the Kellisor Sea have begun to recede. The Kumatin will sense that something has happened to Cheimontyr, and he will begin to make his way back down the Barunaan, back to the ocean. Farimaal's escape to the Mountain will create problems for us, but the Kumatin's escape would be even worse. As it is, he will be very hard to kill, but with the wide ocean open before him, it might prove all but impossible. He must be killed before he reaches the Southern Ocean, or who knows how we will ever find him in the great deep."

"You said the Kumatin *will sense* that something has happened to Cheimontyr," Aljeron said. "Do you know if he has begun his flight yet?"

"I do not know, but if he hasn't, it won't be long."

Aljeron looked to Valzaan, and the old prophet nodded. "Benjiah and I will do what we can to find out."

Aljeron turned back to the giant. "You present a challenge indeed. An army of men and Malekim rides north, and we must catch and kill them. A giant sea creature heads south, and we must also catch and kill him. It would seem that we must divide and conquer, but who to send which direction, that is another question."

"If I may make a suggestion," Amontyr started.

"By all means."

"The Kumatin is a foe beyond the power of men and even Great Bear. He may not move quickly at first, thinking he is safe from immediate harm, but as soon as he realizes he is being pursued, he is capable of moving at great speeds as long as the water is deep enough. Send my brothers and I after him. We can run at a pace ten times faster than the fleetest of men, and we will have a chance where you will not."

"Or perhaps the Kumatin is a matter most safely left to the dragons," Aljeron said, turning to Sulmandir, who had heard the whole conversation.

Sulmandir's deep voice rumbled across the quiet plain. "The creature poses certain difficulties for us. Specifically, as long as he remains submerged, there is little we could do. Water is our one real weakness."

"Perhaps," Valzaan said, and all eyes turned to him, "this is really a task for both Amontyr and Sulmandir, for both the

Vulsutyrim and the dragons. Amontyr and his brothers are not afraid of the water and perhaps might find a way to force the Kumatin to emerge so that the dragons might use their strength and speed from the air. Would both of you be willing, should it be necessary?"

"For my part," Amontyr said, "I would be grateful for any help the dragons would provide. To have any hope of success, we have to force the Kumatin into shallow waters, and the fury of the dragons employed against the creature would be aid most welcome."

Sulmandir was not as quick to speak, but when Amontyr finished, he did add his agreement. "We have agreed to accept the offer of the Vulsutyrim, and we would be willing to help them kill this creature."

"Then perhaps our decision is made for us by necessity," Aljeron said. "The Vulsutyrim and the dragons will head south after the Kumatin, and the Kirthanim and Great Bear will head north after the Nolthanim and Malekim."

"Need we send all the dragons south?" Gilion asked. "If we are to catch Malek's host before the Mountain, we could use the aid of a few dragons to harry the enemy and slow him down."

"Would that be all right?" Aljeron asked Sulmandir.

"That could be arranged."

"Amontyr, does the plan sound good to you?" Aljeron asked.

"Neither task will be easy, but the plan is as good as any we're likely to have."

"Any objections?" Aljeron said, turning around to scan the faces of his captains, but no one spoke.

"I have a suggestion, not an objection," Valzaan said.

"Yes?"

"I suggest that Benjiah and I accompany the dragons and Vulsutyrim. We may be able to help where others cannot."

Aljeron looked at Valzaan, then said, "It may be so, but I would speak to you further about it before we settle the question definitively. All right?"

"We may speak further at your leisure."

"Then at least the main thrust of our plan is settled. We will gather what information we can, discuss what details we must, but by this afternoon, we will depart, each to our own road."

THEIR SEPARATE WAYS

BENJIAH WATCHED AMONTYR head back toward the Vulsutyrim. Even from a distance, the cluster of giants that greeted Amontyr unnerved Benjiah. It was strange to think of them as allies in the war against Malek, and yet somehow it fit. Their grandeur matched their origins as creatures made by Allfather. They were so different from the ugly, brutish Voiceless, the Black Wolves that were far more at ease in darkness than in light, or the Kumatin, the creature of immense size and strength but little purpose other than to kill and destroy. Only the Grendolai, of all Malek's handiwork, came close to approximating the majesty of the giants, but though intelligent and capable, the Grendolai had been hideous like the Malekim and, like the wolves, truly comfortable only in darkness. The Vulsutyrim transcended all these, as did the dragons and Great Bear and the varied Kirthanim. Their repentance might have been unexpected, a remarkable surprise, but they belonged with these armies. They belonged in this final push to set Kirthanin free once and for all.

Now, they gathered around their newly appointed leader, listened for a moment, then began moving about, presumably preparing to head south. They had volunteered for the assignment of hunting down the Kumatin, and now that weighty task was theirs. Theirs and his, possibly, as well.

"Well," Aljeron said to them, and Benjiah turned away from the Vulsutyrim. "Thanks for being willing to discuss this."

"What would you like to discuss?" Valzaan asked.

"I didn't want to question you in front of the others, but I'm not so sure it's a good idea for you and Benjiah to head south with the dragons and Vulsutyrim."

"No?" Valzaan asked.

"No," Aljeron replied. "If you think that Sulmandir and Amontyr could use your help, then by all means, I think you should go, but I think Benjiah should come north with me and the Kirthanim army."

"Why?"

"It's not what you think," Aljeron said, looking from Valzaan to Benjiah and then back again. "I know what Benjiah has been through and accomplished. I know he is more than capable of looking after himself. I want him to come with us because our task will be difficult too. We are fortunate to have two prophets of Allfather, and I don't see why we need to send both of you to the same place. The army is dividing in two directions and there are two of you, so why not let Benjiah come north with us while you go south with the others?"

Benjiah felt a mixture of excitement and anxiety at these words. Aljeron, captain of the army of Kirthanin and his father's close friend, was making a plea to Valzaan for Benjiah's assistance. It was almost unreal. Aljeron, who had all but forbidden Benjiah to be anywhere close to the fighting in Zul Arnoth, was now entreating Valzaan to allow him to go north as a source of aid. At the same time, however, Valzaan's words about walking with him as far as he could go made Benjiah wonder what might await him in the north if Valzaan agreed to their parting.

"Like you, Aljeron," Valzaan said, "I know Benjiah can take care of himself. I do not suggest that Benjiah should come with me because I think he needs my help, but because I have promised to stay with him as long as I am able, until the road he must travel requires him to go on alone. Despite the obvious neatness of the situation as you described it, his road does not yet require us to part ways. I do not then wish to be separated from him, and as one of us at least is needed in the south, I think we should both go."

"You're speaking in riddles," Aljeron replied, frowning. "What do you mean? What road do you speak of, and why must Benjiah travel it alone? The whole Kirthanim army goes north. He shall not be alone."

"The road I mean is not the physical road before you and the Kirthanim army, but the road that Allfather has laid out for him. He and I have spoken of it, and Benjiah knows there will come a point in the journey when he will have to go forward alone, with neither your help nor mine."

Aljeron looked intently at Benjiah, who could not meet his gaze for long. He surveyed the ground beside his feet uncomfortably. He looked back up when Aljeron again addressed Valzaan. "Look, if there is something I need to know here, about what's going to happen to Benjiah . . . "

"There's nothing you need to know, except that Allfather holds all futures in His hands, both Benjiah's and yours, and that of every man in this army."

"I understand that, but though I am concerned for the lives of all my men, Benjiah's is special. Surely you understand that."

Valzaan reached out and placed his hand gently on Aljeron's shoulder. "I understand, Aljeron. I do. Joraiem was special to you. Benjiah is his son, and thus he is also special to you. Even so, the road laid out for him will be neither easier nor harder for any worrying you may do, so as best you can, you must trust his way to Allfather and to me. Can you do that?"

"Do I have any other option?" Aljeron asked, and Benjiah could hear a touch of bitterness in his voice.

"No, I'm afraid not. His way was marked out for him before he was even born. Even should we wish to interfere with Allfather's sovereign plan, we could not." Valzaan paused, only for a moment, then continued in a clear voice. "Now, as for your military concern, it is true that you have a difficult task before you. However, you have a long way to go and many leagues to cover before you can possibly catch Farimaal, and it is certainly possible that once we have accomplished our mission in the south we will be able to join you. After all, should we succeed in catching and killing the Kumatin, we will turn all our might and resources toward the Mountain and Malek's hosts."

Aljeron conceded with a nod. "All right, then you will both head south with the dragons and giants. Even so, would it at least be possible for one or both of you to help me scout out the positions of the Kumatin and Farimaal's hosts? I would like to have an idea of their locations before we part ways, and if you are willing, you could provide that information for me quicker than any other way."

Valzaan turned to Benjiah, "North or south?"

"South," Benjiah replied, and then he was searching in his mind for a windhover to respond to his soundless call.

It did not take long. Within moments he found one gliding effortlessly through the warm spring sky above the westernmost waters of the Kalamin River. The floodwater was noticeably reduced since last he'd seen it. Even so, the water still overflowed the riverbanks, lying in shallow pools for many spans on both sides. Of the Kumatin, Benjiah could see nothing. He needed to see the Kellisor more extensively, and the Kellisor was a large body of water.

From one windhover to the next Benjiah moved, but each windhover he found was near the perimeter of the Kellisor Sea, and urging them toward the center took some concentration. He found a few willing to soar high above, and through their eyes he searched the deep waters for any noticeable disruption. He found nothing. Aside from the wind upon the water, the sea appeared devoid of any and all movement.

He found a windhover near the southern shores, just east of the mouth of the Barunaan, and before long the bird was circling above the ruins of Peris Mil. The city still lay under some depth of water, not so deep that the broken buildings were concealed from the windhover's searching eyes. The bird passed north over the buildings toward the open water of the Kellisor, and there, Benjiah spied at last what he had been looking for.

Cutting through the rippling water of the sea was the long, sleek, dark body of the Kumatin. He moved with an astounding grace for a creature so hideous and large. For a few moments, Benjiah had the windhover keep pace high above the monster, but soon the creature was submerged beneath a wave and was lost from Benjiah's sight. Silently, he thanked the King Falcon for his service, and Benjiah returned to the waking world.

More time had passed than he realized; Valzaan had already given his report to Aljeron. So preoccupied in his search had he been, that he did not notice the conversation going on just a couple spans away. If Valzaan and Aljeron had been waiting long, they did not seem impatient. Rather, when they realized Benjiah was ready to speak, they stepped attentively forward.

"The creature is still in the Kellisor Sea," he said.

"Good," Valzaan replied. "He has not yet begun his journey south. That is fortunate for us."

"But he is not far from the mouth of the Barunaan," Benjiah added.

"That is where you saw him?" Aljeron asked.

"Yes, just north of the ruins of Peris Mil."

"Peris Mil," Valzaan said. Then the prophet stroked his own jaw contemplatively.

"You find the location significant?" Aljeron asked.

"No, not as such, though the proximity of the creature to the Barunaan could mean that he is preparing to go south now that the floodwaters are receding, as Amontyr suggested he would. Of course, it might not." Valzaan said absentmindedly. "No, it was the name, Peris Mil, that prompted my memory."

"Yes?"

"I met a man from Peris Mil during our stay in Tol Emuna. He traveled with Monias. A burly fellow with a strong deep voice. Do you know the one?"

"Garin," Benjiah blurted. "The man who took my grandfather across the Kellisor and traveled with him to Amaan Sul and beyond. That's who you're talking about."

"Yes," Valzaan said. "Garin was his name. He was from Peris Mil, was he not?"

"I think so," Aljeron answered. "Why?"

"Oh, it is nothing definite, only the beginning of an idea. Assuming he has marched out with the Kirthanim army, could you send this Garin to me? If native to Peris Mil, he is no doubt familiar with the waters of the upper Barunaan. He could be valuable to us in the task ahead."

"I will have to ask Gilion where he might be," Aljeron replied. "He usually keeps track of those kind of details. It is possible Garin did not come with us. Monias remained behind in Tol Emuna, after all."

"Monias is past fighting age," Valzaan replied. "This Garin is not. I would be very surprised if he was not somewhere among the army."

"Should I send him to you if I find him?"

"I would be most appreciative."

Aljeron took Benjiah's hand and clasped it tightly. "I will probably see you again before we or you are underway, but if not, best wishes for your road."

"And also to you."

Aljeron headed away, Koshti moving silently at his side.

Aljeron stroked Koshti's furry head lovingly. His battle brother sat proudly beside him. Aljeron was grateful for competent officers. If not for them, directing this large conglomerate of men would have been a nightmare. As it was, the distribution of orders had been relatively easy. The scouts were already riding north along the wall of Amaan Sul. According to Valzaan's report, Farimaal's army was a day northwest of the city, but Aljeron did not feel comfortable going anywhere without sending scouts first. Armies could change directions, and Aljeron did not like surprises.

Gilion appeared at his side, and Aljeron acknowledged his arrival wordlessly. Together the three of them watched as the front of the Kirthanim column moved north off the road.

"Giants on our side," Gilion said as they maintained their focus on the column. "I have to admit I never thought I'd see the day."

"Yes, it is quite a fortuitous turn of events," Aljeron added.

"Of course, I still may not see the day," Gilion said.

"How do you mean?" Aljeron's head turned now as he examined Gilion's impassive face.

"Well, they're all headed south, and we're headed north. If they don't survive their encounter with the Kumatin, or if we force the issue with Malek's hosts before they can return, or if I simply don't live long enough to see their return, I may still never see them in action on All-father's behalf."

"For that matter, then," Aljeron said, "there's no guarantee for any of us, I suppose. Still, just to think of them marching out more or less under our command, it is pretty remarkable, isn't it?"

"That it is," Gilion agreed.

Aljeron smiled, still watching his friend. He'd caught the almost imperceptible reaction. "Come now, Gilion. I know you too well. You want to say something else. What is it?"

Gilion smiled too. "Yes, you do know me too well. I suppose what I wanted to say, though it is likely too late, is that it would be great to have more help for our mission. I understand that the sea creature poses some unique challenges, but both prophets, all the giants and all but four dragons? We could use some of that help, couldn't we? It isn't like our task will be easy."

"No, it won't be easy."

"Then why send so much strength south?"

"Gilion, you heard both the Vulsutyrim and the dragons. Didn't you tell me yourself about how he came up out of the Barunaan and took a dragon from the sky?"

"Yes, but there weren't nearly so many dragons with us then. They could overwhelm him now."

"Perhaps, if he was exposed to them. But if he senses he is outnumbered and likely to be overwhelmed, why come out of the water? Why not just glide through the deep, flooded heart of the Barunaan all the way to the Southern Ocean? And then what will we do?"

"So you think the giants will go into the water and get him out? How are they going to do that?"

"I don't know, but you can see why they'd want to march south in strength. I wouldn't want to be faced with that task and find I didn't have enough help to do it. Besides, Gilion, we've just been harried all over Kirthanin, and before that we fought a long and frustrating war with Fel Edorath. I don't think we'll ever feel like we have sufficient strength. We'll always be looking for more aid 'just to make sure' we have the fight well in hand."

"Maybe, but I still say a few more dragons and a few giants would be very nice."

"There's no arguing that point."

"Well, if not more dragons or some giants, why not at least one of the prophets?"

"I discussed that with Valzaan and Benjiah, and I am satisfied with their reasoning, and for now at least, Gilion, that will need to be sufficient."

Gilion looked closely at Aljeron. Aljeron rarely kept information from Gilion, so he understood the older man's curiosity. Even so, Aljeron felt that the conversation that had passed between the prophets and him was confidential, and he would not discuss it. After a moment, Gilion turned back toward the army and changed the subject without really changing the subject.

"So, you feel that we will be sufficient as we are, without help?"

"I certainly hope so. We have the aid of four dragons, which will be invaluable for scouting and, without the aid of the Vulsutyrim, difficult to defend against. Though the numbers of the Great Bear are somewhat depleted, they have always fared well against the Malekim. I think the outcome may come down to men. Is our Kirthanim army strong enough to defeat the Nolthanim? Will we be able to stand before their dread captain, this Farimaal?"

"The dread captain is an important factor," Gilion said, "and there is of course the other thing, which we all think about but don't dare to speak about, at least not yet."

"Yes," Aljeron said softly after a moment's hesitation. "There is that. What would you ask me about that?"

"I would ask you to be candid with me, that's all. They are fleeing for the Mountain, and we have been charged with catching and stopping them. So, we are going after *him*, and we are not bringing either of the prophets of Allfather providentially given to us for just such a time as this. You will forgive me if I am confused and wary."

"I understand, Gilion," Aljeron said. "Remember, though, if the prophets' mission is successful, the dragons can bring Valzaan and Benjiah back to us. I'm sure they are as aware of our dilemma as we are. I don't think they mean to stop helping us once they've seen to the destruction of the Kumatin."

"That's not really an answer to my question."

"I'm not sure I have another one. You're asking me what my plan is for Malek, but what am I to say to that? His path has been a mystery from the beginning, hasn't it? Where's Malek? Cheimontyr, Farimaal—they are visible on the battlefield, the ostensible heads of the enemy army. And yet, where's Malek? Benjiah says he never saw him. No one in the enemy camp spoke of him. There has been no word of him and no sightings, not that we know of. As far as we know, he may never have left the Mountain."

"Do you think he still lurks there?"

"I don't know, Gilion. That's my point. It is a mystery. However, I would say that the possibility he delegated rule to his captains is not far-fetched. Though captain over the Werthanim forces who fled to Col Marena, I delegated direction of the army to Caan and to you. What's more, did Valzaan not suggest that Cheimontyr's power over the lightning and storm came ultimately from Malek? Even Malek does not have limitless power. Perhaps he has given a bit of himself to this Farimaal, even as he gave some of himself to Cheimontyr. Maybe Malek has little left of his original strength and power for his own use."

"That sounds like wishful thinking."

"It may be, but I do not think Valzaan would endorse this plan if he feared that Malek, unimpaired and undiminished, was waiting to sweep us from the battlefield."

"Well," Gilion said, looking beyond Aljeron. "It seems you will have a chance to ask him yourself. The prophet approaches even now. Tell me what he says later. I have some more things to see to before we're fully underway."

Aljeron turned and saw Valzaan coming. By the time the aged prophet had drawn close enough to speak to him, Gilion was many spans away.

Aljeron spoke first. "Gilion has found this man Garin from Peris Mil. Did he come to you?"

"He did," Valzaan replied. "He knows a great deal about the Barunaan, and I will take him with us. I think he will prove helpful."

"Good," Aljeron said, nodding thoughtfully, but his mind wasn't really on the man from Peris Mil or his eagerness to exact revenge on the Kumatin. "Valzaan, in all our discussion of what must still be done, you have never mentioned Malek."

"I mention him all the time."

"Yes, you speak of opposing his will in a general way, or of fighting his servants and thwarting his purposes, but you do not speak of him, not specifically, like where you think he is or how you think we will deal with him in particular."

"I cannot speak of that which I do not know."

"Then you don't know where he is?"

"I do not know for sure, but I have suspicions."

"Will you speak of them?"

"I will," Valzaan replied. He faced Aljeron. "I think Malek may be moving about Kirthanin in the form of the crippled sailor from Col Marena, Synoki."

"What?"

"That is my suspicion."

"But, how could that be? He deserted us at Harak Andunin, and I don't doubt that Synoki is in Malek's pay. I suspected that myself, especially after Cinjan's attempt on my life, but you're saying Synoki *is* Malek?"

"I'm saying he may be. I'm not sure."

"But, you traveled with us and with him from the Forbidden Isle all the way north of Elnin. Wouldn't you"—Aljeron hesitated, gesturing vaguely with his hand—"you know, have sensed it or something?"

"Don't you remember what I told you before we set sail for the Forbidden Isle? Malek is one of the Twelve. The Titans could not only move among men in human shape, but they could mask their identity so completely that you would not know who they were unless they wanted you to. Just because I am a prophet of Allfather doesn't mean I am exempt from this. No one was exempt from this, not even the other Titans. I can only see what Allfather shows me, and He has not revealed Malek's secret identity to me."

"Then why do you suspect Synoki?"

"There are many reasons, none of them conclusive. It seems clear to me in retrospect that he infiltrated us on the island to spy on us. It also seems clear that he poisoned Rulalin against Joraiem."

"You mean," Aljeron said, his voice trembling a little, "that Rulalin killed Joraiem because Synoki made him?"

"No, I wouldn't put it like that. Rulalin always had a choice. I would say, though, that his thinking was deluded when he did it."

"Why would Synoki want Joraiem dead?"

"For the same reason I sought to take him under my wing. He sensed what I did, and he probably wondered like me at the time if Joraiem was the child of prophecy."

"But Benjiah is. Malek thought he could stop all that Benjiah has done by having Rulalin kill Joraiem?"

"That's right."

Aljeron sighed. "Go on. What are the other things?"

"Despite the fact that Synoki said he was from Col Marena, it is too much of a coincidence that he happened to be there when you went ashore. If he infiltrated us on the Forbidden Isle and had Joraiem killed because he might be the child of the prophecy, why do you think he attached himself to your expedition?"

Aljeron stared at Valzaan. "You don't mean that . . . "

"I do."

"You think he thought I might be the child of prophecy?"

"He sensed something about our group. He'd thought killing Joraiem might take care of things, but at some level, he knew or feared that he hadn't turned Allfather's plan aside. You were Joraiem's good friend, not yet a member of the Assembly when he met you, so in a sense you were a child in that first encounter. Then you became a mighty warrior, chief among the captains of the Kirthanim. I think he attached himself to you to figure out if you might be the child of prophecy, and probably he let things go as long as he did to see what you were up to. Cinjan's failed attempt on your life put you on notice, and the next thing he knew, you found me at the foot of Harak Andunin. He had not counted on that, and it may well have saved your life. I imagine he planned to see if Sulmandir was alive, and after he had the answer to that question, he would have killed you. Even before we spoke of Benjiah in his presence, he probably figured out you were not the one he was after, but he would have killed you all the same. His flight from there was the action that finally opened my eyes, so to speak, to his probable identity."

"By the Mountain, Valzaan. You're saying I journeyed across the Nolthanin waste with Malek as my companion?"

"Maybe."

"I had a knife to his throat, after the Snow Serpent attacked us," Aljeron said, frustration welling up in him. "I could have killed him there and ended all this."

"You had a knife to his throat, but I doubt you could have ended this there. He is not yet so weak he could not deflect your purpose. Whatever he said to you at that point, if it was indeed Malek, I'm sure his words to you were more than just words."

"All right, Valzaan," Aljeron said, "How sure of this are you?"

"I have said already that I don't know for sure."

"I know, but given that, how sure of it do you feel? How confident are you that Synoki is Malek?"

"I am pretty sure. Benjiah shares my suspicions. He was careful in what he said when we discussed the day of his rescue by Sulmandir, but I could tell he also wondered about Synoki."

Aljeron gazed at the prophet, shaking his head in wonder. "Synoki. Right under my nose all that time."

"Aljeron," Valzaan said, "our roads will soon diverge. I certainly hope that we will be able to take care of the Kumatin and meet you in the north in time to aid you in your battle. Even so, I feel confident that Allfather will keep you from the final confrontation with Malek until Benjiah has returned."

"Benjiah?"

"Do you still not see? We have just spoken of the prophecy and of Malek's aim to make sure that the child it speaks of will not live to face him. I don't know what specifically is waiting for you or for me, but I know that Benjiah has a role to play in Malek's ultimate defeat, even though it may come at a cost."

"A cost," Aljeron repeated the words mechanically.

"Yes, do not forget the words of the prophecy:

'With a strength that stoops to conquer
And a hope that dies to live,

With a light that fades to be kindled
And a love that yields to give,

'Comes a child who was born to lead,
A prophet who was born to see,
A warrior who was born to surrender,
And through his sacrifice set us free.'

"He is a not yet of age, so he is a child in the eyes of society if not to us. He is a prophet who has seen many things, even at times things that I have not. He is a warrior, for with a bow he is lethal, and without it he still summoned enough power of Allfather's to destroy the Grendolai and Black Wolves. Only his sacrifice remains."

"Sacrifice," Aljeron echoed, the word barely loud enough to escape his lips.

"As I said before, I know you care for the boy, as do I. What lies before him, he will have to face alone." Valzaan turned his face to the Kirthanim army. "For you, though, I would say that this means you should track down the enemy, then engage and destroy his army. Farimaal, dread captain of the Nolthanim, will prove a challenge, I fear. He is a mighty adversary. I suggest, though, that you be wary of Synoki. He is likely to stay out of the fight as long as possible, but if you should see him on the battlefield and we are not yet back, be careful."

"Of course," Aljeron said, wondering what exactly being careful might mean if Synoki was actually Malek in human likeness.

Benjiah sat on the edge of the road, facing north. The ruins of Amaan Sul were in the distance on his left. In front of him, and stretching far to his right, the Kirthanim army was moving northward. Most of the Kirthanim had passed by, and now the Great Bear moved silently onward. Soon, the Kalin Seir too would pass.

Valzaan approached, and to Benjiah's surprise, settled down on the road beside him. "The Vulsutyrim are well on their way, and the Kirthanim army too."

"Yes," Benjiah said, glancing sideways in the direction of Amaan Sul, where the Vulsutyrim camp had been. "The giants left quickly after our meeting. They've been gone for some time, as have most of the dragons. Why are we still here?"

"Since we don't know how far or how many days we might be traveling with the dragons, I asked Sulmandir if a garrion might be provided for us."

"And?" Benjiah said, not bothering to restrain his excitement.

"A dragon has been sent to fetch one. It will delay our departure a bit, but we will easily catch up to the others, if not tonight, tomorrow."

"That's wonderful," Benjiah said. "I didn't want to complain, but the thought of flying a really long way in the talons of a dragon was almost unbearable."

"I know," Valzaan said. "And now that Garin is coming with us, there will be three who need carrying, and it is easier for a dragon to put all of us in a garrion and be done with it. A dragon must hold a man firmly so that he is not dropped but not so firmly that the man is crushed, and maintaining this delicate balance can be tiring over time. The added weight of the garrion is a nuisance but less worrisome. Sulmandir saw the sense of the suggestion, and I suspect, had already planned on providing one for this journey."

"Where is Garin?"

"He's asleep."

"Asleep?"

"Yes, he's lying in the grass just south of the road, over there," Valzaan nodded to indicate the direction. "I told him we might have a little while, and he promptly stretched out and fell asleep."

"He doesn't seem to be too nervous about being carried around by a dragon, I guess," Benjiah said.

"No, he seems quite unflappable really. I'm glad we'll have him along. Another calm, sensible head is always welcome."

"He's gracious too" Benjiah added. "When I met him in Tol Emuna after hearing about how he guided my grandfather all the way from Peris Mil, I thanked him profusely. He managed somehow to accept my gratitude humbly. I can't really explain it, only it wasn't like those shows of false modesty you sometimes get from people. You know, when they insist it was nothing on and on and you can tell all the while that they're really quite pleased with themselves?"

"Yes." Valzaan chuckled. "I have been around a long time and know exactly what you mean."

"Anyway, it wasn't like that. He just thanked me for my appreciation and said he had enjoyed the adventure."

"There is a kind of balance to him. Courage and humility, honesty and modesty—he seems to possess these in roughly equal measure. It's refreshing."

"Yes, that's right."

They fell silent for a moment, and Benjiah looked back toward the army marching north. The Kalin Seir were there, beginning their march from the road. Benjiah sat up more attentively, realizing too late that he'd wanted to hide his agitation from Valzaan.

"Why don't you go over and see if you can say good-bye?" Valzaan said. "We have plenty of time."

Benjiah looked at him and hesitated. "I'm not sure what to say."

"It may be that the gesture matters more than the particularities of your speech. Now go, before they part ways with us, and she along with them."

Benjiah rose without further hesitation. Had his uncle Pedraan or Aljeron said such a thing to him, he would have died from embarrassment, but Valzaan seemed always able to say what was needed in exactly the right way. Garin indeed was balanced; Valzaan was endowed with balance and then some.

He stopped half a dozen spans from where the Kalin Seir were marching. He watched the men and snow leopards moving along together. Some looked at him as they went past, but most marched with heads held high, eyes focused ahead. They were marching out to face the Nolthanim, the brothers who had betrayed them, and they were sober and steadfast.

Benjiah did not think many had gone past already, but it was certainly possible that Keila was already out of view. It was also possible that she was marching on the far side of the column and might not see Benjiah. It was further possible that she might see him but not come, though that was a possibility Benjiah did not want to entertain.

He spent a few quietly torturous moments examining the passing ranks of the Kalin Seir as inconspicuously as possible, and then Keila detached herself from the main body of the army and began to walk toward him. Relief and nervousness washed over him.

"You're not riding up ahead as you have been?" she asked as she stopped in front of him.

"No," he answered. "I'm not going north, at least not immediately. I'm going south with the Vulsutyrim and dragons."

Keila glanced in the direction of Valzaan. "Both of you?"

"Yes, both of us."

"This is about the sea creature, this Kumatin, isn't it?"

"Yes, we are going to kill him if we can, to keep him from escaping down the Barunaan River into the sea."

"No one among the Kalin Seir had heard of him before we came to Tol Emuna."

"He's not been around very long," Benjiah said. "In fact, he is not much older than I am."

"Then he is old enough to have done mighty and remarkable things," Keila answered, and Benjiah felt a ripple of warmth all over.

Keila stepped closer and put her hand on Benjiah's shoulder. "I have heard he is a formidable enemy. I am glad you will have the Sun-Soarer and his children with you. Take care of yourself."

"Thank you, Keila," Benjiah said. "And the same to you. When we have done what we are being sent to do, we will come back."

"Good," she said smiling, "for the Forge-Foe is a formidable enemy too, and the aid of the prophets of Allfather is much to be desired."

"Farewell," he said as she turned to rejoin her people.

"Farewell," she called after him as she walked away.

He watched as she melted back into the moving mass of men and women and snow leopards. Then, when he could no longer make her out, he turned and headed back to the road.

Farimaal walked back to his tent. He was angry, but as always, he kept his anger locked deep inside.

Malek was sitting in his chair, and Farimaal looked away from him upon entering. Farimaal would have to give his report sooner or later, but he had wanted it to be later.

"Any news from the Vulsutyrim?"

"No," Farimaal replied.

"Nothing?"

"Nothing. There have been no messengers and therefore no messages."

Farimaal knew without needing to look that Malek was watching him intently, so he didn't look.

"What do you make of it?" his master asked.

"Nothing good. Either they have all been slaughtered, which is hard to believe given their orders, or . . . "

"Or what?"

"Or we have been betrayed."

"Betrayed?" Malek did not shout, but a cold intensity echoed in his words.

"It is possible. I sensed something amiss when Amontyr met with us before we left."

"Couldn't it be that they are still engaged with the enemy, that they have neither fallen nor betrayed us?"

"It could be," Farimaal said, "but I doubt it. Even had all the dragons attacked them in force, some would have escaped."

Malek did not at first reply. After a while, though, he said, "Even if the Vulsutyrim have betrayed us, we will not let the enemy catch us before we reach the Mountain. They will pay a high price if they choose to come in after us."

4

THE KUMATIN

BENJIAH SAT BY THE FIRE on the morning of the fifteenth day of Spring Wane, eating. He was hungry. The previous day had been hot, and while this day might soon be also, it wasn't yet, so the fire was not unwelcome.

Benjiah looked at the garrion they had been transported in, which wasn't much more than a big wooden box. No doubt it was once a splendid red, but now the few flecks of paint that remained were all but lost in a sea of discolored brown. That the garrion was little more than a wooden box had been an issue for Benjiah when first confronted with the need to enter it. After so long in a wooden cage among the hosts of Malek, he was not eager to climb into what looked a good deal like another. He gazed at the opening for a long moment, even after Valzaan and Garin entered, until at last he willed himself to step in.

Once inside, his reaction was even stronger than that at the door. He felt claustrophobic and ill at ease. Following

Valzaan's lead, he took a seat along one of the sides and tried to keep himself together, at least on the outside. Looking out through the slats that ran around the top portion of the garrion reminded him far too much of the fragmented view of the world he'd endured in the cage. Closing his eyes, he wrapped his arms around his knees until the dragon took hold of the garrion and lifted it off the ground. Only then did the discomfort and unpleasant associations slip away.

They had slipped away, though, and quickly. Nothing he experienced while carted by cage across Enthanin had felt anything like this. This was flight as it should be experienced, he thought, nothing like the tense, uncomfortable feeling of being gripped in a dragon talon, exposed to the wind and feeling half-crushed. He felt his body relax and found himself smiling broadly at Garin, who watched him good-naturedly from the neighboring wall.

And yet, not everything about their travel in the garrion was good. As the sun climbed higher in the sky, the garrion grew warmer and warmer. The slats were high up the sides, and while the wind flowed freely through the garrion up there, down on the floor it became decidedly stuffy. Even with long stints standing and leaning his head against the slats where he could feel the breeze, it was impossible to completely escape the heat, and sweat flowed continually down his face. It felt like Full Summer.

Now warmed by the fire, Benjiah turned away and put the last bite of bread in his mouth, then wiped the crumbs from his hands. As hot as it might get, the garrion was a blessing, and he would not grumble. He rose, stretched his legs, and looked about for Valzaan.

The prophet liked a good stroll in the morning, so Benjiah had not been surprised when he rose to find him missing. Instead, he'd joined Garin for a silent breakfast. Garin was friendly enough when spoken to, but he rarely offered his thoughts or opinions unless they were solicited, and as Benjiah did not solicit any this morning, there was no conversation.

Benjiah saw Valzaan walking toward them through the rough grass.

"Good morning, Valzaan," he said as the prophet approached.

"Good morning."

"The Kumatin is moving very slowly," Benjiah added, thinking of what he had meant to tell Valzaan when he first awoke.

"I know."

"He seems uninterested in making good time to the Southern Ocean. He seems much more interested in feeding. He devours anything he can find, even if it is only a lone deer that wanders too close to the receding floodwaters. Why would he linger over so small a meal as to seem hardly worth it?"

"The creature is unaware that it is being watched or pursued. While it likely cannot understand why the storm has stopped, it likewise cannot conceive of anything that might threaten its safety. It lingers because it can."

"Which is good for us."

"Which is very good for us," Valzaan agreed. "Even now, if the creature started swimming with all its might south, we'd likely be helpless to stop it. What's more, even with its halting progress, we still lack any good idea of how we will stop it, even if we can catch up to it."

"I have an idea, though I can't say it will qualify as a good idea," Garin said. Benjiah looked at the large man, who stroked his bushy beard of black and grey with a thick hand. He was standing over a depression in the ground that had likely overflowed with water a few weeks before, but now only a shallow layer of water a few spans in diameter peacefully reflected the clear blue sky.

"You have an idea?" Valzaan asked.

"I do." Garin said, but he did not turn or come toward them. Rather, he lifted his foot and then carefully set it down in the water, near the shallow edge of the pool. He gazed down at it for a moment and then looked up and smiled. It was a rare display, and both Valzaan and Benjiah drew closer.

The garrion had only just come to rest on the ground, but Valzaan had already opened the door and was moving out. Garin and Benjiah followed closely behind, and they looked up to see the impressive sight of the Vulsutyrim running toward them across the open plain.

It was only late morning, far too early to stop for the day, but Valzaan had insisted they be flown to the giants as soon as possible so that they could put Garin's idea to Amontyr. After all, without the Vulsutyrim to do most of the work, there was no plan.

The giants slowed to a walk as they approached the three men and the dragon, who stood silent and still beside the garrion. They followed Amontyr, who went directly to Valzaan. "Prophet of Allfather, you have come to speak with me?"

"Yes, Amontyr," Valzaan answered, "with you and with all of your brothers. Garin has shared with us a plan to bring down the Kumatin, and we thought it best to bring the plan to you to see what you think."

The giant looked from Valzaan to the stocky man standing silently between the two prophets. "Go on."

Garin began walking away from them across the plain toward another slight depression filled with water. Benjiah and Valzaan followed him without comment, as did the giants. When Garin reached the small pool of water, he hesitated and started looking around through the tall grass. It took a few moments, but eventually he found what he was looking for, a large stone partially buried in the soft dirt.

"Come, Benjiah," Garin said, motioning to him, "help me with the stone."

Benjiah helped Garin dig around the stone to loosen it. Soon they had excavated it completely, and Garin rolled it up out of the ground and toward the pool.

"Do you need help?" Amontyr asked, and Benjiah wondered if there wasn't some amusement in his voice. He looked up at the giant but could see no hint of insincerity or mockery. In fact, none of the Vulsutyrim faces showed any signs of emotion or impatience.

"Thank you, no," Garin answered. "But if you will hear me out, I'm ready."

Garin came around and stood between the large stone and the small pool. "The Kumatin is nearly unstoppable while submerged in the water, and the Barunaan, though its levels are receding, is still more than deep enough for him to hide in all the way south if he chooses. The problem before us, then, is how to get the Kumatin to come out of the river where he is vulnerable. Would you say this is a fair statement of the situation?"

"It is fair," Amontyr answered.

"Well," Garin continued, "the more I thought about the problem, the more impossible it seemed. The dragons are almost wholly ineffective in water, and almost certainly they cannot go into the Barunaan after this creature and hope to come out again.

"As for you," Garin continued, motioning to show that he meant the whole assembly of Vulsutyrim, "while you may not struggle with water as much as the dragons, the deepest parts of the river are over your head. How you could succeed in forcing the Kumatin out of the water by wading into it, I cannot imagine, though perhaps you have thought of something I haven't."

Amontyr did not speak, so Garin went on. "Anyway, it occurred to me this morning that I was looking at the problem the wrong way. The problem is to get the Kumatin into an exposed position, and if we can't go in and get him, perhaps we can make him come to us."

"And just how do you propose to do this?"

"We lay a trap in the Barunaan," Garin said, and moving back around to the other side of the rock, he lifted it and pushed it over until it rolled down the side of the slight depression into the small pool. It fell with a splash into the water, almost completely submerged with its top sticking out just as it had been in the ground.

"You want to dam the river?" Amontyr asked, looking from the water to Garin, a hint of puzzlement on his face.

"No, not as such," Garin answered. "I don't know that we could do it in time, certainly not well enough that the Kumatin couldn't just break through it and continue on his merry way. He ripped through the walls of Cimaris Rul, so I've heard, and I doubt we could erect anything so sturdy in time. No, my idea is less ambitious and less direct."

"Then what do you propose?"

"About midway down the Barunaan between the Kellisor Sea and the Southern Ocean is a town named Vol Tumian, just north of Elnin Wood. Like Peris Mil, my home, it must have been largely below water at the height of the flooding, and almost certainly its inhabitants have fled for higher ground. My idea is that we take every last brick and stone and even timber in that city and submerge them in the Barunaan over as great a distance as we dare. Submerge it all until the displaced water extends far over the banks in both directions. What do we care how far the water spreads? The river can be as *broad* as it likes so long as it isn't *deep*. When the Kumatin reaches Vol Tumian, he'll be forced to move through the artificially shallow stretch that we've created, and when he does, then you and the dragons can coordinate your attack to take advantage of his exposure."

Amontyr knelt down beside the pool and reached into it, taking up the stone that Garin had struggled to roll. "The Barunaan will not be so easily plugged as this small pool of water."

"No," Garin replied. "It won't."

"We will need days in advance of the Kumatin to have even a hope of being ready for it. I don't know if we can get there in time."

"This is why," Valzaan said, "I have sent word to Sulmandir that he and his sons may need to carry you and most of your brothers ahead to the town. It will likely take two sorties to do it, but they have agreed to try."

"They have agreed to carry us?" Amontyr asked, setting the stone back down and standing up again.

"Yes," Valzaan said. "Each dragon could take one of you at a time, though Sulmandir acknowledged they will need time to recover after each effort. Some should remain behind to spur the creature on and keep him moving forward even when he comes upon the trap. A small band of giants pursuing him will be invaluable. We'll have to coordinate the timing carefully and there is much that could go wrong, but it seems to me the best idea we're likely to have."

"If we have time enough to lay the trap, it might work. It would certainly be easier to attack in water shallow enough to keep our feet beneath us. That way, the dragons could help from the beginning as well. If we all descended upon the Kumatin together, even it could not stop us all."

"No," Valzaan agreed. "I think not, and I have some first-hand knowledge of this creature's strength."

"We will do what we can to move the available rubble into the river, but until we see the town, I can say no more." Amontyr said. "When will Sulmandir and his sons come to take the first group of us?"

"They have been scouting the river ahead of the Kumatin and are far ahead already, but they should be here any time now. Keep moving south, and they will meet you on your way."

"Then we will see you in Vol Tumian," Amontyr said, and he started running south with the other Vulsutyrim running along behind him.

Benjiah watched the powerful strides of the Vulsutyrim, their hair flowing out behind them as they ran.

"Are you coming?" Garin asked, and Benjiah turned to see Valzaan almost back at the garrion already.

"Yes," Benjiah answered. As they walked back to the garrion together, he said, "It will be a thing to see, won't it?"

"What will?"

"The Vulsutyrim, moving a whole town from beside the river to the bottom of it."

"Yes," Garin agreed. "It will be a thing to see."

Benjiah sat beside the still-swollen waters of the Barunaan. He didn't know the river well, certainly not this far south, but he was pretty sure that the place where he was sitting had been for most of Kirthanin's history well back from the river's edge. He was pretty sure in part because of the smattering of small trees that doggedly protruded from the water some ten or more spans away. While they might be remarkable in that they fought to live in their new predicament, they were not so remarkable that they had sprung as seedlings from the waters of the Barunaan.

It was approaching Fifth Hour, and the midmorning sun glowed brightly in the sky. Bright and hot, Benjiah thought, as he wiped sweat from his brow. Though born on the first day of Summer Rise, Benjiah, like his grandfather Monias, had always thought Autumn was the best of all the seasons. The remarkable colors that appeared in earth and sky as a tribute to the failing year, the crisp coolness that blew with the Autumn wind, the relief from the heat of summer—he loved all these. And yet, even as he sat sweating in the hot sun, he could not wish the day other than it was. Though he did not love the heat, and the burning brightness of the sun made it hard for him to look into the expansive sky, he was glad of it all the same. Spring Wane was passing and summer would soon be here. The heat was part of the natural progression of seasons, and as such, it spoke to Benjiah of the reign and rule of Allfather over the heavens and the earth. The storm with which Cheimontyr deluged Kirthanin was a malicious aberration. This heat and light was a gracious gift, despite Benjiah's personal preferences.

The river glistened, and Benjiah admired its shimmering flow. His mind reached back for days that seemed longer ago than they really were, days when he'd been able to sit long hours in forest glades and beside babbling brooks with nothing more on his mind than the beauty of his surroundings. Some days he contemplated the slow movement of the sun across the sky, the shifting shape and sizes of clouds as they appeared on the horizon, or even the way the wind whisked playfully through the grass of an open plain. He believed such days would return for Kirthanin. He was convinced of that. Allfather was bringing to pass even now what all had yearned for, the final defeat of Malek and the restoration of all things. He didn't know exactly how it would all be accomplished, but that didn't prevent him from believing firmly that it would be. What Benjiah did not know, and what was increasingly in his thoughts, was whether such days would return for him. The sun might be rising over Kirthanin's future, but a dark cloud hung over his own. The thought of facing it was hard, but the thought of facing it alone was worse.

He rose and turned back toward Vol Tumian, or at least, toward what had once been Vol Tumian. The town no longer existed in any functional sense. In places here and there, partial structures still existed on dry ground, but for the most part, the visible components of the town had already been forcibly removed and were either on their way toward the Barunaan or already submerged in it.

The work of the Vulsutyrim had indeed been something for Benjiah to see. They'd begun to arrive in Vol Tumian on the evening of the fifteenth day of Spring Wane. Though little daylight remained, some of the giants immediately surveyed the town. They examined the structures and scavenged for things like rope, logs, and poles on which to roll what they were removing, and more. All was in adequate if not plentiful supply. As a port town on a river, rope was not hard to come by, but many of the mooring lines and ropes used to help river barges negotiate the extensive port system of Vol Tumian had been submerged for a long time. The long-term soaking had rotted some to the point of uselessness. A similar situation existed for the logs and poles, but Elnin Wood was not too far south and trees grew in clusters not far from Vol Tumian. Accordingly, some of the Vulsutyrim began immediately to harvest timber for the work.

Other Vulsutyrim ignored the town altogether and went immediately to the river. They waded in and took measurements of relative depth as they sought to figure out the width of the section where the Kumatin could fully submerge, and how much of the surface expanse covered places already shallow enough to expose the creature. They moved farther and farther from shore until at last they could not stand and so dove, over and over again, swimming to the bottom in order to survey the channels of the great river.

It was well after dark before all the Vulsutyrim quit for the day, and by sunrise on the following day, the work began in earnest. Now, on the third full day of labor since arriving in Vol Tumian, the eighteenth day of Spring Wane, Benjiah could see the enormous progress that had been made. As

Benjiah understood it from Garin, a stretch of the Barunaan close to thirty spans long had been sufficiently clogged with debris that there was no way for the Kumatin to pass through without being exposed. The Vulsutyrim had placed the materials in the river to preserve channels of open space perhaps a span or so wide here and there. These trenches were too small for the Kumatin to pass through but were useful for the Vulsutyrim, enabling them to cover more total area with the trap. Their goal was to create a zone some fifty spans long, but Benjiah feared that there was insufficient supply to meet that goal. If the Kumatin did not hesitate as he passed over the debris, there would not be much time for the dragons and giants to ambush him.

The Kumatin had to pause, though. The sheer bizarreness of the situation would surely make the creature pause. Even if he suspected danger in the rocks and stones piled on the bottom of the river, he would surely be cautious in approaching what to do about it. If he tried while submerged to simply push through the obstruction, he would find the mass of it too great to move entirely. Sooner or later, the creature would realize that if he wanted to continue south, he'd have to go over, and when he did, the dragons and Vulsutyrim would be ready.

The main fear, other than the fear that the creature might overcome their trap, was that he would turn back toward the Kellisor Sea. His turning north might be a short-term victory of sorts, but it would only delay the necessary confrontation. After all, if the Kumatin did elude them, he could try via the Kalamin to reach open water again. No one relished the thought of another long journey to build a similar trap in order to keep him from reaching the ocean in that direction.

Benjiah walked toward the excavations going on in Vol Tumian. Several Vulsutyrim had spent a portion of the previous evening retrieving great trees from Gyrin and then shaping them into enormous levers to pry up the buildings' foundations. Though many buildings in Suthanin were designed with cellars for cool storage in the warm climate, the buildings of Vol Tumian generally were not. Like any riverside town, the possibility of flooding meant that paying too much attention to ground floor or cellar storage wasn't especially wise. Most people of Vol Tumian stored their cherished goods well above ground level.

This also meant that many of the larger buildings were built on foundation stones and slabs of substantial size and weight. These foundations were the anchors, as it were, keeping Vol Tumian safe from the vicissitudes of the Barunaan. They did the job admirably; many of the houses and buildings, though not those closest to the water's edge, had survived the rising waters of the previous season. Now those same buildings, which had resisted being pulled into the river by the floodwaters, were forcibly placed there by the Vulsutyrim, and the foundations that anchored them were soon to follow.

Benjiah surveyed the Vulsutyrim at work. Some were busy trying to pry up more stone, others were engaged in carrying and rolling it down to the water's edge, and still more were in the water, actively working on setting the materials just so on the river bottom. Benjiah felt, as he had most of the last three days, like he wasn't serving much of a purpose. He knew that it was best for him to simply stay out of the way, and that he was here for other reasons, but it didn't make him feel entirely better. The dragons helped with the early work of demolishing what was left of the standing buildings, and they were further engaged in scouting from high above the Barunaan. They wanted to keep watch over the creature's progress and gather any information that might help them should the trap fail and the Kumatin escape.

Even Garin had found something useful to do, as he began surveying the outlying areas in search of any stone formations that might be quarried for the work. He found some rocks and stones of moderate size, and though nothing grand, Benjiah imagined it helped him to feel useful.

Benjiah appointed himself as a sort of watchman, and he spent much of the last three days beside the river, keeping an eye on the Barunaan as far north as he could. He frequently moved between this job and seeking out windhovers to help him locate the Kumatin and track its progress, but as the creature seemed to be virtually crawling down the river, it was a tedious task.

"Deep in thought, Benjiah?" Valzaan said from behind him.

Benjiah turned to see the prophet standing a few spans away. "Yes, I suppose so. Not much else to do these days but think."

"Well," Valzaan said, "the time for action will come soon enough. Have you seen the Kumatin today?"

"Yes, and he's not much farther along than he was yesterday. What's he doing, Valzaan?"

"Do you mean why isn't he moving faster?"

"Yes. I know we've discussed this, but if I were fleeing to the ocean, I'd be doing it faster than this. He certainly doesn't seem to be all that eager to get there."

"The creature almost certainly doesn't believe itself to be in any danger, so why rush?"

"But the Bringer of Storms is dead. Isn't it afraid?"

"We can't even be sure it knows about that. In fact, it might have been the plan from the beginning to flood Kirthanin so the thing could enter the Kellisor Sea and help Malek with his conquest, then return to the ocean. Who knows?"

Benjiah rubbed his hands through his hair. "Even if that is the case, why go so slowly? It's like he's deliberately slowing himself down so that it takes longer."

"I think that's true."

"But why?"

"I think it's going as slowly as it can because it's doing what it was made to do. It's eating whatever is close enough to be eaten, uprooting whatever is close enough to uproot, and knocking down whatever can be knocked down. It is a creature designed to destroy, and that is precisely what it is doing. Rushing back fearfully to the ocean is not what it is thinking."

"That may prove a catastrophic mistake," Benjiah said, then added, "for the Kumatin, I mean."

"Let us hope it does."

Benjiah lay against the side of the trench the Vulsutyrim had dug a couple days before. With the work on the river bottom complete, the giants had turned their attention to preparing the ambush, and this trench and another like it on the far side of the river were the result.

The trenches were very deep, perhaps three spans from top to bottom, and Benjiah lay near the top so he could peek out between the tall grass that grew along the ridge. Unless the Kumatin came down the river raised to his full height, he would not be able to see the trenches. About twenty Vulsutyrim lay on either side of the Barunaan waiting for him.

Valzaan and Benjiah both believed the Kumatin would arrive today. Amontyr had been in contact via Sulmandir with the party of Vulsutyrim who were following the Kumatin down the river. They knew at what point they were to initiate hostilities with the Kumatin. They were armed with spears to try to penetrate the creature's thick scales, so there was some hope they would strike a solid first blow to the sea monster.

Of course, wounding the Kumatin was a secondary goal. Their primary goal was to anger, fluster, and if fortunate, frighten the creature. Any confusion and perhaps panic they could generate in the Kumatin before it reached the trap in the river was desirable. In the best of all possible scenarios, the Kumatin would move cautiously out onto the debris, angered by the unexpected attack of the Vulsutyrim and annoyed by his inability to simply submerge and leave the trouble behind. Then, as he moved hesitantly, the hidden Vulsutyrim would launch their attack, aided by dragons swooping from high above where neither man nor giant nor sea monster could see them.

This was the plan, a plan that all of them had been over again and again, both quietly in their own minds and collectively. It was hard not to be confident, but that was itself a fear. *When you think you've thought of everything*, Benjiah reflected, *that's when you've surely missed something.* Or at least that was what he feared.

It was early afternoon on the twenty-second day of Spring Wane, and it was by all appearances a peaceful day. Benjiah allowed his mind to wander, and he found himself wondering what was going on in the north. He wondered if Aljeron had caught up with Malek's forces, or if the latter had succeeded in reaching Gyrin without battle. He had hoped that the Kumatin would move faster and that this matter would be resolved favorably by now. He hoped to return north and aid in the battle, to arrive with many dragons and bring help to the Kirthanim there. If things went well here today, they might yet arrive in time to help. How likely that was, Benjiah couldn't say. They'd all been so preoccupied these last several days that none of them really spoke much of matters in the north. Benjiah had seen the Kirthanim army through the eyes of a windhover moving around Amaan Sul, but that had been six days ago on their first full day in Vol Tumian.

A great bellowing howl shattered the silence of the hot afternoon, and Benjiah's thoughts returned to the river. He peered out at the placid water. There was no sign of the Kumatin.

His mind reached out for a windhover, and he found one. The falcon soared high above the river, moving upstream.

Soon, he found what he was looking for. Vulsutyrim, moving along either bank, were running, some with spears in hand. The Kumatin was thrashing about in the middle of the river. It appeared to Benjiah that it was trying to reach a shaft partially buried in his side. One of the spears of the Vulsutyrim had struck home.

In a moment, the Kumatin removed the spear and smashed it into splinters with its great, clawlike webbed hand. The creature, now facing north, stopped thrashing and shot up out of the water, lashing out first to his right at the giants on the east bank and then at the giants on the left bank. These latter were surprised by how quickly the Kumatin reversed himself, and two of them were crushed by a powerful downward stroke. The others recovered quickly and threw their spears. The weapons struck but fell to the water, and as quickly as he had attacked them, the creature leaped southward into the water, disappearing beneath the surface and leaving nothing but ripples behind.

"He's coming," Benjiah whispered to the Vulsutyrim nearby.

"How long?"

"Not long," Benjiah answered. The point designated for the Vulsutyrim to attack the Kumatin was just a few hundred spans beyond a slight bend in the river, which marked the farthest point north they could see from Vol Tumian. Benjiah shivered as he realized that even now, somewhere out there under the water's surface, the creature was likely speeding toward them.

Then he saw the waves, unmistakably moving toward both riverbanks and growing in size. The Vulsutyrim had seen it as well, and he could feel them strain at the edge of the trench, waiting for what the creature would do. Their brothers appeared around the river bend, running south as they had been instructed to do, hoping to deter the creature from turning back when he encountered the debris.

The rippling waves moved farther and farther south until they spread out sideways over the obstacle. Benjiah waited, holding his breath, staring at the water. Nothing happened. In fact, if anything, the waves seemed to be smaller, and the surface of the water was calmer.

He looked upstream to see if there were any signs that the creature had reversed itself, but he could see none. The Vulsutyrim in pursuit had slowed to a walk some fifty spans upstream, and Benjiah could see that they had the same thought he did, for they moved cautiously, peering into the water, looking for evidence the Kumatin was coming their direction.

For a long, dreadful moment, there was silence and stillness, and panic spread through Benjiah's mind in half a dozen different ways. Perhaps the creature had disappeared upstream before any of them had noticed, or perhaps he'd shoved the debris aside with little difficulty and slipped downstream without revealing even a single hand-width of his ugly exterior. Surely something had gone wrong.

Then the Kumatin shot upward out of the water. Water sprayed outward in every direction as the creature stood, his head and torso and arms completely exposed. The Vulsutyrim did not move. Their discipline was impeccable. They were waiting, as they must, for the creature to move forward onto the debris so that he might not easily evade their attack.

Benjiah peered up at the towering form, incredible in its size and strength. Water shimmered all over the creature's body, which seemed almost black in the bright sun, a striking contrast with the bright blue sky. Benjiah held his breath in wonder as he gazed upward, reminded afresh of the Kumatin's immensity.

And then it happened: the creature began to slide forward on top of the stone that littered the river's bottom. His front arms reached out and pulled him across the artificially shallow Barunaan. At last, his legs appeared and he was spread out fully as they had all hoped he would be, visible fully except for his long dark tail, which still lay in the deeper waters.

The Vulsutyrim leapt up and out of the trench. There was no battle cry, for it would have been foolish to give the creature warning. Even so, the sight of the giants sweeping in a line toward the water's edge with swords and iron spears raised was magnificent to see. Benjiah followed more slowly with Garin, for Valzaan, who was on the other side of the Barunaan with the other Vulsutyrim, had been clear that Benjiah was to stay well back from the water's edge.

The giants on both sides reached the river and splashed through the shallows toward the great beast. The Kumatin raised himself up as though on his knees and swung a massive claw toward the line of Vulsutyrim approaching from Benjiah's side. As they were almost waist deep in the water, it was a devastating blow. They could not move fast enough to dodge it, and they were not able to withstand it. Four or five of them were flung well upstream, and by the look of them in the air, Benjiah believed they were dead already.

And yet again, the Vulsutyrim showed their remarkable discipline. The giants near this stroke who nevertheless avoided it, drove toward the extended arm, and Benjiah saw them drive at least a few swords and spears into it. Another bellowing howl confirmed that their strokes hit home, and the backlash of the arm knocked another couple of Vulsutyrim away.

The creature writhed and swung to face the far bank, but Benjiah couldn't see exactly what was going on. What he did see was a host of golden flashes falling out of the sky with remarkable speed. The dragons were coming.

They sped downward, their great wings outstretched as they shot toward the dark, immense form of the Kumatin. Without any forewarning that Benjiah could see, the creature leapt from where he stood on the east side of the river. His outstretched hand reached for one of the dragons and closed upon it. At the same time, blasts of fire from the others swirled about his body so that he was lost for a moment in flame and smoke. Even so, as the flame and smoke cleared, Benjiah saw him still standing on the debris of Vol Tumian, unaffected, his great hands wringing the long neck of the dragon he'd caught. He flung it away, and it landed in a golden heap, half-submerged in the shallows.

Benjiah was stunned—not that the Kumatin had killed a dragon, he'd seen that before. He was stunned that the blasts of fire had not hurt the Kumatin more. He felt a surge of despair. If the dragons couldn't do more damage than this, what hope did they have of stopping the creature from crossing the short trap?

As though on cue, the creature turned back southward and moved in that direction carefully. The Kumatin was fully aware this was a trap laid for him. He was being attacked from both sides and above, and he was only vulnerable because he had been forced out of the water. Intuitively, he must have realized that the trap could not be large. Further south, the waters of the river would offer both protection and an uninterrupted passageway to the Southern Ocean.

The Vulsutyrim on Benjiah's side of the Barunaan renewed their attempts to slow the creature. The Kumatin's eyes and arms seemed focused on the dragons, but he brought his massive tail to bear against the giants, and it came whipping just a half a span above the surface of the river. Benjiah watched several Vulsutyrim submerge themselves to avoid the blow, while others moved closer to the body, hoping the stroke couldn't reach the monster's side. The tail swept back and Benjiah saw that it spanned almost the whole distance from the Kumatin to the riverbank, and he was glad he was well back from the water. He would not have survived the blow had he been struck by it.

BROKEN

As it retracted, several Vulsutyrim leapt out of the water onto the tail, and a handful managed to gain a tenuous position on top of it. Benjiah watched them, holding on for dear life and stabbing downward repeatedly. Again came the howl, and the Kumatin instinctively turned his body toward the near bank where the giants had leapt upon his tail. The tail thrashed wildly out of Benjiah's sight, but when the Kumatin turned southward again, the giants were no longer there.

For a brief moment, the Kumatin appeared to have an unimpeded path. Several dragons swooped, blowing fire at the back of the Kumatin's head, but as before, the fire failed to do anything that Benjiah could see to hurt or halt the creature's movements. Now the dragons were regrouping, and the number of Vulstuyrim available to actively oppose the creature had been reduced. It was far harder for them to keep pace with the Kumatin in the waist-deep water. As Benjiah stood on the bank, the Kumatin dropped back onto all fours and pulled itself across the debris toward the open river.

Then, just as it appeared to Benjiah that the creature would slip past the trap into deeper waters, the Kumatin hesitated. Benjiah could not see why. The giants were struggling to regroup and the dragons were circling above. What was holding the creature back?

The Kumatin's massive head swiveled toward the eastern bank. The deep dark eyes covered with a slightly grey film peered down at Benjiah. They were peering at him, Benjiah realized—not Garin or the remains of Vol Tumian or anything else—at him. For a moment Benjiah froze. The Kumatin's stare held him fixed to the spot, and unable to move, Benjiah watched the creature turn away from the south, away from the open river and freedom, toward the very place where he stood. A wave of fear washed over him, but as quickly as it came it left. He felt rushing in behind it a wave of light and heat, such as he had felt before in the dragon tower, on the plain beside the Kalamin, and above Tol Emuna. He felt a surge of joy and power, and raising his arms to shoulder height as the Kumatin came closer, he swept them forward until his hands met in a thunderous clap. What happened next he found hard to describe afterward. Something like a ripple of air, but more than air, like a rip through the very fabric of the air, shot forward from his hands across the surface of the Barunaan at the Kumatin. Benjiah could see it move, like a wave rippling through the open sky, distorting the objects on the other side of it, namely the Kumatin. It struck the Kumatin squarely in the chest and sent the creature reeling. It teetered for a brief moment, then fell backward with a splash into the water.

Benjiah watched as the golden forms flying above seized on that opportunity and flew down like carrion from a distant treetop. They fell upon the Kumatin's head, arms, legs, tail and torso, upon every exposed piece and patch. Talons and teeth ripped into the creature again and again. Twice more the bellowing howl of the creature rang out over the expanse of the Barunaan waters, then there was relative silence. A few moments later, the dragons left their bloody perches on the Kumatin's body, and the creature's corpse lay unmoving upon the artificial river bottom of the stones of Vol Tumian.

The rush of light and heat that had filled Benjiah was gone, and he sank to his knees on the ground beside the river, awash with relief that the Kumatin was dead.

5

SAEGAN

THE EVENING WAS WARM, though it wouldn't have mattered much if it wasn't. Leaving the campfires behind each night to walk alone a while was just part of his routine, and Saegan didn't really care what temperature it was.

In Nolthanin, things had been different. He'd not wandered far from their fires then, not because of the cold, but because he felt it wouldn't be safe to leave Cinjan and Synoki alone with the others for too long. This was especially true after Evrim lost his arm. In short, the common good had militated against his indulgence of habit for a while, but now he was free to be himself. So he walked on, moving north of the camp and enjoying the warm evening air.

He didn't turn to look at what lay behind him. He didn't need to. Dotting the horizon would be the scattered campfires of the Kirthanim. The men, and in some cases women, who sat around those fires would be talking, perhaps late into the night. They would talk of almost anything, save only the long march and the enemy they pursued. Of that they would not speak, because to do so would invite the many fears they held at bay to come in closer and stay awhile, and if they did that, then they would not sleep. No, they would talk as though they sat here on this empty plain north of Amaan Sul for no greater reason than to enjoy the warm spring air, and then they would each lie down and close their eyes, where at last they could not fill completely the empty spaces with idle chatter.

Saegan understood the routine of the camp; he just couldn't endure it without the respite of these quiet walks. His soul craved silence and solitude, which was hard to obtain when marching with an army. That was a large reason why he had taken the post as a captain of the scouts during the early years of the war against Fel Edorath. As a scout, his work required silence and stealth, and even when he traveled with the other scouts, silence was usually not hard to find. Bryar on the other hand, well, she'd had her reasons too.

He remembered the day when Bryar went to Aljeron. The Assembly had sanctioned Aljeron's request that military action be taken against Fel Edorath if the city would not produce Rulalin in chains to stand trial for the murder of Joraiem. Many believed that the simple threat of war would break down Fel Edorath's stubbornness, but when it became apparent that actual fighting was required, Aljeron began to build his army.

Saegan, with his parents both dead, no siblings and no wife, rode west from the Assembly with Aljeron to lend what aid he could. He was with Gilion and Aljeron when Bryar came to see them, asking that she be allowed to march with the army, and Aljeron refused. Bryar did not take no for an answer. They went back and forth, not exactly angrily, but they were two strong-willed people with a lot of determination and not much willingness to yield on either side.

It was Saegan who suggested Bryar serve under him with the scouts. His rationale was simple. If Aljeron objected to thrusting Bryar into the heart of battle, then perhaps she could serve alongside him in a position that was more . . . indirect. Aljeron objected along predictable lines, specifically that serving with the scouts could be just as dangerous as the normal infantry, however indirect their engagements might be. Even so, Saegan pressed him to see that this was a way to utilize Bryar's acknowledged ability without putting a woman in the front lines, something Aljeron was reluctant to do. Whatever these wild Kalin Seir practiced, it was not the Kirthanim way to send women off to battle. Yes, Bryar fought alongside both Saegan and Aljeron on the Forbidden Isle, but that was an unforeseen conflict. Any man or woman would have been justified in taking up the sword in a situation like that. In the end, Bryar received her commission as a captain of the scouts under Saegan, and for seven long years they served in the saddle together, first against Fel Edorath and ultimately against Malek.

Why was Bryar so eager to join the war? At first, Saegan assumed what everyone else who knew her did, that she was weary of life and sought an honorable way to lose it. To be sure, her conduct in battle suggested a certain disregard for her own safety, but this could just as easily be explained by the simple fact that Bryar was courageous. In fact, during their service together, Saegan came to see that she was as courageous as any man in the army, himself included. He came to see that it wasn't desire for death that motivated her. No, much like Aljeron himself, she was driven by a deeply rooted hunger for justice.

Though Rulalin's murder of Joraiem was not in any way connected to Kelvan's death in the streets of Nal Gildoroth, the two events had in some strange way become connected in Bryar's mind over the years. Perhaps it was because both had died so close together, or perhaps it was because, having lost her own love, she identified strongly with Wylla. Saegan suspected that whatever the reason ultimately was, Bryar herself probably did not fully understand it. What was clear, though, was bringing Rulalin to justice became for Bryar a case of avenging Kelvan. So, while Aljeron, Evrim, Brenim, and the others fought for Joraiem's memory and honor, Bryar carried Kelvan with her into battle in much the same way.

That she carried Kelvan in her heart was something Saegan learned the hard way. As they served together, Saegan fell in love with her. Perhaps it was her stoic nature, quiet and assured and in so many ways like his. Perhaps it was a growing appreciation for her intensity, drive, and sadness. Perhaps it was simply being in close quarters all the time. Whatever it was that attracted him, love had come as something of a surprise. Saegan spent little of his first thirty-plus years thinking of things familial. And yet, he reached a point during the third year of their campaign against Fel Edorath when he could no longer deny his feelings. When he finally admitted it to himself, he decided not to delay but take the situation directly to Bryar. They were straightforward people, and whatever she might say, Saegan had no doubt that speaking openly about it with her was the right thing to do.

That night, a cool night in Autumn Rise, he asked Bryar to accompany him on his walk near the scouts' camp. As they walked, talk came, to his surprise, easier than usual. They were neither one loquacious, but this night they talked and laughed with ease. Mistakenly, Saegan took this as confirmation that Bryar was aware of his intentions and felt much the same way.

He stopped walking and turned to Bryar, saying abruptly as he changed topics, "When this war with Fel Edorath is over, Bryar, let's get married."

She looked at him wide-eyed, and he either did not see or did not heed the wariness bordering on dismay that must have appeared on her face. All he saw were her eyes, gazing intently into his, and he leaned in to kiss her.

Their lips met, but he realized immediately that something was wrong. He pulled back and saw at last the truth of the situation. As he looked at her, understanding dawned on him, even as Bryar took a step back. "I'm sorry, Saegan, I can't do that."

He watched her walk away in the darkness, and the next day they returned to business as usual. They never spoke of that night, and as time went on, Saegan, by sheer strength of will, put away any thought of Bryar as something more than a friend and fellow officer in Aljeron's army. At least, he put it mostly away. Every so often, perhaps a handful of times each year, he'd find himself gazing at her, and he'd chastise himself for indulging in fantasy and turn his attention to something else. Almost five years had passed between that night and this one, and Saegan could think of it for the most part dispassionately.

Saegan had known of men disappointed in love who carried around their disappointment like a burden, weighing them down at every turn. They were often poor company, allowing a shade of bitterness to creep into all their conversation. Saegan was determined that he would not be such a man. They were, after all, prosecuting a war in order to apprehend a man who had murdered his friend over a lost love. Accordingly, Saegan never breathed a word of either his interest in or rejection by Bryar to anyone, and he was reasonably sure she never did either. To his friends, he was simply a confirmed bachelor, at home in the saddle and the martial world of the battlefield, uninterested in or unfit for all things domestic.

Saegan stopped walking. He had probably gone far enough from the Kirthanim camp. Still, he hesitated before turning back and stood, gazing eastward. Somewhere out there, the great walls of Tol Emuna stood. Whatever else Malek and his minions had taken from the Kirthanim and even from his fellow sons and daughters of Tol Emuna, the city still stood. Of that, he was justifiably proud.

And yet, so much had been lost in this catastrophic war. The toll in both lives and destruction was high, and Saegan felt again the fiery anger welling up in him. He hated Malek and all that the fallen Titan represented with a passion. It was time he was stopped. It was time he was killed. Saegan drew his sword and felt the warm steel with his fingertip. He was fortunate to own an Azmavarim, and every time he wielded the Firstblade in battle, he was most grateful. Even so, he wanted nothing more than to finish what they had started, so he could lay it down once and for all.

Malek had to be stopped, and soon. Saegan hated the thought that he and his hordes might escape into the Mountain, where they would be extremely difficult to root out and defeat. However, in order to be stopped, the enemy had first to be caught, and there was no good news on that front as yet.

Saegan turned and walked back toward the camp. He would approach Aljeron in the morning. It had to be done.

On the morning of the seventeenth day of Spring Wane, Saegan arrived early at Aljeron's tent. Inside, Evrim was already sitting with Aljeron, and they were talking quietly, for Aelwyn was still asleep. Aljeron pointed Saegan toward an empty seat at the table. Saegan entered but did not accept the offered seat.

Aljeron looked curiously up at him. "What's on your mind, Saegan?"

"We have to catch Malek's army before Gyrin."

"That's just what we were discussing," Aljeron said, looking over at Evrim.

"You have good news then?"

"No," Aljeron answered. "None. We're no closer than we were."

"Then you were discussing an idea to close the gap?"

"No," Aljeron replied again, shaking his head. "We were simply acknowledging that we are moving as fast as we can if we hope to be in fighting condition, should we catch our enemy."

Saegan nodded. "It is as I thought."

"Then what did you have in mind?" Aljeron asked. "You wouldn't come simply to tell us what we already know."

"No, I didn't." Saegan replied.

"Then?"

"Give me permission to take the scouts. We can ride much faster than the army can march. We'll arc around below the enemy until we are between them and Gyrin."

"You must be joking," Evrim said at this, incredulous.

"I am not joking."

"You'll be overrun," Aljeron said, echoing Evrim's disbelief.

"We won't be."

"Saegan," Aljeron said, "no one knows better than I how capable you are. You're the best captain I have, without question. But there are not enough of you to stand between our enemy and Gyrin. You will be overrun."

"No, we won't be," Saegan repeated. "because we aren't going to stop Malek's army, just slow him down. We'll harry them, not enough to engage in any real battles, but enough that they have to progress more slowly, put up their guard. While they're doing that, you'll catch them. You'll catch them, and together, then, we'll destroy them."

Aljeron stood. "You're sure you want to do this?"

"Yes."

"You know the risks. It won't be as easy as you make it sound."

"I know, but it needs to be done."

Extending his hand, Aljeron clasped Saegan's hand tightly. "Go, as soon as you're ready, and may Allfather go with you."

Evrim rose and walked to Saegan, then placed his arm around him and hugged him for a moment. Standing back, he said, "We'll see you in a few days."

"Until then," Saegan said, then he turned and left the tent.

He made his way quickly through the camp. The sun was just peeking up over the eastern horizon, but Saegan thought he could feel already that it would be a hot day. Even so, it would feel good to finally be in the saddle and to ride hard. He passed the tents at the edge of the encampment and approached Bryar, wisps of her brown hair fluttering in the morning breeze as she held the reins to her horse and his. She watched him with her nearly expressionless face and then handed him his reins when he drew near enough to take them.

"Well?" she asked.

"We ride," Saegan said, and mounted.

Aelwyn sat on the ground inside the tent she shared with Aljeron and, most nights, with Koshti as well. At the moment, the tiger lay curled up at her feet, and she was running her hands through the soft fur on top of his head. The great cat had his eyes closed and was, by all appearances, sleeping peacefully.

Aljeron knew he wasn't asleep though, the same way he knew when Koshti was tired, on edge, or hungry. Aljeron turned back to the world beyond the tent, gazing out into the darkness. Another day of marching and still no sign of the enemy. Another day, and still no word from the south.

"Aljeron?"

"Yes?" he said, turning back toward his wife and battle brother.

"Do you still want to be off before dawn?"

"Yes," Aljeron said, nodding in understanding. "I'll come to bed now."

"What's on your mind?"

"Only the usual," he replied as he sat down beside her. "I am anxious that we are so close to Gyrin and haven't caught our enemy. I am anxious with each day that passes without word from Suthanin. It's the twenty-second of Spring Wane. There should be some word from Benjiah and Valzaan by now."

Aelwyn put her hand on his. "You know they can take care of themselves. Perhaps there is no news yet because there is nothing to report, good or bad. Perhaps no news is nothing sinister, maybe it just means there really is no news. Even if something catastrophic had happened, someone would have survived to bring us word, don't you think?"

"Yes," Aljeron sighed. "I know you're right, but it is so hard not to know."

"I know," Aelwyn agreed, "but you have enough on your plate right now without worrying about them."

She stroked Aljeron's hair. "Do you still think tomorrow is the day we will catch Malek's army?"

"It has to be. When we stopped tonight, the dragon said we are only a few hours behind. We're only a few hours behind, and they are less than a day from Gyrin. If we don't catch them tomorrow, we won't catch them before they reach the Mountain."

"Then what you need is sleep."

"I know, but I don't know if I can."

"Lie down, and see what comes."

Aljeron lay down and Aelwyn curled up beside him, leaning her head against him. They lay together in the dark tent until he could hear her smooth, rhythmic breathing. He listened to her and looked through the shadows at her beautiful face and her soft brown hair. He gazed at her, but his mind soon wandered through the darkness toward the Forest of Gyrin.

The next day, the twenty-third of Spring Wane, they were on their way west before dawn as Aljeron had ordered. By Second Hour, they had been on the move for some time and covered many leagues. The signs that Malek's hosts had recently moved through the same area were unmistakable. They'd not been this close before. If the Kirthanim pressed hard today, they just might catch the enemy after all.

A dragon came swooping down from the sky, and Aljeron broke off from the army. The beast descended quickly in a broad arc, and Aljeron could see the faintest glint of blue in his scales as they caught the morning sun. When the dragon was down, Aljeron addressed him. "What news, Dravendir?"

"Malek's hosts are not far ahead," the blue responded. "Prepare yourselves for battle, for you should catch them in a few hours."

Aljeron felt his excitement rise. "What news can you bring of our scouts? Have you seen them? Are they all right?"

"The last I saw they were. They have engaged Malek's hosts several times in the last three days. Each time, they strike and retreat before the enemy can respond. They have succeeded in slowing the enemy down. Each time they engage, however, the enemy reacts a little faster. They play a dangerous game. The last time, we had to show ourselves in order to help them disengage, and even with our help they were fortunate to escape."

"Can you take them word to pull back and wait for us? Can you tell them we will engage the enemy today?"

"I can try, but I wouldn't be surprised to find them already in the saddle."

"Then fly, Dravendir, fly! Tell them we are coming."

"I will do what I can do," Dravendir replied, then leapt into the air.

Aljeron turned to Evrim, who had ridden with him from the ranks of marching soldiers and waited behind him the entire time. "We need to push on. Today is the day. Spread the word, Evrim. Double time, weapons at the ready. By the Mountain! Today is the day."

Saegan sat in his saddle, looking across the plain. Not far beyond the horizon, the right flank of the enemy army lay. They'd ridden through the dark before sunrise for several hours until he was quite sure they were well north of their enemy. They had swooped in from the west the first time they attacked, and they never came from exactly the same direction more than once. The enemy had come to expect their periodic charges and might possibly suspect attack from the north this time, but they couldn't be absolutely sure of it. At least Saegan hoped they couldn't. Their lives might well depend on it.

He turned to Bryar, mounted beside him. "We don't have to do this, you know."

"I know."

"We may have pushed our luck far enough. The last time, we almost didn't get away."

"I know."

"No one would be able to say we didn't do everything within our power. We've slowed them as much as we dared. Aljeron will either catch them today, or they won't be caught, not on this side of Gyrin, anyway."

Bryar turned and looked at Saegan. "Saegan, I know all this, and I will defer to your decision. We both know the risks, and we both know what may be lost if Aljeron doesn't arrive soon. Only you, though, can decide."

"Yes, but it is more than my life at stake."

Bryar met his gaze and did not look away. "Saegan, there isn't a scout under your command who will question the order you give. If we pull out, they will do so knowing that we have done all we could. If we ride, they will do so knowing that too much is at stake not to risk it."

Saegan pulled his gaze away from Bryar and looked back south. "I know you will follow me, and all the other scouts with you. What I don't know, Bryar, is what you would do if you were me. Would you ride, knowing that they may be waiting to spring a trap? Would you hold back, knowing that forcing them to spring that trap may be the only thing that slows them down enough to keep them out of Gyrin until Aljeron gets here? This is what I must face, what I must decide. I'm asking you, not as your captain, but as your friend who respects your opinion. What would you do?"

"What would I do?" Bryar answered easily. "I would ride. I would give the command, and I would ride. I would swoop down upon them, trap or no trap, and I would do all that was in my power to keep them on this plain. I would do all this and more besides if I was able. If we fall, we fall. We can't let them reach the Mountain."

Saegan smiled at Bryar, and the smile broke some of her surface cool. "What? Why are you smiling like that?"

"I knew that was what you would say," he said, almost laughing. "If I had tried to predict the words you would use, I would not have been far off. You would not be you if you had said anything else."

"Then why did you ask?"

"Because," Saegan started, growing more serious, "I wanted to hear your marvelous fortitude and certainty one more time, just in case we do fall. I wanted to ride to war with your voice echoing in my head. I wanted to see the look on your face, fierce and determined and so full of confidence."

Bryar nearly blushed, or so it appeared to Saegan, but she caught herself. "Saegan, this is no time for jokes."

"I do not jest, Bryar. We stand on the brink of death, perhaps, and I apologize for indulging myself if it offended you. I am the captain, though," Saegan added, a slight smirk on his face. "Some allowances for rank must be made."

"Yes, Captain," Bryar said, mock subservience in her voice. "What then do you command?"

"What do I command?" Saegan said, turning back to the broad plain. "Pass the word. It is time."

Saegan whirled his horse to meet the attack coming from his left. Raising his sword, he blocked the blow from the Nolthanim. The man was a competent rider and swordsman, so it took Saegan some time, but eventually he unhorsed his enemy, sending the body slumping to the ground to be trampled underfoot.

Things had not gone well. Saegan should have known from the beginning that something was wrong. When the scouts crested the hill, their enemy appeared too unaware, too surprised. Of course, the Nolthanim had been expecting them, but their appearance of being caught off guard gave Saegan and his scouts just enough encouragement to swoop in a little too directly. Before they could wheel away, Nolthanim on horseback attacked their left flank, and Malekim appeared from somewhere off to their right, hemming them in on three sides.

Saegan tried immediately to reverse his direction and get the others to follow, but already their lines were being broken as his men turned to whatever danger seemed most immediate. Nolthanim on horseback and on foot, and ever-multiplying Malekim, seemed to be pressing in on them en masse. Soon Saegan's attempts to rally the scouts to retreat were abandoned as he fought to survive.

For several moments, moments that felt like hours, Saegan held the scouts together with his skill and bravery, but he could feel the battle slipping away. Every moment they delayed, the enemy's number increased. If they did not carve their way out, and soon, they might well slay five for every scout that fell and soon be completely massacred, trampled underfoot like the man Saegan had just knocked from his saddle.

Three golden forms plummeted from the sky, and Saegan looked with relief at the dragons who flew low over the fray, blowing fire and smoke at their enemy. Saegan saw the area where they concentrated their efforts, and wheeling his horse that way, called to the scouts within the sound of his voice to follow.

Nearby, he saw Bryar, wielding her own sword deftly and capably, fending off attack from a Nolthanim soldier on the ground. The infantryman looked up and seemed to realize he was fighting a woman, but any thought that his job would be the easier for it died in an instant, because a short swift stroke slit his throat. He sank down upon his knees.

"Bryar!" Saegan called. "This way. The dragons are trying to open a way for us."

She rode abreast of him, and together they pushed through the mayhem. A Malekim leapt in front of them, his sword flashing, and Saegan charged, driving his Azmavarim home before the Silent One could defend against his stroke. He turned only to see three or four more Malekim crowding in around them, a few in front of him and a few beside Bryar. He struck down at the one nearest him, and then he slipped sideways as his horse stumbled and fell.

He was lucky not to have his leg crushed under the weight of the horse, but he was able to push himself free of the dying animal. The Malekim on the other side had given the beast a fatal blow and sent Saegan to the ground. He rolled, rose, and blocked the stroke that was aimed at his head. The creature was strong but slow, and Saegan drove his sword home, and with a firm shove from his boot, he dislodged the Malekim from his blade.

Again the dragons swept low, and again the fire blew across the line of their enemies, this time much closer. Saegan could feel the heat of the flames, and the smoke drifted his way across the tumultuous field. He turned and looked for Bryar, just in time to see her horse struck down by a Silent One. The horse stumbled forward, and Bryar flew over its head and landed with an awkward thud.

Saegan ran across the intervening distance and interposed himself between Bryar's still form and the Malekim. The blow he intercepted knocked him backward, and he fell on top of her. Again he rolled and raised his sword, blocking another blow. He looked up at the senseless eyes in the dense, grey Malekim hide, a thin strand of wispy black hair floating above the ugly face. He slashed his sword across the creature's knees. The Voiceless almost dropped his sword, and Saegan rose, his adrenaline flowing, and quickly slew him.

He turned to Bryar, who was moaning, and helped her onto her feet. "Come, we must go. We won't last long here without our horses."

Again the dragons came, and now Saegan could see a perceptible gap in the line of their enemy. He pointed Bryar, now aware and moving on her own, in that direction and bid her run, which she did. He followed to keep himself between her and any harm from behind. As she ran, though, a terrible figure stepped through the thick but clearing smoke. It was the dread captain of the Nolthanim.

Saegan had not been this close to him before, and he could see the details of the odd armor, singed and blackened, perhaps by the fire of the dragon. In any case, the man inside walked undeterred through the fire and smoke, personally clogging the escape route that the dragons had labored to open. Through the narrow slit in the bizarre helmet, two intense and piercing eyes gazed out at the world.

Bryar saw him emerge even as the dread captain saw her. She dodged a vicious stroke that surely would have killed her. She managed a partial block with her own sword, but the blow caught her off guard and her sword was knocked several spans away. She slipped, lost her footing, and fell.

Once more, Saegan ran to intervene. Here was a chance not only to preserve Bryar's life but to strike more than an incidental blow to the forces of Malek. Farimaal, he thought Benjiah had called this man. Captain of the Nolthanim, second only to Malek in the hierarchy of the enemy. Saegan's chances of surviving the day were disappearing rapidly, but his fall might well be worth it if he could take this Farimaal with him.

The dread captain was aware of his approach, for while he had aimed as though to dispatch Bryar, he adjusted his position to fend off Saegan's attack. For all the seeming inflexibility of the strange armor, he moved more quickly than Saegan anticipated. Even so, he closed with the man and, sword flashing, succeeded in driving him a few steps backward.

Saegan had always been exceptional with the sword. His reflexes were clean, his instinct impeccable, and his discipline unwavering. He did not make mistakes in battle, ever, and he pressed the Nolthanim captain only as much as he could without making himself unduly vulnerable. It was sufficient to give Bryar, if she was still capable of moving under her own power, time to get up and hopefully, get away.

A surge from his opponent put Saegan on the defensive. Farimaal had allowed Saegan to drive him back so he could watch his mode of attack and consider how to direct his own efforts. Saegan wielded his blade furiously in defense and had to trust his feet to navigate the treacherous ground.

Then, as he fell backward, Saegan saw an opening, and whirling to the side struck a solid blow against the dread captain's armor. His Firstblade made contact but put no dent in the blackened armor. Farimaal's counterstroke was already on its way as Saegan dodged, and it came within a hair's breadth of separating Saegan's head from his shoulders. He regrouped as Farimaal came on again.

From off to the side, Bryar came rushing in, sword slashing. Saegan called out for her to turn back, but Farimaal had already sensed her attack. He did not bother trying to dodge it, rather, he lifted his gauntleted hand and caught her blade as his other hand drove his sword right through her. Saegan watched in horror and dismay as she sank slowly, lifelessly to the ground.

Rage and fury flowed through him and he charged. Farimaal turned, but not in time to be fully on guard, and with a series of strokes, Saegan had the dread captain stumbling back over the ground he had yielded. He landed several strokes but had no further luck with the man's armor. All he could think of was to try for the man's eyes, the slat in the helmet being the only visible weakness in his armor.

Saegan pressed in, but the dread captain's defense intensified whenever Saegan maneuvered to a place where he might strike at Farimaal's face. For a long time they dueled, moving back and forth, until at last Saegan felt his legs beginning to give. He knew his limitations, and he knew he was losing his edge. He had to bring this to an end now, or he would not have the strength to finish it.

Putting everything he had left into a renewed surge, he beat back the dread captain. With a sudden flurry of blows, directed at the sword hand and not Farimaal's body or face, he succeeded in knocking the dread captain's sword free. He looked into Farimaal's eyes and saw what might have been the faintest glimmer of fear. Moving in, he lunged hard at the opening in the helmet.

Farimaal ducked and struck out with his fist. The blow caught Saegan in the chest and hit like a rock thrown by a giant. It knocked him backward more than a span, and he fell onto the ground. He struggled to get up, but he was winded and could feel that several of his ribs were cracked. He wheezed, but he had to stand.

As he rose, he saw two things simultaneously. Farimaal had retrieved his sword and was turning toward him. Beyond Farimaal, though, Saegan saw something else, something as beautiful as anything any other Spring day had ever produced. A great host was marching across the plain. Aljeron and the Kirthanim had come.

Farimaal moved, and Saegan struggled to lift his sword. A swift blow from Farimaal sent the sword flying out of his hand, but Saegan kept his feet and smiled as Farimaal closed the gap.

The smile must have angered the dread captain, for he lifted his fist again and hammered Saegan in the face. He fell hard, spitting blood and teeth as he rolled over and tried to push his heavy body up off the ground. His eyes were having trouble focusing, but he could hear the voice ring out above him.

"You might as well stay down." This time the dread captain's foot came swiftly down, and Saegan hit the ground again.

His body barely responded to the command his mind sent it to move, but it did move. He began to push his way up, and once more the foot came down and he fell again.

His hands were splayed out on the ground. He thought they were pushing, but he wasn't going anywhere. His neck was in incredible pain, and he couldn't turn his head. His mouth was warm and salty, and he felt blood sliding down the back of his throat.

"They've come," he mumbled, still trying to get up.

"What's that?"

Saegan struggled with all the energy he had to push himself up, just a little bit. He would strike no more blows, but he would be heard before he died. "They've come. We've won."

"You've won nothing. We will deal with them, as we have dealt with you," came Farimaal's voice, calm, cold and eerily confident. "You are a worthy warrior, but you have died in vain."

Pain radiated outward from a point in his back, and Saegan's head rested in the coarse grass. He closed his eyes, Bryar's voice echoing in his head. *If we fall, we fall.*

6

ALL ROADS LEAD TO THE MOUNTAIN

PEDRAAN LOOKED DOWN as Aljeron knelt over Gilion. The slash across Gilion's thigh was bleeding profusely, and Aljeron struggled with the torn fabric of Gilion's pants, trying to tear an adequate strip to tie off the wound and slow the bleeding. Gilion clenched his teeth and grunted, trying to stay still despite the pain of Aljeron's expeditious but rough handling of his wounded leg.

"You really must head back, Gilion," Pedraan said as Aljeron drew the strip of cloth tighter around Gilion's upper thigh.

"Yes," Aljeron jumped in before Gilion could reply. "I won't hear anymore foolish protests. This wound is serious and the women can help you. Head back. You can be cared for properly there. On this leg, you won't be much help here."

If Gilion intended to protest again, he thought better of it and eventually nodded. Pedraan helped Aljeron lift him to his feet, and when both were sure he could move under his own power, they turned back toward the ongoing fight. They were fortunate that Gilion had been cut near the edge of the fighting and was able to limp and crawl away from the heat of the battle.

Koshti paced impatiently, waiting for them to reenter the fray. Even Pedraan could sense the tiger's eagerness for battle. Aljeron looked to Pedraan and said. "Are you ready to head back?"

"Are you kidding?" Pedraan said, hoisting his hammer to his shoulder. "I didn't lug my hammer all these leagues after spending all day looking for it just to stand here and watch. There are still plenty of Voiceless around to pay for Pedraal's death. This reprieve has just given me a chance to gather my second wind."

"All right, then," Aljeron said. "Let's go."

Pedraan walked beside Aljeron, the din of battle growing louder. The sun was hanging low over Gyrin. What a day it had been, Pedraan thought, but there wasn't much of it left.

Since their arrival earlier in the afternoon, the bloody scuffle had escalated into a battle of ferocious intensity. The Kalin Seir swept across the plain against the ranks of Nolthanim, their snow leopard battle brothers leading the way. Without the presence of Black Wolves to counteract their charge, the attack proved devastating—too fast and ferocious for the Nolthanim to adequately defend themselves. The Kalin Seir likewise dealt the Nolthanim a serious blow. Pedraan saw in action what Aljeron had tried to explain in words, namely the centuries of pent up rage against their treacherous "brothers."

Pedraan marveled at both the men and the women. Though he thought their wooden spears surely too weak and flimsy to be effective, the Kalin Seir proved him wrong. Not only were they accurate from a distance with both their bows and arrows and their spears, they were deadly at close range with the latter, light weapons that were nonetheless capable of skewering a man.

He didn't watch too long, however, for he and his hammer were required elsewhere. He moved in with the contingency of Great Bear, who were assigned the fundamental task of trying to separate the Malekim from the Nolthanim. This would allow the Kirthanim and Kalin Seir a chance to devastate their merely human enemies. Aljeron thought that the destruction of the Nolthanim would likely result in the dissolution of Malek's forces. Despite their might and prowess in battle, the Malekim seemed fundamentally designed to follow, not lead, and left to themselves he thought they would be more easily dealt with without their human captains. What's more, Aljeron still hoped that some of the Vulsutyrim and dragons would return from the south to help them, and exterminating what was left of the Silent Ones would surely be easier then.

Pedraan was one of the few Kirthanim to accompany the Great Bear on this task. The other men with them carried Azmavarim, the Firstblades, swords from the end of the First Age, strong enough and sharp enough to cut through Malekim hide and deliver a fatal wound even when wielded by a man—something no ordinary Kirthanim sword of later make could do. Pedraan, though, did not carry one of these Firstblades. Instead, he carried the great war hammer that Caan had given him while sailing to the Forbidden Isle. He'd thrown his war hammer down in disgust after Pedraal fell, determined that come what may, he was through with it. After their deliverance from Malek's hand, though, he decided to find his war hammer and bear it to war once more. When this campaign was over, however, he intended to lay it down for good, despite how natural it felt in his hands as he wielded it against the Malekim. He meant to make good his unspoken vow. He would lay it down.

It had felt natural, though, that much could not be denied. He'd jogged along behind the Great Bear as they tried to drive a wedge between the ranks of Nolthanim and Malekim. Their great staffs struck with lightning speed, crushing Voiceless on every side. Even so, there were far more Malekim than Great Bear, and some of them slipped under or around the furious attacks of their ancient foes. Pedraan found plenty of opportunity to wield his war hammer against Silent Ones, each of whom initially found itself delighted not to be face-to-face with a Great Bear. Initially, that is, for not one of them survived Pedraan long enough to land a single blow of its own. Pedraan, smaller and faster than any of them, nevertheless wielded his hammer with remarkable power. An unblocked blow from his war hammer could crush a Malekim's chest or skull or whatever it struck, and many a Silent One was laid low in the midst of its surprise that a mere man could strike it so fast and so hard.

The push against the Malekim was greatly aided by the few dragons who accompanied them. They too focused on the Malekim, leaving the Nolthanim to the Kirthanim and Kalin Seir. Pedraan watched the dragons swoop in time after time, the flame from their mouths sending the Malekim scurrying in any direction that might lead them away from the suffocating heat. Pedraan began to believe that they might not simply hold back the Malekim but defeat them outright before the day's end.

This was not to be, however, in large measure because the Malekim produced a strategy and a weapon against the dragons that Pedraan had not yet seen. A band of Malekim arrived, bearing strange weapons. They appeared to be a combination of some kind of bow and pieces of sturdy wood. The bows lay horizontally across the end of the wood, and the bowstrings were drawn back along the shaft, on which were placed what seemed to Pedraan to be something like bolts of iron or steel. Then, when the dragons passed overhead, the bolts were shot with great force straight up at them, and Pedraan saw with some dismay that these bolts were capable of penetrating the dragons' scales. This became clear after one flew overhead, several metallic bolts sticking through the golden scales of his underbelly, and again after one of the dragons plummeted heavily to the ground, a great metal bolt protruding out of its neck.

And so the tide of battle had been not so much turned as halted. The Malekim, composed and able with their new weapon to keep the dragons at bay, rallied against the Great Bear, who were far outnumbered by the seething mass of Voiceless. Pedraan's work with his war hammer grew more desperate, and he began to grown weary. Moving along the perimeter set up to hold the Malekim back, he came across the fallen Gilion being tended to by Aljeron. Now, having enjoyed his brief reprieve, it was time to get back into the fight.

They were drawing near to the battling Great Bear when Aljeron reached over and grabbed his arm. He followed Aljeron's extended sword arm, which pointed up into the sky, and he turned to see a remarkable sight. A dozen dragons flew ever closer, each one bearing a Vulsutyrim in its talons. Pedraan had to blink and look again to make sure he was seeing what he thought he was seeing. Sure enough, the dragons had giants gripped under their armpits.

At the front of the approaching dragons flew Sulmandir, his completely golden form shining brilliantly in the setting sun. He flew in low with Amontyr, who had barely been set down and released before he was leading a charge of determined giants right into the heart of the reorganized Malekim. The dismayed Voiceless were something to behold as the giants came charging into them; they seemed unable to register that they were being attacked by the Vulsutyrim. When they recovered at last, some of them were able to get a few shots off with their strange, horizontal bows, but though one of the giants took a metallic bolt through his shoulder, the others quickly drove the responsible Malekim back, and now all the Malekim were fleeing toward Gyrin without pretense of fighting any longer.

The newly arrived dragons sped over the plain, roasting the Malekim that lagged too far behind. Pedraan turned toward the area where the Kirthanim were engaged with the Nolthanim, and there also the enemy seemed to be in full retreat. Everywhere he looked, as far as his eyes could see, the enemy lines had broken and they fled helter-skelter, broken and defeated.

Benjiah emerged from the garrion and looked over the battlefield, now devoid of battle. The dragons that carried Vulsutyrim had flown ahead, and by the time the men arrived, the battle had broken up. The Kirthanim, Kalin Seir, and Great Bear had routed as many of the stragglers as they could without heading into Gyrin themselves. Benjiah imagined that Aljeron had made it clear that the pursuit was to end there, at the edge of the dark wood, at least for now.

By the time Garin, Valzaan, and Benjiah reached the Kirthanim captains, who gathered with Amontyr and Sulmandir, the discussion of what to do was under way. Benjiah noted the absence of several normally present in these meetings: Gilion, Saegan and Bryar most obviously, but he did not interrupt the proceedings to find out where they were. He hoped they were merely occupied elsewhere, though it was a little alarming to see all three of them missing.

The captains made room for them, and they found themselves standing before Aljeron, with Evrim on one side and Pedraan on the other. His uncles were both lathered with sweat, and Pedraan especially appeared weary, leaning on his war hammer's long handle.

"Valzaan," Aljeron said. "What news from the south?"

"The Kumatin is dead."

Smiles and sighs of relief rippled around the small gathering. Aljeron allowed himself a rare smile as well. "I had hoped from your timely return that this was so. We give thanks for both the help and the news you have brought."

"You are welcome," Valzaan replied. "I see that the enemy was caught and engaged here. What is the report?"

"The main body of Nolthanim has been defeated, right here on the plain." That the intensity of battle had not quite left Aljeron, despite the fact Daaltaran was sheathed, was evident in the way he gestured to emphasize his point. "Even so, a core of the Nolthanim was held together by the leadership of their captain, Farimaal."

"And the Malekim?"

Turgan, the greying Great Bear who succeeded Sarneth, answered this question, his deep voice rumbling over the quieting plain. "They were hit hard as well, but more Voiceless remain than Nolthanim. They will need to be hunted down in the wood or in the Mountain, if they get there."

"Our casualties were minimal," Aljeron added. He hesitated. "Except for the scouts. They rode ahead to delay the enemy so we could catch them, which they did successfully. However, they were trapped today, and we arrived too late to save many. Saegan and Bryar are among the fallen."

Benjiah felt his heart sink. He knew neither of them well, but he had heard his uncles speak often enough of both, especially of Saegan, and he knew their fall was a serious loss for the Kirthanim. He felt a surge of anger spread through him. He was angry that this war was happening at all. Angry that Malek had ever warped and ruined so much of Allfather's good creation. Angry that so many lives had been laid on the altar of sacrifice to defeat their ancient enemy. He felt a great desire to kill Malek with his own hands, to spill his lifeblood and watch it slowly drain away. The anger boiled up in him, and he felt it seething, threatening to burst out in some sudden, violent act.

He looked up to see Valzaan, his head turned sideways so that he was facing Benjiah. His white, eerie eyes appeared to penetrate Benjiah from beneath his wild white shock of hair, and Benjiah felt a chill. Valzaan turned back toward Aljeron and the other captains, and as quickly as they had come, all the emotions and sensations passed.

"Though we rightly mourn their fall," Valzaan was saying, "I tell you all, be comforted! The time draws quickly near when all things shall be made new. All roads lead to the Mountain. There, on Agia Muldonai, Malek's treachery began, and there it shall end, and soon. So says Allfather!"

Murmurs rippled through the captains again, even more excited than before, and they continued until Valzaan spoke again. "That is the report of what has happened. What have you decided to do in response?"

"We need to catch and mop up as much of the enemy as possible, before they reach the Mountain." Aljeron turned to look toward Gyrin, and all the captains shifted to gaze at the border of the great wood. "Since the scouts are devastated, my plan is as follows. I am hoping that the main body of the army could push in along the road. I hope that the Great Bear, with the aid of the Kalin Seir and any Vulsutyrim who are available, might sweep in through the wood north and south of the road. I want all the Nolthanim and Malekim who might be hiding to be corralled and swept ahead of us, so they have no where to go but further in, toward the Mountain.

"The dragons, if Sulmandir agrees and is willing, will fly to the foot of the Mountain and post themselves around its base.

Their job will be to hold the enemy as Malek's hosts come into the open, and we will finish them there at the Mountain's base. Then all will be finished."

"Sulmandir?" Valzaan said, looking up to the Father of Dragons.

"We are willing," Sulmandir replied. "We will secure the base of the Mountain, and we will finish what started on the Mountain so long ago."

"Good, then it is settled," Valzaan replied. "Let us not tarry. In Gyrin, it is dark by day and by night. The enemy will not rest, for desperation has overcome him. We will not be able to rest either. Those who grow too weary to continue will need to stay behind, unless they can catch up to us after they regain their strength. No captain is to refuse any man who asks to be left behind. Only those with strength to keep going will go on. There will be strength enough among us to do what must be done. Now go!"

Immediately the assembly began to break up, and Benjiah watched as men who had run or fought all day moved quickly in all directions to rally their men. Soon, the main force of Kirthanim would plunge into Gyrin along the road, and the rest of them would move inward through the wood itself, he along with them. His road had brought him here, and he had no desire to turn away.

Soon, all the captains but Aljeron had gone to be about their business, and now only Valzaan and Benjiah stood with him and Koshti, who lay panting peacefully on the ground beside them. If it wasn't for the bloodstains on the soft fur around Koshti's jaws, Benjiah would not have known he had been in the battle at all.

"Aljeron," Valzaan began, "I have one question for you that I did not wish to discuss in front of the others."

"Yes?"

"Synoki, did you see him on the battlefield today?"

"I did not," Aljeron replied.

"I don't like it," Valzaan replied. "I suppose he might have gone ahead, but I would have thought he'd be here."

"You mean Malek, if he's Synoki, might have been moving ahead of his army? He might have already slipped into Gyrin and be on his way to the Mountain?"

"It is possible, if he felt it imperative that he reach Gyrin or the Mountain safely and believed the army might slow him down," Valzaan replied. "Of course, I don't know that he did this. He may have simply been staying out of harm's way, directing things from a safe distance."

"Then all we can do is go after them and see," Aljeron said.

"Yes," Valzaan agreed. "At this point, that is about all we can do. Head start or not, Malek is running out of places to hide. He will face his reckoning. In a week it will be Summer Rise, and I say this to you both: Malek will not live to see it."

Returning to Gyrin after his journey through Taralin with Sarneth was fascinating for Benjiah, if less than pleasant. Having discussed with Sarneth the connection between the life of the wood and the draal of the Great Bear, he noticed details now that he had missed earlier. The trees showed signs of rot, like cracks stretching in zigzags up their trunks from the gnarled roots. The leaves, even those highest up and closest to the life-giving light, showed signs of blight despite the temperate weather of spring. A faint putrid odor hung close about them as they moved beneath the trees, a scent that permeated so much that Benjiah could taste it in his food. There was, in everything around him, a palpable decay.

It was the twenty-sixth day of Spring Wane, and for three days they had been traveling through Gyrin. The darkness of the place shadowed Benjiah's mind. Although it was a little after midday, the perpetual twilight fueled his dark thoughts and feelings. Every step that led him farther into the wood led him closer to the Mountain. *All roads lead to the Mountain*, Valzaan had said, and Benjiah believed it was true. But how many roads would end there, and would his be one of them?

With both hands, he held the bow he'd taken off a fallen Kalin Seir. It was lighter than Suruna but well made. He'd taken two shots at the edge of Gyrin with it, enough for him to get its feel and be satisfied that if he needed to use it, he would be prepared. He hadn't known how it would feel to carry a bow again, but he was surprised, both by how comfortable it felt in his hand and by how uncomfortable that comfort made him.

Benjiah was moving through Gyrin, some distance north of the road. Skillful with a bow, he felt he could be of more service here than in the mass of Kirthanim marching along the road. Valzaan had insisted on coming with him, though the prophet at times drifted. He seemed to have an uncanny sense for when Benjiah wanted company and when he did not, and he always honored that sense. At present he was not where Benjiah could see him.

He and Valzaan moved westward with the others but angled steadily northward as well. Benjiah was now convinced that they were close to the top of the line of Great Bear and Kalin Seir shepherding their enemy closer and closer to the Mountain. Progress had been slow, at least slower than Benjiah anticipated. Valzaan's words to the captains had spurred everyone on, but the actual work of moving in this fashion through the dense wood was easier to imagine than to do. While a large part of him dreaded arriving at the foot of the Mountain, which loomed ever closer with each sighting through the canopy of leaves, Benjiah had come to think that the journey might be worse than the arrival.

"Benjiah?" a voice called, and Benjiah looked back to find Keila walking toward him between two great trees.

"Keila," Benjiah said, pausing to allow her to catch up. "It's good to see that you're all right. I saw many fallen Kalin Seir on the battlefield when we arrived."

"Yes," Keila said, coming alongside him. "Many of our people and many of our battle brothers fell."

"I'm glad you weren't one of them," Benjiah said. "I hear that the Kalin Seir were magnificent."

"We have done what we can to support the Master-Maker against the Forge-Foe," Keila said. "And along the way, we have taught our wayward brothers a lesson about fidelity."

"I think you have," Benjiah said, smiling through the dim light at the evident satisfaction Keila took in that fact. "I see you carry a bow of the Kalin Seir."

"I do," Benjiah answered. "I hope you don't mind, but I had no other weapon with me."

"Does a prophet need a weapon?"

"Not always. The power I have wielded belongs to Allfather, not me, and it is not really mine to command. It seems prudent for me to carry a weapon as well."

"I am glad you chose one of our bows, rather than a sword," Keila said, and Benjiah could see her shaking her head in wonder. "It still startles me to see servants of the Master-Maker who are Blade-Bearers."

"I never really took to the sword," Benjiah began to explain, but a small commotion grabbed their attention. Both headed in the direction of the noise, and came upon a trio of Malekim being pursued by a handful of Kalin Seir and a Great Bear. Benjiah drew his bowstring, and the arrow that he had carried, knocked, all the way through Gyrin, flew straight and true. It struck the Malekim with a thud in the arm, but not being cyranic, Benjiah knew it would not bring the creature down.

Even so, the Malekim had been hit many times, including an arrow that Keila had managed to land during the same pass, and the wounds slowed the creature enough that the Great Bear caught it before long. Benjiah and Keila hurried after and arrived in time to see the Great Bear wielding his staff with great effectiveness against his wounded enemies. Soon all three of the Malekim were tracked down and killed. The line reassembled itself, and Benjiah walked slowly beside Keila as before, a new arrow at the ready.

"The last time I walked through Gyrin, I shot a few Silent Ones with my own bow, Suruna," Benjiah said, remembering the Autumn day that felt so long ago now.

"You've been in this wood before?" Keila asked.

"Yes, once."

"Once is enough," Keila said, disgust evident in her voice. "I hate this place. It doesn't feel like a living place, as a forest should."

"No, it doesn't," Benjiah agreed. "A Great Bear friend told me that since the destruction of the draal that was once here, Gyrin has been dying. Perhaps when Malek is defeated and Allfather makes all things new, perhaps then Gyrin will live again."

"It is hard to imagine, but perhaps it is so. That feels a long way away right now."

"Does it?" Benjiah said, genuinely surprised. "Not to me. It feels so close, like coming within view of home after being on a long journey. There may be some fighting left, but it can't be long now. Malek is almost finished."

"I hope so, Benjiah," Keila said. "That will be a great day, won't it?"

"It will be a day of rejoicing for all Kirthanin," Benjiah replied wistfully, "but it may come at a steep price."

"A steep price has already been paid."

"Yes, that's true," Benjiah said, wondering if he should say more. The weight of his fear hung heavily upon him, and he decided to share it. "I was speaking not of the price Kirthanin has paid, but of the price I may have to pay."

"What do you mean?" Keila asked, and Benjiah saw her steps falter slightly, though she recovered.

"Valzaan believes I am the fulfillment of a prophecy connected with Malek's fall, and that the role I have to play in what is to come is a role that I may not survive."

"How long have you known this?" Keila asked, and Benjiah met her steady gaze.

"For a while."

"You've been carrying this with you then, all this way?"

"Yes."

"By yourself?"

"No, Valzaan has helped me carry it."

"I am sorry," Keila said, placing her hand lightly upon his shoulder. "I have been insensitive to you at times."

"No need to apologize," Benjiah answered. "I have enjoyed your company."

"Even so, it must have been hard to carry this knowledge. It must still be hard."

"Yes," Benjiah replied. "Increasingly I feel like I'm being led back up the stairs of that great scaffold, back to the poles and chains that bound me."

"But Valzaan has only indicated that you *may not* survive, right? I mean, there is a chance that you will survive?"

"I suppose so, but that isn't the feeling I've gotten from our discussions."

"No?"

"No, Valzaan doesn't seem optimistic about it at all."

"Well, even so, he has not said you *will* die, only that you *may* die. That is true of all who march into battle. Who knows, you may live and I may die. Who can say?"

"I certainly hope you won't die," Benjiah said, suddenly turning toward her.

"I hope not too, but it is possible."

"It would be a great loss," he said softly.

"As would you," she said as she stepped toward him. He was standing in a small depression in the ground that put her just slightly above him. She leaned over and kissed his forehead. "That is why, whatever happens, you cannot die. You would be missed."

As they approached the Mountain, Benjiah felt his pulse quicken with every glimpse of it. Now the trees were thinning, and Agia Muldonai remained constantly within view. Still, Valzaan's voice echoed in his head. *All roads lead to the Mountain.*

The sound of battle, though distant, floated unmistakably upon the evening breeze, and Benjiah began to run. The great trees of Gyrin parted, and the space before him opened. After a few moments, he left the wood behind and emerged north of it, near the eastern foot of the Holy Mountain.

He could see the fighting in the distance. Dragons were active in the skies, flying in tight circles, bursts of flame and smoke erupting at steady intervals as they blocked the Voiceless' advance up the Mountain. Snarling Great Bear and towering Vulsutyrim emerging from the wood caught the Malekim from behind, trapping them.

A number of Kalin Seir and Great Bear moved westward along the foot of the Mountain toward the battle. Benjiah had lost track of Keila earlier in the day when he paused to have a word with Valzaan, but he imagined she was among those moving to join the fray. As for Valzaan, Benjiah had not seen him since, and he wondered where he was. Being here, at the foot of the Mountain, with dragons, Vulsutyrim, Great Bear and men all fighting together to finish Malek and his hosts was chilling. It was wonderful, certainly, but Benjiah felt the finality of it, and it shook him.

"Benjiah," Valzaan called, as though appearing in answer to his own wishes, and Benjiah turned to see the prophet hurrying across the open ground from the edge of Gyrin.

"I wondered where you'd gotten off to," Benjiah said.

"I may be a prophet, but I'm also very old," Valzaan said, a glimmer of amusement in his voice. "Keeping up with you is a challenge to road-weary legs."

"The battle has already been joined," Benjiah said, looking back to the unfolding spectacle.

"We should be on our way."

"Valzaan," Benjiah said before the prophet could move off. "Yes?"

"I've had a sense of something the closer we've come to the Mountain. At first I thought it was just the foreboding that has been growing since Tol Emuna, but it is different, I think."

"I know," Valzaan replied. "I feel it too. The Mountain is drawing us."

"The Mountain?"

"More properly, the One who made it, who formed it from nothing by the might of His power. He is summoning us back."

"Allfather is drawing us back here? I thought Malek was drawing us here."

"In a sense, but Malek is himself being drawn here."

"I thought Malek came here because this is where he can escape us."

"That is also true. What Malek believes does not contravene the plan of Allfather. What's more, Allfather may well be using Malek's fear to maneuver events in such a way that what must happen, happens here."

"Because this is where it started?"

"That is one reason. Malek's rebellion against Allfather began here. It was conceived in his heart in the blessed city, Avalione. But there is more to it than that."

"May I ask what?"

"Can you not see what? Can you not figure out why All-father would draw men and Great Bear, Vulsutyrim and dragons all to the foot of Agia Muldonai? You are young, but surely the Mound rites are well known to you."

Benjiah thought of Valzaan on the mound in Tol Emuna, pouring water down its sides and speaking the words of the ritual. Then he understood. "We need cleansing."

"We do indeed. Kirthanin has not only been long oppressed by Malek and his machinations, it has long been tainted by its own corruption. Malek's fall alone will not remedy Kirthanin's ills. Kirthanin needs to be cleansed."

"So Allfather draws us back to the Mountain," Benjiah said, turning his face from the battle to gaze up the side of Agia Muldonai.

"Even so."

Just then, as Benjiah gazed at the Mountain, a ripple of coldness overwhelmed him and he staggered, almost falling to his knees. He swayed and collided with Valzaan, who instinctively took hold of him and held him up so that he did not fall.

"What is it?"

"He's here," Benjiah said, sure of what had happened. "The limping man, Synoki, he's here."

"Where?" Valzaan said, concern and urgency in his voice.

"Up there," Benjiah said, pointing up the side of Agia Muldonai.

"Are you sure?" Valzaan asked. "Have you seen him?"

"I have not seen him," Benjiah answered, "but I am sure."

Benjiah scanned the base of the Mountain. The portion he could see was limited, extending both left and right beyond his vision and ever upward, far into the sky. Scraggly bushes and small trees dotted the lower regions of the Mountain, offering numerous hidden vantage points, and somewhere up there was the limping man.

"He's not far away," Benjiah added.

"He's probably watching us."

"Yes," Benjiah said, nodding. "He is."

Looking quickly back toward the battle, Benjiah stepped toward the Mountain. As he did, he dropped the Kalin Seir bow on the ground. "I need to go after him, and I won't be needing this anymore."

"No, you won't."

"It would only encumber me," Benjiah added, thinking of the ineffective arrow he fired across the battlefield at Synoki.

Benjiah looked back to Valzaan. "Is this what you meant when you said you couldn't go all the way with me, that the last part of my journey I would need to take alone? Must I go up while you stay here?"

"No, Benjiah," Valzaan said, placing his hand gently on Benjiah's shoulder. "It is not what I meant. I am coming up the Mountain with you."

"I'm glad," Benjiah said, then he turned back to the Mountain and began to move quickly up over the loose rocks.

All roads may lead to the Mountain, he thought, *but mine actually goes up it.*

7

UNDER THE HAMMER

ALL WAS GOING WELL, better even than Aljeron had dared to hope. The dragons were virtually omnipresent in their defense of the Mountain, and smoke from their frequent blasts of flame drifted in dark clouds over the open field. Everywhere a cluster of men or Malekim attempted to make a break for the foot of the Mountain, a dragon appeared and drove them off, back toward the chaotic battlefield.

To say the battlefield was chaotic was not an exaggeration. The fighting was spread out over a great distance and the enemy lacked almost any semblance of a line or coherent defense. Having been driven before the Kirthanim through Gyrin, they became separated and were now fighting, more or less, each man and Malekim for himself.

The battle was only clearly delineated on two sides. To the north, the dragons marked an absolute boundary at the foot of the Mountain. To the south, the Great Bear had taken up positions all along the northern edge of Gyrin to prevent retreat. The Great Bear were more at home in the forests of Kirthanin than any other race or creature, and they moved stealthily along its border, punishing any Nolthanim or Malekim who came too close, so much so that most of the enemy seemed equally terrified to move too close either to the Mountain or the wood, though the hope of escaping certain death eventually drove most of them to try one or the other.

The consequence of this terror was that the Nolthanim and Malekim caught in the open ground fought desperately, but they were disorganized and dismayed. The dismay came just as much from the visible work of the Vulsutyrim, who wreaked havoc primarily among the Voiceless. Aljeron watched a single giant, his great curved sword in his hand, completely destroy a small band of half a dozen Malekim with just a few skillful strokes. Everywhere the Vulsutyrim roamed, the Nolthanim and Malekim fled, but with exits to the north and south cut off, they could only run toward other enemies waiting to take advantage of their panic.

Aljeron was moving along the southern edge of the battle with Koshti, not far from Gyrin, where he could see the looming forms of Great Bear moving among the trees. After a hectic afternoon of moving here and there to make sure everyone understood their roles and that all went as planned, Aljeron found himself almost a spectator in the fight, watching the plan unfold in reality much as he had envisioned it. That it did so was a rarity. He was almost unsure what to do with himself.

He looked down at Koshti, the great cat prowling silently at his side. He could see the tiger's great excitement in his rapid pace, which meant that Koshti frequently retraced his steps so as not to leave Aljeron too far behind as they walked together. Aljeron knew it must be difficult for his battle brother to be so close to a fight and not be involved. Aside from a few light skirmishes early on, they had not been involved, really, and though Aljeron knew he had been fortunate, he also felt an itch to be a part of this final battle.

He hesitated. It was the final battle. He was quite sure of it. The numbers of Malekim had been visibly reduced by the dragons and Vulsutyrim, as well as by the pursuing forces of Great Bear, who had hunted and killed so many in Gyrin that far fewer emerged from the wood than had entered it. This was it. The war between Malek's hosts and the Kirthanim ended today.

It was a striking thought, both wonderful and strange. Aljeron knew, intellectually, that eventually this would all end, for better or for worse. That it appeared to be ending for better was of course delightful, but it also meant that a lot of things were going to change. He looked down at Koshti, pacing with his eyes trained on the fighting. If Koshti was frustrated now, spoiling for the fight in view, how would he cope when all fights were ended? He was a tiger, after all, and all he'd ever known was hunting and fighting. What would a promised age of peace mean for him?

"A rest, perhaps," Aljeron said out loud, and Koshti turned and looked at him. It was only a brief glance, and it seemed to communicate impatience that they were not moving out from the relative safety of the wood. "All right, Koshti, we'll go to war together one more time."

As Aljeron started away from the trees, much to Koshti's evident delight, a voice calling Aljeron's name stopped him.

"Aljeron?"

Pedraan came toward him with his war hammer in hand. Aljeron jogged out to meet him, Koshti running slowly at his side. "Pedraan, what news?"

"Nothing," Pedraan said as he drew nearer, "except that everything seems to be going very well."

"Very well, indeed," Aljeron answered. "I think today is the day we finish this war, once and for all."

"I think so." Pedraan nodded as they came together at last. "I'm almost having trouble finding a fight out here. Fear has complete possession of our enemy. Some of them will hardly stand still long enough to fight. They flee and find their end wherever a sword is ready to greet them."

"It is remarkable disarray from an enemy who was so well-organized once, and whom we so greatly feared."

Even as he said the words, a thought occurred to Aljeron, and he looked up to the Mountain, towering above everything going on at its foot. He continued, "I wonder . . ."

"You wonder what?"

"The Mountain," Aljeron began, then tore his eyes from it and looked back at Pedraan. "It seems to me odd that everything is going so smoothly today, but I wonder if being here, at the foot of the Mountain—I wonder if that isn't somehow a reason for it. Perhaps this fear you speak of has come upon our enemy because they stand in the shadow of Agia Muldonai. After all, wasn't it here that Malek met his defeat during his second attempt to conquer Kirthanin?"

"Yes, it was," Pedraan said. "Sulmandir killed Vulsutyr somewhere near here, didn't he?"

"He did," Aljeron said, looking back up at the Mountain. "Life and death revolves around the Mountain. Malek desired to rule from the Mountain, and his actions defiled it. Alazare cast him from the Mountain and broke him at the foot of it. Even so, it was to the Mountain that he returned, even after Vulsutyr was defeated and killed at its foot. It was inside the Mountain that he dwelt, these long years, preparing to come out again, but his purpose was always to return, wasn't it? Not running in defeat, as he has, but to rule from Avalione, from the top of the Mountain. Now his army is here, being destroyed at its base."

"Yes, but is he here? And if so, what will he do?" Pedraan asked.

"Aljeron!"

Both men turned to see Evrim moving quickly toward them, his sword held tightly in his left hand, which was by now quite adept at wielding it.

"What is it, Evrim?" Aljeron replied as both men and Koshti moved toward him.

"The enemy is all but broken and defeated," Evrim began.

"So we were discussing."

"But a pocket of stiff resistance remains, a few hundred spans west of here."

Aljeron and Pedraan exchanged a quick glance.

"What holds this pocket of resistance together when all the rest of our enemy is in disarray?" Pedraan asked.

"Farimaal. Only those Nolthanim close to him hold their ground and fight together with anything like order and determination. Everywhere else the enemy gives way."

"Is that so?" Aljeron asked.

"It is," Evrim answered. "I have come to find you, that you might rally our men."

Aljeron turned to Pedraan. "Will you come with me, Pedraan? This may be our last chance to fight together. Let us go to war once more, side by side."

"I will come," Pedraan said, smiling. "This dread captain, Farimaal or whoever he is, is making me mad. It's about time he met his match."

Benjiah looked back over his shoulder at Valzaan, scrambling up behind him a good bit farther down. They still weren't that high, but the loose rocks made the ascent tricky even though the slope wasn't steep. Valzaan, for his part, came on steadily if a little slowly, and Benjiah was so glad to have him along that he didn't even consider bidding the aged prophet to hurry up. There was inside him no small amount of conflict. He felt strongly that Synoki, or Malek, or whatever he should call the limping man, was somewhere up ahead and that he should hurry after him. At the same time, he also felt that catching up to the limping man was something that he would rather avoid.

What was he doing, chasing Malek up a mountain, up *the* Mountain? He was not quite a seventeen-year-old boy. Malek was one of the original Twelve, a Titan who had helped rule Kirthanin from the beginning of time. What was Benjiah supposed to do if he caught him? Malek had eluded capture for more than two thousand years. What was Benjiah supposed to do that would change all that?

The question had occurred to him before, of course, but there had always seemed time to answer it later. Now he was actually on the Holy Mountain, in hot pursuit of Malek, and he could no longer defer or avoid it.

He had heard assurances in various forms from the beginning of his journey that Malek was, perhaps, a shadow of his Titan self. Perhaps, some said, enough of his power had gone into his creations or been entrusted to Cheimontyr that Malek was not what he once was. As far as Benjiah knew, these murmurs and rumblings might well be true, but he had seen the limping man avoid Benjiah's arrow and then cast him through the air with apparent ease from the far side of a battlefield. Whatever power Malek had lost, he possessed enough to best Benjiah. Benjiah had felt no rush of light and warmth face-to-face with this enemy. Of course, if Valzaan was correct, it made sense that he hadn't. Allfather wanted Malek to come here. In fact, He was drawing Malek and the rest of them to the Mountain, so evidently a showdown between Malek and Benjiah or anyone else for that matter at Tol Emuna had not been the plan.

Benjiah knew that he was supposed to trust in Allfather and His plan. The same omnipotent will that had orchestrated history to bring Malek back to the Mountain was at work to draw Malek and Benjiah up it. If it was Allfather's will that

Benjiah should be given the power to strike Malek down, then he supposed he would be able to do so, but was victory sure? Was it guaranteed? Not according to Valzaan, who evaded straight answers about this subject even more than he normally did. So the questions lingered in his mind. When Benjiah caught up to the limping man, to Malek in the guise of this mysterious Synoki, what was he supposed to do?

Valzaan, by now, had almost reached him, but he was still a moment away. Benjiah allowed his eyes to flicker closed, and he pushed the strong sense of Malek's presence not far above them on the slope away from his consciousness. *I don't know what I'm supposed to do, but give me strength to go forward and to do it.*

The prayer was quick and silent, but it was sufficient. He opened his eyes in time to greet Valzaan, who had joined him and paused to catch his breath. For the moment, at least, the questions and doubts did not overwhelm Benjiah, and he could focus once more on the task at hand.

"How are you doing?" Benjiah asked as Valzaan rested.

"All right," Valzaan answered between deep breaths. Benjiah waited.

"I have seen him," Valzaan added after a moment. Instinctively, Benjiah turned and peered up the mountainside. Valzaan continued, "Not in the waking world."

"Is he beyond our sight, then?"

"Yes, but not too far. He is keeping a good pace, despite his defective leg."

"Yes, the leg," Benjiah murmured as he and Valzaan renewed their progress up the Mountain. "Why a lame man?"

"Pardon?"

"Well, you've said that Malek could take a variety of human forms. In fact, you said that if he wanted to, Malek could pass unnoticed and unknown among men, which he apparently did for some time. Why as a lame man? Is he really lame?"

"I think he is," Valzaan answered. "Otherwise, I don't know why he would maintain the illusion now that it serves no purpose. Surely he would abandon it and flee all the quicker on two strong legs. When he was thrown from the Mountain perhaps his body was so broken that his capacity to shift human likenesses was limited as well. Perhaps he can only adopt broken human forms like that of Synoki. I had thought it just a clever trick. After all, who would suspect a broken man of being the greatest of Titans? Certainly it runs counter to what we know of Malek's personality in the First Age, when he walked among men as a large and powerful man. It now seems to me, however, as though it was no trick at all. It appears to be the truth of Malek's physical limitation."

"One he cannot overcome?"

"I think not, though I should not be surprised. He is not all-powerful."

"Not all-powerful, perhaps, but powerful, despite his brokenness."

"Yes, he is powerful," Valzaan answered.

Benjiah wrestled with himself for a moment, working up the nerve, then he asked his question. "So what should I do if I catch him?"

"I don't know, Benjiah," Valzaan answered softly. "But you must trust Allfather. He who guided you with the Grendolai and Black Wolves will guide you with Malek himself."

"But you have said this may cost me my life. How can I trust that this will be like those other times?"

"I did not say it would be like those other times in terms of the outcome," Valzaan answered. "I have only said that Allfather will guide you. Of that I am sure. That doesn't mean that it won't cost you your life."

Benjiah resumed his trek up the Mountain, and he did not reply to Valzaan's statement. There was nothing new in it.

"The Kirthanim at the foot of this Mountain have followed Allfather's guiding, and rightly so, and it has brought them here," Valzaan continued. "For many of them, it will cost them their lives. You are a prophet of Allfather, and through you mighty deeds have been done. Even so, the same truth applies to you. When all is said and done, the servant of Allfather is required to go where he is led and do what he is instructed, neither more nor less. What happens to him when he obeys, is beyond his control, even beyond yours and mine. In the end, we are both only servants."

"That's not terribly reassuring right now."

"I understand," Valzaan answered. "Perhaps at this point you may only find reassurance in this: What is beyond your ability to comprehend is perfectly clear to Allfather and is within His plan. Whatever waits ahead may be a surprise to you and to me, but it won't be to Him. Trust is all we have."

Aljeron ran behind Evrim with Koshti at his side and Pedraan coming on a little behind. As they ran, they passed a larger group of Malekim than they had yet seen pushing toward Gyrin. It was not hard to reconstruct the situation. A pair of towering Vulsutyrim followed, and their path from the battlefield toward the great wood was strewn with dead Malekim.

At Gyrin, however, the Malekim were met by a unit of Great Bear under Turgan himself. Turgan's teeth were bared, and after slamming a Malekim against a tree with his great staff so hard that the tree shook and the crushed Malekim crumpled to the ground, Turgan gave a great growl. The Voiceless were so affected by the Great Bear's frenzy that they turned and ran straight back into the Vulsutyrim, whom they had apparently forgotten in their haste to escape the new threat. They did not get far.

"They're something to see, the Great Bear," Pedraan said from behind him.

"They are indeed," Aljeron answered. "So gentle in life and so deadly in battle."

They ran on, and Aljeron's thoughts drifted back to the possibility that this was the end of the war against Malek. The Great Bear, he thought, for all their ferocity on the battlefield, didn't seem to *need* to fight. Not like Koshti seemed to. Not like Caan had seemed to. Not like, well, like he seemed to.

They reached their destination, and there was no more time for reflection. The fighting here was considerably more organized than anything Aljeron had encountered all day, and it was easy to see why. Sitting atop a great, sturdy stallion, Farimaal in his bizarre armor was out in front of his soldiers, holding them together against a larger force of Kalin Seir and Kirthanim, who were nevertheless having no success in taking down the dread captain.

The greater their distance from Farimaal, the more success the Kalin Seir and Kirthanim had. Snow leopards darted in and out of the skirmishes, sleek and fast, white streaks of snarling teeth and razor-sharp claws. Without Farimaal's leadership, Aljeron realized almost immediately, the enemy would collapse.

Koshti, able to wait no longer, sped away from Aljeron's side. Aljeron thought of calling after him but stopped when he realized what was happening. The tiger caught up to one of the snow leopards that was pursuing a Nolthanim, and together the two cats took down the man, who was able only to give a brief, startled cry before he was pulled to pieces.

"Come, Pedraan," Aljeron said, unsheathing Daaltaran and turning to his friend. "Let's do what we've come to do."

"Let's," Pedraan replied, and together they moved forward.

Evrim followed, but Aljeron turned to him. "Evrim, no."

Evrim shot Aljeron a look burning with anger, but Aljeron held firm. "You've come a long way, but you're not ready for this. Maybe none of us is. Stay back."

For an instant Evrim glared at Aljeron, but then he stepped back. Aljeron turned toward Farimaal.

Between Aljeron and Farimaal, a contingency of Nolthanim soldiers fought like crazed men against Kalin Seir and snow leopards. With Aljeron's and Pedraan's aid, however, these men were quickly dispatched. Soon nothing stood between Aljeron and Farimaal but open ground.

Pedraan was with him, and they paused instinctively, evaluating the man they had come to kill. Then, without a word, they moved a few steps apart. Divide and conquer. It hadn't worked for anyone else who had engaged this enemy captain, but Aljeron and Pedraan weren't just anyone. They were, in Aljeron's estimation, the best fighting men among the Kirthanim.

Farimaal wheeled on his horse to face them, and he looked down upon them for an instant before he spoke.

"Have you come for me?" His voice was quiet but clear, and Aljeron thought he detected a note of bemusement.

"We have," Aljeron said as he and Pedraan continued forward.

"Do you still not know? You cannot kill me."

"We can't?" Aljeron answered calmly, despite the fear that knifed his gut. What if this man was not really a man? What if he was . . . something else?

"No, you cannot," Farimaal replied. "You will soon fall under the hammer, as do all who come for me. My armor is made from the hide of the Grendolai that I killed a thousand years before you were born. I cut it from his dead body with my own hands. Your blades will not penetrate it, so come on if you wish to die, for death is all you will find here."

The horse charged Aljeron, and he had to dive to the side to avoid the sword stroke that almost took off his head. He heard a scream like that of a horse in pain, and Aljeron got up in time to see the horse bearing Farimaal wheel around, his rear left leg dragging. Pedraan had struck the flank of the horse. The blow had landed and crushed the bones at the top of the leg. The horse struggled to keep its feet under the weight of the heavy rider, but it stumbled around, its flank drooping like its rear legs were about to buckle and break.

A flash of orange flew by Aljeron and leapt into the side of the faltering creature, and it collapsed under Koshti's weight. Farimaal, though momentarily down, was soon on his feet, surprisingly agile despite the full body armor of, if Aljeron could believe it, Grendolai hide.

Both Aljeron and Pedraan had moved in instinctively when the horse went down, and they continued with their attack. Farimaal dodged Pedraan's war hammer and blocked Aljeron's stroke, whirling away from them both and even launching a counterattack on Aljeron that he was only barely able to deflect. Aljeron realized at that moment that whatever Farimaal was, he was more than just a soldier in a suit of armor.

Back and forth the fighting continued, and now both men and Koshti were circling Farimaal. Cautiously they moved, all aware that there was no margin for error. Make a mistake against this man and someone would die, maybe all of them. Farimaal lunged toward Pedraan, initiating an offensive strike that Pedraan could only partially block. The downward sword thrust caught him on the left side and left him bleeding through his torn shirt.

"Stay back! I'm all right," Pedraan called as Aljeron started to move to assist him.

As he called out, Pedraan had started in toward Farimaal, angered by the wound, his war hammer swinging so viciously and fast that it forced Farimaal backward. Aljeron came in as well, and though he landed a blow against Farimaal's back with Daaltaran, the first really solid blow he'd managed to strike, the blade didn't cut the Grendolai hide at all. Aljeron stumbled, dismayed. He hadn't believed that his Azmavarim would do nothing at all against the armor. Now he knew that the opening in the visor was the only real weakness in the man's defenses. How he would be able to get a shot at that, though, he had no idea.

Again, Koshti flew in, taking advantage of the attacks by the other two. He launched himself and hit Farimaal with all his weight in the shoulder, pushing the man hard enough that he fell over. The tiger tumbled down with Farimaal, and Aljeron could see his powerful jaws working to rip through the armor around Farimaal's neck.

It must have startled the tiger to find that he could not rip open the protective hide. Aljeron had never known Koshti's teeth to fail him. Even Malekim hide could not withstand those powerful jaws, as Koshti's first encounter with one had shown. Now, though, through the bond they shared as battle brothers, Aljeron could feel something of the surprise and anger that rippled through Koshti as he tried harder to rip through the Grendolai hide.

Farimaal, though down and with the full weight of the tiger upon him, was not inactive, and having gathered himself for the blow, swung his gauntleted arm and struck the tiger on the side of the head, managing to dislodge Koshti. As they both rolled to the side, Farimaal raised and drove home his sword. The blade swiftly and fatally penetrated the tiger's chest.

Aljeron felt the shudder that wracked the tiger's frame, and he attacked Farimaal with renewed wrath. Farimaal was already rising to his feet, turning to meet Aljeron, the writhing tiger prostrate on the ground. Before they could come together, Pedraan landed a blow with his massive war hammer to the side of Farimaal's head. It was a crushing strike, and Farimaal was knocked completely off course.

Pedraan followed hard after. He was raining blows with the war hammer now, trying, Aljeron thought, to crack through the dense Grendolai hide. Blow after blow connected, and Farimaal stumbled across the open space but kept his feet despite the brutal intensity of every shot. One of those blows against any ordinary man without armor would have been an instant kill, but Farimaal struggled on, no longer able to dodge the hammer, but not collapsing under the punishment.

After more than a dozen hits, Pedraan paused to gather himself. Sweat was pouring down his face and indeed, his whole body was soaked with perspiration. He had swung as hard and fast as he could, landing rapid and thunderous blows, and still no sign of a crack or break appeared in the Grendolai hide. For his part, Farimaal stood dazed, his sword, still held weakly in his hand, dangling downward.

Aljeron circled warily to face Farimaal, wanting to be sure this apparent lack of defensive posture was not a deception. Farimaal did not move to meet him or raise his sword. His blank eyes gazed out through the slit in his Grendolai helmet. Pedraan looked at Aljeron, who returned his glance with a shrug, hardly taking his eyes off of the motionless form of the dread captain.

Pedraan, stepping back, slid his hands all the way down to the bottom of the hammer's long handle. He tightened his grip, and cocked the great war hammer. Still, Farimaal did not move. Aljeron, seeing out of the corner of his eye what Pedraan was preparing to do, held his ground. He didn't want to be anywhere near the receiving end of this blow.

The stroke that Pedraan landed was, if possible, even more crushing than any Aljeron had ever seen from him. The arc of the blow was slightly upward, the head of the hammer beginning on a level with Pedraan's knees and moving swiftly upward until it connected with the front of Farimaal's helmet. At that moment, something remarkable happened. The Grendolai helmet which covered all but Farimaal's eyes flew up and off of him. It flew across the battlefield and landed a fair distance away, bouncing a little in the grass, while Farimaal reeled and then dropped, finally, to his knees.

"That's for my brother," Pedraan said as he gathered his breath and gazed down at his stunned enemy.

Aljeron did not hesitate. Farimaal had somehow survived the stroke from Pedraan's war hammer, but he did not live long. If his eyes were still functioning, the last thing they must have seen was Daaltaran flashing toward them. The blade slid smoothly and easily through Farimaal's neck, which was but flesh and bone after all, and his head landed midway between the body and the helmet.

Aljeron stooped and began to wipe Farimaal's blood off of his sword, which he wiped carefully, even lovingly, whispering so that no one but Pedraan could hear. "Death comes to all."

When his blade was clean, he sheathed it and crawled to the place where Koshti now lay still. He took the tiger's great, furry head in his arms, with his two deep eyes staring straight ahead, no longer bright but dark, and he wept. He thought of the little tiger cub that he had freed from the hunter's arrow, of the fear and terror in its eyes as he had bound the wound. He thought of the way Koshti had saved him from the Malekim and licked the wounds on his face. He thought of all the years behind them, and of all the leagues they had traveled together. He thought of the powerful connection and bond they had shared, and he felt the emptiness inside him now where the ever-present sense of his battle brother had always been.

"My brother," he murmured almost incomprehensibly as Pedraan stood over them. "My brother."

8

STRENGTH THAT
STOOPS TO CONQUER

NIGHT FELL ON THE HOLY MOUNTAIN. A clear
sky full of brilliant stars smiled down on them, but only a thin
slip of a moon shone, its pale light faint and eerie on the
stones around Benjiah's feet. It was late in the lunar cycle, and
in just four days there would be no moon at all. In five days it
would be the first day of Summer Rise, Benjiah's birthday.

Benjiah tried not to think of his birthday as he pushed his
weary legs to keep moving up the Mountain. The smell of warm
iced cakes wafting through the palace in Amaan Sul swept over
him, and he found his mouth watering. Birthdays had brought
him many different things over the years, but one thing that
tied them all together was a mountain of iced cakes. The older
he grew, the less he needed help eating the mountain. Right
now, he felt as though he would not have needed any help at all.

He couldn't remember when he'd eaten last, and he wished he hadn't begun to wonder. The thought of food was making him even more hungry.

He turned his mind outside himself, refocusing on the reason why he was here, climbing this Mountain in the dark. He could sense that Synoki had not stopped, and he was not willing to stop either—for rest or for food, though he was quite sure he had none of the latter anywhere near him. Even if he had tried to stop, the sense that he had to move onward, forward, farther up the Mountain wouldn't allow him to. It was a compulsion. He had to catch Synoki.

They were closer now. Benjiah knew that for sure. He had not seen Synoki, though at moments he felt sure that Synoki could see them. He heard sounds and noises from up ahead, too, sounds that could represent nothing other than Synoki's own desperate scramble up the Mountain. Occasionally, the sound of displaced rocks would greet his ears, and at such moments, Benjiah would push on harder and more determined than ever.

Valzaan, for his part, was doing a better job of keeping up. It was as though Benjiah had spent whatever adrenaline he had on the lower portions of the Mountain and tired in the hours since, while Valzaan somehow maintained the same pace. It was probably a trade skill of prophets that Valzaan had developed during his thousand years of life that he had not yet taught Benjiah. Whether it was or not, Benjiah knew that there was in fact at least one such skill that Valzaan had not taught him.

As it had grown dark, Benjiah saw Valzaan carrying something clenched in his hand that was shining out in a small radius. Benjiah stopped to see what it was, but when Valzaan caught up to him, Benjiah saw that it was nothing but a compact ball of light nestled securely in Valzaan's palm. Benjiah asked how Valzaan could do that, produce and sustain the small globe, but the older prophet had merely smiled and said, "We'll save that discussion for another time."

"What other time?" Benjiah asked darkly as they continued up the side of the Mountain. "For me, there may be no time to learn but this."

"If that is true, then spending what little time you have on this would be a waste of your final hours. And if it is not true, well then, it isn't worth worrying about, is it?"

Benjiah did not have anything to say to this, but Valzaan continued with little more than a pause. "What I have said to you just now, Benjiah, is the answer of the head, but come, you should hear also the answer of the heart. As a living creature made by Allfather, we are creatures of hope. You are able to climb this Mountain tonight in the dark because you are alive. You breathe in the air and take each step because the gift of life is yours. You don't know how long you have it, but that is not the point; no one else does either.

"What I am saying is simply this—you must go up this Mountain as though you are going to come down it again. You must, because that is what it means to be alive. Come, ask me no more about this light, but walk in it awhile with me. It will serve us better as a guide to our feet than as a topic for our conversation."

And so they walked awhile together, talking about many things, but as the slope grew steeper and more difficult, talking also grew more difficult. Eventually they stopped talking in order to conserve their breath. So Benjiah eventually found himself a few spans ahead of Valzaan, but the steady glow of light continued to cast his shadow faintly forward upon the rocky mountainside, showing him that Valzaan was keeping up.

And then, even as they were struggling with a particularly steep and unpleasant part of the mountainside, they found themselves upon a wide, ledgelike surface. Benjiah stopped and turned, reaching down to give Valzaan a hand up onto the ledge. The mostly flat surface was perhaps three spans across with thin wisps of grass growing out of it. On the other side, the mountainside moved steadily upward again with as steep a slope as the portion they just traversed.

"This is a strange ledge," Benjiah said, turning back to Valzaan, who stood in the middle of it, facing neither up nor down the Mountain but along the level portion.

"This is not a ledge," Valzaan answered, raising his hand higher. The light glowed brighter. He started walking along the ledge, and Benjiah started after him, catching up quickly and walking beside him, realizing after a moment that the ledge was not in fact flat as he first supposed. They were headed, even if only slightly, upward.

"What is this?"

"This is a road," Valzaan answered.

"A road?" Benjiah asked, but he said no more, for up ahead he saw what appeared to be a vast opening in the side of the Mountain. It was black and cavernous, more than three times his height and easily as wide as the three-span road that lead into it. "Valzaan, maybe you should stop walking now."

"It's an opening into the Mountain," Valzaan said, stopping as Benjiah had suggested. "Isn't it?"

"It is," Benjiah said, looking from the opening to the prophet. "Can you see it?"

"I can sense it. Not only that, but I can smell it too. It exhales its less-than-savory breath onto the world, as it has these many hundreds of years."

"This is the place where Malek's hosts emerged?"

"It may well be, though there is no doubt more than one way in and out."

"But," Benjiah said, a little confused, "if this heads into Malek's lair, why did Synoki not go in? I can still sense him moving up the Mountainside."

"I can sense him too," Valzaan answered. "He did not go in."

"I thought he was fleeing here, back to his ancient lair."

"So did I," Valzaan answered, "but we must have been wrong."

"If we were wrong," Benjiah said, "then that can only mean he's—"

"—headed to Avalione."

"The blessed city," Benjiah whispered, trembling a bit. "He's going all the way up."

"It appears as though he is," Valzaan answered. "And it looks as though we won't be getting any rest tonight."

"Ugh," Benjiah groaned. "My legs are already so heavy. I don't know how long I can keep this up."

"Well," Valzaan said at last, as though he had been considering Benjiah's words as a request rather than a complaint. "I suppose that we can take a brief rest."

"I want to, believe me, Valzaan. I just don't know that I can," Benjiah said. "I know that sounds bizarre, but all day I've felt this urgency. I don't think it, or He, or whatever is going on inside me, will let me sit down and rest."

Valzaan placed his hands gently on Benjiah's forehead. A sense of peace and calm washed over him. "Sit here, with your back to the Mountain, and rest. Sleep if you can, just for an hour. I will keep watch, and when you awake, we will renew our pursuit."

"Are you sure?" Benjiah asked, but already his eyelids were heavy.

"I'm sure," Valzaan said. "Rest."

"All right," Benjiah said, settling down and yawning. "I don't need to be told twice."

"I just told you twice," Valzaan said, almost laughing, but Benjiah heard his words as a distant echo, because he was already falling fast asleep.

The sun was pleasantly warm upon his face, and Benjiah did not want to open his eyes. The grass he was lying in was thick and lush and just a little bit ticklish. A faint scent of daisies drifted on the breeze, and he inhaled it gladly. An ant crawled up out of the unseen world beneath the grass, onto one of his fingers, but he didn't want to move so he let it cross. Eventually it descended the other side and disappeared back into the grass from which it came. His body felt very tired, though he couldn't remember what he'd been doing to wear himself out so thoroughly. At any rate, he supposed it didn't really matter. It was summer now, and his days were his own.

"It's good to see you relaxed and enjoying yourself," a light-hearted voice said.

Benjiah's eyes flickered open and he rolled onto his side to see the speaker, who was silhouetted a bit by the bright sun shining behind him. As his eyes adjusted, Benjiah sat up. "Father?"

"Yes, Benjiah," Joraiem said, laughing at Benjiah's surprise. "Sorry to sneak up on you like that."

The hint of a thought that somehow this meeting was unusual passed through Benjiah's mind, but as he reached out to grab hold of it, it was gone. He smiled at his father and said, "It's nice here in the grass, isn't it?"

"Yes, it is," Joraiem answered, lying down on his side and propping his head up on his left hand, his elbow buried in the grass. "Sleeping outside on a warm summer day is one of my favorite things."

"Mine too," Benjiah answered, relaxing again and closing his eyes as he lay down once more. "It's like, well, I'm not sure how to describe what it's like. Sleeping in the summer sun is like dreaming, I guess."

Joraiem laughed again. "Yes, it is very much like that."

Benjiah laughed too. He laughed and lay still, letting the warm sun continue to smile down upon him.

"Benjiah, we need to keep moving."

Benjiah opened his eyes again, but the sun was gone and Valzaan was leaning over him, shaking his shoulder gently. Benjiah pulled away from Valzaan's grip and tried to lie down flat on the ground, mumbling, "Just a little longer."

"No," Valzaan answered, taking hold of Benjiah's wrist and pulling his arm up much less gently. "I'm sorry, you can't have any longer. We need to be going."

Reluctantly, Benjiah sat up and rubbed his eyes. Valzaan was standing beside him in the pale moonlight, a thousand stars glittering above his head. The sight was beautiful in its own right, but somehow depressing. It had been so nice to sleep. What's more, he was pretty sure he'd been dreaming when Valzaan woke him. He couldn't quite recall what about, but he felt sure it had been pleasant.

Benjiah stretched and stood, yawning. "How long did I sleep?"

"An hour, as I promised."

"It didn't feel like an hour."

"It never does. Now come, we must go on."

Benjiah felt the presence of Synoki growing on his mind again, and he realized at once that the lame man was a good bit farther away from them than he had been. "He's still moving up."

"I know," Valzaan answered as they started walking along the upside of the road, looking for a good place to climb up onto the Mountain face. "However, I think he sensed that we were resting, and though he didn't stop, he did slow down a bit."

"Does he get tired, like we do?"

"Maybe not entirely like we do," Valzaan answered, "but he shares the limitations of his human body. He can go long periods without sleep or even food, but he does grow weary and hungry eventually."

"Valzaan?"

"Yes?"

"I know they are needed down below, but maybe we could borrow a dragon for a few hours? That would get us up this Mountain in a hurry."

"That certainly would," Valzaan agreed. "But, we cannot do it. The Mountain is closed to the dragons as it is closed to all Kirthanin. Synoki is here in violation of that command, and we are here because stopping him is a task appointed to us. This task, all of it, is for us. We can look to our friends below for no further aid."

"You say *us*, but there will still come a point when I have to go forward alone."

"There will," Valzaan replied. "Now let us go."

They found a place where the embankment wasn't as high as elsewhere, and after helping Valzaan to climb onto it, Benjiah scrambled up. The slope was steep and the going difficult, and they did not go far before his muscles ached. They felt as tired and sore as they had before stopping. The rest had been lovely, just too short to make any real difference.

They labored through the rest of that night and early morning, and the coming of the dawn found them still climbing, one foot after the other, steadily higher and higher. As the light of morning began to spread, even though the sun had not yet shown itself, Benjiah began to feel somehow more hopeful about the venture. They were a good way up the Mountain now, and Valzaan was still with him. Whatever lay ahead might not be as bad as he feared.

After a particularly difficult stretch, they found a small outcropping of rock and sat down to catch their breath. For the first time since early the evening before, Benjiah looked down. What he saw took his breath away. They were so high that the ground far below was little more than a swirl of blurry colors shrouded by a faint mist in the early morning light. Had

Benjiah been scared of heights, he would have had trouble with the view.

"The fighting at the foot of the Mountain is over," Valzaan announced as they sat, looking down.

"Over?"

"Yes, the hosts of Malek have been defeated."

"Completely?"

"Utterly. The Malekim have been exterminated, except for a handful that are even now being hunted by Great Bear and Vulsutyrim. They will not survive the day. In effect, if not yet completely, the Voiceless are no more."

"Just like that," Benjiah said, peering down the Mountainside. "They were a mighty army a few days ago."

"They were, but they are no longer."

"And what about the Nolthanim? Have they been exterminated too?"

"No, though many of their number are dead, as is their captain, Farimaal."

Benjiah thought about the man in the dark, gruesome armor, and he shuddered. "I am glad he is dead. He was . . . oh, I don't know even know what word to use. Unnatural."

"He was indeed, but he also is no longer."

"And what about the Nolthanim who aren't dead? What will happen to them?"

"That is up to them," Valzaan said. "They are men, after all, and not creatures made by Malek. It may be that Allfather will grant them mercy, but whether they take it, well, that is another matter."

Benjiah wondered what this chance for mercy would be, and he thought of the proud Nolthanim he had seen in Malek's camp while he was in the cage. Would they bend the knee? At first the idea seemed impossible, but he wondered what might happen with Farimaal now dead. After all, the

Vulsutyrim turned after Cheimontyr's fall. Might not some among the Nolthanim do the same?

"We should start out again," Benjiah said after a moment, placing his palms on the smooth rock to push himself up.

"We should," Valzaan answered. "Help me up."

Benjiah helped pull the prophet to his feet, and without even thinking about it consciously, he turned and looked upward. His first thought, as he glanced higher and higher, was that this part of the Mountain face did not seem as unforgiving as some of the portions they had climbed in the night, and Benjiah was relieved. A stretch of slope that was not quite so steep was very welcome.

What he soon noticed, though, took his thoughts entirely away from mundane matters such as the grade of the slope. Far above them, he could see what looked to be a portion of a wall or spire stretching into the sky, just a little below the twin peaks of the Mountain. Even at this distance, the white stone gleamed in the morning sunlight.

"Valzaan," Benjiah said, putting his hand on Valzaan's arm. "Is that Avalione I can see?"

Without even glancing up, Valzaan answered. "I should think so. We are high enough by now that it should begin to be visible, though you may not get a very good glimpse until we have a better angle."

"The blessed city," Benjiah murmured, half under his breath. "How remarkable!"

"It is a remarkable place, to be sure," Valzaan answered, starting ahead of the still motionless form of Benjiah. "But let us not hang around here, staring at bits and pieces of it. After all, you're going to see it right up close before too long. For now though, we have work to do. Let's climb."

From sunrise to sunset they climbed. Benjiah's mind wandered less than it had the day before, in large measure because he was far too tired to think of anything more than where he should put his foot down next. He spent much of the day in something of a daze, with only the determination to keep going and the hope that they had closed the gap on Synoki. His hope seemed to be based in fact, for his sense of Synoki's presence indicated that they were closer. However, the farther up the Mountain they went, the fainter that sense grew, for a sense of something else began to overshadow it.

Benjiah could not describe it except to say that Avalione loomed increasingly large in his consciousness. The city was occasionally visible when clear vistas opened up over the course of their climb. However, even when no portion of the city was within view, the thought of Avalione was never far away. He felt as though he was being drawn to the city, even as he had felt he was being drawn after Synoki. What's more, the farther they went, the more the two feelings seemed to merge.

Afternoon became evening and evening became night. Now with only three days until there was no moon at all, the light was even paler. And yet, things did not seem oppressively dark. Perhaps his eyes had compensated, but Benjiah did not feel as though it was as dark as the night before, and he noticed that Valzaan no longer produced the light in his hand. Benjiah wondered if Valzaan was somehow aware that Benjiah could see more clearly this night.

Benjiah realized that it was probably no longer the twenty-seventh day of Spring Wane; rather, they had most likely slipped into the early morning of the twenty-eighth. It was his third day of climbing. Surely today he would reach Avalione, and whether he would find rest there or not, it would at least mean an end to this interminable ascent.

Almost as though in answer to his thought, they crested a ridge and found themselves on ground that was considerably less steep. The ground moved upward, but progress could be made at a brisk walk. Benjiah stretched his back, which ached from all the bending over that their climb had necessitated.

Several hundred spans away, a large white structure waited. It was, of course, Avalione. They moved steadily toward it, and Benjiah, despite the dim light, made out the grandeur of its walls and buildings.

"Valzaan," Benjiah said, excitement in his voice. "We're almost there."

"Yes," Valzaan replied. "We have made good time."

"I can't see where the gate is."

"It is in the center of the wall ahead," Valzaan answered. "The city is built into the lower portions of the twin peaks. This wall that you see is less than a half circle, and the gate in the middle of it is the only way in."

"Yes, I can see it now," Benjiah said, straining his eyes in the darkness. "It is a little over to our left."

He took the prophet's arm and adjusted their course just a little, and he felt his own pace quicken. He could see the open gateway, and the excitement of having achieved this goal, having reached Avalione, filled him.

They were still some fifty spans away, though, when something to the side of the gates moved. Benjiah stopped instinctively, as did Valzaan, without even needing Benjiah to warn him.

"What was that?" Benjiah asked. "It isn't Synoki. I sense that he has gone into the city."

"So he has," Valzaan answered.

"Then what is this?"

"I would guess that this is his gatekeeper, appointed to wait and watch."

"A gatekeeper? You mean he brought someone with him?"

"It may be something, not someone, and no, I don't think he brought it with him. I think it was already here, and perhaps it has long been so."

As Valzaan spoke, Benjiah caught sight in the moonlight of the thing. It walked out, directly in front of the gate, and gazed in their direction. Benjiah had no doubt that the creature could see them.

It was a creature—that was clear now. It looked to Benjiah very much like a Black Wolf, but it was far larger than any Black Wolf Benjiah had ever seen. It was bigger than Koshti, and it stood almost as tall as a man. Even from this distance, Benjiah could see its eyes glowing eerily in the darkness, a luminous, pale green.

"It's a wolf, I think," Benjiah said. "An enormous one."

"I think you're right," Valzaan said. "Allfather has granted me an image of the creature."

"But I thought I killed all the Black Wolves," Benjiah said.

"You did," Valzaan answered. "This is no child of Rucaran the Great. This wolf is too large to be descended from that line."

"Then what is it?"

"My guess is that it was made by Malek while he dwelt here in the Mountain. Under the Mountain he would have been limited in what animals were available to him, so perhaps he scavenged what he needed from wolves he already had."

"But why? What did he make it for?"

"To guard these gates? To ensure that no one but he could go in?"

The great wolf began to lope across the ground between them, and it was accelerating with every step.

"It's running this way, Valzaan!" Benjiah cried.

Benjiah reached inside, desperately searching for the light and heat that came with manifestations of Allfather's power. He felt nothing, though, and he turned in terror to see the wolf closing the ground between them rapidly. It occurred to him almost as an afterthought that he might run.

There was, though, no time to run. The great creature was almost upon them when Valzaan raised his arms and cried, "Hold, come no further!"

Immediately the wolf stopped. For a long moment, Benjiah looked at the beast, but it did not move. Its eerie green eyes were trained upon them. Benjiah believed the creature was straining against an invisible barrier, but it did not move.

"You must go on into the city," Valzaan said, with obvious exertion.

"What will you do?" Benjiah said, looking from the immense wolf to the prophet, whose hands remained lifted in front of him.

"I will hold him for as long as I can."

"And when you can't?"

"I said you must go!" Valzaan cried out. "We are here that you may face him in there. Waste no more time and go!"

Benjiah did not waste any more time. He found fresh energy and strength flowing through him, and he ran up what remained of the slope until he stood at the gate of the city. He paused at the threshold, looking in at the white roads, one of which ran along the inside of the city wall, and the other of which seemed to lead directly into the city.

Benjiah looked back over his shoulder. The prophet and the creature were frozen in the moonlight. Taking a deep breath, Benjiah turned around and plunged into the blessed city.

The wailing coming from the camp of the Nolthanim continued. Aljeron stood beside Pedraan, gazing at nothing in particular in the darkness.

"What is that?" Pedraan asked at last.

"I don't know," Aljeron answered. "Let's wait for Evrim to return. He will bring word."

They stood in the chilly, late-night air, listening to the wailing and weeping that rose from the camp of the Nolthanim captives. The two men were not alone, either, for Kirthanim encircled them in the darkness, staring in silence across the distance as they were. The battle was over, and this bizarre interruption of their peaceful evening had been unexpected. Their intent was simply to keep the captured Nolthanim under guard until Valzaan and Benjiah, or at least one of them, returned to give direction about what should be done. For their part, the Nolthanim seemed to accept this fate, disappearing into their own camp, not to be seen again or heard from, until now.

A figure moved up ahead, and they gradually made out Evrim coming their way. He stopped before them, and Aljeron could see the consternation in his friend's face. He seemed to be searching, unsuccessfully, for words.

"Evrim, what is it?" Aljeron asked, impatiently. "What's going on?"

"I don't know," Evrim said, lifting his hands in a despairing signal of uncertainty. "No one really knows."

"What do you mean no one knows?"

"The Nolthanim . . . "

"The Nolthanim what?"

"It seems like a large number among the Nolthanim survivors are dead. There are bodies all over their camp, in the tents and out."

"What?"

"That's what I'm trying to tell you, no one knows what's happening. The guards have tried to get answers from the living, but they're not saying anything that makes sense. I think you should come."

A rush of images poured into Benjiah's consciousness. He saw an immense figure wielding a great hammer charge another, but his arm was seized by opponents, and the hammer stroke was caught and stopped. Around this group, other

Titans—for Benjiah realized that must be what they were—fell upon one another. Some of the Titans were slain and fell, while others fled that place, running along the wall. Then the Titan with the hammer—Malek, Benjiah supposed—wrenched his arm free and turned back into the city with a pair of Titans coming after.

As quickly as they had come, the images faded. Benjiah recalled sitting with Valzaan in the Autumn, hearing the story of the battle among the Titans in Avalione at the end of the First Age, but these images were like nothing he'd ever conceived of on his own. He knew that they were real, like memories, though not his own. How he could see them, he did not know. Neither did he know what they were supposed to mean, and there was no time now to think any further about it.

He looked around him, searching for any sign of where to go, but he saw nothing that helped. There was nothing moving in the empty, white streets, and he could hear nothing other than the whistling sound of the breeze blowing across the Mountain. He felt a sense of urgency again, and not wanting to delay, he started moving up the street that seemed to lead into the heart of the city, even as the three Titans in the last image that flashed before him had done.

He moved silently up the street, and it was up, for the street had a definite incline. Benjiah worked hard to resist the urge to run. He did not know where Synoki had gone, and he needed to be absolutely quiet, both so he could hear anything that might give Synoki's location away, and so he did not betray his own location. He moved to the left side of the street, which seemed to afford more shadow because of the angle of the moonlight, and he moved steadily up and into Avalione.

The eeriness of the white city illuminated by moonlight began to play upon his nerves, and his hands began to tremble. The empty stillness of the place added to his growing anxiety, and he felt an urge to scream, just to hear some human sound.

Loneliness overcame him, and only the driving compulsion that had almost literally pulled him up the Mountain kept him moving forward.

The street opened up into a wider area, and he found himself staring into a vast, open square. Some distance away, in what must have been the center of the square, a long, low wall encircled a defunct fountain. Benjiah's trembling intensified. He'd been here before.

The images of his recurring dreams flashed before him. There was the familiar storm, the rain pounding constantly in the darkness. After the storm came the blinding flash of dazzling light, and Benjiah threw his hands up in the dim moonlight to block the light that was only shining inside his mind. After the light came the slats of the wooden cage, and then they too passed. Benjiah found himself standing in the great white square of the great white city. He blinked and looked around him—the great white square and the great white city were just as he had dreamed. Without exception, down to the smallest detail, everything he saw in the waking world was consistent with the images he had been seeing for years.

This was the square, and the eruptions of water he had seen at the end of his visions, then, must be connected to the famous Crystal Fountain of Avalione. He thought of Valzaan, standing on the Mound of Tol Emuna, pouring water down the sides, repeating the words of the Mound rite. It was all about cleansing, and it anticipated the day the Crystal Fountain would flow again. That was what he had been dreaming about all these years. Allfather had drawn them here, to Avalione, not only that Malek might be defeated but that the great deep might be opened again and that the waters of the Crystal Fountain might flow once more and cleanse the Mountain. There was blood upon the Mountain, and it needed cleansing.

The thought of blood on the Mountain sent a shiver down Benjiah's back. He had come here to face Synoki, or Malek, as he supposed he should really think of him. Whatever happened, it seemed unavoidable that there would be more blood on the Mountain before the night was through.

Benjiah started moving slowly out from the shadow of the wall. It felt strangely bright to be walking in the open, spotlighted by the slim moon, but he continued toward the low fountain wall. As he drew closer, he caught his breath and stopped. Malek was there, at the wall, sitting motionless upon it, watching.

When Benjiah stopped, the man must have realized that he had been spotted, and that there was no reason to remain immobile, for he rose and stepped away from the fountain, walking a short distance toward Benjiah.

"So," Malek said, his voice deep and laced with scorn, "You are the child of prophecy. I'm supposed to fear your coming, am I?"

Benjiah did not answer, for everything he thought to say suddenly sounded silly. As Keila had pointed out, he was just a boy not yet seventeen. Why would the last and greatest of the Titans fear him? The idea was clearly ridiculous.

"You have somehow found your way past my gatekeeper," Malek said, more matter-of-fact this time. "It appears your elderly companion, that doddering prophet Valzaan, has not been as successful. He did not enter the city with you, which means we are alone here, you and I."

The trembling of his fingers increased, and Benjiah felt his legs quivering, so he shifted uneasily. He wiped his sweating hands on his pants and refrained from reaching up to wipe the sweat off of his brow, even though he could feel it rolling toward his eyes.

"You are very quiet," Malek said, stepping not toward Benjiah but laterally, his eyes trained upon him. "I suppose that's to be expected, for you have been taught, I'm sure, to be silent before your elders."

A surge of what Benjiah could only describe as raw power made visible erupted from the man's outstretched hands and flew across the square in Benjiah's direction. It struck him in the chest and threw him into the stone building behind him, where he landed in a heap with a crash. He rolled over and stood up, amazed to find that not only had he not been crushed by the blow, the pain was minor. He turned back toward Malek and started walking back into the square.

If Malek was surprised that Benjiah survived, he hid it by the time Benjiah drew close enough to see his face. This time, though, he did not waste any energy speaking but again cast a wave of energy or force or power or whatever it was at Benjiah. This time, the wave of light and heat that signaled Allfather's power did ripple through Benjiah's body, and he felt the blow strike him, split, and veer off in two different directions so that at the same moment, two of the structures behind him were hammered with the impact.

This time, Benjiah could see in Malek's face the failure of his second attack. For a brief moment, there was surprise, and then it was replaced by rage. "Not bad, boy," he taunted, emphasizing the final word, and then he ran forward.

Benjiah also ran toward him and they met, locking arms in a struggle of strength and will. Benjiah could feel the power of Allfather pulsing through him, and yet he could also feel a very real and terrible power coursing through Malek. It was a long and awful moment as they stood, arms locked and faces so close he could see the glare of eager malice in Malek's eyes.

Benjiah felt a surge of power and realized Malek was weakening. With a great push he threw his enemy backward. Malek tumbled over on the white stones of the square, though he did not stay down long. He rolled and rose in a single, fluid motion, and before Benjiah could lay hold of him again, he was off and running, and quickly too, despite the limp.

Malek ran out of the square by a different road than the one that had brought Benjiah in, and though he was focused on his pursuit, Benjiah realized that they were headed west.

This road passed a number of smaller buildings set off from the road on either side, and Benjiah quickly realized that Malek was headed for the enormous building that rose straight ahead. If Benjiah remembered Valzaan's tale of the betrayal of the Titans, this then was the Council Hall, the place where Balimere had been slain by Malek. In through the open door Malek disappeared, and Benjiah dashed in after.

Benjiah was struck by the loss of light, but he moved carefully in and found himself in an enormous room with moonlight streaming through a towering western window. Immense pillars rose at intervals through the hall, and aside from the shadows cast by these, he was able to see the room reasonably clearly, for his eyes had adjusted to the change.

To his right, a raging fire sprang up in a huge fireplace, and Benjiah could see the dark silhouette of Malek, standing before it. He moved closer, cautiously, watching to see what Malek was up to. The man stretched up toward the mantel, took hold of something, and then turned to face him.

In the bright firelight, Benjiah saw clearly what Malek was holding. It was a long spear, its shaft long and solid, with an especially wicked blade protruding in a jagged fashion. Benjiah, who was only perhaps ten spans away, stopped.

"Do you know what this is?" Malek asked.

Again, Benjiah held his tongue. Of course it was a spear, so he realized that there was something else behind the question.

"This is Ruun Harak," Synoki said. "It is the first spear ever made, bearing the first blade ever forged. And do you know who made it? I did. I made it, for I am Malek, the first and greatest of the Titans, and you are dead."

With that, Malek reared his arm and hurled the spear at Benjiah. In the moment that Ruun Harak left his hand, Benjiah, with remarkable presence of mind, stepped into *torrim redara.*

Once in slow time, Benjiah moved forward toward Ruun Harak. He walked all the way around the place where it hung immobile in midair, examining it carefully and gazing down its shaft toward Malek's hand, which had released it just an instant before. He was not looking out of curiosity or fascination. He was trying to determine, as best he could, the trajectory of the spear. His examination proved fruitful, for he realized that the spear had already, in the short distance since leaving Malek's hand, begun to drift across Malek's body. That meant that for Benjiah to dodge in real time, he would need to move to his left. He'd need to be fast, but armed with this knowledge, he could successfully avoid being skewered.

He returned to the place where he'd been standing and steeled himself for the maneuver. After taking a deep breath, he stepped out of *torrim redara* into real time and dove left. Ruun Harak sailed past him, missing his right shoulder by a hair, and struck a massive column, where it lodged itself.

Malek, stunned by his miss, nevertheless started forward when he saw Ruun Harak sail past Benjiah. Even so, Benjiah, despite his evasive maneuver, had too great a head start, and he reached the spear first. Placing his foot up on the column, he wrenched Ruun Harak free and turned on Malek, raising the spear in his own hand.

Malek came to a halt only five spans away. A genuine look of terror came over him as he looked from the dark blade to Benjiah's angry face. Benjiah took a cautious step closer, and Malek, as though trying to keep pace, took a cautious step backward.

"So," Benjiah said, breaking his silence at last. "No more bravado? No terms of derision? No? Nothing?"

It was Malek's turn not to say anything. They both took another step.

The pent-up rage that Benjiah had felt earlier about the ruin Malek had brought to Kirthanin swept over Benjiah. He shook with it as he cocked the spear back to throw it. As he did so, though, he heard, calm and quiet but also clear as could be, the voice that had first spoken to him in the storm. *Lay it down.*

He hesitated, and Malek, uncertain of the meaning of the delay, took another step backward. Benjiah did not move. The voice continued. *Remember the words of the prophecy.*

> *"With a strength that stoops to conquer*
> *And a hope that dies to live,*
> *With a light that fades to be kindled*
> *And a love that yields to give,*
>
> *"Comes a child who was born to lead,*
> *A prophet who was born to see,*
> *A warrior who was born to surrender,*
> *And through his sacrifice set us free."*

Born to surrender. The words echoed in Benjiah's mind as he stood in the Council Hall of the Titans, trembling. *I was born to surrender.*

Yes, you were. Lay it down, and through your sacrifice, set Kirthanin free.

With a trembling hand, Benjiah lowered Ruun Harak while Malek watched with amazement. When the spear was down, Benjiah forced his fingers to loosen their grip, and the spear clattered to the stone floor.

Malek pounced. He covered the spans between them with alacrity as he snatched up Ruun Harak in his hands. Benjiah stepped backward and raised his hands instinctively to his face, but Malek was not aiming at his face, and he drove the spear through his gut in a single, swift and brutal motion. Benjiah felt pain sweep over him as he sank to his knees, Ruun Harak having passed all the way through. Malek leaned over him, leaning his weight on the spear, and Benjiah groaned as the light departed from his eyes.

"You utter fool," Malek whispered, the scorn dripping from every word. "You *are* dead, and I have won."

9

THE LAST TITAN

MALEK STOOD OVER BENJIAH, staring down at the
dead boy. His death throes had been brief, and his face already had that wan look that came so quickly upon men at
the moment of their passing. His strength and resilience in
the city square had been impressive, as had his lightning-
quick reflexes in dodging Ruun Harak, but he died like a
very ordinary man—nothing exceptional there.

Malek's mind roved back over the two millennia since his rebellion, and he thought of how he struck down Balimere in this
very room. He looked up from the dead boy and gazed toward
the western wall. It had been a little closer to the window, the
place where Balimere stood defiant. He listened to Malek's offer
but refused to submit to it, as Malek suspected he would. But
even up to the very last, when Malek brought his hammer crashing down and ended his life, Balimere showed no fear. That fact
greatly disappointed Malek, for he had secretly nursed the de-

sire to see his brothers cower before him, and even over the long centuries, the memory that they had not cowered vexed him.

He looked back down at the boy, this Benjiah, the so-called child of prophecy who would break his hold on Kirthanin and be his demise and death. At least he had showed his fear. He raised his arms in a fleeting, instinctive act of self-defense, and Malek saw the fear in his eyes as he braced for the killing blow.

But why had the boy laid Ruun Harak down? What could he possibly have been thinking? Ruun Harak could never have threatened the real Malek, the Malek of old, the Master of the Forge and greatest of all the Titans, but when his fall from the Mountain trapped him in mortal form, he was quite vulnerable to the power of the blade. He had been exhausted by his confrontation with the boy in the square, and Ruun Harak thrown straight and true might well have killed him.

But the boy did not throw the spear. He seemed about to— Malek did not doubt that. He saw the flash in his eyes, the intense desire to destroy, but then, without warning, the emotions dissipated. Just like that, they melted away and something like submission and surrender replaced them. Then the boy simply lowered the spear and dropped it. He didn't even bother to throw it away or run; this so-called child of prophecy just stood and watched as he retrieved and used it.

That also vexed him. Malek defeated the boy, but only because the boy surrendered. He had essentially lost the fight, and he cursed his diminished powers. With every new creation since leaving Avalione, he had become weaker. That was why he had struggled so hard, not only to subjugate Kirthanin, but to achieve Avalione—in hope that returning to the blessed city would rejuvenate his power, even though admittedly his first return here had not done so.

He took hold of the shaft of Ruun Harak, gave it a stiff tug, and wrenched it free of the boy. Taking it up, he looked at the blood running down the jagged blade. How fortunate for him that he had brought the spear with him upon his return to Avalione at the end of the Second Age.

Shortly after retreating into the Mountain after the fall of Vulsutyr, he ascended alone to the gates of Avalione. He took no one with him and carried only Ruun Harak, which had come during the long years of his exile to symbolize his quest for sovereign rule over Kirthanin.

He'd stood a long time at the threshold of the city, hesitant to go in. He recalled all the stories from his spies, which had moved to and fro in Kirthanin during the Second Age, about the pronouncements made in Kirthanin by men who called themselves prophets, pronouncements that claimed the Mountain was closed and that anyone who walked upon it would invoke upon themselves the wrath and curse of Allfather. He heard the stories and dismissed them, but once he actually arrived at the gates of the city, he felt strange about going in.

But he eventually did and had found that nothing happened as he walked around the city. Confident that nothing stood between him and occupying Avalione, he deposited Ruun Harak on the mantel in the Council Hall before returning to his lair in the Mountain, fully intending to return to Avalione with his hosts. However, he discovered upon reentering the Mountain that at about the same moment, if not at exactly the same moment, he had stepped across the threshold of the city gates into Avalione, a thousand Malekim had suddenly dropped dead. So it was that Malek returned to Avalione and placed Ruun Harak upon the mantel of the Council Hall at the cost of a thousand lives. Malek realized, of course, that even with his great hosts, he could not afford to pay that price too often, and he determined not to return to the blessed city until Kirthanin lay at his feet. Then he could afford as many lives as necessary to regain the city.

He wiped Ruun Harak's blood-soaked blade upon his cloak. The blood stained his garment, but the weapon was soon clean. Malek ran his finger along the dark metal and admired his own craftsmanship. He thought back to the day when Andunin had taken up this very blade and killed the bleating lamb. Ruun Harak, in all this time, had not lost its edge, for it had once more killed a sacrificial lamb with ease.

Malek looked down at Benjiah, lying cold and still on the stone floor, and he laughed. He'd amused himself with his joke. Sacrificial lamb. That was a good description of the foolish boy. Had he not crossed Kirthanin, climbed the Mountain and pursued him into this place, just to lie down and die?

"Baa!" Malek mocked, prodding the dead body with his foot. Again he laughed, and this time the laughter overcame him. He laughed so hard that for a moment, no sound came from his mouth. He shuddered so hard with the violence of his laughter that his face began to ache. Then sound returned to him, and his laughter burst forth like water breaking through a dam. He laughed and laughed and laughed until tears rolled down his cheeks. He'd not laughed for a very, very long time.

His laughter echoed through the Council Hall and broke out into the stillness of the early morning. The peals rolled through the city streets and even out through the gates. They cascaded down the sides of the Mountain, and the animals and men at the foot of Agia Muldonai heard the roaring laughter and thought that a strange and supernatural thunder was falling from the Holy Mountain. They heard the awful sound and covered their ears, unsure of what it meant and afraid to know.

Outside the gates of Avalione, the warm night hung heavily upon Valzaan, who was still locked in a battle of will and strength with the great wolf, Malek's gatekeeper. The stars had all but disappeared, and Valzaan knew it was almost morning.

Even so, in the nether region of night, after the stars and moon receded and before the sun rose, a dark lull hung over the land like an inverted twilight.

Throughout his long, silent struggle with the wolf, those piercing green eyes were trained upon Valzaan, roving over his unmoving form until they settled in on his throat. Valzaan, though granted a glimpse of the scene from above, could more sense than see the piercing eyes. He could feel them, searching him in a probing way, looking for a weakening of the mental grip with which the creature was being held.

That weakening came with the echoing laughter that spilled out of the city. It came, faintly at first, like a distant echo of a small brook or stream, reverberating off of a canyon wall, but soon it grew until it filled the mountainside, and Valzaan's heart trembled and his body shook at the sound.

He knew it was Malek. More than that, he knew as he listened to the uncontrollable peals of laughter that Benjiah was dead. An image of the boy's lifeless body collapsing to the floor appeared before him. Whether it was Benjiah's death moment in truth, revealed to him by Allfather, or just a semblance of the awful moment produced by his own weary mind, he didn't know. A wave of darkness that felt much like despair washed over him. Sadness and weariness also spread over him in an instant, and slowly at first, but then more rapidly, his shaking hands began to droop. In a moment the gatekeeper would be freed from his hold, but there wasn't much he could do about it.

The wolf, so long held at bay, seemed to spring to life. Every part of it was in motion, and it was not walking or loping toward him but running, its powerful legs ripping up grass, dirt and stones—whatever lay under its feet. It was magnificent in its strength and stride, covering the distance between the place where he'd been halted and the prophet in the briefest of moments.

It gathered itself from over a span away and leapt. The great, dark mass of the wolf flew through the air, its forelegs outstretched and its massive jaws open wide. Valzaan, who patiently awaited the attack, reacted with speed and precision. He raised his no longer weary arms, for the power of Allfather was flooding through him in force, and his aged fingers grasped the upper and lower jaws of the creature and caught him midair. He was not knocked over and the wolf did not fall to the ground, for in the blink of an eye the prophet had sealed his grip upon the brute.

His wizened fingertips slipped inside the huge wolf's warm, moist mouth and felt the sharp teeth that had been so eager to devour him. For just an instant, he sensed through his physical contact, in the midst of the creature's confusion and shock, a residual desire that the prophet might be his dinner. The creature did not yet understand that his death was upon him.

With a quick, fluid motion, Valzaan pulled the wolf's jaws in opposite directions and ripped the creature apart. The rending of the jaw produced a violent cracking that echoed against the walls of Avalione, and Valzaan gladly released the wolf and allowed his body to crash to the ground, the eerie green eyes now empty and dull.

For a moment Valzaan just stood there, gazing down at the gatekeeper. Until the very last moment, he had no idea how he would be delivered, but he had survived too many difficult situations over the long years to doubt that Allfather would provide a way if he was meant to continue forward. That Allfather had provided a way meant it was time to be moving again.

He lifted his countenance to the blessed city. The laughter had died away, and now silence ruled the Mountain once more. Silence but not peace, for Malek was still in the city. Valzaan could feel it. He was still there, reveling in his triumph.

He was still there, profaning and defiling the Holy Mountain. Valzaan walked around the wolf's decaying body, for the fur and skin seemed to be contracting, dissolving, and started up toward the gate. It was time, time to find Malek, the ancient betrayer and destroyer. It was time to find Malek, who forged the blades that had for far too long bound the men of Kirthanin. It was time to confront him at last.

Valzaan hesitated at the threshold and peered in. He reached out and felt the stone of the tall white wall beside him. The stone was smooth and warm to the touch. His fingers trembled a little, and slowly he lowered himself onto one knee and whispered a short prayer to Allfather. *Thank you for bringing me to this day, and for allowing my return to the blessed city. There were days, too many days, when I wondered if I would ever behold it again, but you have brought me back alive, and for that I thank you. Guide my footsteps, I ask, and give strength to my hands to do what must be done. Let it be finished at last, once and for all.* Rising, Valzaan stepped into the city.

He listened but he could hear nothing that indicated where Malek might be. He had a vague sense of Malek's presence further up and further in, but he couldn't pinpoint the location exactly. The image he'd seen of Benjiah falling to the ground appeared to Valzaan to be in the Council Hall, and even though he didn't know for sure that the image was an actual picture of what happened, he thought he might as well start there as anywhere. So, without spending too much time debating with himself, he started up the main road that led to the heart of Avalione.

As he walked quietly up the street, a faint glimmer of early morning light appeared to come from the east. He felt the excitement that the light brought to the King Falcon he had been using on and off again most of the night. He turned his face to the horizon as he walked past the buildings that lined that side of the street in even intervals, but he could not sense the warmth of the sun yet. Only the faintest rays of light slipped irresistibly over the horizon and into the morning sky, a harbinger of the rising sun. Though his own world would remain dark as the sun appeared and rose higher into the sky, it was encouraging to think of light breaking once more upon Kirthanin. He quickened his pace.

He arrived at the entrance to the enormous central square of Avalione and paused, hanging close to the large building at the corner of the street. He directed the windhover far above to circle over the fountain. Peering through its eyes and seeing nothing moving in the square, he started into it. Here the sound of his feet upon the stones resounded a little more, and he took care not to make too much noise. He knew the fountain was ahead and to his right, and the road that would take him to the Council Hall would be on his left.

He felt fear radiate through the connection with the King Falcon, and peering once more through its eyes, he saw that the bird was flying above Malek, who was making his way east from the Council Hall toward the great square, carrying a great spear in his hand. He was only a few spans from the square and would soon be in it, and Valzaan knew that there was not enough time to hide, even if he had been inclined to do so. He decided to stop where he was instead. He would meet his enemy calmly.

Valzaan kept very still, and he sensed Malek's arrival easily. He did not doubt that Malek had also sensed him, so he knew that he would not catch his enemy by surprise. The windhover flying above them both granted Valzaan a better look at Malek, and the increasing morning light allowed him with each passing moment to view his enemy more clearly. He could see the blood smears on the front of Malek's cloak, and Valzaan felt anger rise within, though he quickly pushed it down that it might not cloud his thinking.

Malek had stopped, perhaps fifteen to twenty spans away, and he was looking silently at Valzaan. Neither had yet spoken, and for a long moment, both men did not move. Eventually, Valzaan decided to speak. "You trespass here where you are not welcome."

"I think you have things turned around," Malek said, making no attempt to restrain his condescension. "You are trespassing in my city, where you are not welcome, Prophet."

"This is not your city, though once indeed you did live here, and as for being welcome, I am not the one who defiled Avalione with the blood of my brothers, traitor. You were cast out of the city by Alazare, and you only reentered it at the end of the Second Age at the cost of a thousand lives."

"How did you know that?" Malek said, his voice cold.

"I know many things that you know," Valzaan replied, "as well as many things you do not."

"Your boast may be true," Malek scoffed, "or it may not. It is no matter. Your knowledge will be of little use to you here, where only power greater than that which you possess could save you."

"How do you know what power I possess? Have you measured it? Have you measured yourself against me and found me wanting?"

"You could not stand before Cheimontyr, and he was only my servant. He blasted you into the sea."

"That he did, but as you can see, I am still here, while Cheimontyr lies rotting."

"My point remains, your strength was inferior to his, and he was himself inferior to me. What makes you think you can stand against me?"

"Your time has come. Your army is defeated and destroyed, and it is your turn."

"Is it?"

"It is."

Malek took a couple steps and stopped again. Valzaan did not move a muscle but waited for whatever might come next. Malek held the spear firmly, but he did not make any overtures with it.

"Tell me, old fool," Malek began again. "Why should I be afraid of your shuffling feet, wrinkled hands and sightless eyes when the boy you sent to do your dirty work—no doubt because of your own weakness and frailty, or perhaps even cowardice and fear—this 'child of prophecy' that you have been so concerned about, is dead? All the drama outside Tol Emuna with Sulmandir to rescue him proved ultimately of no use. He pursued me all the way to this place only to die at my hand. He has failed, as have you. My army may be defeated and my captains slain, but after I slay you, who will dare come up after me? I may not have Kirthanin, but I have myself and Avalione, and that will suffice."

"You might have a point, if Benjiah had indeed failed, but he did not fail. For a moment he tottered on the brink of failure, but in the end, he chose rightly. He has won a great victory."

For the second time that morning, Malek laughed. He laughed loud and long. When Malek had finally ceased laughing, he spoke again. "I suppose you can define winning any way you like. If you want to call wallowing in a pool of your own blood as you die *winning*, who am I to correct you?"

"Mock if you like," Valzaan replied. "You are free to do as you please with what little time you have left."

"Again, the empty threats," Malek replied, his voice turning cold once more. "All right, I'll humor you. Tell me how this day can be seen as anything but a complete defeat for you?"

"Benjiah did what he was born to do," Valzaan answered. "Laying down the blade was his great victory, and your response, killing him, could not undo it."

"That's ridiculous."

"Not so. Had he taken up the blade, you would be dead, but the binding of the blade would have continued. Now the cords of bondage that have bound all Kirthanin since Andunin first took up the blade have been broken, and you're about to die."

"Am I? I'll show you, prophet, that the blade has endured your boy's pathetic 'sacrifice.' We'll see just how meaningless this victory of his really was."

"You won't live long enough to see if it was meaningless or not."

"Don't you understand who I am?" Malek raged. "Don't you know what I can do to you?"

"I know who you are," Valzaan replied. "Did I not just acknowledge that you are guilty of shedding your brothers' blood? I know who you are, defiler of Avalione, corrupter of Agia Muldonai and all Kirthanin."

"Your actions don't show a proper respect for the danger in which you stand. I am not the helpless sailor you found stranded on the Forbidden Isle. I am Malek, Master of the Forge, first and greatest of the Titans, and now, the last of them as well. No man can stand before me."

As he spoke, he lifted the arm that held Ruun Harak and for the second time that morning, he hurled it with great force. As the spear sped across the square in the early morning light, Valzaan raised his hand and Ruun Harak shattered—both the shaft and the blade. A thousand pieces fell to the stones and dissolved into nothingness. No trace of it was left to show that it had ever been there in the first place.

Malek, perhaps unconsciously, stepped backward as he watched the remnants of Ruun Harak disappear. Valzaan could sense a whirl of emotions emanating from him. He was angry and bewildered, but stronger than either of those was a sense of concern and even fear.

"I know who you are," Valzaan repeated, stepping forward. "It is you who don't know who I am. You will learn who I am, momentarily, but can you not now guess? Come, I will give you a clue. We have been here before, you and I. Yes, you begin to understand. We have been here before, and now I have returned to finish what we started here, so very long ago."

Then, before the trembling form of his enemy, Valzaan felt elation at the surge of a dazzling power inside him like no other he had experienced in the last two millennia. Light began to filter into his eyes, and he blinked as he suddenly became aware of the white stones of the square and city and of Malek cowering some distance away. He was seeing, not a vision inside his head granted by Allfather, nor a view from above through the eyes of a King Falcon. He was seeing with his own eyes, for the first time in a very, very long while. What's more, his aged body was transforming, growing younger and stronger and bigger, until he stood towering over the square and the still human form of his enemy.

"It can't be," came the half-whispered words of despair that slipped from Malek's lips. "It is impossible."

"It is not impossible," Valzaan, now Alazare in all his Titan glory, replied. "I am Alazare, and I am the last of the Titans."

Malek turned to flee, running through the ever brightening morning light, back in the direction of the Council Hall. Alazare took a few giant steps and cut him off, and Malek doubled back, heading east. He was not entirely powerless, Alazare knew, and he moved with greater than human speed. For the moment, Alazare was content to let him spend his energy. He moved across the great square and cut Malek off from any escape to the east.

For a moment, Malek wavered, unsure of where to go. Alazare stood due south of him, watching him closely. The only possible way out of the square was the road to the north which led past the temple toward the long stairs that wound up between Agia Muldonai's twin peaks. He had no desire to go there, but it seemed the only way out. He turned and fled.

Alazare moved after him, staying close enough that Malek was aware of his pursuit. Malek reached the foot of the long winding stair and began to climb. Up and up and up he climbed, and Alazare climbed after. Alazare could sense the weariness burning in Malek's limbs, yet his enemy did not slow down. Desperation drove him, and he continued with all his remaining might.

When they reached the top, there was of course no where for him to go, and Alazare could see Malek considering leaping from the precipice. He reached out for him, not with his arms, but with a restraining power that Malek could not resist. Malek was frozen at the edge.

Alazare spun Malek around to face him. Fear now mingled with uncontrollable rage, and Alazare could feel the hate radiating out from his enemy.

"There is nowhere for you to go now," Alazare said. "It is time for you to face the hour of your judgment."

"This can't be," Malek growled, his body still held still by the force of Alazare's will. "I would have known."

"You would have?"

"I would have."

"But you didn't," Alazare replied. "I knew you survived your fall, and the fact that I didn't know where you were or what form you had taken convinced me that you were capable of cloaking yourself from me. You never seemed to consider that I could do the same. When you ceased sensing me in my Titan form, the day after I threw you from the Mountain, you assumed wrongly that I had died from the blow you gave me with your hammer. After I buried my brothers, I left Avalione and assumed human form. Allfather removed from me my ability to take Titan shape, saying only that it would be restored when the binding of the blade had been broken and

He began to make all things new. This has happened, and now you must face the consequences of your treachery."

Malek strained to say something, but Alazare raised his hand and Malek's mouth was sealed shut, and little more than muffled sounds escaped. "You will not speak. You have said all that you will be allowed. You are not here to offer a defense, not that you have one. You are here to be sentenced."

Stepping forward, Alazare reached down and picked Malek up in his great hand and moved to the precipice.

"For spilling the blood of your brothers, for tempting Andunin to take up the blade, and most of all, for rebelling against Allfather and plotting to crown yourself lord and king of Kirthanin, you are hereby sentenced to death. You are sentenced to be once more cast from the Mountain, and this time, you will not survive. Your sentence is final and will be carried out immediately. Go now to your doom, to the flames long ago prepared for you."

With that, Alazare cast Malek from the Mountain, and his broken body fell writhing down the mountainside. The seal on Malek's mouth was broken and the once mighty Titan could be heard screaming all the way down. At the foot of Agia Muldonai, a yawning chasm opened wide, revealing a roiling pit of flame. Malek dropped into its center, and the chasm closed with a boom. The dust settled, and there was no sign to Alazare that anything had even happened there.

A single windhover alighted beside Alazare on the ledge, settling in beside him and appearing to gaze down the Mountainside as well. Alazare looked to the little creature, and then noticed another landing not far away from it. He turned his face to the heavens and looked up to see a myriad of dark specks moving to and fro in the sky, coming lower and lower. Soon, a whole flock of King Falcons dropped down all over the ledge, and one of them, a little larger than the rest with hints of age in the coloring of his feathers, landed on Alazare's shoulder. Alazare turned away from the precipice and looked to the hosts of windhovers that were now assembled, covering the ground.

"My, what a greeting." Alazare laughed and then looked at the King Falcon sitting on his shoulder, peering at him with its dark, piercing eyes. The birds stood as though listening, their wings folded at their sides. Alazare thought of how they had ministered to him on this very ledge, so very long ago, and of all the years they had been his window to the world. "Welcome, my little friends, and thanks for your many years of faithful service. You have been the light in my long darkness.

"Now," he said after a long moment. "I can linger here no longer. The Master of the Forge has been consigned to the flames. This portion of my task, at last, is complete, but there is more left to do."

10

THE CRYSTAL
FOUNTAIN

ALAZARE DESCENDED the long stair from the precipice that rested between the twin peaks of Agia Muldonai. The hosts of windhovers that surrounded him there had flown back up into the sky, spreading out in all directions like brown leaves blown from Autumn trees by a whirlwind. The sun was steadily rising, and the morning light was warm and encouraging. He of course felt satisfaction from having finally defeated his ancient enemy, but he also felt sadness and heaviness of heart at the prospect of returning to face Malek's handiwork. His first and last victims waited in Avalione, and it was time to begin the process of undoing the damage that Malek had done.

Several things needed attending to, and he didn't honestly know which should come first. Benjiah lay slain in the

Council Hall, and in his heart, Alazare felt a responsibility to attend to him. He wanted to head there immediately and leave Benjiah alone no longer, for Alazare had been unable to accompany him on his final journey, unable to walk beside him on the last leg of his lonely road to death. On the other hand, there were his brothers, lying where he had buried them two thousand years before under the trees of the orchard. Long had they waited for the promise he'd made to them to be fulfilled. Now that day had finally come, and he did not want to delay.

And yet, despite both these desires, he felt instinctively that he should begin his work at the Fountain. All these years, the great hope of Kirthanin had been not only that Malek would fall, but that the Fountain would flow again, bringing cleansing to the Holy Mountain and all Kirthanin. Surely this was the day. Surely today was the day that the blood that had long stained the Mountain would be washed away.

He reached the bottom of the stair and walked back into Avalione. He passed the temple, and joy sprang up in his heart; soon the Mountain would be clean and the temple could be opened again. Soon all the faithful creatures of Kirthanin could come and worship Allfather together on the Holy Mountain—men and Great Bear, Vulsutyrim and Titans together. No more would they be divided, but as Allfather made all things new, He would restore the harmony among His creations that He had intended from the beginning. Alazare had not set foot in the temple since the First Age, and his own heart longed to return. Not yet, though, he thought as he walked past it and kept on toward the center of the city. There was work to be done first.

Alazare reentered the great white square of Avalione and moved toward the Fountain. He had not seen the Fountain pool empty before, for he had not been here since he'd washed his brother Volrain's blood off of his dead body. He knew that the large, circular pool area had been dry all these long years of exile. Even so, in his memories of Avalione, the Crystal Fountain was always alive, bursting with the pure, clear waters that gave it its name, and the pool was always beautiful and tranquil. Of course, he envisioned the city with the Fountain stopped and the pool empty, but it was a different thing to actually see it that way. It looked barren and desolate, and he wanted it to live again.

He approached the long white wall that encircled the pool. He stopped at the wall and gazed into the empty interior. The Fountain itself was a simple white flower, and only the uppermost petals protruded above the surface of the pool when it was full. Still, because of the water's crystal clarity, the whole flower was always visible, shimmering in its elegant beauty beneath the surface for all to see. Now Alazare could see the bare and inactive Fountain, dry but still beautiful, resting in the center like a flower in the springtime, opening to the sun.

Get the boy.

"Benjiah?"

Yes, bring him to the Fountain.

Alazare turned and walked briskly to the road that led to the Council Hall. His heart beat quickly, churning his competing emotions. He'd not been to the Council Hall since removing Balimere's body for burial, and the place was dark with painful memories. What's more, now that he knew the Council Hall was where Benjiah was slain, his approach to the building weighed upon him even heavier. Despite all this, though, the words of Allfather brought hope. Whatever His instructions might mean specifically, they brought a measure of light to Alazare as he entered the dim chamber.

Though the sun was well up in the eastern sky by now, there was still little light in the Council Hall. The main window faced west, while smaller windows around the top of the hall let light in from all directions, but not much. The smell of smoke from a recently burning fire greeted Alazare as he entered. Finding Benjiah was not difficult, for the boy lay out in the middle of the open floor, his body curled up in a somewhat defensive position, as though his last impulse had been to contract in a vain hope of self-protection.

Alazare stood in the Council Hall doorway and assumed human shape once more. His body took on the long white hair and aged form of Valzaan, but his eyes remained functional. He made haste to his protégé and stooped beside him. With trembling fingers he touched the dead boy's skin, which was smooth and waxen and cold to the touch.

Unbidden, tears began to stream down his face, dropping in dark splotches on the light stone floor. His hand moved to Benjiah's blond hair, and he brushed back the loose strands that had fallen in his face. He thought of the overwhelmed and frightened boy he'd first met in Amaan Sul in the Autumn, standing there with his mother, trying to make sense of all he was hearing and all that he felt. He'd come so far and through so much. Valzaan had wanted to watch over and protect this boy, so eager to do what he was called to do and to become what he was called to become.

Valzaan slid his hands under the boy's shoulders and hoisted him up. Whatever aches and pains he used to feel in his human form were far removed now, and he found new strength and energy as he lifted the lifeless body and cradled him closely. Holding him tightly that way, Valzaan turned and walked from the dim Council Hall out into the morning light.

He walked with the rising sun directly ahead, shining brightly and warming his tear-stained face. Looking down at Benjiah, he saw that while the boy looked just as deathly pale in the full light of day, there was a look of peace on his face that had not been obvious in the Council Hall. Perhaps in the moment of his death, Allfather had spoken peace into his troubled heart and eased his passing, that he might the more readily endure the common fate of all men—at least until now.

Reentering the city square, he clutched Benjiah as his feet quickened toward the Fountain. With every step, his excitement grew. He could feel something remarkable coming, something beautiful, overwhelming, joyous and fantastic. He hurried faster across the square and, reaching the Fountain wall, rested Benjiah upon it and climbed over. He took the boy back up in his arms and all but ran to the center of the pool.

When he reached the Fountain, he laid Benjiah upon the hard stone basin. He reached out instinctively to touch the Fountain and felt the smooth surface of the nearest petal. He knelt once more beside Benjiah, and taking hold of his blood-stained shirt, ripped it open and pulled it back from the gaping wound that Malek had made with Ruun Harak.

Benjiah was a mess, and the torn flesh almost made Valzaan sick. Even so, he did not turn aside from what he had come to do. He placed his right hand over the great wound and closed his eyes. He felt the great searing pain that had spread through Benjiah like wildfire when the spear struck him, and Valzaan groaned at the vicarious blow. Once more, the tears that had come unbidden in the Council Hall returned, and he wept, sobbing over the broken body of this beloved and beautiful boy.

I have brought him, Valzaan prayed silently. *He has done all that You asked him to do. The binding of the blade is broken. Now Kirthanin can be free. Malek has been defeated and destroyed. Now the Mountain can be cleansed. O Allfather, open the great deep and call forth the waters of the Crystal Fountain! Let it flow again. Let the water rain upon us and flow down the Mountain. Cleanse Your land and make all things new!*

Even as the prayer was running through Valzaan's mind, a great rumbling shook the ground under his knees. He felt a mighty surge, like the trampling of a stampede of giants.

The ground shook and shivered. The Mountain heaved and groaned. Then, with a mighty roar, water exploded from the Fountain, erupting hundreds of spans into the air and showering not only the pool but the entire square and much of the rest of the blessed city with the first drops of water to burst from the Crystal Fountain in two thousand years.

Valzaan turned his face upward and closed his eyes as the water fell, cascading over him. It was cool but not cold, delicious and refreshing, like life itself in liquid form flowing from out of the great deep. In the pure water of the Crystal Fountain, his tears were washed away. They were washed clean from his face and disappeared amid the flood of joy that burst within him at the same moment that the Fountain came alive. It felt like he was taking a breath for the first time after being submerged for as long as he could bear, like waking to find the cold, dark night gone and a warm, new day begun, only it was far more beautiful and glorious.

He opened his eyes and looked down at the rising water. It had risen several hands already as the water continued to gush from the Fountain. Benjiah's body had been lifted up and was now floating on the surface of the rising water, his golden blond hair floating in a swirl around his pale face.

Valzaan stood as the water rose, now knee level, now up to his waist, now approaching his chest. With his arms underneath Benjiah, he kept the body from floating away in the swirling waters of the rapidly filling pool. The water was now cascading over the walls of the pool out into the square. The water was seeping outward in all directions, running over the white stone and into the buildings and down the streets.

He looked back from the spreading flood to Benjiah. Something moved. Perhaps he had imagined it, but he thought he saw a flicker of the boy's eyelids.

Benjiah's eyes opened wide and he gasped, taking a long, deep breath.

Benjiah had gradually become aware that he was floating. Where he was or where he had been before was not exactly clear. He felt like it was somewhere cold, dark, and alone, but he couldn't recall and didn't especially want to. But where he was now felt lovely and cool, a welcome respite from pain and toil and weariness. Gradually, he also became aware of light, slowly filtering in from somewhere outside of himself, and he thought that perhaps he had better open his eyes and see what was going on. So he did, and as his eyes fluttered open, he found someone like Valzaan and yet not like Valzaan gazing down at him.

The face and hair were very much like Valzaan, but the signs of age seemed to be gone, and clear, piercing blue eyes gazed at him warmly. Did Valzaan have blue eyes? Benjiah couldn't remember.

"Valzaan?"

"Yes?"

"Are you Valzaan?"

"I am Valzaan," the smiling man answered. "I am Valzaan, and I am more than Valzaan."

"Oh, I see," Benjiah answered, but even as he said the words, he knew that he didn't see.

"Come, stand up and come with me out of the Fountain."

Benjiah felt Valzaan remove his arms, even just as he realized they supported him. His legs drifted down through the cool water until his feet touched bottom. He stood on his own, and when Valzaan started out toward the edge of the Fountain pool, he followed.

At the side, Valzaan lifted himself up onto the wall, where he sat, the water still cascading over the side in all directions. Benjiah did the same, and for a moment he sat beside Valzaan, taking in the great white square of the blessed city, awash in the clear waters of the Crystal Fountain.

"The Fountain is flowing again," Benjiah said, as though just now realizing the significance of what was going on.

"Yes, it is," Valzaan answered. "The Mountain is being cleansed, as is all Kirthanin."

"Then," Benjiah began, memories of his final moments in the Council Hall coming back to him, "Malek is dead?"

"Yes," Valzaan answered. "I cast him from the Mountain. He has been consigned to the flames and is no more."

Benjiah looked down at his chest and stomach, pulling aside the tattered remains of his torn shirt. There was no sign of the gaping wound he had received from Ruun Harak.

"That's strange," he said. "I could have sworn Malek struck me here, and that I was dying."

"He did strike you there," Valzaan answered, "and you did die."

"I died?" Benjiah answered, looking up with wonder and amazement in his face.

"You died, but now you are alive. You have been bathed in the life-giving waters of the Crystal Fountain. You are the first of the faithful dead to return, but you will not be the last, for Allfather has already begun the work of making all things new."

"I really died?" Benjiah repeated.

"You really did."

"I'm sorry," Benjiah said after a moment, "I just don't understand. I remember taking up Ruun Harak to strike Malek, and I remember being told to lay it down, that I'd been born to surrender. Then Malek took it up and struck me, and everything was dark. Now I open my eyes to find that I'm alive again, and Malek is dead. I don't understand. I thought I was somehow supposed to be instrumental to all this, but it seems to have happened without me."

"You were instrumental."

"How?"

"When you refused to use Ruun Harak against Malek, you rejected the blade that Andunin embraced. You laid down what he took up. Even as one man brought ruin upon Kirthanin by freely taking it, so you brought release by freely laying it down. The binding of the blade that held Kirthanin fast for over two thousand years was finally broken. You set in motion the events that led to Malek's ultimate defeat."

"What happened then, after Malek killed me?"

"My hold upon the gatekeeper weakened and he attacked me, but Allfather granted me strength to strike him down. Then, I entered the city to finish what I had started so long ago."

"Finish what you'd started?"

"Yes," Valzaan said, looking intently at Benjiah, "for I am Valzaan and yet more than Valzaan. I am Alazare, Benjiah, the Titan who threw Malek from the Mountain at the end of the First Age."

"Alazare!" Benjiah said, staring now in amazement. "Have you been Alazare all this time?"

"I have." Valzaan laughed. "And I haven't. It was only when I returned to Avalione this morning that my body was restored and I could once more take Titan form, which is why I am no longer blind, you see."

"Did you assume your Titan form to defeat Malek?"

"I did."

"I should like to have seen that," Benjiah answered, smiling broadly. "I bet he was surprised."

"He was indeed," Valzaan answered, and they laughed together. "He was so sure he had won. Even right up to the moment I threw him from the Mountain, he didn't seem fully able to accept what had happened."

"What did happen, Valzaan, or Alazare—what should I call you?"

"Call me whichever you wish," Valzaan replied. "Or, if you prefer, call me Valzaan in this human form and Alazare when I am a Titan."

"All right," Benjiah answered. "Can you answer some of these questions, now that it is all over?"

"Sure," Valzaan answered. "It's pretty simple, really. When I had finished burying my brothers after throwing Malek from the Mountain, I left the blessed city under cover of darkness and assumed human form. Allfather told me that I would not be able to resume my Titan form until I returned to the city, which was not until this very day. I took the form of Erevir, and from the end of the First Age until the end of the Second, I moved in that form among the world of men and Great Bear. I did what I could to guide the affairs of the age, but the Kirthanim would not always listen, and I could not prevent the civil war that opened the door for Malek's return.

"After that war and Malek's escape to the Mountain, Allfather granted me power to change my form and I became Valzaan, the prophet of the Third Age of Kirthanin, and the rest of the story, I think you know."

"That's incredible," Benjiah said. "All this time, I've been walking and talking with a Titan!"

"Yes," Valzaan answered, "but that really isn't so incredible. During the First Age, men walked and talked with the Titans all the time."

"I suppose, but it still seems pretty incredible."

"I can see how it would seem that way. In time, you will grow used to it."

"Perhaps in time," Benjiah echoed, as though he just now remembered something else. "Shouldn't we go down the Mountain and tell everyone that Malek is dead? They'll be wondering, won't they?"

"We will go down," Valzaan answered, "when we have finished all that must be done here."

"There's more?"

"There is," Valzaan replied. "But don't fear, things are proceeding nicely at the foot of the Mountain without us. The fighting is completely over and the Kirthanim are already re-alizing it is time to reforge their weapons for the coming age of peace."

"But what about the Nolthanim and Voiceless who survived?"

"The Malekim died with Malek. When he went into the flame, his children were no more. We may find bodies of Malekim here and there, but I doubt it. I think they more likely have simply ceased to exist."

"And the Nolthanim?"

"That is a different story," Valzaan said, a hint of sadness in his eyes. "When Malek set foot in the blessed city last night, he did so despite the fact it was forbidden to him. The last time he entered the city, it cost the lives of a thousand who followed him. When he set foot in the city last night, all the Nolthanim who lived and still defied Allfather also died."

"They died?"

"Yes, they paid the blood price that the curse required. They paid the final price for following their master."

"But some of them lived, right?"

"Yes," Valzaan said, "A few. Allfather knows the hearts of all men, and He knew the Nolthanim who despised Malek and wanted to be forgiven."

"And He saved them from death?"

"He did."

"And now those who remain are loyal to Allfather?"

"Yes, that is so."

"So there will be no more fighting."

"None," Valzaan said eagerly. "War is ended."

"That's wonderful," Benjiah said, considering the beauty of the words.

"So it is," Valzaan answered, standing up from the low pool wall at last. "But we have not yet finished our task here. One more thing remains to be done. Will you come with me while I attend to it?"

"Of course," Benjiah said, standing as well. The water running over the pool wall and through the square was a little deeper than his ankles, but it did not provide any serious impediment. Valzaan started walking around the pool and Benjiah followed. "Where are we going?"

"Come and see," Valzaan replied, and his voice was cheerful and happy, full of life. "Allfather is making all things new. Come and see."

They walked together, east through the city. The water was flowing at their feet in all directions, and the sun, rising ever higher in the eastern sky, shone brightly so that the running water sparkled with its rays. It was visually dazzling, and though Benjiah knew that what was happening was real, he kept thinking how much like a vision all of this was. Like a vision, though happier and more glorious than any vision he'd ever had.

The street they were on opened up to a verdant grove of lush trees, full of ripe fruit and rich green leaves. The grass was thick and plush, but even here the water ran freely in all directions. Valzaan led him into the grove to a place where seven mounds lay side by side, and Benjiah understood without needing to ask what they were.

"I remember digging these graves as though it were yesterday," Valzaan said quietly, looking down at them.

"Can they not live again, as I do?"

Valzaan turned to Benjiah, his eyes sparkling with tears, though not tears of sadness, Benjiah thought. "Oh yes, Benjiah, they can. That is why we are here."

Valzaan walked closer to the mounds, and stooping, put his hand on one. For a long time he stayed there, lost in his own silent reverie, and Benjiah waited patiently. The sun was warm and the water rushing past his feet cool, and he felt a restful relief unlike any he'd ever known. He was in no hurry to be anywhere other than where he was or to do anything other than to wait upon Valzaan for as long as the prophet saw fit.

"When I laid them in the ground here," Valzaan said after a while, "it was like dying myself. These were my brothers, and we had dwelt together in harmony for over a thousand years. As Allfather's first creation, we watched the unfolding dawn of Kirthanin and walked freely through this land, knowing nothing of betrayal or hatred or fear. Malek ruined all that, and as much as I have long desired to see him pay the full price for his actions, I have even more deeply longed for the restoration of all that was taken from me as well as from all Kirthanin. You were the first to be restored, but now it is time for my brothers to receive the fulfillment of the promise.

"When I laid them in their graves, I spoke words of promise over them. I told them they would rest until the day the Mountain was cleansed and the way was prepared for their return. I told them these things as I buried them, and when all were laid in the earth, I leaned over Balimere, and I whispered into his ear the word that is the great hope of all the faithful dead—*resurrection*."

Valzaan stood and backed a few steps away from the graves. Benjiah moved back with him. Valzaan raised his arms so that his hands stretched outward and up, and leaning his head back, faced the heavens. Benjiah watched as his form changed and grew, and he understood that now he was looking at Alazare, the Titan, and he marveled at his immensity and grandeur.

"Allfather!" Alazare called aloud. "The Crystal Fountain is open, sending forth the waters of life to cleanse the Mountain and Kirthanin. The time of renewal and restoration has come. Awaken my brothers, who were the first to pay the price of Malek's betrayal and are to be, along with your faithful prophet Benjiah, the first fruits of the restoration. Make them new, Allfather, and let them arise and be an earnest of the work that you are already doing across the length and breadth of this land."

As Alazare's words faded away, a great wind came swirling upon the Mountain. The trees swayed and bent, and Benjiah felt for a moment as though the wind was going to lift him from the very ground, but it did not, and after a time, it passed. With the wind came a fog and mist that also swirled about them, layering the trees and sky with white wisps against the green and blue, but as the wind passed, so did the fog and mist. A silence ensued, all the more profound after the rustling wind, and Benjiah noticed a growing brightness. It grew in intensity until Benjiah could see none of the colors of the world around him, and only Alazare. The water and grass at his feet and the trees around them disappeared from view. All was whiteness and illumination, but much to his surprise, the light did not hurt Benjiah's eyes or compel him to look away.

And then, as he stood in the wonder of the brilliance, he saw men walking toward them in the light. They towered above the earth as Alazare did, and he knew from their majestic faces as well as their size that they were not men but the fallen Titans. The light began to fade and gradually the colors of the sky and trees and grass returned, but the Titans did not disappear. They remained, seven figures clothed in white, those Titans faithful to Allfather throughout Malek's Rebellion.

Alazare took the closest one in his arms, and Benjiah could hear the joyful greeting. "Balimere, my brother."

"Alazare, at long last," came Balimere's laughing response.

Benjiah watched as hugs and greetings were exchanged all around. One by one Alazare greeted them all—Rolandes, Volrain, Therin, Eralon, Stratarus, and Haalsun. Tears and laughter mingled, and it seemed to Benjiah that he could feel the joy that radiated from the eight who stood before him, the energy in the air.

When they were finished, Alazare turned around and walked to Benjiah. Standing between them, he turned to his brothers and said, "This is Benjiah, faithful servant and prophet of Allfather. Through him, much of what Allfather orchestrated in this final war with Malek was accomplished. It was Benjiah who laid down Ruun Harak and sacrificed himself that Kirthanin might be free. It is Benjiah whom Allfather raised first, along with you, to be the first fruits of the Age of Restoration. Welcome him, brothers, for he has done well."

The Titans gathered about him, and Benjiah felt no shame or embarrassment by their congratulations. Rather, he felt merely pleasure at their welcome, and he acknowledged their words with gratitude as each of the seven individually greeted him and said, "Well done."

When this exchange was finished, Benjiah turned to Alazare and asked, "Are we finished with the work that must be done here, Alazare? Will we now descend from Avalione, and will your brothers come down the Mountain with us?"

"They will come down the Mountain, Benjiah," Alazare replied, "but probably not just yet. I will go down with you, and we will tell those who are gathered at its foot what has happened. I will reveal myself to them and tell them of my brothers, but it would perhaps be overwhelming for them to see all of us at once. We will let them get used to the idea first. There is no rush anymore. We have all the time in the world.

"Now," Alazare continued, looking from Benjiah to his brothers. "Let us return to the Crystal Fountain. Come and see what Allfather has done. Come and see what Allfather is doing."

As they started out of the grove, back into the city, Alazare became Valzaan again, and he walked beside Benjiah, ahead of the others, who talked among themselves as they followed. Benjiah turned to Valzaan and asked, "Valzaan, I would like to ask a question about you and your brothers, and about Avalione."

"Ask."

"The Fountain pool, the wall around it, the buildings in the city, the trees in the grove, they all appear normal size to me, and yet it seems to me they shouldn't. They should all be enormous. The Fountain wall should be so high I couldn't possibly scale it, and yet I stepped up and over it with little difficulty. What's more, when I look at you as Alazare, and at your brothers, I see that you are far bigger than I, but the trees in the grove were not dwarfed by you. When I look behind me at your brothers, I see that the buildings of the city are just the right size for them. All seems to fit them, as it should, and yet the same buildings seem to fit me. This cannot be."

"It cannot?"

"I don't see how," Benjiah asked. "Can the same tree be two or three times my height and also be two or three times the height of a Titan, or the same wall be half my height and yet half your height, when you are Alazare?"

"If not, how do you explain what you have seen?"

"Perhaps there is something about this place which adjusts to your eyes, so than when you see it, you see it in perfection, regardless of scale."

"But you haven't just seen the wall of the Fountain pool; you've touched it and sat upon it and crossed over it. Can it be that you simply saw yourself crossing it or sitting upon it?"

"I don't think so," Benjiah said.

"Also, let me ask you this, since it is the realm of what is possible that we are discussing. Can it be that you were dead and are now alive?"

"It seems so."

"It is so, for you are here, and you live, though you were dead." Valzaan said, laughing, and then he continued. "You were very nearly right. Avalione is unlike any other place in

Kirthanin. It is perfect in both size and appearance to any who enter at its gates. A small child who desired to bathe in the Fountain pool would find it as easy to access as you did to exit. This would be true, whether the pilgrim in search of washing was a Great Bear or a Vulsutyrim."

"That is amazing."

"It is the work of Allfather, and all His works are amazing, though we understand some of them better than others."

They reentered the square, wading to the Fountain, which continued to shower the city. The Titans gathered at the wall that encircled the pool and gazed at the Crystal Fountain, and they stood quietly, letting the refreshing water rain down upon them.

"When will we be going?" Benjiah asked Valzaan.

"Not until tomorrow," Valzaan answered. "The sun is already high in the sky, and we have one more thing to do."

"What's that?"

"Celebrate," Valzaan answered. "Today is a day of celebration, and we will feast this afternoon like you have never feasted."

"That sounds wonderful," Benjiah answered. "Though I no longer feel hungry, as I did on our way up the Mountain, the thought of eating is welcome."

"Good, for the table will soon be laid," Valzaan answered. "It will be time then to eat and drink and remember our sorrows no more."

The preparations for the feast were largely a mystery to Benjiah, who saw the Titans going here and there but did not partake in the preparations. He was told simply that it was not necessary. When he was at last ushered into the building, he beheld a glorious table laden with food from one end to the other. There were plates and bowls overflowing with the fruit of the groves he had seen east of the city. There were vegetables too of all varieties, as well as fresh warm bread and soft delicious cheese and exotic nuts and berries he had never seen before. In the great fireplace near the table, two immense spits turned slowly, and the smell of roast meat wafted across the room and whetted Benjiah's appetite.

He was shown to the head of the table, where he was seated as though a guest of honor with Valzaan and Balimere beside him and the rest of the faithful Titans along either side. They ate and ate and ate, and when they finished, he was neither full nor hungry, only satisfied and contented. All the way through the meal, they drank only the water of the Fountain, and it was better than any milk or cider Benjiah had ever tasted. It felt, in a way, as it ran down his throat, like the light and heat that ran through his body when Allfather's power had come upon him. It felt like that, but it wasn't that. It was an echo of what that had been and a fulfillment of what it could be, and Benjiah savored every sip as he enjoyed every bite.

When the feast was finally over, Benjiah noticed that it was now night, and emerging from the feasting hall, he looked up to see the stars were already out and the thin sliver of moon was hanging high overhead. He had no idea how much time they had spent feasting, but it was already well into the evening. He turned to speak to Valzaan, but when he opened his mouth a great yawn emerged. His eyes started to flicker closed, and the last thing he remembered was Valzaan smiling.

The next thing he knew, he was lying in a bed after a deep sleep, and the mattress was deliciously soft and warm and comfortable. He lay for a long time with his eyes closed, just enjoying the pleasure of it, and when at last he opened his eyes, he saw bright sunlight pouring in through the window.

11

THE UNMAKING

B ENJIAH WALKED OUT into a glorious morning. It was,
if he reckoned the time correctly, the twenty-ninth day of
Spring Wane. In two days it would be his birthday, as well as
the first day of Summer. He was pretty sure about that, anyway.
He felt a little hazy about the days in Gyrin and the trip up the
Mountain. Though he knew those events hadn't happened
very long ago, they felt dreamy and distant, like something remembered upon waking. In fact, there was something like a
veil over all his memories of the events before Valzaan took
him into the Fountain and woke him, though he realized,
strictly speaking, that waking up wasn't really what happened.
It was a bit strange to think of what had happened as coming
back to life.

It wasn't that he couldn't remember life before awakening
in the Fountain, of course. There was no discontinuity in his
recollection of those things now, at least none that he was

aware of. Memories of his childhood were all there, as were the memories of the many leagues traveled, the battles fought, and adventures undertaken. There was, though, a kind of vividness about what had happened since, a vividness that surpassed the simple truth that the events of the previous day were more immediate than the events of days prior. He wondered what exactly made the difference. It could have been that he was somehow qualitatively different in this new life he possessed, similar perhaps to Valzaan, who seemed somehow to be every bit as old as before, but without the tell-tale signs of age. Or maybe it was being in Avalione, walking its streets and drinking the water of the Crystal Fountain. Maybe everything was more real in this place. Or maybe the sense had to do with Allfather making all things new. Now that Malek was fallen and the binding of the blade was broken, perhaps everyone would wake up to a world more real than the world they had known.

Whatever the cause, Benjiah thought as he gazed up at the deep blue sky and the thick white clouds sailing through it, the effect was most welcome. The past was not so hazy that he didn't remember how hard it had been. Long awful marches in the rain, long wearying journeys, long desperate battles, usually against superior forces, and of course, the long weeks spent in the cage. He would have welcomed almost any reprieve, and this was so much more than an ordinary reprieve. This was rest and comfort beyond all reasonable expectation or hope. He thought he could quite easily get used to such a life, if such was the life available to him.

As he stood in the doorway of the house where he'd slept, leaning against the doorpost and gazing contentedly at the empty square of Avalione, for he saw none of the Titans about, it occurred to him that he wasn't at all clear on what all these changes would mean for Kirthanin. Malek was dead and his forces were defeated. The binding of the blade was broken.

Allfather was already at work making all things new. What would life look like now, for Kirthanin as a whole and for him in particular? How would he spend his days and nights? It was an obvious question, but there had been so much to do and so much to occupy his mind, he'd never really considered it carefully or for very long.

Maybe life would be like it had been in the First Age, before Malek's Rebellion, before Andunin took up the blade. Maybe everyone would return to farming and commerce and their normal daily routines, now free to go about them without fear of the Mountain and all who dwelt within it, without fear of the Black Wolves that ran by night or fear of the legendary Grendolai lurking in the ancient dragon towers. Whatever it would be, Benjiah felt sure the Titans would help to show them all the way. Eight of the Twelve had returned—the faithful eight. Maybe they would once more oversee and guide, leading and advising as they once did.

Even if the role of the Titans changed, Benjiah thought, Allfather would not leave them without guidance. Benjiah had come far enough as a prophet, lived through enough, that he knew Allfather was firmly in control of the affairs of Kirthanin and would not allow them to wander aimlessly in this new era of peace. If Allfather had led them with timely aid and direction through their darkest hours, He would not abandon them in the light of a new day.

Benjiah shrugged off the whirling thoughts and moved out beyond the doorstep of the building. The stones of the city square were now dry, and as he approached the pool of the Crystal Fountain, he saw that it was no longer overflowing. The Fountain was still spouting water, though not as high or as voluminously. The cleansing of the Mountain must be complete and the fountain returned to normal operation, Benjiah thought, as he looked at the surface of the clear water sparkling in the morning sun.

"Yes," Valzaan said from behind him, "the cleansing of the Mountain is complete."

Benjiah turned, smiling. "How'd you know that was what I was wondering?"

"It was, you could say, an educated guess," Valzaan replied with a smile. "How did you sleep?"

"Very well, thanks," Benjiah replied. "I hardly even remember going to bed."

"You fell asleep on your feet." Valzaan laughed. "We took you to your bed and you didn't even last until we laid you in it. I am glad you rested well, though I'm not surprised. Avalione is, in its very nature, a place of rest."

"Are we going down the Mountain today?" Benjiah asked.

"Yes."

"Will it take us as long to get down as it did to get up? I mean, are we likely to end up spending tonight on the Mountainside?"

"No," Valzaan answered. "We are not going down the same way."

"There's a different way?"

"Yes."

Benjiah looked at Valzaan, feeling a little puzzled, but he didn't have time to ask any questions before Valzaan pointed toward the sky. "Look."

Benjiah looked up and saw the golden form of a dragon circling above Avalione, making its descent toward the blessed city. "Is that Sulmandir?"

"It is," Valzaan answered. "Now that the cleansing has taken place, he is able to return. He's come with a garrion to take us down the Mountain. He was only too glad to do it, knowing what you did for Kirthanin."

"Knowing what I did?"

"Yes, knowing how you laid down Ruun Harak and sacrificed yourself."

"How does he know?"

"He came last night while we were gathered here in the square, after you were fast asleep. He came because he saw the waters of the Crystal Fountain flowing down the Mountain, and he flew up to investigate."

"What did he say when he saw you and your brothers?"

"He greeted us warmly," Valzaan said, again laughing. "If *warmly* is the right word for a dragon. There was no fire involved, after all. If he was surprised by our presence, he kept it to himself. Dragons are like that, you know."

"I'm beginning to," Benjiah said, laughing too. "What did Sulmandir say when he found out you are Alazare as well as Valzaan?"

"Only that he'd thought there was something about Valzaan that reminded him of Alazare. He thought that perhaps it was simply the hand of Allfather at work in Valzaan for so long during the Third Age, but learning who I really am answered some questions for him I think. When I spoke with him in his gyre in Harak Andunin, I could tell that he was searching me out, with his penetrating eyes, but I also knew that whatever he might think or suspect, Allfather veiled knowledge of my identity from all, even the Father of Dragons, who sees much and knows more."

By now, Sulmandir was slowing as he circled, coming in low. Soon, he set the garrion down in the great white square, and he landed nearby. Valzaan and Benjiah approached.

"Greetings, Sulmandir," Valzaan said. "Thank you for coming with the garrion. We both appreciate it."

"You are welcome, Alazare," Sulmandir answered. "As are you, Benjiah. It will be an honor to serve you both."

Benjiah was taken aback, but he managed a polite thank-you as he looked up into the deep golden eyes of the Father of Dragons.

"Were you able to gather the information I desired?" Valzaan asked.

"Yes," Sulmandir replied. "I sent several of my sons for leagues in all directions. Every Water Stone we found—in Enthanin, Suthanin, Werthanin, and even Nolthanin—they're all flowing, just like the Crystal Fountain."

"I expected they would be," Valzaan replied, "but it is good to know it for sure. It is especially good to know about the Water Stones in Nolthanin. That will help if anyone thinks we should not venture into the northlands. They too are being made new, and they too will be cursed no longer. They will once again be home to men, who will dwell there in peace and safety and without fear of the wild and dangerous creatures that have long held dominion."

"The Kalin Seir, at least, will be eager to head back north," Sulmandir said. "I think that even now they are preparing for the march."

For the first time since emerging from the waters of the Fountain, Benjiah found himself thinking of Keila. It made sense, of course, that the Kalin Seir would be eager to head back north, but he wanted very much to see her before she went. He hoped she was all right, that she'd not been hurt in the battle. Thinking of her made him eager to head down the Mountain, and he was glad when he saw Valzaan move toward the garrion.

"Well, let's go down," Valzaan said as he moved away.

Soon, both Benjiah and Valzaan were inside. They were not resting on the ground for long before Sulmandir picked up the garrion and lifted it up into the sky. After several widening circles, Benjiah forced himself to stand up, though it did take some effort. He peeked out the window slats and looked out over the wide land of Kirthanin. It looked warm and green and happy, though Benjiah suspected he was reading his own emotional state into what he saw. As the circles grew wider, he was able also to see Avalione. The blessed city viewed from the air was just as splendid and wondrous as it was viewed from within. He was glad to be headed down the Mountain, to see his uncles and friends and Keila, but he hoped he'd be able to come back to Avalione some day.

Aljeron walked along the northern border of Gyrin, the shade from the trees falling pleasantly on his head. The sun was rising in the eastern sky, and the day looked like it would be a beauty. Evrim and Pedraan were walking beside him, for they had just discussed with Gilion the mysterious deaths of so many Nolthanim the night before last.

"It's true," Gilion had said, confirming the story that came Aljeron's way. "Each of the Nolthanim who remain profess loyalty to Allfather."

"All of them?"

"All of them," said Gilion.

"Well, all the same," Aljeron said, "keep an eye on those until we have some sort of guidance on the matter. Perhaps we'll have word on Valzaan or Benjiah today."

As Aljeron walked with Evrim and Pedraan, he felt more certain that the matter would have to be left until Valzaan or Benjiah or both came down from the Mountain. If neither of them returned, then he supposed he'd have to make a decision, but that could wait a while longer. He wasn't willing to give up on the prophets' safe return yet. Three days and nights was a long time, but he knew it might well take that long just to get up and then back down. They might still be descending, even now.

He looked up and across the busy field at the Mountain rising high beside them. He couldn't help but wonder what had happened upon it. The water flowing down its side had slowed to a trickle, but it certainly seemed to be a good sign. Most of the Kirthanim had greeted the flow with rejoicing, and excited murmurings that the Crystal Fountain flowed again, just as the Mound Rite predicted, cycled around the camp. Aljeron would have more readily joined in the celebration, had he not known that Valzaan believed something difficult lay ahead for Benjiah. Aljeron was concerned for the boy, and while he hoped that soon both men would return from the Mountain, he braced himself for the possibility that Valzaan would return alone.

"The work is proceeding quickly," Pedraan said as they walked, and Aljeron turned his eyes from the Mountain to the scurrying Kirthanim.

"Yes it is," he replied.

They approached the place where three makeshift forges had been quickly erected. As was true in any army, a certain amount of metallurgy was always going on. Many of the soldiers who marched with them had been blacksmiths in their previous civilian lives, and these readily met the needs of the army as it marched with what equipment they had. That scale of work, though constant, was nothing like the work that was going on now, however, and Aljeron couldn't help but marvel at what he was seeing.

The first day after the battle, during what might be called the mopping up—pursuing and killing the remaining Voiceless, and pursuing and capturing the remaining Nolthanim—everyone was intent on the work at hand. The next day, though, after they awoke to find so many Nolthanim dead, a conviction grew among the men that Aljeron could only describe as a feverish compulsion to melt down and destroy all their weapons.

At first, Aljeron thought that the men meant they desired to go home and turn their swords into things more useful for their erstwhile occupations, but he quickly discovered they meant to do it now. Several sent through officers of differing ranks the request that they be allowed to start collecting the blades and gear they would need to reforge them. Aljeron, strangely confident that the Malekim menace was no more, and that the few remaining Nolthanim could be easily handled if they chose to rebel, agreed. Dragons were dispatched with men in garrions to the partial ruin of Amaan Sul, where they gathered blacksmith tools and gear for the forges, and the work began pretty much immediately. By sunset of the previous day, three fairly sizeable forges had been built, and three just as sizeable piles of weapons had been collected. Aljeron stood with Pedraan, looking at this work, and Pedraan said, "These piles remind me of those that were made outside of Tol Emuna, except that those were a sign of defeat, and these are a sign of victory."

Afterward, Pedraan walked over and hurled his war hammer onto the pile. Without so much as a look back, he returned to Aljeron. "I'm glad to be done with it," Pedraan said. "I thought I'd thrown it away for good at Tol Emuna, and it was hard to take the burden of it up again, though I admit I was glad to have my war hammer when we faced Farimaal."

"You wielded it most effectively," Aljeron had agreed. He laughed and added, "Indeed, you have forever altered for me the meaning of the old saying, 'under the hammer.'"

"It was a fitting final use," Pedraan said. "Even so, it is a relief to put it down, once and for all."

Aljeron nodded and felt that perhaps he should follow suit and take Daaltaran to the pile, but as he fingered the smooth, familiar handle, he hesitated.

That was the previous night, and this morning, he was still wearing Daaltaran, though both Evrim and Pedraan were completely unarmed. For that matter, he didn't think he'd seen anyone bearing a sword or weapon all day. Even so, the piles of weapons being melted down were still enormous. He felt no rush to deposit Daaltaran now—the smiths couldn't possibly get through all the weapons for some time. Besides, if some sort of danger did continue to lurk around the camp, it might not be a bad idea for at least a few of them to remain armed.

The three men paused where they were, gazing at the work of the forges. Aljeron could feel the heat emanating from them and wondered how the bare-chested men in their thick aprons could stand to be working so close, but the work went on and the ringing of many hammers upon blades and anvils echoed across the open field. Despite the loud and at times cacophonous sound of the work, there was something regal in it, like the tolling of many bells calling imaginary townspeople and workers in the field to come and hear their summons. Maybe, in a sense, these hammers were a tolling bell, sending a message that would soon be heard through all Kirthanin. The long war was finally over. Malek had lost.

Aljeron looked up from the three forges to see Turgan and Erigan coming his way. They were walking, side by side, and Aljeron was again reminded of the strange combination the Great Bear possessed, gentleness and grace on the one hand, and strength and speed on the other.

"Turgan, Erigan," Aljeron said, greeting them. "It is good to see you this fine morning."

"And you," Turgan said, and it seemed to Aljeron that there was something different in the Great Bear's manner. He wasn't mirthful, exactly, but the sobriety and seriousness that had marked Turgan in their march from Tol Emuna seemed absent. Aljeron wondered if he also seemed different to the men, lighter and less burdened. He didn't seem to feel in himself the same change he was witnessing in so many others.

"We've come to take our leave of you and the army," Turgan added.

"Oh?" Aljeron said, not so much surprised that Turgan and the others would leave but that they were doing so already. "Heading home?"

"Eventually, but not yet," Erigan said. "First, we intend to explore Gyrin in search of the remains of Gyrindraal."

"The remains of Gyrindraal?" Aljeron said. "Do you expect to find any?"

"There will be something," Turgan said. "Much evil has befallen Gyrin, but the fact that the wood remains at all means something of the draal remains. We will find it, so that we may take word back to the other draals of what is needed to restore it."

"So," Pedraan said, "the Great Bear are going to restore Gyrindraal."

"Yes," Turgan said, "and in time, Gyrin itself will be restored, and then it will be a place of majesty and beauty, as it once was."

"That would be wonderful," Evrim said. "It felt so dark and foreboding as we passed through."

"It did," Erigan agreed, "but in time, with the healing that will come with the return of the Great Bear, the health and vitality of the wood will also return."

"Well," Aljeron said, "then I wish you all speed and success in your journey. All Kirthanin looks forward to the transformation of Gyrin."

"Thank you."

"And," Aljeron said, "I want you both to tell all the Great Bear that travel with you and all the Great Bear that wait for you in your own draals, how much we appreciate all that you have done and all that you have sacrificed. We could not have survived Malek's hosts without you."

"I speak for the Great Bear when I say," Turgan began, "that we did nothing but obey the word of Allfather, as you did. We were not the only ones who sacrificed, and we know that it was only our combined strength and Allfather's power that kept any of us standing. We also are grateful to you."

"Will there now be more connection between men and Great Bear? Are the old wounds and rifts forgiven?"

"Indeed," Turgan replied. "They are. Farewell."

"Farewell," they replied, and Turgan and Erigan started away.

Aljeron and the others watched the Great Bear disappear inside Gyrin and were about to head on from there when a soft voice called out to Aljeron. He turned to see Aelwyn running across the field toward him, and with only enough time to open his arms, he caught her in an embrace.

"It is so good to see you," she said after a moment, when he had held her close and then at last relaxed his grip.

"And you," Aljeron answered. "Have you all come?"

"We have," Aelwyn replied. "You didn't expect us to just linger behind forever, did you?"

"Knowing you and your sister," Aljeron said, laughing, "I'm surprised you lingered as long as you did."

"Well, we're here now," Aelwyn said, "and I'm very happy to see that you are well. I was so worried."

"There's nothing to be worried about any longer," Aljeron said. "The war is finally over."

Benjiah stepped out of the garrion into the afternoon sunshine. The flight had been pleasant enough, though longer than Benjiah expected. At Valzaan's request, Sulmandir circled around the Mountain and took them over several large Water Stones so Benjiah could see them, now that they were active again. Benjiah did not regret the delay, for he was fascinated to look down on these great rocks, cascading water flowing down their sides and forming tiny pools at the bottom. Eventually, Valzaan said, small streams from the Water Stones that once watered the land of Kirthanin in the First Age would return and again cut their winding way through the fertile soil.

Now that they were back at the foot of the Mountain, he was glad to be on solid ground. He did not have long to relish the feeling in peace, though, for several voices called out to them, and he looked up to see his uncles, Pedraan and Evrim, running toward them with Aljeron and Aelwyn, and Mindarin following behind. Benjiah ran toward his uncles, and reaching Pedraan first, threw his arms around him. Pedraan laughed out loud as his strong arms held Benjiah tight. Then Benjiah turned to Evrim and hugged him as well.

Valzaan followed at a distance, smiling at the reunion. Only after Benjiah was thoroughly greeted did anyone look up and see Valzaan's face clearly. In the end, it was Mindarin who spoke, putting their surprise into words. "Valzaan, your eyes! Can you see now?"

"I can."

"What happened?" Aljeron asked as they crowded nearer to hear Valzaan's story.

"The whole story is long, and there will be time for it later, but suffice it to say that Allfather healed me."

"On the Mountain?"

"Yes, in Avalione," Valzaan said. "He promised me long ago that when I came home, he would restore me."

"Home?" Pedraan said first, though several others echoed the word. "What do you mean?"

"I mean that Avalione is my home," Valzaan said. "It is time you all understood what I have not been at liberty to explain until now. Though I have been known to you as Valzaan, prophet of Allfather during the Third Age of Kirthanin, in time, most of you will come to know me simply as Alazare."

"Alazare!"

After their initial shock and incredulity subsided, Aljeron continued. "You are Alazare, who threw Malek from the Mountain at the end of the First Age?"

"Yes," Valzaan replied, "and I am Alazare who threw Malek from the Mountain again at the end of the Third."

"So," Aljeron said, "Malek is finally dead?"

"Malek is defeated," Valzaan replied. "He will bother Kirthanin no more."

There were a few moments of sober silence as this fact sunk in, and it was Mindarin who broke the silence, laughing nervously with her hand raised to her mouth as she spoke. "I can't believe you're Alazare!" she said. "Remember all those years ago, on the road to Sulare, when I was rude to you and you shut me up, literally?"

"Yes," Valzaan said.

"How could we forget it?" Aljeron added, laughing.

Mindarin ignored him and continued. "I can't believe, well, that I treated a Titan like that."

"That debt was paid long ago," Valzaan replied, "do not let it trouble you."

Valzaan smiled warmly upon Mindarin, and the nervous laughter became real laughter as she shook her head over what she had done. Benjiah could see though, that the embarrassment over it was gone. Valzaan had set her at ease.

Valzaan had stepped closer to him, and he put his arm around Benjiah's shoulders. "There is more to our story than you have heard, much more, and we will tell you all in time, but there is something else you should all know now. The binding of the blade that ensnared Kirthanin when Andunin took up Malek's gift was broken the night before last when Benjiah voluntarily laid down the blade and sacrificed his life that Kirthanin might be free."

"Sacrificed his life?"

"Yes," Valzaan answered. "Benjiah laid down the blade, but Malek took it up and struck him with it. Benjiah was dead but is now alive. He has been bathed in the living waters of the Crystal Fountain, and his wounds have been healed."

Benjiah saw the eyes of those gathered searching him anew. Normally he would have felt embarrassed to be at the center of so intense a scrutiny, but he did not feel embarrassed now. He understood their curiosity, for it had been his own when he realized what happened. They too, in time, would understand and accept what had happened to him.

After a few moments, they walked together toward the center of the camp, where the clanging of the forges could be heard echoing across the open area between Gyrin and the Mountain. As they walked, Valzaan told the story of their climb, of the gatekeeper who tried to attack them, of what he found when he entered the city, and of Malek's fall. Benjiah then told his own story at their request, and they listened, most of them with tears in their eyes at the news of his fall. When he finished, Valzaan took up the story again and narrated Benjiah's resurrection and also that of the other faithful Titans.

"Eight of the Titans, alive!" Evrim said. "Imagine that! Will they also come down from the Mountain?"

"In time," Valzaan said. "I will prepare the way for them first. When Kirthanin is ready to receive them, then they also shall come."

"Now," he continued, "What of things here? Sulmandir told us something of what has been going on in the camp, and we saw from our ride in the garrion the Water Stones flowing."

Aljeron started filling them in on the events of the previous days. As he did, Valzaan explained the deaths of the Nolthanim and the reason why they need not fear the possibility of any surviving Malekim.

"So that's why we've all been so confident that we are safe," Aljeron said, almost under his breath.

"It is why. Malek's children perished with Malek."

Aljeron spoke of the desire that had swept over the army to erect the forges and break down the weapons they had carried to war. By this point, they were near enough to see the forges and the steadily dwindling piles of swords.

"The work seems to be progressing well," Valzaan said.

"It is," Aljeron answered. "It is going very smoothly."

"And yet," Valzaan added, turning to Aljeron, "you still wear your sword. Why?"

"No real reason, I guess," Aljeron said after a moment, appearing taken aback by the question. "I didn't know for sure until just now that there was no longer any threat."

"You know now," Valzaan said gently. "You could put Daaltaran in the pile over there. We will wait for you."

"Oh I will," Aljeron said, strangely adamant. "I certainly will. I'm just waiting for the smiths to work through the rest of them. I thought I'd wait until the rest were done before throwing mine in. You know, as the captain of the army, I thought it could be some kind of sign that it's all over."

Valzaan nodded with a smile, and they kept walking. Benjiah looked at Aljeron and saw that he seemed a little pale. For some reason, the exchange had flustered him. He soon covered that fact with a detailed report of other things that were also underway.

"The Great Bear have left to explore Gyrin," Aljeron started. "They want to find the remains of Gyrindraal and take word home about what will need to be done to rebuild it."

"Good," Valzaan replied. "The work of restoration is proceeding very well."

"It is," Aljeron hastily agreed. "In fact, a large number of Enthanim have left as well with a core of Vulsutyrim. They are headed back to Amaan Sul to begin work on rebuilding the city."

"Really?" Benjiah said, surprise and delight mingling in his voice.

"Yes, they left just a few hours ago," Aljeron said. "And at about the same time, a group of Suthanim left for Cimaris Rul with Talis Fein and another core of Vulsutyrim to help them do the same there. And, when things are finally wrapped up here, I plan to lead a similar expedition back to Shalin Bel."

"Did the Vulsutyrim volunteer to help?" Benjiah asked.

"Yes, as a matter of fact they did," Aljeron answered. "Why?"

"I think it is interesting that they have offered to help rebuild the three cities that were devastated by the war. Some might be tempted to see their surrender to us as self-serving, changing sides to save themselves, but this offer to help those who suffered at their hands has the ring of authenticity, doesn't it?"

"I would say it does," Pedraan agreed. "But, having watched them fight alongside us a few days ago, I wouldn't be inclined to doubt them anyway."

"Yes," Valzaan joined in. "And had you seen how they worked to set the trap and then kill the Kumatin, you would be even more convinced. I would hope it is now clear to all that Amontyr and his brothers are genuinely devoted to serving Allfather."

"That reminds me," Aljeron said. "Gilion confirmed that the surviving Nolthanim all profess a desire to serve Allfather, which is consistent with your account of who survived Malek's entry into Avalione and who didn't, but I'm still wondering what we should do with the survivors."

"Do with them?" Valzaan replied.

"Yes," Aljeron said, fumbling with his words a little bit. "Technically, they are still prisoners of war. Are they to be put on trial or kept under guard or what? When we all leave here, where should they go?"

"When we all leave here," Valzaan answered, "they, like you, should go wherever they wish. As for a trial, there will be no need. The moment Malek set foot in Avalione, they were already tried in the only court that really matters. They have been acquitted and granted a new life in a new world. They should be released and set free."

"I wonder what they'll do?" Evrim mused.

"Or where they'll go," Pedraan added.

"I guess, like most of us, they'll go home," Valzaan replied.

"If by home you mean Nolthanin," Aljeron said, "I wonder how the Kalin Seir will feel about that."

"The war is over," Valzaan said, "and the Kalin Seir will learn, if they haven't already, that there is no further need to revile their estranged brothers."

The mention of the Kalin Seir again brought Keila to Benjiah's mind. He thought of her beautiful face, and he wondered when he might be able to see her again or if she might already be gone.

After the evening meal, Benjiah made his escape from the amiable company of his uncles and friends, though not without considerable effort. No one came right out and asked why he wanted to go for a walk, but that only seemed to confirm his suspicion that they might well know. In the end, Valzaan had to step in and encourage the others to "let the boy have a few moments of peace." At that point, they let him wander off, but Benjiah felt sure he had been the topic of their conversation ever since leaving.

He wandered in the direction where he thought the Kalin Seir were camped, and the presence of a half dozen snow leopards lying in the grass ahead of him confirmed his guess. He was relieved, for he had feared that in the hours since learning the Kalin Seir had not yet left, they might actually do so. Now he just needed to find out if Keila was with them. Knowing her, she had thrown herself into the battle, and he hoped that despite this she was all right. It would be ironic if he survived Malek only to find that Keila had not survived the battle with Malek's lesser minions. This unpleasant thought had lingered in the back of his mind all day. However, he did not have to wander long in doubt, for he had barely approached the exterior ranks of the encamped Kalin Seir when an excited voice called out to him. A slender figure rose from beside a fire and walked toward him.

If he was at all concerned about how he might be received after the strange and surreal events of the past few days, those fears were alleviated when she threw her arms around his neck. He felt her hands clasp tightly and hold fast upon him, and he found himself after a few moments rubbing her back and saying, over and over, "It's all right. I'm all right."

After a few moments, she relaxed her grip and stepped back. Tears were shining in her eyes. "I'm so glad you're all right. I had the most terrible dreams."

"What dreams?"

"The night before last," she said. "They were horrible."

"What happened in them?"

"I don't really want to talk about it," she said, shuddering. "Could we speak of something else, anything else? You could tell me where you've been and what happened."

"I could."

"Would you?"

"Sure, do you want to walk together awhile?"

"I do," she answered, and they walked away from the Kalin Seir encampment toward the foot of the Mountain. A large stone sat at the base of the Mountain, and Benjiah walked toward it.

"Maybe we should sit," he said. "We might get some privacy here."

"All right," she said, and they sat.

"The day we arrived here," Benjiah began at last, for all the way from the Kalin Seir camp he had wondered how to tell his story. He decided to keep it simple and brief. "I ended up going up the Mountain with Valzaan."

"After the Forge-Foe?"

"Yes, he was fleeing up the Mountain."

"The coward," Keila said with clear disdain. "He didn't even have the courage to fight with his army."

"No," Benjiah said, agreeing. "As it turns out he didn't. He didn't care about his army at all, not like Aljeron or one of our captains."

"So go on," Keila said. "I shouldn't have interrupted."

"That's all right," Benjiah said, smiling at her apology. She seemed different, softer maybe than she had. "Well, we climbed all day and night, and all the next day. We finally reached the gates to the blessed city, Avalione, the night before last."

"The night I had my dreams," Keila said.

"Yes," Benjiah said. "A great wolf guarded the gate, and Valzaan held the beast somehow in a battle of wills, and I went past him into the city."

"On your own?"

"Yes, but Valzaan had warned me it would probably come to that. Anyway, I'll make a long story short. Malek tried to strike me down with Ruun Harak, the spear he gave to Andunin at the end of the First Age, but he failed. I took up the spear and was about to turn it on him when Allfather spoke to me. He spoke the words of the ancient prophecy that Valzaan always said was a prophecy about me, and I understood that I had to lay down the spear. Whatever happened to me, I couldn't use the blade that Malek had made, even to strike Malek down. I had to refuse it. So I laid it down, and Malek picked it up and killed me."

Keila stared at him, her lips trembling. "What do you mean, he killed you?"

"Just that, he speared me right here," Benjiah said, putting his hand over the place where Malek had struck him.

"But how can that be?"

Benjiah shook his head. "I know, it sounds crazy, but it isn't. Valzaan ended up killing the wolf and entering the city. He killed Malek."

"Valzaan did?"

"Yes," Benjiah said, trying to figure out how to best explain it. "Valzaan is really Alazare, the Titan who threw Malek from the Mountain at the end of the First Age. Allfather restored his Titan form when he entered the city, and Alazare did it again."

"I know you must be telling the truth," Keila said, wonder in her voice. "I can feel that you are, but it is a lot to swallow."

Benjiah nodded. "It is, but that is what happened. It was Alazare, once more in the human form of Valzaan, who took me up in his arms and carried me to the Crystal Fountain. He bathed me in its waters, and life returned to me. The water healed me."

"And now you have returned to me," Keila said. "The Master-Maker is merciful."

"He is," Benjiah agreed.

"May I see your scar, where the spear struck you?"

"There is no scar."

"None?"

"No, look for yourself." Benjiah raised his shirt and showed Keila the smooth unbroken skin. There was absolutely no sign that he had ever been cut, let alone ripped open by the jagged edge of Ruun Harak.

"It is amazing," Keila said. "You've been completely restored."

"I have, and I've been eager to see you. I am as glad to find you well as you are to find me well. Maybe more so."

She smiled. "You aren't as shy and awkward as you used to be."

"And you seem to be smiling and laughing more than you used to," he answered. "You seem . . . oh I don't know, happier, perhaps?"

"I am," she said, laughing again, apparently amused at the idea that she was now laughing more. "Especially now."

"I was worried that you'd be gone," Benjiah said. "When Aljeron said the Great Bear left to search for Gyrindraal and that men went to Amaan Sul and Cimaris Rul, I thought maybe the Kalin Seir had left for Nolthanin. I was so worried that I'd find you gone."

"The Kalin Seir are leaving," Keila answered, the smile fading a bit from her face. "Tomorrow, in fact. We leave in the morning."

"You're going too?" Benjiah said, realizing that he hadn't even bothered to mask the disappointment in his voice.

"Sure, we all are," Keila said. "It is what we've waited all these years for, the defeat of the Forge-Foe and the chance to resettle Nolthanin and reclaim it, to cultivate the ground and make it habitable again. It has been our great hope."

"Would you consider staying behind?"

"I would," she answered, quietly. "Would you like me to?"

"Very much," Benjiah answered. "I need to find my mother and let her know I'm all right, and when I've seen her and perhaps seen to the rebuilding of Amaan Sul, ensured that it is proceeding all right, maybe we could journey together to Nolthanin."

"I would love to see your home with you," Keila said. "And I would love to travel to Nolthanin with you as well. Let me go and speak to the elders. I am of age, of course, so I don't need their permission, but it is the courteous thing to do. I will stay with my people tonight, then tomorrow I will come and find you in your camp."

"All right," Benjiah said, and Keila stepped toward him and leaned in, kissing him gently on his cheek.

She turned to go, and Benjiah reached out and took her hand. She stopped and looked back at him. He pulled her to him as he stepped closer and kissed her in return.

The following day passed dreamily for Benjiah. Keila arrived not long after breakfast and they spent the day together—

walking, sitting, lounging, talking, and doing nothing at all that was pressing, essential, or urgent. Benjiah had worried that Keila might be a little down with the departure of her people, but she seemed quite happy and contented to spend the day with him, doing little or, more often, nothing. She even took quickly to the others, especially Mindarin, which might have been a little worrisome to Benjiah had he not felt so overwhelmingly happy at Keila's presence.

The large open area between Gyrin and the Mountain was by evening almost devoid of movement and life. The Great Bear were all gone. The Kalin Seir too. Almost all the Kirthanim had moved on as well. The Enthanim from Tol Emuna had turned east. Though they did not have a city to rebuild, it seemed to them about time to head home. The Suthanim had all left with Talis Fein, and a few hours earlier, the Werthanim from Fel Edorath and Shalin Bel had left together, except for Aljeron, Gilion, and few others who planned to catch up after saying their final farewells to Valzaan and their other friends and brothers in arms.

The clanging of the smiths at the forge had persisted all day, but within the last hour or so, the work ground to a halt. Benjiah was camped too far from the forges to see the work that had transpired there, but close enough to deduce that the work was complete. Benjiah was glad, not only because the cessation of the work meant a cessation of the clatter, but because the unmaking and reforging of the blades was a very real sign that his sacrifice had not been in vain.

"What a beautiful day it is," Keila said. She was lying in the grass beside Benjiah, resting with her head against his legs. They were sitting with Valzaan, Aelwyn, and Mindarin. Gilion had been scouring the battlefield all day for any blades that had been overlooked, while Aljeron, Evrim, and Pedraan had been gone since not long after lunch, when they went to the forge to see how the work there was progressing. "It may only be the last day of Spring Wane," Keila continued, "but this is as beautiful a summer's day as there ever was or will be, I would say."

"Summer may not officially begin until tomorrow," Valzaan said, "but a new age is already here. This age will be different than all the others, and the beauty and delight of this summer will never end."

"It's the real Summerland," Mindarin said. "I thought today felt like being in Sulare, and now I think I understand why."

"Tomorrow is my birthday," Benjiah said absently, "if birthdays really mean anything anymore."

Keila shifted her position as though to say something to Benjiah, but then she sat up as they all did when they noticed Evrim running toward them. On a day that had been nothing but peaceful and relaxed, they easily recognized that something had Evrim concerned.

"Valzaan, Benjiah, all of you," he called out as he drew nearer. "Come quickly to the forges."

Each rose as Valzaan spoke. "What is it Evrim?"

"It's Aljeron," he said in reply as he stopped before them. "He has threatened Pedraan with Daaltaran."

"What?" several of them said together, looking at one another in wonder.

"Tell us exactly what happened," Valzaan calmly directed.

"We went to see how the work was progressing, and Aljeron was saying all the way there how he was going to turn over Daaltaran, but when we got there he said they didn't seem quite ready for it, though there weren't that many swords left. So we all hung around and watched the smiths for a while, but even when all their other work was finished a little while ago, he still refused.

"In fact," Evrim continued, "he went so far as to tell the last few blacksmiths to go on and leave when they asked about his sword, adding that he wanted to take care of Daaltaran himself. They offered to stay in case he needed a hand, but Aljeron got angry and sent them away. Still, even after they left he delayed, making excuses. He said that it would be easier to carry Daaltaran back to Shalin Bel in the form of a sword, and once he was home he would find a suitable use for the metal, and then he would find a blacksmith to take care of it.

"Well, when he said that, Pedraan started to object. When he did, Aljeron got really mad, mad like I've never seen him. Pedraan didn't like that too much, and he said that he was going to take Daaltaran off him and melt it down himself. At that, Aljeron drew his blade, and that was the impasse they were in when I left them—Pedraan standing empty-handed and staring at Aljeron, and Aljeron standing with Daaltaran, staring at Pedraan."

"Lead on," Valzaan said after a moment. "We'll follow."

They all hurried after Evrim, who half walked, half jogged back to the forges. From a fair distance away, they could all see that the stalemate continued, and as they approached, neither Pedraan nor Aljeron budged. Both men stood within a few spans of the other, neither saying a word. It was clear from the way Aljeron was holding Daaltaran that Pedraan was not in any immediate danger, but it was also clear that Aljeron did not intend to allow Pedraan to come any closer.

Aelwyn made as though to move toward Aljeron, but Valzaan signaled for her to stop. He stepped a little closer to the two men, though neither turned to acknowledge his presence. "It is time to lay down your sword, Aljeron. In fact, it is past time."

"I don't want to."

"Why not?"

"I just don't."

"That's not a reason," Valzaan said. "You don't need it anymore."

"Then what does it matter? What's one sword, after all? It isn't like the world will fall apart if this one piece of metal remains in the shape of a sword."

"Are you so sure it won't? Have you so quickly forgotten what happened to Kirthanin when Andunin took up Ruun Harak, just one spear?"

"It isn't the same thing. I don't plan to use it on anyone. I just want to keep it."

"But that is forbidden, or have you forgotten the prophecy?

> *"On that day, the Fountain will flow again.*
> *The Mountain will be cleansed*
> *And all will be made new.*
> *All instruments of war will be destroyed.*
> *They will be unmade;*
> *They will be reforged.*
> *Recast as implements of peace, as plows*
> *These blades will work and till*
> *The ground forevermore.*
> *No one will ever harm or kill again,*
> *And Peace will be restored*
> *On All My Holy Mountain.'*

"So you see, Aljeron," Valzaan continued. "I can't take your refusal so lightly. It is time to lay Daaltaran down."

Valzaan's voice had not grown louder, but his words seemed more forceful. Benjiah was sure that Aljeron would obey, but he held on stubbornly, though it looked to Benjiah as though he might have wavered a bit.

"Is the sword so dear to you that you would hold onto it despite all that Valzaan has said?" Aelwyn added. "So dear that you would threaten your friend and worry your wife?"

"It's not that Daaltaran is dear to me, though it is dear," Aljeron said, still holding Pedraan in his gaze. "It is more than that. Daaltaran is who I am."

"What do you mean?" This time it was Evrim asking the question.

"The other soldiers—those who joined my army and followed me—they were soldiers only by necessity. They were really farmers and merchants, blacksmiths and cobblers. They were bakers and innkeepers, stonemasons and stewards. I am none of those things. I am a soldier, like Caan was. That's all that I am. The sword is my life. It always has been. Without it, what am I?"

"You are a man," Valzaan replied.

"A husband," Aelwyn added, speaking tenderly, "and perhaps one day a father."

"Daaltaran is not who you are," Pedraan said, speaking at last. "I thought my war hammer was who I was, but it failed me, and I watched my brother die before my eyes. You took up your sword to do a job. It's done. Lay it down."

"Aljeron," Benjiah said at last, walking past the others and in between his uncle and this man who had been one of his father's closest friends. "I laid down my life to free Kirthanin from the blade. Will you not lay down your blade?"

Benjiah stopped in front of him and stretched out his hand. Aljeron looked at him and then at his hand for what seemed a long time, then slowly he lowered Daaltaran and rested it in Benjiah's palm. Benjiah received it and turned to Pedraan. "You are a reasonably skilled smithy, Uncle. Would you deal with this?"

"Gladly," Pedraan replied, and taking Daaltaran, he turned and walked over to the nearest of the forges.

Aelwyn walked past Benjiah and put her arms around Aljeron. Tears were in her eyes. "Thank you, Aljeron."

"I'm so sorry," Aljeron said after a long moment, looking ashamed. "It just felt so hard, letting it go, like losing a piece of myself."

"You haven't lost anything," she replied. "You have gained, as we all have. The binding is broken. We're free." The loud ring of a hammer on steel emanated from the nearby forge, and Benjiah watched Pedraan's muscular arm striking the sword tip that was just beginning to glow with the heat. A disconnected movement caught his eye.

"Look," he said, pointing out beyond the forge. A long, graceful tiger was loping toward them across the open field.

"Koshti!" Aljeron called out, amazed.

Soon the tiger was in their midst, and Aljeron dropped to his knees and threw his arms around his battle brother. The greeting was warm and the joyful reunion lifted the cloud from the small group. All the while, the ringing of the hammer at the forge continued, and soon, the unmaking was complete.

EPILOGUE:
ALL THINGS NEW

VALZAAN WALKED BEHIND the others with Benjiah and Keila. The sun was sinking low on the western horizon and a pleasant breeze blew out of the south, rustling the tops of the Gyrin's outermost trees.

"Pedraan did a good job with Daaltaran," Benjiah said.

"Yes," Valzaan agreed. "It will make a fine plow."

"Valzaan?"

"Yes?"

"Why was letting go of Daaltaran so hard for Aljeron?"

Valzaan looked at the boy and Keila, who were both searching his face for answers to what they had just witnessed.

"I think," Valzaan said after a moment, "that the blade bound some to itself more firmly than others. You, for instance, never really took to it and essentially abandoned it long before the binding was broken. Aljeron, though, was quite proficient with it. Yes, he took it up and used it in Allfather's service, to oppose Malek and his will, and it was right that he did so, but in the process he lost sight of the fact that the blade was an unfortunate necessity of a broken world. He learned to love the blade too much, and consequently, life without it was hard to imagine."

"Will he," Keila started, "you know, will he be all right?

"Oh yes," Valzaan replied. "Any lingering hold the blade had on him was effectively broken when he handed it over. He'll be fine. Remember, Allfather is making all things new, not just dead things and long-lost things—all things."

"So," Benjiah said, looking around him at the towering Mountain and the shadows stretching from the forest across the field. "I suppose the work here is finished. What comes next?"

"Next?" Valzaan said, almost laughing. "Next comes eternal summer, where Kirthanin experiences the restoration it has long desired."

"That sounds wonderful," Keila said.

"Yes, very," Benjiah said.

"It is," Valzaan agreed, "but though the work, as you put it, is finished, there is still one more thing that we need to attend to."

"What is that?"

"Look," Valzaan said, pointing into the sky.

They looked and saw Sulmandir descending with a garrion. He circled around them and set the garrion down in the field close by, then landed himself.

"Greetings, Sulmandir," Valzaan said.

"Greetings, Alazare," Sulmandir replied.

"Is everything prepared?"

"Yes," the golden dragon replied.

"Valzaan, what is going on?" Benjiah asked.

"You'll see," Valzaan said. "Now trust me, and get into the garrion."

"Are we all going?"

"No, just you."

EPILOGUE

"But what about Keila?" Benjiah protested. "I can't just leave her behind."

"I will look after her until we meet up again, which will be soon. Don't worry."

Benjiah looked from the prophet to Keila, who smiled and laughed. "Don't worry. I'm sure Valzaan will take good care of me. Go, do what you need to do."

A little mystified, Benjiah looked from them to the garrion, then back. "All right," he said at last. "I'll go. I'll see you both soon, I suppose."

"You will," Valzaan assured him, a twinkle gleaming in his clear blue eyes.

Benjiah hugged Keila, then turned and walked to the garrion. Opening the door, he stepped inside. Sulmandir took the garrion in his firm grip and lifted it from the ground as he circled upward into the sky, his golden scales gleaming in evening sun.

For a few moments, Valzaan and Keila stood below, watching the dragon circle up and up, then Keila turned to the Titan. "Where is he going?"

"To get an early birthday present."

Keila thought about asking another question, but she noticed that a large man was walking toward them from the east, the direction in which the dragon had flown away. She watched, and as he drew nearer, she realized that she recognized him. She turned to Valzaan. "How did Pedraan get all the way over there? He went back to the camp with Aljeron and the others, didn't he?"

"He did," Valzaan said. "That is not Pedraan. That is his brother, Pedraal."

Keila raised her eyebrows in surprise and turned from Valzaan to the man who was drawing nearer.

"Greetings, Pedraal," Valzaan said. "Follow this girl here. She'll take you to Pedraan."

"What about you?" Keila asked.

"Oh, I'll be along after a while," Valzaan answered, smiling.

Keila and Pedraal walked off after the others, and Valzaan found a good-sized stone and sat down. The warm sun smiled down upon him, and he closed his eyes and sat for a time, feeling the warmth upon his face.

A shadow fell over him, and he opened his eyes as a voice said, "Valzaan? Where am I?"

Valzaan smiled as he rose and embraced the man standing before him. When he had stepped back he said, "You stand at the foot of the Mountain, Rulalin. Come, let me take you to the others, that they may welcome you, for behold, Allfather is making all things new."

It did not take Sulmandir long to cover the leagues between the Mountain and Amaan Sul, and as the dragon circled the city, Benjiah leaned against the garrion's wall and peered out the slatted window to get glimpses of the ruins below. The damage was extensive, but the thought of rebuilding was not overwhelming. They had all the time in the world, now, to put things to right. Valzaan's words reassured him. All things new—it was quite a promise.

Sulmandir set the garrion down in the northern quadrant of the city, just outside the gates that had led to the palace. One gate was twisted and broken, lying on the ground, and the other dangled from a broken hinge. Even so, Benjiah felt his heart race as he felt the surge of familiarity. He was home.

For a moment he stood there frozen. He'd left so long ago and been through so much, it was odd to be suddenly dropped back in the place where he'd grown up. He looked to Sulmandir, who stood beside the garrion, but the dragon did not speak. In the end, Benjiah turned and walked through the gateway.

The courtyard was a bit of a mess, littered with debris. The fountain at least was working, and the sound of the cascading water soothed him. He walked over and scooped some up to drink. It was cool and refreshing, and he walked on toward the palace.

The damage was not total, but it was significant. The building had been set on fire by the hosts of Malek, but much of the stone, though scorched and blackened by smoke, still stood. The roof seemed a total loss, but it could be replaced.

As he approached the building, he saw stewards working, sorting through the debris and separating things that might be salvageable. As he drew closer, they stopped and stared at him, wide-eyed.

"Good evening," he said.

"Good evening," they answered.

"Is my mother here, by any chance?" Benjiah asked.

"She's inside," one of them said, pointing through the door into the palace.

"Thanks," Benjiah answered, moving away from them and heading through the door. He didn't look back, but he was pretty sure they continued to stare at him all the way into the palace. He wondered if something was visibly different about him, having died and been brought back to life.

He walked toward the great hall, where he heard the sound of voices. Missing its roof, the great hall felt even more open and immense than it normally did, and for a moment, Benjiah stood in the entrance to it, surveying the walls and open sky.

"Benjiah?" It was his mother. He recognized the voice immediately.

He looked across the room at the place where she was standing amid stewards and smiled. "Mother," he said as he walked toward her. "I've—"

He stopped short, trembling. One of the men near his mother had moved away from the rest and gone to stand beside her. He was young, blond, and handsome, and Benjiah recognized him immediately.

"Benjiah," Wylla said softly, "this is your father."

"Father," Benjiah said, mouthing the word slowly. Then something inside him broke free, and he ran across the open room and fell to his knees before his father, throwing his arms around his waist and holding him close, as though he might disappear if Benjiah did not hold on tightly.

"Well done, my son," Joraiem said, gently stroking his son's golden hair. "Welcome home."

So ends the Binding of the Blade.
The songs of the Age of Peace are not here recorded,
For they cannot be, by us, comprehended.
It is enough to know that they are real,
And both are and will be heard by many.

GLOSSARY

Aelwyn Elathien (ALE-win el-ATH-ee-un): Novaana of
  Werthanin, Mindarin's younger sister.
Agia Muldonai (ah-GEE-uh MUL-doe-nye): The Holy Mountain. Agia Muldonai was the ancient home of the Titans,
  who lived in Avalione, the city nestled high upon the
  mountain between its twin peaks. Agia Muldonai has been
  under Malek's control since the end of the Second Age,
  when he invaded Kirthanin from his home in exile on the
  Forbidden Isle.
Alazare (AL-uh-zair): The Titan who cast Malek from Agia
  Muldonai at the end of the First Age when Malek's Rebellion failed. Severely injured in his battle with Malek,
  Alazare passed from the stage of Kirthanin history and was
  never seen again.
Aljeron Balinor (AL-jer-on BALL-ih-nore): Novaana of
  Werthanin (Shalin Bel), travels with his battle brother
  Koshti.
Allfather: Creator of Kirthanin, who gave control of Kir-
  thanin's day-to-day affairs to the Council of Twelve. To ac-
  complish this task, He gave great power to each of these

Titans. Since the time of Malek's Rebellion, Allfather has continued to speak to His creation through prophets who remind Kirthanin of Allfather's sovereign rule.

Amaan Sul (AH-mahn SUL): Royal seat of Enthanin.

Anakor (AN-uh-core): Titan, ally to Malek, killed by Volrain in the Rebellion.

Andunin (an-DOO-nin): The Nolthanim man chosen by Malek at the Rebellion to be king over mankind.

Andunin Plateau: Wasteland of northwestern Nolthanin.

Arimaar Mountains (AIR-ih-mar): Suthanin's longest range, which runs between Lindan Wood and the eastern coast of Suthanin.

Assembly: The official gathering of all Kirthanin Novaana who are appointed to represent their family and region.

Autumn Rise: See *seasons*.

Autumn Wane: See *seasons*.

Avalione (av-uh-lee-OWN): Blessed city and home of the Crystal Fountain. It rests between the peaks of Agia Muldonai and was once the home of the Titans. Like the rest of Agia Muldonai, the city was declared off limits by Allfather at the beginning of the Second Age.

Avram Gol (AV-ram GALL): Ancient ruined port city of western Nolthanim known in the First Age as the City of the Setting Sun.

Azaruul butterflies (AZ-uh-rule): Green luminescent butterflies.

Azmavarim (az-MAV-uh-rim): Also known as Firstblades, these swords were forged during the First Age by Andunin and his followers.

Balimere (BALL-ih-mere): Also called Balimere the Beautiful. The most beloved of all the Titans to the lesser creatures of Kirthanin. It is said that when Allfather restores Kirthanin, Balimere will be the first of the faithful Titans to be resurrected.

Barunaan River (buh-RUE-nun): Major north-south river between Kellisor Sea and the Southern Ocean.

Bay of Thalasee (THAL-uh-see): Bay off Werthanin's west coast.

Benjiah Andira (ben-JY-uh an-DEER-uh): Joraiem and Wylla's son.

Master Berin (BARE-in): Master of Sulare.

Black Wolves: Creatures created by Malek during his exile on the Forbidden Isle.

Mistress Brahan (BRA-HAN): Rulalin's housekeeper and chief steward.

Brenim Andira (BREN-im an-DEER-uh): Novaana of Suthanin (Dal Harat), Joraiem's younger brother.

Bringer of Storms, the: See Cheimontyr.

Bryar (BRY-er): Novaana of Werthanin, Elyas's older sister, who fights for Fel Edorath under Aljeron's command.

Caan (KAHN): Combat instructor for the Novaana in Sulare.

Calendar: There are ninety-one days in every season, making the year 364 days. The midseason feast days are not numbered and instead are known only by their name (Midsummer, Midautumn, etc.). They fall between the fifteenth and sixteenth day of each season. These days are "outside of time" in part as a tribute to the timelessness of Allfather; they also look forward to the time when all things will be made new.

Calissa (kuh-LISS-uh): Novaana of Suthanin (Kel Imlarin), Darias's sister.

Carrafin (CARE-uh-fin): The captain of Tol Emuna, known as the "Captain of the Rock."

Charnosh (CHAR-nosh): Titan, ally to Malek, killed by Rolandes during the Rebellion.

Cheimontyr (SHY-MON-teer): The Bringer of Storms, most fearful of the Vulsutyrim who can control the weather.

Cimaris Rul (sim-AHR-iss RULE): Town at the mouth of the Barunaan River where it pours into the Southern Ocean.

Cinjan (SIN-jun): Mysterious cohort of Synoki.

Col Marena (KOLE muh-REEN-uh): Port near Shalin Bel.

Corindel (KORE-in-del): Enthanim royal who attempted to drive Malek from Agia Muldonai and betrayed the Great Bear at the beginning of the Third Age.

Corlas Valon (KORE-las vah-LAHN): Fel Edorath captain whose troops join Aljeron's to face Malek.

Council of Twelve: The twelve Titans to whom Allfather entrusted the care of Kirthanin. The Council dwelt in Avalione on Agia Muldonai, but frequently they would transform themselves into human form and travel throughout the land. The greatest of these was Malek, whose Rebellion ultimately brought about the destruction of the Twelve.

Crystal Fountain: Believed to be the fountainhead of all Kirthanin waters, this fountain once flowed in the center of Avalione.

cyranis (sir-AN-iss): A poison of remarkable potency that can kill most living things almost instantly if it gets into the bloodstream. Consequently, the cyranic arrow—the head of which is coated in cyranis—is one of few weapons that the people of Kirthanin trust against the Malekim.

Daaltaran (doll-TARE-an): Aljeron's sword, a Firstblade whose name means "death comes to all."

Daegon (DAY-gone): Titan, ally to Malek, killed by Alazare during the Rebellion.

Dal Harat (DOLL HARE-at): Village in western Suthanin, Joraiem Andira's home.

Darias (DAHR-ee-us): Novaana of Suthanin (Kel Imlarin), Calissa's brother.

Derrion Wel (DARE-ee-un WELL): Town in southeastern Suthanin.

draal (DRAWL): A tight-knit community of Great Bear.

dragon tower: These ancient structures were built in the First Age as homes away from home for dragons who naturally live in the high places of Kirthanin's mountains and prefer to sleep high above the ground.

dragons: One of the three great races of Kirthanin. All dragons are descended from the golden dragon, Sulmandir, the first creation of Allfather after the Titans. All dragons appear at first glance to be golden, but none except Sulmandir are entirely golden. Three dragon lines exist, marked by their distinct coloring: red, blue, and green.

Dravendir (DRAV-en-deer): A blue dragon.

Eliandir (el-ee-AN-deer): A red dragon.

Elnin Wood (EL-nin): Forest of central Suthanin that straddles the Barunaan River, home to the Elnindraal clan of Great Bear.

Elyas (eh-LIE-us): Novaana of Werthanin, Bryar's younger brother, who died fighting for Amaan Sul in one of the first campaigns against Fel Edorath.

Enthanin (EN-than-in): Kirthanin's eastern country. Residents are Enthanim.

Eralon (AIR-uh-lahn): Faithful Titan killed by Malek and his allies during the Rebellion.

Erefen Marshes (AIR-i-fen): Swampland boundary between Werthanin and Suthanin.

Erevir (AIR-uh-veer): Major prophet of Allfather in the Second Age.

Erigan (AIR-ih-gan): Great Bear, Sarneth's son.

Evrim Minluan (EV-rim MIN-loo-in): Joraiem's best friend and close friend to Aljeron.

Farimaal (FARE-ih-mal): Leading general of Malek's, who brought the Grendolai into submission.

Fel Edorath (FELL ED-ore-ath): Easternmost city in Werthanin; the first line of defense against attacks from Agia Muldonai.

Fire Giant: See *Vulsutyr*.

First Age: The age of peace and harmony that preceded Malek's rebellion. Not only did peace govern the affairs of men in the First Age, but the three great races of men, dragons, and Great Bear coexisted then in harmony.

Firstblade: See *Azmavarim*.

Forbidden Isle: After Malek's failed Rebellion at the end of the First Age, he was driven from Kirthanin and took refuge on the Forbidden Isle, home of Vulsutyr, the Fire Giant.

Forest of Gyrin (GEAR-in): Forest south of Agia Muldonai, home to the Gyrindraal clan of Great Bear.

Forgotten Waters: Passage across the Southern Ocean from Suthanin to the Forbidden Isle.

Full Autumn: See *seasons*.

Full Spring: See *seasons*.

Full Summer: See seasons.

Full Winter: See *seasons*.

Garek Elathien (GAIR-ick el-ATH-ee-un): Novaana of Werthanin, Mindarin's father.

Garring Pul (GAR-ing PULL): Southernmost city of Enthanin, where the Kalamin River meets the Kellisor Sea.

garrion (GARE-ee-un): Mode of transport common in the First Age used by the Titans and some Novaana. Garrions came in many shapes and sizes, but they all functioned similarly: A dragon would pick up the garrion with his talons as he flew.

giants: See *Vulsutyrim*.

Gilion Numiah (GIL-ee-un new-MY-uh): Captain of Shalin Bel's army.

Gralindir (GRAY-lin-deer): A blue dragon.

Great Bear: One of the three great races of Kirthanin. These magnificent creatures commonly stand two spans high and are ferocious fighters when need calls. Nevertheless, they are known for their great wisdom and gentleness.

Grendolai (GREN-doe-lie): The joint creation of Malek and Vulsutyr, these terrifying creatures were used to attack the Dragon Towers when Malek invaded Kirthanin from the Forbidden Isle. The dragons call them Dark Thieves.

gyre: A manmade dragon den built on top of a dragon tower.

Haalsun (HAL-sun): Faithful Titan killed by Charnosh during the Rebellion.

Halina Minluan (huh-LEE-nuh MIN-loo-in): Evrim and Kyril's older daughter.

Harak Andunin (HARE-ack an-DOO-nin): Mountain in Nolthanin whose name means "Andunin's Spear."

Hour: See *time*.

Invasion, the: Malek's second attempt to conquer Kirthanin.

Joraiem Andira (jore-EYE-em an-DEER-uh): Novaana of Suthanin (Dal Harat) and a prophet, murdered by Rulalin.

Jul Avedra (JULE uh-VADE-rah): Coastal town of Enthanin about midway between Tol Emuna and the Kalamin River delta.

Kalamin River (KAL-uh-min): River separating Enthanin from Suthanin.

Kalin Seir (KAY-lin SEER): The "true sons" or "sons of truth," a loyal contingency of Nolthanim who went into hiding after Andunin's rebellion and stayed hidden for two thousand years.

Karalin (CARE-uh-lin): Novaana from Enthanin (near Amaan Sul), crippled left ankle.

Keila (KEE-luh): A warrior woman of the Kalin Seir.

Kellisor Sea (KELL-ih-sore): The great internal sea of Kirthanin that lies directly south of Agia Muldonai.

Kelvan (KEL-vin): Novaana from Werthanin who died on the Forbidden Isle while battling Malekim and Black Wolves.

Kerentol (CARE-en-tall): Great Bear, elder of Taralindraal.

King Falcon: See *windhover*.

Kiraseth (KEER-uh-seth): Father of the Great Bear.

Kirthanin (KEER-than-in): The world in which the story takes place. Kirthanin comprises four countries on a single continent. Each country is defined by its geographic relationship to Agia Muldonai.

Kiruan River (KEER-oo-an): Marks the boundary of Werthanin and Nolthanin.

Koshti (KOSH-tee): Aljeron's tiger, battle brother.

Kumatin (KOO-mah-tin): Sea serpent created by Malek under the Forbidden Isle.

Kurveen (kur-VEEN): Caan's sword, a Firstblade whose name means "quick kill."

Kyril Minluan (KEER-il MIN-loo-in): Novaana of Suthanin (Dal Harat), Joraiem's younger sister and Evrim's wife, mother of Halina and Roslin.

Lindan Wood (LIN-duhn): Forest in eastern Suthanin, just west of the Arimaar Mountains, home to the Lindandraal clan of Great Bear.

Malek (MAH-leck): The greatest of Titans whose betrayal brought death to his Titan brothers and ruin to Kirthanin. Since the end of the Second Age and his second failed attempt to conquer all Kirthanin, he has ruled over Agia Muldonai and the surrounding area.

Malekim (MALL-uh-keem): Also known as Malek's Children, the Silent Ones, and the Voiceless. These creatures were first seen when Malek invaded Kirthanin at the end of the Second Age from the Forbidden Isle. A typical Malekim stands from a span and a third to a span and a half high and has a smooth thick grey hide. "Malekim" is both a singular and a plural term.

Marella Someris (muh-REL-uh so-MAIR-iss): Wylla's deceased mother, former Novaana and Queen of Enthanin.

Merias (mer-EYE-us): Captain of the army of Amaan Sul.

Merrion (MAIR-ee-un): White sea birds with blue stripes on their wings that can swim short distances underwater in pursuit of fish.

Mindarin Orlene (MIN-duh-rin ore-LEAN): Novaana of Werthanin, Aelwyn's older sister.

Monias Andira (moe-NYE-us an-DEER-uh): Novaana of Suthanin (Dal Harat), Joraiem's father.

Mound: Central feature in the midseason rituals that focus on Agia Muldonai's need for cleansing.

Nal Gildoroth (NAL GIL-dore-oth): Solitary city on the Forbidden Isle.

Naran (NARE-un): A leader of the Kalin Seir.

Nol Rumar (KNOLL RUE-mar): Small village in the north central plains of Werthanin.

Nolthanin (KNOLL-than-in): Kirthanin's northern country, largerly in ruin during the Third Age.

Novaana (no-VAHN-uh): The nobility of human society in Kirthanin who at first governed human affairs under the direction of the Titans but have since adapted to autonomous control. Every seven years the Novaana between the ages of eighteen and twenty-five as of the first day of Spring Rise were to assemble from the first day of Spring Wane until the first day of Autumn Wane. Sulare is commonly referred to as the Summerland. "Novaana" is both a singular and a plural term.

Nyan Fein (NYE-un FEEN): Novaana of Suthanin (Cimaris Rul), married to commander Talis Fein.

Parigan (PARE-ih-gan): Great Bear, lead elder of the Taralindraal.

Pedraal Someris (PAY-drawl so-MAIR-iss): Novaana of Enthanin (Amaan Sul), Wylla's younger brother, Pedraan's older twin.

Pedraan Someris (PAY-drahn so-MAIR-iss): Novaana of Enthanin (Amaan Sul), Wylla's younger brother, Pedraal's younger twin.

Pedrone Someris (PAY-drone so-MAIR-iss): Last king of Enthanin, deceased.

Peris Mil (PARE-iss MILL): Town south of Kellisor Sea on the Barunaan River.

Ralon Orlene (RAY-lon or-LEAN): Mindarin's late husband.

Rebellion, the: Malek's first attempt to conquer and rule Kirthanin by overthrowing the Twelve from Avalione.

Rolandes (roll-AN-deez): Faithful Titan killed by Daegon during the Rebellion.

Roslin Minluan (ROZ-lin MIN-loo-in): Evrim and Kyril's younger daughter.

Rucaran the Great (RUE-car-en): Father of the Black Wolves.

Rulalin Tarasir (rue-LAH-lin TARE-us-ear): Novaana of Werthanin (Fel Edorath), who murdered Joraiem in jealousy over Wylla.

Ruun Harak (RUNE HARE-ack): A spear given to Andunin by Malek.

Saegan (SIGH-gan): Novaana of Enthanin (Tol Emuna) who fights alongside Aljeron.

Sarneth (SAHR-neth): A lord among Great Bear, one of the few to still hold commerce with men, of Lindandraal.

seasons: As a largely agrarian world, Kirthanin follows a calendar that revolves around the four seasons. Each season is subdivided into three distinct periods, each of which contains thirty days. For example, the first thirty days of Summer are known as Summer Rise, the middle thirty days as Full Summer, and the last thirty as Summer Wane.

Second Age: The period that followed Malek's rebellion and preceded his return to Kirthanin. The Second Age was largely a time of peace until a massive civil war devastated Kirthanin's defenses and opened the door for Malek's second attempt at total conquest. Any date given which refers to the Second Age will be followed by the letters SA.

Shalin Bel (SHALL-in BELL): Large city of Werthanin.

Silent One: See Malekim.

Simmok River (SIM-mock): Nolthanin north-south river that pours into the Great Northern Sea.

slow time: See *torrim redara*.

Soran Nuvaar (SORE-an NEW-var): Friend and officer of Rulalin.

span: The most common form of measurement in Kirthanin. Its origin is forgotten but it could refer to the length of a man. A span is approximately 10 hands or what we would call 6 feet.

Spring Rise: See *seasons*.

Spring Wane: See *seasons*.

Stratarus (STRAT-ar-us): Faithful Titan killed by Anakor during the Rebellion.

Sulare (sue-LAHR-ee): Also known as the Sumerland. At the beginning of the Third Age the Assembly decreed that Sulare, a retreat at the southern tip of Kirthanin, would be the place where every seven years all Novaana between the ages of eighteen and twenty-five were to assemble from the first day of Spring Wane until the first day of Autumn Wane.

Sulmandir (sul-man-DEER): Also known as Father of the Dragons and the Golden Dragon. He is the most magnificent of all Allfather's creations beside the Titans. After many of his children died during Malek's invasion of Kirthanin at the end of the Second Age, Sulmandir disappeared.

Summer Rise: See *seasons*.

Summer Wane: See *seasons*.

Summerland: See *Sulare*.

Suruna (suh-RUE-nuh): Joraiem Andira's bow, previously his father's, whose name means "sure one."

Suthanin (SUE-than-in): The largest of Kirthanin's four countries, occupying the southern third of the continent. Ruled by a loose council of Novaana. Residents are Suthanim.

Synoki (sin-OH-kee): A castaway on the Forbidden Isle.

Tajira Mountains (tuh-HERE-uh): Nolthanin range in which Harak Andunin is located.

Talis Fein (TAL-is FEEN): Commander of the armies of Cimaris Rul.

Taralin Forest (TARE-uh-lin): Western forest of Suthanin and home to the Taralindraal clan of Great Bear.

Tarin (TARE-in): Novaana of Enthanin, Valia's cousin.

Tashmiren (tash-MERE-in): Servant of Malek, originally from Nolthanin.

Therin (THERE-in): Faithful Titan killed by Malek and his allies during the Rebellion.

Third Age: The present age, which began with the fall and occupation of Agia Muldonai by Malek.

time: Time in Kirthanin is reckoned differently during the day and the night. Daytime is divided into twelve Hours. First Hour begins at what we would call 7 AM and Twelfth Hour ends at what we would call 7 PM. Nighttime is divided into four watches, each three hours long. So First Watch runs from 7 PM to 10 PM and so on through the night until First Hour.

Titans: Those first created by Allfather who were given the authority to rule Kirthanin on Allfather's behalf. Their great power was used to do many remarkable things before Malek's rebellion ruined them.

Tol Emuna (TOLL eh-MUNE-uh): Heavily fortressed city of northeastern Enthanin's wastelands.

torrim redara (TORE-um ruh-DAR-uh): Prophetic state of being temporarily outside of time.

Turgan (TER-gun): Great Bear, elder of Elnindraal.

Ulmindos (ul-MIN-doss): High captain of the ships of Sulare.

Ulutyr (OO-loo-teer): Vulsutyrim captor of the women on the Forbidden Isle.

Valia (vuh-LEE-uh): Novaana of Enthanin, Tarin's cousin.

Valzaan (val-ZAHN): The blind prophet of Allfather.

Voiceless: See *Malekim*.

Volrain (vahl-RAIN): Faithful Titan killed by Malek during the Rebellion.

Vol Tumian (VAHL TOO-my-an): Village along the Barunaan River between Peris Mil and Cimaris Rul.

Vulsutyr (VUL-sue-teer): Also known as Father of the Giants and the Fire Giant. Vulsutyr ruled the Forbidden Isle and gave shelter to Malek when he fled Kirthanin. At first little more than a distant host, Malek eventually seduced Vulsutyr to help him plan and prepare for his invasion of Kirthanin. This giant was killed by Sulmandir at the end of the Second Age.

Vulsutyrim (vul-sue-TER-eem): Name for all descendants of Vulsutyr; both a singular and plural.

War of Division: Civil war that weakened Kirthanin's defenses against Malek at the end of the Second Age.

Water Stones: Stone formations created by the upward thrust of water released from the great deep at the creation of the world.

Werthanin (WARE-than-in): Kirthanin's western country. Residents are Werthanim.

windhover: Small brown falcons that are seen as "holy" birds in some areas of Kirthanin because of some stories that associate them with Agia Muldonai.

Winter Rise: See *seasons*.

Winter Wane: See *seasons*.

Wylla Someris (WILL-uh so-MAIR-iss): Queen of Enthanin and widow of Joraiem.

Yorek (YORE-ek): Royal advisor to Wylla.

Zaros Mountains (ZAHR-ohss): Mountain range bordering Nolthanin on the south.

Zul Arnoth (ZOOL ARE-noth): Ruined city between Shalin Bel and Fel Edorath; sight of many battles during Werthanin's civil war.